W9-BCP-273

Praise for Taffy Cannon's Nan Robinson mysteries!

A POCKETFUL OF KARMA

"Will leave readers eager for a sequel ... Cannon's skeptical heroine and her elusive villain stake out the wilds of L.A. in an auspiciously flavorsome foray."
—*Publishers Weekly*

"Taffy Cannon, I predict, shortly will be recognized as one of the genre's heavy hitters. . . . Cannon is a gifted writer, adept at plot and people, making her debut an event that readers everywhere should cheer."
—*The San Diego Union-Tribune*

TANGLED ROOTS

"Tense, entertaining, and satisfyingly thorough."
—*Library Journal*

"*Tangled Roots* is likely to turn more readers into Nan Robinson (and Taffy Cannon) fans."
—*Booklist*

By Taffy Cannon:

Fiction
CONVICTIONS: A Novel of the Sixties

Nan Robinson mysteries
A POCKETFUL OF KARMA*
TANGLED ROOTS*
CLASS REUNIONS ARE MURDER*

Young Adult Fiction
MISSISSIPPI TREASURE HUNT*

*Published by Fawcett Books

Books published by The Ballantine Publishing Group
are available at quantity discounts on bulk purchases
for premium, educational, fund-raising, and special
sales use. For details, please call 1-800-733-3000.

CLASS REUNIONS ARE MURDER

Taffy Cannon

FAWCETT CREST • NEW YORK

Sale of this book without a front cover may be unauthorized. If this book is coverless, it may have been reported to the publisher as "unsold or destroyed" and neither the author nor the publisher may have received payment for it.

A Fawcett Crest Book
Published by Ballantine Books
Copyright © 1996 by Taffy Cannon

All rights reserved under International and Pan-American Copyright Conventions. Published in the United States by Ballantine Books, a division of Random House, Inc., New York, and simultaneously in Canada by Random House of Canada Limited, Toronto.

Library of Congress Catalog Card Number: 95-96234

ISBN 0-449-22389-2

Manufactured in the United States of America

First Edition: May 1996

10 9 8 7 6 5 4 3 2

This book is dedicated to
the Morgan Park High School
classes of 1966 and 1967

ACKNOWLEDGMENTS

Special thanks to:

Officer Bill Cannon of the Wheaton Police Department, Tim Metcalfe of Earth and Environmental Engineering, Al Zuckerman of Writers House, and, as always, Bill Kamenjarin.

CHAPTER 1

There were probably, Nan thought as she walked into the Spring Hill Inn, a thousand more odious ways to spend an August Saturday night. She could be staring down a swarm of killer bees, stark naked. Turning her vintage Mustang over to a crack-addled carjacker with an automatic weapon. Trapped in a stalled elevator with three insurance salesmen. Clinging to a scrap of wood in shark-infested waters.

Nope, she'd taken the easy way out. She'd come to her twentieth high school reunion.

Nan hesitated just inside the doorway, feeling a momentary wave of panic, wishing she'd arranged to meet Janis somewhere beforehand. It was 6:37, barely seven minutes into the designated cocktail hour, but already the lobby was jammed with people. She shook her head slightly, smiled as she felt the dangling earrings graze her neck. It was downright silly to work herself into a swivet about this. It was just a party, after all, and if she didn't like it she could always leave.

Then, without warning, a projectile came hard and fast from the right, smashing sharply into the lobe of her recently pierced ear, knocking her momentarily off balance.

Recovering, she planted her feet solidly and looked around in confusion. Picked up the Frisbee that had nearly taken her out before she could even get a name tag. Read SPRING HILL IMPORT MOTORS in green on white, with a scattering of shamrocks and, in smaller print, WALLY SHEEHAN, GENERAL MANAGER. And smiled again, despite herself.

1

By now Wally himself was at her side, solicitously taking her elbow. "Nan!" he exclaimed. "Nan Robinson! Forgive me, I had no idea it was loaded!" He raised his hands to the heavens. "Wow! I can't believe you're really here."

Nan's laugh carried an undeniable element of relief. There was nothing here to be afraid of, for heaven's sake. "Maybe I should have sent a stunt double." Nan rubbed her ear and returned Wally's casual hug of greeting. He wore a blue satin jacket covered with Alfa Romeo logos, a suede jockey's cap perched at a jaunty angle, and a pair of leather racing gloves.

Nan had seen the class clown occasionally over the years, and she was fascinated by how little time had changed him. Wally was one of those short guys who claim to be five-ten, with the general contours and agility of a fireplug. But boy, was he ever peppy. His roly-poly exuberance had always made him extremely popular with both sexes: the boys didn't feel threatened and the girls, to Wally's eternal chagrin, considered him the finest sort of buddy.

"Doggone, you gorgeous little eye-candy, I was afraid you wouldn't come. But then I said, hey, she'll probably be delighted to get out of old Shakytown for a spell. Must be nice to get to where the terra's a little firma." Wally was a natural salesman, brimming over blarney. His blue eyes sparkled, and beneath the cap his wiry red hair seemed vibrant as ever, though possibly a bit thinner. His complexion, a wild mass of merging freckles, had an underlay of summer sunburn. He's be a regular at the dermatologist's.

"You bet," Nan told him with a grin as they crossed to the registration table. "I was hoping you'd have a nice flood while I was here. One of the ones that wash away entire towns. Or maybe a tornado?" As she walked, she made mile-a-minute assessments and recognitions. The anxieties melted away, and she realized with a start that this might even be *fun*.

"We'll do our best to oblige," Wally answered. "But me, I was kind of hoping for sunshine. And then you walked in that door and brought it." Anyone else being so hopelessly corny would set off Nan's gag reflex, but somehow from Wally it was all right.

They reached the registration table, where Rose Crosby, née Jenner, sat beneath a huge banner announcing SPRING HILL HIGH SCHOOL TWENTIETH REUNION. Rose flashed a quick, self-conscious smile of greeting. "Why, Nan, you're really here! Edwin is *so* looking forward to seeing you." She ran her pencil down a list of names and made a triumphant black X beside "Robinson."

Nan had quickly noticed that, by and large, her classmates were fairly youthful and well preserved. Rose Crosby, however, was another matter. She looked matronly, thirty-seven going on sixty-two. Though Rose had been *born* matronly, come to think of it, born to be the minister's wife she now was. There had to be endless flesh-pressing and public contact involved in that role, but Rose retained her adolescent air of shyness. Maybe, Nan realized with sudden insight, it was simply a matter of her teeth, an awful clutter of horse corn packed willy-nilly into a narrow, delicate jaw.

"We have lots of catching up to do," Nan said. Rose was married to Edwin Crosby, pastor of the same Methodist church where he and Nan had moved in tandem from preschool stints in the Sunday morning nursery to teenage MYF hayrides. "I'm really excited about seeing you both," she went on, less truthfully.

Wally Sheehan shifted his weight. "Oops, there's somebody I need to see. Catch you later, Nan."

Rose handed Nan a name tag featuring a large reproduction of her graduation photo. The girl in that picture beamed brightly toward the camera, projecting far more presence and confidence than Nan recalled ever truly feeling in high school.

"Edwin wanted me to ask you to join us at dinner," Rose said, almost but not quite smiling. Bugs Bunny, the boys had called her in grade school. *What's up, Doc?*, they'd say as they passed Rose on the playground. Might orthodontia have changed her life? Rose cocked her head and looked over Nan's shoulder. "Mary Lee, look who's here!"

Mary Lee Webster, sleek and vivacious, popped up beside the registration table and squealed with delight as she embraced Nan. Mary Lee's glistening black hair was cut short and feathered toward her face, a modern variant of the pixie cut she'd always worn. Her porcelain complexion glowed translucent against the passage of time, and her amber eyes were bright and intense. She wore a creamy silk flapper dress splashed with abstract scarlet roses, matching red sling-back pumps, and a long knotted string of pearls. Real, at a guess. Mary Lee had always had money.

Mary Lee still had that cheerleader aura, the perennial perkiness Nan herself had never been quite able to properly muster. She believed it was something you were born with, like knock-knees or a tendency toward hypertension.

Behind Mary Lee, a tall geeky fellow homed in on them, camcorder to his eye. In high school, he'd been one of the A-V Club boys who brought the film projector to the classroom where a teacher had scheduled *Passport to Bulgaria* or *The Miracle of Digestion*. He had two last names, Nan remembered from her previous night's cram session with her senior yearbook. Kirby. That was one of them. Something Kirby. Or Kirby Something. Taylor? Martin? No, Grant. Grant Kirby.

"You look wonderful," Nan told Mary Lee. "I had this terrible fear that I wouldn't recognize a soul." Actually, she was realizing, everyone seemed disturbingly familiar. Maybe she hadn't traveled as far and wide from her roots as she liked to think.

"Nonsense, girl!" Mary Lee had been voted "Most Popular" two decades earlier, and her effervescence had to be a tremendous asset for the wife of one of Spring Hill's more prominent young movers and shakers. Mary Lee would be an ebullient natural at fund-raisers, political rallies, Rotary dinner dances, and supermarket ribbon-cuttings.

Mary Lee's eyes widened as Nan felt a strong arm around her shoulders. Without releasing Nan, Jim Webster drew Mary Lee to him with his free arm and grinned broadly.

At first glance he appeared totally unmarked by time. On closer inspection, however, he was slightly thicker through the middle, and there were permanent crinkles around those ever-smiling brown eyes. His boyish shock of thick brown hair was flecked with just enough silver at the temples to suggest maturity. Jim and Mary Lee had worn each other's class rings and been voted "Cutest Couple," then gone together to the University of Illinois and married as juniors, some six months before the birth of their oldest daughter.

Jim made eye contact with professional ease, seemingly oblivious to Grant Kirby—or was it Kirby Grant?—and the camcorder five feet away. "Mary Lee's been poring over lists of names for weeks," he said. "You were one of the folks I most wanted to see, Nan."

"It's been ages, hasn't it?" Nan told him cheerfully, wondering where the bar was. "I never even had a chance to congratulate you on your political ascendancy. Of course I always did fantasize that I'd know a mayor someday."

"But you figured his name would be Richard Daley, I bet. A safe enough fantasy as the torch passes in these parts." Spring Hill was forty-three miles west of Chicago.

Nan laughed. "It was a generic mayor. I never tried to put a name and face to the person. Just like I fantasized I'd know a movie actress and a professional athlete and a congressman."

"And do you?" Jim asked.

She thought for a moment and grinned. "Oddly enough, yes."

"Confidante to the stars," Jim said with a wink and a twinkle. "I want to hear all about it at dinner. Say! Fellows!" And he was gone, glad-handing his way toward some old football teammates.

"I guess you must know all sorts of famous people."

Mary Lee sounded downright wistful. "Los Angeles is *such* an exciting place. I really love it when we go out there for conventions. We always stop off on the way to Hawaii, too. One time I saw Ed McMahon in the Polo Lounge, eating a hot fudge sundae for breakfast."

"Yuck," Nan responded involuntarily. "That's life in L.A., all right. A cavalcade of stars."

She felt rather silly, and a bit fraudulent. Of course, she made the occasional celebrity sighting; it was inevitable in a city where so many famous people lived, worked, and hung out. But the actress Nan had alluded to was her buddy Shannon, a former child star now peddling real estate. The pro athlete was a Laker she'd literally bumped into outside a restaurant, and as for the congressman, he'd been up to his campaign buttons in a messy influence-peddling scandal. By the time Nan's investigation for the California State Bar was finished, he was humbly grateful for the opportunity to hand over his law license, resign his House seat, and slink away into the desert. No ritzy place like Palm Springs, either. He was probably living out of an elderly Airstream on a concrete slab outside Plaster City.

"Actually, I always thought Los Angeles sounded terribly scary," Rose Crosby told her apologetically. "Seems like there's always something horrible happening there. Fires and mud slides and riots and earthquakes. We're *always* taking up a collection at the church for one catastrophe or another."

"It *is* mildly flawed," Nan admitted. She had a feeling this conversation would repeat itself on an endless loop through the evening. "But I can't imagine living anywhere else."

"You *will* sit with us at dinner, now," Mary Lee said firmly.

"She already agreed," Rose Crosby said, turning to check in Señor McNamara from Nan's tenth-grade Spanish class. He'd gone totally bald.

"Super!" Mary Lee said. "Now, don't forget your bid."

Mary Lee handed Nan a program book and an eight-inch brass sword, symbol of the Spring Hill Pirates. "Be sure to get one of Wally's Frisbees, too." She reached into another carton and handed one over.

"Thanks," Nan said, "and . . ."

She was cut off by a welcoming cry as Janis Levin dashed up, a margarita sloshing in one hand, a yachting cap perched on strawberry-blond curls. Janis, a twice-divorced Atlanta health care executive, had been one of Nan's few close friends in high school, where both considered themselves misfits. They'd remained in sporadic contact over the years.

"Not a moment too soon," Nan told Janis, with a wry grin. The divorcées would have to stick together. Nan couldn't quite shake the notion that without a husband on her arm and a brace of youngsters bunking at Grandma's, she was an abject failure in hometown eyes. Even though she knew from her mother's frontline reports that marital disaster was rife in Spring Hill.

"Is there room at your table for Janis?" Nan asked Mary Lee, who seemed on the verge of slipping away. There were people to greet, things to do. Besides, Mary Lee and Nan had never been particularly close friends, though both were part of a vaguely defined clique of class leaders.

"Of course. Hi, Janis. You look wonderful. Are you with somebody?" Mary Lee peered hopefully around.

Janis nodded. "Nan."

"Well, by all means join us," Mary Lee chirped automatically. "We're the center table all the way across the dance floor." Then she fluttered away.

"You know," Nan told Janis as they headed away, "until the very moment I walked through that door, I thought these folks were all forever seventeen."

"When, in fact, we represent several millennia-worth of life experiences." Janis giggled. "Ain't life grand?"

As they walked into the ballroom, Nan had the sense of people watching. Which was okay, really. They both looked just fine. Janis, once ridiculously thin, finally had some meat on her bones and looked almost robust in her sailor dress. And Nan herself had dieted and worked out for weeks, had shopped endlessly to find a dress sufficiently sophisticated yet artfully casual. She had, uncharacteristically, dropped a bundle on it.

She felt a momentary flicker of self-doubt. Janis was deeply tanned, and beside her Nan was washed-out and anemic, first cousin to last week's boiled potatoes. She caught herself: Think positive. Skin like alabaster, that's what she had.

She smiled and walked straight ahead into her own history.

Things got very busy then, almost blurred. For the next forty-five minutes, Nan nursed a Heineken as she talked to people she hadn't seen or thought about for more than half of her life.

Almost every face was familiar, and each one opened floodgates of ancient, irrelevant memories. These were boys and girls she'd known from grammar school, home room, Student Council, gym class. She found herself recalling seating patterns in long-forgotten classrooms, a group history project on the Panama Canal, an awful football date, her locker combination.

The skinny boy who had given her that mortifying hickey after the freshman homecoming dance now had a belly like a whiskey barrel. At the opposite end of the caloric spectrum, Jill Rockwell—at Nan's elbow through four years of alphabetized gym classes—was terribly frail and appeared to be recovering from either chemotherapy or anorexia.

Some folks were reticent, unsure of themselves, tentatively offering glimpses of their lives only when coaxed and prodded. Most, however, rambled on delightedly in monologues liberally studded with the first-person singular. Nan vastly preferred hearing these new tales to telling her own story—which was, after all, extremely familiar. But a surprising number of people had already taken a perfunctory flip through their program books and wanted to hear all about Nan's life.

They fell into two decidedly different camps. There were those who could not fathom living in a place that suffered from smog, mudslides, urban uprisings, uncontrollable wildfires, and seismographic nightmares. Most of these folks had never visited California and announced firmly that they never would.

But there were others who had passed through the Golden State at one time or another. Had driven the breathtaking Coast Highway between Morro Bay and Carmel, ridden cable cars through San Francisco fog, seen celebrities on Rodeo Drive, strolled the winter Southern California beaches in shorts. Their responses were more wistful.

Spring Hill must seem awfully dull, they said. Though of course, they added quickly, there were the new expressway and the Webster Center and lots of folks commuting into the city now.

Oh, but California, they added, their voices trailing off. It must be wonderful.

Indeed it was, she assured them proudly, hearing the unarticulated jealousies, laughing off the predictable fruits-and-nuts jokes, the awkward shake-and-bake quips. Realizing that the mere notion of California still had the power to intoxicate.

Remembering how it had intoxicated her twenty years ago, had seemed to be some kind of Promised Land, had been—not at all coincidentally—the farthest one could get from Spring Hill without actually leaving the continental United States.

By the time everybody sat down for dinner, Nan felt a pleasant buzz from the beer and welcomed a moment of relative solitude to glance through the program book herself.

The Reunion Committee had reprinted old class information, current demographics, lyrics to the Spring Hill fight song, and the senior class will. After so much time, the will was largely incomprehensible, full of arcane bequeathals of late passes, history notes, morning cheerfulness, and gym socks. On the list of class superlatives, valedictorian Nan Robinson was listed as "Most Likely to Succeed," "Most Studious," "Most Serious," and "Biggest Brownie," a title which still made her cringe.

Inside the back cover five names were listed in a simple black-bordered list labeled IN MEMORIAM. There were probably other dead classmates, too, among the lists of the MISSING. Physical malfunctions, overdoses, suicides, accident victims. Nobody would have dreamed that gregarious Melody Larsen would succumb to breast cancer, that Jerry Leffingwell would crash in a military plane, that Skip Watkins and his family would be wiped out on a Wisconsin highway, that studious Francine Graystone would be found hanged in Bora Bora. There *had* to be some kind of amazing story attached to that one, but nobody seemed to know it, not even Mary Lee.

The Reunion Committee had located two hundred sixty-two former Pirates: "Nearly two-thirds," the program book crowed. Something like half of those were here tonight, most with spouses.

At the round table for eight, Nan continued gossiping with Janis Levin. Janis was a joy—funny, irreverent, full of outrageous opinions and wild ideas. It was nice, this chemistry that allowed a truly significant friendship to resume instantly after years of separation.

"The good ones are always married," Janis sighed, "and the best of the best are faithful to boot. But when they're divorced, criminy. Guilt, confusion, bitterness. And of course, if they have kids, it's a hundred times worse."

Nan nodded, vividly recalling an interminable Disneyland day with a mortgage banker and his whining, petulant offspring. "I'm almost at the point where I don't even want to go to lunch with guys who have children, unless the kids are off at boarding school."

"Preferably in Switzerland," Janis said. "Even so, I'd rather have a divorced guy than a bachelor. Any straight man who gets to our age without at least taking a crack at marriage always has some kind of horrible flaw."

"In a perfect world they'd be wearing sandwich boards that say THERE'S A *REASON* WHY I'VE NEVER BEEN ABLE TO FULLY COMMIT MYSELF TO ANYBODY."

Janis laughed. "In a perfect world, they wouldn't exist."

Beyond Janis, Wally Sheehan was using lots of gestures to relate a story to Mary Lee while Jim Webster leafed through his program book, remarking occasionally to the Reverend Edwin Crosby. Edwin wore the mildly dazed look he had sported since kindergarten, along with sixty pounds he'd put on since high school. Rose Crosby, folding and refolding her napkin, periodically announced that she was having a wonderful time. Not that anyone would have guessed. She looked spectacularly dowdy in a striped brown and beige dress that bunched across her shoulders, screaming made-by-loving-hands-at-home. An empty chair between Rose and Nan was piled with sweaters nobody needed in the hot, smoky ballroom.

The noise level had risen gradually and relentlessly during the cocktail hour, then dropped to a more subdued level as people found their tables. Now waitresses started bringing platters of iceberg wedges, lazy-Susan salad dressing selections, and nasty-looking bowls of cold potato soup. Nan was so keyed up she wasn't sure she could even eat. It would be the standard Wedding Special anyway: mostaccioli, fried chicken, and tough gray beef in gummy tan gravy. She felt a fleeting craving for chile rellenos and a nice bowl of spicy salsa with chips.

"It never mattered a rat's ass to Fred what I said," Janis was complaining. "He never paid attention to a single word I uttered."

What, was he crazy? Janis was *always* entertaining, even

if you disagreed with every word she said. If Nan had learned nothing else in twenty years, she knew that having ready access to a genuinely funny friend was a gift beyond price.

"Testosterone poisoning," Nan suggested.

"I could tell him there was a troupe of Comanches riding down the driveway armed with laser arrows, and he'd say 'That's nice, honey, have you seen my crescent wrench?' " Janis made a face and poked through a basket of rolls.

There was, Nan realized, a depressing universality to the litany of divorce. Even an alleged no-fault, like Janis and Fred's. Nan had never met Fred, and now she never would; Janis, if her luck held, would never run across Nan's own ex. Whole major chapters had passed unwitnessed in each other's lives, but Nan would still have unhesitantly described Janis as a best friend.

As Janis stopped to take a sip of her fifth or sixth margarita, Nan realized that the ballroom had fallen strangely silent. Across the table she heard Mary Lee's sharp intake of breath and Jim's muttered "Good God."

Nan twisted around and watched a woman cross the empty dance floor toward their table in a cloud of glitter: golden tan, platinum hair piled high, tight white satin dress dusted liberally with rhinestones. Her heels were very high, open-toed, and sprinkled with more rhinestones. The satin dress was low-cut, and she had the sort of cleavage which sets a certain type of man to automatic salivation.

Sure enough, a male voice came clearly from a nearby table. "Hubba, hubba."

Obviously this woman was lost, looking for some other party or maybe some parallel universe. She certainly didn't look as if she'd be the least bit interested in reminiscing about the Great Blizzard or the senior production of *Showboat* or the football team that came *this close* to the playoffs.

But, still. There was something hauntingly familiar about her walk, a screw-you defiance that took a moment to place. By the time the woman came to a stop beside their table, Nan knew exactly who she was, and smiled at her.

"How nice to see a familiar, friendly face," the woman said to Nan. Her voice was rich and deep and throaty. She tossed her head and flashed a dazzling smile around the table. Slowly and deliberately she pulled cigarettes from a rhinestone handbag and lit one with a silver lighter.

"Hello, everybody," she said. "Remember me? I'm Brenda Blaine. I'd've got here sooner, but I had to stop for gas. Say, this looks like an empty chair here. Mind if I join you?"

CHAPTER 2

"I don't quite understand," Nan said carefully, a little later. Talking to Brenda Blaine was a distinct challenge. She was like a boutique chocolate chip cookie, crisp and brown outside, with an interior full of odd little chunks and nuggets. "If you don't like to gamble, why stay in Las Vegas?"

Brenda shrugged and shook her head. The rhinestone clip that anchored the platinum curls shimmered. "In Vegas nobody gives a damn what you do, nobody's minding your business for you. Unlike some places we both know. Not naming any names."

Nan laughed. One of the first things she and Brenda had discovered in their conversation tonight was a mutual teenage eagerness to forever flee the confines of Spring Hill. Brenda had likened it to an old C&W song, "Happiness Was Lubbock, Texas, in my Rearview Mirror."

Brenda had been a real trip in high school. Most of the girls in Nan's class were either primly conservative or had nervously embraced a vaguely defined counterculture. Oblivious to both factions, Brenda Blaine had lacquered her beehive, troweled on eyeliner, carried a half pint of gin in her purse, and done it in backseats.

She had been a bona fide Bad Girl.

And twenty years later, she seemed to have no regrets or second thoughts.

"L.A.'s the same way," Nan agreed. "Everybody's crazy, so nobody notices. You can be walking down the street with blue hair in a string bikini, carrying a cigar-store

14

Indian. And unless you whip out an Uzi, nobody'll really pay attention."

"Yeah, I know. I spent a few years in L.A. Took some acting lessons and everything. But it was too hard, with a little kid to support."

"So how'd you end up in Vegas?"

"I had a boyfriend who was a dancer, probably the only straight boy dancer ever. He got a gig, and me and Ryan came along. Didn't work out with the dancer, but I liked the town okay. So me and Ryan just stayed."

"And you became a blackjack dealer." Brenda had earlier announced her occupation as if mentioning she taught kindergarten, or sold Avon.

"Shit, Nan, you gotta do something. It's a living, and the hours suit me. You meet a lotta people, see a lotta stuff."

"Hmmph," Nan answered noncommittally. She had been to Las Vegas three times in her life, and on each occasion was ready to leave after fifteen minutes. Proximity to all that desperation terrified and depressed her. Nan's idea of a gamble was whether or not the office soda machine would be out of Diet Coke.

"I like living on the edge," Brenda explained. She'd been downright garrulous since her dramatic entrance, directing most of her comments to Nan and Janis. Now, however, Janis was laughing over something with Wally Sheehan, who sat on her other side. Meanwhile Rose Crosby, on Brenda's right, industriously cleaned her plate, chewing each mouthful several dozen times. She never looked at Nan or Brenda and made no effort to join the conversation. But she was definitely listening.

"And being around folks who live on the edge," Brenda went on. "One of the things I loved best about drinking was getting myself to the edge and trying to stay there."

Nan still didn't get it. "But didn't all that change once you stopped drinking?"

Brenda had explained, early on, that she was a nine-year veteran of AA. She sipped her Perrier. "Not as much as I expected. They tell you to stay away from the things you used to do, the people you used to see. But I couldn't stop going to work now, could I? It was tough at first, but then I found out I could get the same kind of rush just being around the high rollers. Kind of a contact high. And I took up skydiving, too."

Of course. Just like all the girls do when they dry out. Brenda's cockiness was fascinating. Nan could picture her skydiving into Beirut and surfacing with a sugar daddy and a million bucks.

Wally Sheehan set his glass down suddenly and made a big show of noticing his watch. "Show time, Jimbo," he announced. Jim Webster took a couple of fast bites of mostaccioli while Wally looked around the table. "I *did* tell all of you about the party at my place after this is over, didn't I? It oughta be a blast."

Jim Webster wiped a trace of tomato sauce off his lip, stood, and straightened his jacket. He seemed suddenly nervous. "Back soon," he said, bending down to kiss Mary Lee. She presented her cheek for Jim's casual peck, then turned and spoke conspiratorially to the table at large.

"Now make sure you pay attention when he starts talking," Mary Lee stage-whispered.

"Well, of course," Nan said mildly.

"We have a choice?" Janis muttered into her mashed potatoes.

"No, I mean *really* pay attention," Mary Lee insisted coyly.

Wally was at the bandstand now, picking up the mike. "As chairman of the Reunion Committee," he began, "I made a unilateral decision to skip the after-dinner remarks tonight." A cheer came from somewhere in the back of the room. Wally held up a hand. "Not so fast. We're going to have some *during*-dinner remarks instead. That way we'll all have plenty of time to socialize later." He looked around and grinned. "But before I go on, let me say that I noticed some of you are driving automotive machinery that can't *possibly* give you the pleasure and reliability you deserve when you sit behind the wheel."

Some laughs and a couple of groans came from tables near the door. When Wally Sheehan started selling Toyotas in Spring Hill, Nan's auto-dealer dad—and plenty of other folks—had howled. *Foreign* cars in Porter county? Not bloody likely. But times had changed. Phil Robinson was dead, for one thing, and the Ford dealer now sold cars assembled on foreign soil by people who spoke no English. Back when everybody was still guffawing, Wally and his silent partner Jim Webster had quietly picked up a handful of unwanted franchises. Now Wally's Japanese, Swedish, Korean, and German cars dotted all the nicer neighborhoods in town.

Wally told a few jokes and went on for a while, as befitted one of the mainstays of the Porter County Toastmasters Club. Grant Kirby stood nearby, getting it all down on videotape. Grant was pretty pathetic. His suit fit badly, his hair was too greasy, and he kept getting in everybody's way. After all these years, he was still an outsider, chronicling events he was only peripherally part of. Not all nerds, it seemed, had grown up to invent interesting microchips in Silicon Valley. Some were still just nerds.

Then Wally paused dramatically.

"Friends, senior year there was a guy who did it all. He was president of the class and captain of the football squad. The Homecoming Queen was wearing his ring. He married that girl and came home from the U of I determined to make this town greater. We've seen the results: the Webster Center, the Sunny Acres subdivision of Rocky Glen, and of course Potawatomi Industrial Park, taking shape for tomorrow at this very moment. Three years ago, Spring Hill thanked this man by electing him mayor. But we already knew twenty years ago that he was somebody pretty special. Ladies and gentlemen, our own Jim Webster!"

Amid the applause as Jim stepped onstage, Nan watched Mary Lee's right fingers tap her left palm in a light and ladylike fashion. Her head was slightly tilted, her lips were slightly parted, and a look of sublime adoration radiated toward her husband. Nan wanted a barf bag.

"I'm not going to keep you from each other's company for long," Jim promised. He spoke with natural ease, had undoubtedly spent thousands of hours addressing Kiwanis and Rotary clubs, homeowner associations, and high school econ classes. "Too many folks have come too far to see each other. Wally and the Reunion Committee have done a terrific job pulling this thing together, don't you think? Let's have the Committee members stand up for a moment, and give them a hand!"

Mary Lee bounced to her feet, beaming and waving, before Rose Crosby could even set her fork down. Rose did stand finally, along with half a dozen others scattered around the room. Her napkin stuck to her dress.

"Thanks, everybody," Jim said. "We've been through a lot these last twenty years, all of us, good times and bad. Those of you who live around here may know that last year I had a serious illness, and for a while it was touch and go. While I was lying up there in Spring Hill General, I did some serious thinking. I'd been extremely fortunate, and it was time to give back some of what I'd been given. The new addition at the Y is part of that pledge. But I wanted to do more."

Grant Kirby videotaped merrily away, with the confident air of one saving a truly significant event for posterity. Nan longed for another beer. But there was no way to slip out unnoticed, not with Mrs. Mayor parked right across the table.

Jim Webster paused. "I look around here tonight and think of all the things I shared with you people, all the memories we made together. I want to make another memory with you here tonight. I've decided to do something that I only wish my parents could have lived to see, something they dreamed of when I thought it was impossible. I want to take the things we've always cherished and believed in here in Spring Hill, I want to take those values and ideas to Washington, D.C. I plan to be on the Republican primary ballot in April, and with your help I hope to go on and represent Spring Hill in the United States House of Representatives."

Nan was flabbergasted. This wasn't history-in-the-making so much as unabashed chutzpah. What came next, Mary Lee passing the hat? Bumper stickers on the dessert plates?

Applause began somewhere behind her. Mary Lee jumped up again, and this time there was nothing sedate about her clapping. Two decades had dropped away, and she was on the Spring Hill gridiron, ready to lead the crowd in "Two Bits."

Others started standing up around the room. Nan took her sweet time getting up, and Janis was even slower. But they weren't the last to rise. When nearly everyone in the room was standing, Brenda Blaine finally rose languidly to her feet and began clapping slowly, in dirge-like cadence. But a vein at the base of her neck throbbed in double time.

After Jim came back to the table, a waitress appeared with a tray of chocolate sundaes and began distributing them. Brenda seemed to literally shake herself back into sociability, like a terrier just in from the rain, and turned to Nan with a smile.

"Jeez, I've been talking way too much about me," Brenda said. "What about you? I thought for sure you'd be married and have a bunch of kids, same as all the rest of the socialites." She waved an airy, dramatically manicured hand around the table.

Nan laughed. "Socialite" had been a term of disparagement used by the greaser crowd in high school. But there'd never been anyone resembling a true socialite within the town borders, then or now. "You sound like my mother," she answered dryly.

"Nobody ever told me I sounded like nobody's mom," Brenda shot back. "Not even my own kid."

"How old is he?"

"Ryan's nineteen." Brenda seemed genuinely proud of her son, though unlike other classmates, she didn't automatically lunge for photographs. "He's a real smart boy, gonna be a sophomore in college next year."

"Really? Where's he go to school?" Nan heard her own patronizing tone with embarrassment. Was she expecting Brenda to announce that her child was enrolled at the Las Vegas School of Dice Repair?

But Brenda didn't notice. "He's at the University of California in Santa Cruz." Her pride was unmistakable now. "He's an A student. I want him to be a doctor."

"That's really great," Nan told her. She hesitated a moment. Brenda had made no mention of a spouse. "You're divorced?"

Brenda's eyes narrowed. "Yeah."

The silence was suddenly awkward. "Me, too," Nan volunteered. "It made me a little nervous coming back here without a husband. I guess . . ." She trailed off uncertainly. Auld lang syne was fine and dandy, but there was no reason on earth to share the details of her marital failure with Brenda Blaine.

But Brenda was cheerful again. "You thought everybody'd be like me, expecting you to have it all." Her tone grew more serious. "Your dad still here in town, Nan?"

Now *that* was a land mine. Despite all the lighthearted earlier reminiscence about chem lab, both women had delicately skated around their one genuine teenage bond. Now Brenda had plopped it right down on the table like some smelly, half-dissected frog: alcoholic parents.

Nan shook her head. "He died a few years ago." She swallowed. "Wrecked his car on a bender."

Brenda cocked her head. "Anybody else . . ." The question was cautious, unspoken.

Nan shook her head again. "No, thank God. You always knew, didn't you?"

Brenda's smile this time was warm and personal. "Well, sure."

"I always wondered just who knew . . . I guess I figured you did, on account of . . ."

"On account of my mom," Brenda finished flatly.

Brenda's mother had been a notorious lush, her alcoholism one of those tidbits of small-town info that everybody knew but never really discussed, except occasionally to wonder that she remained in Spring Hill at all. Brenda didn't have a father, at least not that anybody knew about. She had lived with her mother and maternal grandmother in a run-down little white clapboard house at the edge of town.

This was strangely unsettling. Nan had somehow expected, in the back of her mind, that her father's death would come up during the course of the evening. She'd heard others asking folks about their parents, was braced simply to announce he had died a few years back. Period. In her wildest fantasies she wouldn't have imagined discussing the particulars with somebody else who had truly been there.

"I used to read Ann Landers," Nan said slowly, "and sometimes there'd be letters from kids whose parents drank. 'Go to Alateen,' she'd tell them. And I'd think, how in the hell could I do that without letting everybody know my secret? Not that there was an Alateen in Spring Hill anyway. Or was there?"

"You're asking *me*?" Brenda gave a little hoot of amazement. "Shit, Nan, I didn't know nothing. I was starting to put it away pretty good myself by then. Booze, pills, you name it. But I gotta tell you something. Folks looked down on my family, I knew that. And this may sound awful, but it helped, knowing about you. I got a real kick out of knowing the high and mighty Nan Robinson had an alkie for a Pop."

A shiver of horror passed through Nan. Who else had known? What had they said, and thought? And who else, she wondered suddenly, had been carrying around the same secret shame? Simple statistics made it obvious that plenty of her classmates had been in the same miserable boat, fearful to bring home friends, never certain what the next turn of the doorknob might bring.

"I spent a lot of time in ACA," Nan told Brenda quietly. "Starting back before he died. In the days when bookstores didn't have a whole section labeled 'Recovery,' and they looked at you a little funny when you bought the one book on the subject you found on some bottom shelf. I'm pretty much out of ACA now, but I went back a couple times this last month." She looked steadily at Brenda. "I don't come back to Spring Hill often, and it's a lot harder here."

Brenda pushed away her chocolate sundae untouched. "No shit, Sherlock," she answered fervently. "But jeez, Nan, let's set it aside for now, okay? I did the ACA bit too. Hell, between that and AA, I was spending half my life at meetings. And I really didn't mean to bum you out. We're supposed to be having fun, remember?" She gave a throaty laugh and raised her voice slightly. "I been telling folks the last couple weeks I was coming here. Half of them said, 'Man, you're crazy trying to go back.' But the rest said, 'Hey, fuck 'em all. Go back, party, get laid, have yourself a blast.' "

Brenda turned suddenly to Rose Crosby, who had long since given up any pretense of not listening. "That's what *you're* planning on, aren't you, Rose? Why, I'd bet old Edwin there is hell in bed."

Rose's eyes widened, and a flush of crimson raced from her neck to her hairline. She started to open her mouth, then clamped it shut. Beyond Rose, Edwin was dipping a cookie into his sundae. He looked up, stunned.

"Just teasing, honey," Brenda said lightly. She stood and stretched, a motion that flashed showers of light in every direction from her jillions of rhinestones. It was one hell of a dress. "Hey, guys, this is a party! Let's see a little action . . ." She stopped, peered across the room, and grinned. "Why, I do believe I see old Frank Finney over there, makes me downright nostalgic."

As Brenda shimmered away, Nan felt herself slowly exhale.

The DJ played rock and roll from twenty years ago and longer. It was music that Nan had made out to in rec rooms, danced to stoned, cranked up *loud* despite parental protest. *It'll never last,* her father had always warned. *Take Sinatra, now,* there's *an entertainer. You're not going to want to listen to this garbage in twenty years.*

Wrong again, Dad.

Nan wasn't really interested in dancing, but she welcomed the sound track as she meandered around the room, talking to people she had once known, meeting spouses, admiring photographs of children who all looked curiously alike. Wondering, at intervals, who else had alcoholic parents. Hating herself for wondering.

She danced once or twice with the particularly insistent, but generally held back. She couldn't help but notice Brenda Blaine on the dance floor, however, moving her voluptuous body with supple grace and seductive prowess.

And then there was a light hand on her shoulder, a soft voice in her ear. "Hello, Nan."

She froze. It was eighteen years since she'd last heard that voice, the summer when he told her he'd met a girl at Purdue he was serious about, when she found the confession an unexpected relief even as she wept.

Henry.

She turned and looked at him, stared into the dark eyes she had once loved with sixteen-year-old fervor, felt Henry Sloane's strong hands take her shoulders as he smiled gently at her.

"I thought you weren't coming," she said, as he pulled her into his arms in a fierce and familiar hug. But softer somehow. He wasn't quite so bony anymore. "I looked for you."

Henry kept his arm snugly around her, his fingers playing gently on her bare shoulder as he looked down. She'd forgotten how tall he was. He looked the same, but different, as if he had somehow grown into his looks. Henry had never really looked boyish, at least not once his braces came off. Now his hair was much shorter than she remembered, just barely flecked with gray. The angles of his nose and cheeks seemed softer.

"I almost didn't make it," he answered. "My little boy's been sick. But I was being such an insufferable mope about the whole thing that Amy insisted that I just get in the car and come." He gave a sardonic smile. That smile was part of why he'd always looked older. It was so knowing, so vaguely superior. "She said she didn't want to hear for the next twenty years what a martyr I'd been."

Nan had read Henry's bio in the program book, had turned directly to it when she'd finally sat at the table and had a moment of privacy. Henry Sloane was a high school principal in some downstate town she'd never heard of, married to a former teacher, father of two sons and one daughter. Nan had pictured the Sloane family sitting snowbound on a hand-hooked rug in front of the stone fireplace in a white frame house with green shutters, wearing hand-knit sweaters and eating chocolate chip cookies still warm from the oven. Amy, she presumed, was a paragon.

Well, now she'd find out. The evening had suddenly slipped into another gear altogether, and she felt an odd giddiness, a flash of adolescent anxiety.

They got fresh drinks at the bar, Henry noting with amusement that Nan ordered another Heineken. "I remember you *hating* beer," he told her, "drinking those awful soda-pop wines instead." Henry himself was drinking bourbon, very manly. In high school he'd preferred Seagram's 7.

They found an empty table, apparently abandoned. A forlorn Frisbee lay on it, next to a spilled glass of water. For the next twenty minutes they talked. Easy talk, mostly, a comfortable update on each other's past two decades. His parents had retired to Florida, and his sister was married and living in Milwaukee. Amy wasn't the girl he'd fallen for at Purdue, it turned out. That romance had ended badly, and he'd met Amy when he began teaching high school math in Bloomington. They'd been married fourteen years, and their youngest child was seven.

It was, Henry said, a good life.

Henry had been a brain in high school, and the only reason Nan consistently outranked him in class standings was his unfortunate inability to master any language other than English. As they talked now, she remembered sharing honors classes with him, considering him rather a geek. As a freshman and sophomore he was all elbows and angles, with enough orthodontia to build a train trestle.

Then, when he was down to just a retainer, they were assigned to do a history project together, spring of junior year. They began dating, and later—midwinter of senior year, after interminable discussion and much painstaking analysis—lost their virginity together in the Sloanes' rec room on a cold January night. She could still remember the black-and-white checkered couch, the knotty pine walls, the green linoleum floor. In one corner was a table where his father built intricate ship models, and the finished products were shelved on every wall. The room smelled of Mr. Sloane's Flying Dutchman pipe tobacco. And dogs. The Sloanes always had black labs.

It hadn't been the torrid passion Nan had fantasized, but it was pretty nice, all things considered. Henry was considerate and caring and had wanted her desperately. *First love* might be a bit strong to describe their relationship, but it wasn't entirely inaccurate either. A couple of times since then she had smelled Flying Dutchman tobacco, and invariably it made her horny.

Now, as she looked around the room tonight at her assembled classmates, she realized she could have done a whole lot worse.

It was nearly eleven, and Nan was starting to feel hot and a bit dizzy. She wasn't exactly sure how many beers she'd had through the evening, never a good sign.

"I'm sweltering," she told Henry. "Let's take a walk." He gave her an odd look, and she rushed to assure him that she merely wanted some fresh air and if he wanted to stay inside and mingle while she went out, that was fine, too. She was gabbling, she realized, but she couldn't stop.

"I've mingled enough," Henry told her, with that slow sardonic smile. She was sure he'd been remembering the rec room too. After that first time, they'd returned there with considerable regularity. Henry's parents, bless their hearts, had season tickets to several theater and musical series, and his sister did a lot of baby-sitting. "You're the main one I wanted to see anyway."

Which was exactly what she wanted him to say, superficial hussy that she was.

They stopped at the bathrooms on their way out. Nan splashed water on her face and neck, combed her hair, and repaired her makeup. It amused her to be getting fixed up for Henry Sloane. She remembered other nights and other ladies' rooms from long ago—fluffing on blusher, meticulously applying mascara, not bothering with lipstick because it would just get all over Henry's face and shirt collar.

Henry was leaning against the wall outside when she came out, looking rather prep and far too young to be a high school principal, a species Nan recalled as having one foot in the grave. They ambled down the hall, passing Wally Sheehan, who offered a cheery "About-time-you-showed-up" to Henry before turning into the men's room.

The night outside was sultry, but still substantially cooler than the ballroom inside. There was an occasional indolent breeze. Everything was soft and still and timeless, bathed in crystalline light from a nearly full moon. They walked along the sidewalk without speaking, heading away from the street, aiming vaguely toward the wooded area behind the various hotel buildings. At the end of the walkway, Henry took her hand and led her half a dozen yards into the woods.

Nan was pretty sure she knew where this was headed, and not at all certain how she felt about it. Safely in the shadow of the trees, Henry dropped her hand and turned to face her.

"I know," he murmured, his dark eyes staring down intensely into her own. "This is *extremely* irresponsible of me. And I won't have my feelings hurt if you call me an adulterous masher and slap me upside of the head." He grinned suddenly, his teeth white in the darkness. "Though I'd prefer you not leave any bruises. I was just wondering, though, what it might be like to kiss you again." His smile broadened. "You were really a *great* kisser, Nan."

And eternally susceptible to flattery, too.

"You weren't half-bad yourself." Nan had probably spent the equivalent of three weeks necking with Henry Sloane, if you added it all up. And with the wisdom of hindsight, she recognized him to be a champion kisser. The world was full of slobberers. Some of them were, of course, quite skilled at *other* sexual ventures, but not nearly enough men excelled at simple face-to-face contact.

So without thinking too much about it, she stepped forward, leaned up, and kissed him. Then kissed him some more. He hadn't lost his touch at all; if anything, he'd improved.

Nan realized, in a moment, that he wasn't making any effort at all to break away and that she was getting a good deal more aroused than she'd anticipated. Henry's hand, in fact, was slipping down her back, and it felt kind of nice, exactly like it belonged there.

It was time to bail, or at least to discuss parameters. With considerable reluctance, Nan pulled herself away.

"I'm not sure this is a good idea," she told him.

"Did I suggest it was?" His voice was softer than before, and she wondered if he'd set this up as some kind of test and if so, of what. And for whom. "Thanks. That was nice."

A car door slammed and an engine started somewhere in the hotel lot just beyond the edge of the woods. Nan walked a few steps away from Henry, realizing for the first time that she'd probably totally destroyed a brand-new pair of shoes with this little jaunt into the forest. On balance, it was well worth it. It was nice to know she could still turn on her high school boyfriend.

"Are you going back home tonight?" she asked.

He shook his head and the wry smile returned. "I checked into the hotel before I came to the ballroom. *Not* that it matters to you, of course." He paused. "Or does it?"

"I don't know."

And she didn't, and wasn't *that* a fine how-do-you-do. She was planning to go to Wally Sheehan's after-party party with Janis. But Janis would still be around tomorrow and besides, there would probably *never* be another chance for this. Whatever it might be. She was more likely to be elected president of the American Bar Association than to find herself in Henry's hometown, wherever the hell it was. If they met at another reunion, he'd surely have Amy with him. And if he ever brought his family to L.A., they'd all be off on nuclear family adventures at Universal Studios and Knott's Berry Farm, maybe watching the taping of some dreadful sitcom.

Nan thought fleetingly of Brenda Blaine. Brenda wouldn't hesitate under circumstances like these, she was quite sure. Brenda would jump his bones. Though Brenda probably wouldn't be off in the woods with a principal from Podunk.

"Let's go back inside," she said softly, after a moment. "And then I think I'd like to go to Wally's party. With you, if you're interested. And after that I just plain don't know. Is that all right?"

"Fair enough," he told her, "Eminently fair." He took her hand, holding it until they reached the edge of the woods. A car was pulling out of the parking lot at the far end. Henry made an exaggerated show of dropping Nan's hand, moving a discreet distance away. "You have a reputation, Ms. Robinson."

She shot him a sidelong look and laughed. "Maybe so, but *you* have a wife, big boy." They walked on toward the side entrance to the building. They were coming up, she realized, to her own rental car. As she wondered what Henry was driving—probably some kind of van, big enough to hold the whole Little League team—she saw an odd glint on the front seat of her dark blue rented Taurus, on the driver's side.

What on earth?

"Just a second," she told Henry and stepped toward the car, growing more and more puzzled. She opened the door on the passenger side and blinked as the bright light illuminated the interior.

It couldn't be.

But it was.

She felt her entire body begin to shake uncontrollably as she willed herself not to scream.

Brenda Blaine lay supine across the navy plush front seat, her platinum hair splayed out against the steering wheel. A scarlet stain spread down the rhinestones on the bodice of her white satin dress.

A brass sword, one of the replicas distributed as reunion souvenir bids, had been thrust to the hilt into the tanned mound of her left breast. Her eyes were closed, her lips parted slightly.

Nan cautiously reached in, lifted Brenda's warm and flaccid wrist, felt frantically for the pulse that wasn't there.

Brenda would not be going off into the woods with anybody. Ever again.

She was quite dead.

CHAPTER 3

When Detective Brian Delahanty arrived at the Spring Hill Inn shortly after midnight, he found chaos. Substantially subdued by the hour, of course, and by the oceans of alcohol this crowd had been soaking up, but still a mess.

No time to deliberate, to size things up before moving. Action was called for here, and fast. Delahanty spoke briefly with Officer Jack Pukowski, the young and clearly overwhelmed uniform who'd been first on the scene, took a quick glance at the body, and stepped inside to meet the hotel manager, a no-nonsense woman in her fifties disheveled enough to suggest she'd been rousted from bed by the news.

As had he.

He felt a strange kind of rush—half from the murder and half from being wakened abruptly after only twenty minutes of sleep. Saturday had been his day off, and he'd spent almost all of it aimlessly driving and walking the streets of Spring Hill and its environs, trying to find the damn dog. Thursday, while Delahanty was on duty, Jamison had broken through the screen in the bedroom window and split.

The crime-scene techs were working on the car and the body. He had one of them bring in a fingerprint kit and then took a deep breath and commandeered the disc jockey's microphone. The first cops on the scene had closed the bar and gathered everybody in the ballroom, including people who'd been trying to leave the parking lot and those with rooms upstairs. Most of them were plenty pissed.

31

"I'm Detective Brian Delahanty of the Spring Hill police," he announced, with screeching feedback. The DJ fiddled with something and the feedback vanished. "As you probably all know by now, we've been called here to investigate a sudden death. I'm told that this party was supposed to be ending right around now, but I'm afraid we'll have to ask you to stick around for a bit longer."

Groans from all around the room. Delahanty recognized a number of local faces including, God help him, the mayor and his wife. Swell.

"With everybody's cooperation, we should be able to get you home at a reasonable hour. Mrs. Quaintance, the hotel manager, is arranging for coffee to be served for anyone who'd like some." As if on cue, a waitress wheeled in a large coffee urn through a back door. Most of these folks were pretty blasted, and pouring coffee into them wasn't going to sober anybody up. It might, however, prevent some folks from passing out before they could be questioned.

Delahanty looked around the room. A twentieth reunion. Whoop-de-do. He'd skipped his own, in Lansing a few years back.

"The deceased has been tentatively identified as Brenda Blaine." And from her looks, no shrinking violet. Which should make things easier.

A low murmur through the crowd. They all had to know by now, of course, but there was something almost cathartic about Official Information.

"We have three conference rooms open down the hall," he went on. "You'll be asked to wait in one of those to be interviewed by myself or another officer. We're also going to ask everyone to leave us their fingerprints. You're under no legal obligation to provide fingerprints, but we hope you'll be willing to cooperate and expedite our investigation."

A louder murmur. Fancily dressed women stared at their manicures in consternation, including, front-row center, the mayor's wife. With luck, nobody would put up any half-assed civil libertarian bullshit.

"If you have any information you feel might be useful to the police in our investigation, please tell the officer as you leave this room. If you were acquainted with the deceased, or had contact with her tonight, we need to know that also. Does anybody have any questions?"

A woman raised her hand. "My baby-sitter expects us home," she announced with righteous indignation.

"And I gotta go to the can," came a male voice from somewhere in the back of the room. Laughter followed, more than was warranted.

"We can take care of both problems," Delahanty said. "If you need to notify somebody you're delayed, tell the officer as you leave this room. Ditto the rest room."

He sighed and left the stage, signaling to Tank Thiswell and Lance Thompson to join him at the door. Tank was twenty-seven, the youngest detective on the force. He had made detective over Delahanty's objections at the insistence of the police chief, a family friend of the Thiswells. Tank's sole qualification beyond nepotism was a lifelong commitment to TV cop shows. With an IQ in the high two figures, he had great difficulty examining a problem from even one angle. He could probably, however, be depended on to watch somebody taking a leak.

Delahanty assigned Lance Thompson to sort out the now grim merrymakers. Thompson, in his mid-thirties, was a bit short on manners but plenty smart, and he had a superb bullshit detector. His prejudices were legion. Lance hated punks, uppity women, homosexuals, persons of color, and the Syndicate. Just for starters. Fortunately, this white-bread crowd seemed unlikely to push too many of his buttons.

And he himself would start with the couple who'd found the body. Nan Robinson and Henry Sloane. He'd separated them and stashed them in administrative offices. It was the Robinson woman's car. Maybe he'd get lucky. Maybe it was a simple lovers' triangle, and the Robinson woman was already sobbing in remorse.

Somehow, he doubted it. This had all the earmarks of a very long night.

"What I don't entirely understand," Detective Brian Delahanty told Nan, "is why somebody you claim you barely even knew twenty years ago would glom onto you for no particular reason, and then talk your head off for a couple of hours."

It was nine-fifteen on Sunday morning. Nan had slept maybe four hours before crawling out of bed to come to the police station as promised. Detective Delahanty, of course, probably hadn't slept at all, so it wasn't surprising that he was a bit cranky. It was hot and humid inside his tiny office. Nan moved slightly to get within range of the overburdened ancient wire fan that angled down from atop a file cabinet.

She smiled politely. They'd been over and over this, and it seemed time to move on. "That's the entire point of a reunion, isn't it? Bringing people back together. Besides, I don't think Brenda really knew anybody else any better. She made a big point about how she hadn't set foot in Spring Hill for twenty years."

Delahanty's windowless lair looked like every government office since the dawn of time: scarred gray metal furniture, walls painted that peculiar shade of bilious green manufactured by the carload for institutional settings, ripped Naugahyde seat cushions unsuccessfully mended with a Fix-Ur-Self vinyl repair kit. Bare walls except for a well-framed Canadian Pacific Railway poster of a gleaming train snaking through the Rockies. Still, everything was tidy. Papers were piled neatly in squared stacks, the stacks set in carefully labeled baskets and slots.

Brian Delahanty seemed much too lively and good-looking for this office, actually. He had thick sandy hair and a moustache the color of buckwheat honey. Dark blue eyes, pale skin lightly dusted with freckles. If he was over forty, a picture in a closet somewhere was taking a real beating. He stood at least six-two, and last night at the Spring Hill Inn, he'd seemed large and physically intimidating. Here behind his desk he looked constrained, too big for the allotted space.

"She has to have known *somebody* better. She didn't ram that sword into her own chest. She walks into that ballroom and heads straight for you. Four hours later, her body turns up in your car."

Nan raised an eyebrow and swallowed her irritation. "Are you suggesting that *I* had something to do with her murder?"

Delahanty's smile was genial. "Did you?"

She laughed. "Of course not!"

"Then what's the problem?"

She hesitated a moment. "Spring Hill isn't the kind of town where people get murdered, is it?"

He shook his head, and the smile broadened. "Not really. We've had a couple domestics since I've been on the force, but that happens everywhere. Spring Hill's basically a pretty clean little town. No organized crime, no major drugs, no gangs." He grimaced. "Then some hometown honey bops in from Vegas and gets herself stabbed with a party souvenir." He shook his head. "That's gotta be a first: death by party favor. I *still* don't understand what the point of those swords was."

Nan smiled slightly. "Kind of goofy, I know. I don't have any idea if they still do this, but when I was in school here, every big dance at Spring Hill High always had to have souvenir bids. Homecoming, the prom, Spring Frolic, whatever. The bids were usually something junky, but that never seemed to matter. It's just a tradition, and I suppose the Reunion Committee wanted to maintain tradition."

"Does that mean somebody will have to be killed at the twenty-fifth?" He looked startled, as if the question had popped out on its own.

"I hope not," Nan answered, with an appreciative laugh. "What have you been able to find out about Brenda, anyway?"

"Inquisitive, aren't we?"

"Sorry." Nan knew she didn't sound remotely apologetic. "I do a lot of investigative work myself. I suppose it's just a habit."

"Ah, yes." Delahanty flipped open the reunion program book and read aloud. *"Nan Robinson graduated with honors from Stanford University before attending UCLA Law School. After a few years at a major law firm in Los Angeles, Nan joined the Trial Counsel's Office at the California State Bar.* I am not sure I understand what that means."

"Naughty lawyers," she answered lightly. "Shysters, crooks, ambulance chasers. We're the disciplinary arm of the state bar, trying to keep the profession honest. A thankless task, really."

"I'd say hopeless is more like it. You bust lawyers on the take?"

"That, and all sorts of other things. Embezzlers, people who steal from escrow accounts or estates or trusts. General incompetents. Substance abusers who get particularly sloppy. And the occasional truly original sociopath."

He looked puzzled. "Why would you want to do that kind of work?"

She waved an arm lazily around his office. "Why would you want to do this kind of work?"

He smiled. "Your point, counselor. And I like the idea of nailing some of those scumbag lawyers. But this is a murder investigation, and if it's all the same to you, I'll handle it myself."

"Look," she told him, "I know that as far as you're concerned I'm just another California crackpot. But I do feel a kind of ... well, not responsibility, but maybe anger is a better word. About what happened last night. I'm going to be seeing and talking to a lot of the people who were there anyway, so I don't want you to take it the wrong way if I ask people questions. I'm not trying to do your job, just to satisfy my own curiosity."

"Forget it," he told her flatly.

"Look. You can't stop me from talking to people, we both know that." She glanced at her watch. It was seven-thirty in L.A. In the A.M. "I have a friend who's a homicide detective with LAPD. Maybe it would save us both some time and aggravation if you just gave my friend a call and checked up on me?"

He sighed and reached for a pen. "What's his name?"

Nan smiled sweetly. He'd walked right into it, and she savored such moments of petty sexist triumph. "Rosalie O'Brien." She dug out her address book and gave him the numbers.

"So tell me about Brenda Blaine," he said, a moment later.

Nan closed her eyes for a moment to organize her thoughts. This was a subject she'd been considering non-stop since the moment she first saw the body. Even in her sleep, full of troubled, jumbled dreams.

"I never really knew Brenda personally until our senior year," she began slowly. "She was usually in some of my classes. Brenda was pretty smart and a good student when she felt like bothering. But she didn't seem particularly comfortable with her intelligence. Tried to hide it, in fact. With the wisdom of hindsight and therapy, I'd say she had terrible self-esteem. But, of course, that was perfectly understandable."

Delahanty raised one eyebrow into an inverted V. It was going to be tough to get this next part across.

"Let me try to explain," Nan went on. "Brenda's mother was a real rummy. Now, I don't think I ever heard the words alcoholic or alcoholism spoken out loud while I lived here, and believe me, I'd have remembered."

The eyebrow went up again, but Delahanty remained quiet. He knew, Nan admitted reluctantly, how to listen. By no means a given for a cop. She inhaled. It should be easy to talk about this. She'd spent enough time belaboring the issue in therapy and ACA meetings, after all.

But the old taboos held strong, even after twenty years. This was still Spring Hill, and everybody still remembered Phil Robinson.

"My father was an alcoholic, too." There, she'd said it. She could almost hear her father's drunken laugh. He'd always been a happy drunk, a charming and gregarious salesman who never met a stranger. "Phil Robinson. He owned Robinson Ford. How long have you been on the force here?"

"Three years."

"Then he was before your time. He's been dead for five. He knew all the cops here, cut them all great deals on new cars, gave them terrific trade-ins. In return, they'd bring him home when he was too bombed to get his key in the ignition." She could remember looking out her bedroom window and seeing the squad car pull up, watching the officer help her father stumble up the front walk. Frequently he'd be singing, loudly and off-key. Sinatra standards, for the most part. The next morning, a tight-lipped June Robinson would drop him off wherever he'd left his car.

"Mostly, he was a binge drinker," she went on. "He'd stay relatively sober for weeks and then one day he'd go down to the Lemon Twist Lounge and we'd barely see him for a week. Midway through one of those binges he wrapped himself around a telephone pole at Washington and Third downtown, going fifty-five. He was killed instantly." She had always wondered why he didn't call the station house for a ride that night.

"I'm sorry." He sounded sincere.

Nan smiled a little wryly. "It would be harder to live with if he'd taken out somebody else at the same time."

He nodded, then shifted his weight. "You were talking about Brenda Blaine."

"Yeah. Well, I always knew about Brenda's mother, and it turns out she always knew about my father. I suppose, looking back, that everybody else in town knew, too, but that's not something you want to dwell on too much when you're fifteen. When Brenda and I were seniors, we were lab partners in chemistry, random assignment. Amazingly, we really hit it off."

It *had* been amazing. Brenda revealed a slightly kooky sense of humor and a genuine interest in chemistry. She loved the experiments, reactions and reagents, watching liquids change colors and precipitate. By the second week of class, she had memorized the entire periodic table.

"Did you see her, um, socially?"

Nan chuckled and shook her head. Outside the classroom, she and Brenda Blaine had never shared a lot of common interests. Brenda was never terribly keen on student government and Nan hadn't been much into blow jobs. "Never. It wasn't something that even occurred to me. Brenda was ... well, I don't know what people have been telling you about her."

"The words that keep coming up are things like slut and tramp."

"*Nil nisi bonum*, eh? Brenda was ... let's just say she was easy. She had a *terrible* reputation. Everybody was always astonished that she didn't get pregnant sooner."

"Sooner than what?"

"Hasn't anybody told you? The summer after graduation, Brenda left town, p.g. Until last night, that was the last time anybody ever saw her here. At least, that I know about."

"Very interesting," he said. "More coffee?" He indicated the small machine on the tiny refrigerator in the corner of his office.

"I'm fine, thanks. But it's awfully good."

"My private stash," he admitted. "Rank has its privileges."

He refilled his own cup, adding sugar and pouring milk from a pint in the refrigerator. As he walked, with a light, springy bounce, he seemed to visibly displace the sticky office air.

"I thought cops always drank their coffee black and bitter," Nan commented mildly.

"Yeah, right. Like a pimp's heart. Who was the father of Brenda Blaine's baby?"

Nan shrugged. "No idea. It could have been anybody. There were rumors, but I always had the feeling nobody knew for sure. And who's to say whether Brenda even knew herself? I didn't ask her the obvious question last night, but like I told you, she talked about a nineteen-year-old son. Ryan."

"Yeah. We're trying to find him."

Nan considered. "You think Brenda's murder had to do with that pregnancy?"

"The timing is interesting. Did she get along with people?"

"In high school? Not really. Brenda kind of reeked attitude, and she mostly kept to herself. She had a lot of . . . I guess you could call them boyfriends. But you wouldn't see her at the prom, or a homecoming dance. I always felt sorry for her."

"What did you two talk about last night?"

"Alcoholic parents."

"Come on."

"Really. That wasn't all, of course, but it was really the only thing we had in common back then, and we'd *never* discussed it, not for a second. It felt very natural somehow. We'd both been in ACA."

"Adult Children of Alcoholics." Interesting that he knew.

"Yeah. It wasn't always considered chic to come from a dysfunctional family, and back when I first discovered ACA, there was nothing very trendy about it. But it was a real revelation." The amazing sense of not being the only one. Descriptions, paragraph by paragraph, page by page, seemingly scripted by a fly on the wall of the Robinson home. Checklists of traits that defined them all, like it or not.

Delahanty looked unconvinced. "You see this girl, this

virtual stranger, after twenty years apart—leading what I suspect were rather different lives—and you start yakking about your drunk parents?"

"No, not the way you're saying. But it *was* the first time we ever acknowledged to each other that we'd shared a problem. I always felt so *lonely*, not having anybody to talk to about it when I lived here. Turns out Brenda felt the same way."

I got a real kick out of knowing the high and mighty Nan Robinson had an alkie for a pop.

Delahanty shifted some papers on the desk from one tidy pile to another, straightened both piles unnecessarily. "Uh-huh. Did Brenda tell you why she was at the reunion?"

"Only that she thought it would be a real kick to come."

"Did she mention anybody she particularly wanted to see?"

"Nope. Oh, wait, after dinner she went dashing off across the room to see Frank Finney. She sounded kind of excited about seeing him."

Delahanty seemed to perk up. "And he is?"

"Just some guy. I never really knew him, and I didn't talk to him last night." It seemed gratuitously snobbish to report her teenage impression of Frank Finney: a bag boy shaped like a Shmoo.

"Hmmm," he said, making a note. "Anybody she *didn't* want to see?"

"Not that I know about."

"So why was she here?"

Nan smiled. "To show off, I'd imagine. To thumb her nose at everybody, say 'Fuck you, Spring Hill.' Brenda always had a well-developed capacity for nose-thumbing. She told me once in high school that she was born flipping a bird. I never forgot that."

Abruptly Delahanty switched tacks. "Why did you go to your car?"

"I hadn't intended to. Like I told you, I went out for a walk with a friend and on the way back in, I glanced over at the car and noticed something shiny. When I went over to check it out, there she was."

"You weren't planning to leave yet?"

She shook her head. "I think there was about an hour left of the formal reunion. And then some of us were going to go to Wally Sheehan's for a post-party party."

"Did you go?"

Nan stared at the detective. "Wally was talking to you at two-thirty this morning, while I was still cooling my heels in the Sunrise Room at the hotel. I can't imagine that he went home and threw a party after that."

"Inconsiderate of Brenda Blaine to get herself killed." Delahanty was offhand, light. "The guy you were with, this Henry Sloane, who's he?"

A missed opportunity, Nan thought sadly. It was small comfort to be spared guilt pangs over Amy Sloane and the kiddies. Henry might still be in town for the picnic this afternoon, but daylight changed a lot of things.

"Like I told you before, he's a high school principal downstate. We dated each other a bit in high school, but I hadn't seen him in eighteen years." And might not ever again.

"You left about—when?"

Nan gritted her teeth as she went through the entire story again. Brian Delahanty wore such an insufferable little smirk when he grilled her about the brief side trip into the woods. She and Henry had been separated almost immediately after they reported finding the body, and she hadn't seen him since. For all she knew, he'd already left town.

Finally Delahanty seemed satisfied. "Let's back up a little," he suggested. "Tell me about the rest of the people at your table."

For twenty minutes, Nan told him everything she remembered about her tablemates the night before, stopping midway through to pour herself more coffee. When she finished, she offered a beguiling smile.

"By all means, corroborate everything. This time on a

Sunday morning, a good place to start might be the First Methodist Church. Edwin Crosby will be delivering some incredibly dull sermon, and Rose will be singing in the choir. Mary Lee and Jim Webster are probably very visibly seated in the third pew, on the aisle. Wally Sheehan's Catholic, so if you want him, check Queen of Sorrows. Janis Levin had a room at the Spring Hill Inn. And if she isn't asleep, I bet she wishes she were. She's going to have one monster hangover today."

"Are you just in for the weekend?"

She shook her head. "I'll be here through the week. I leave on Sunday."

"Keep in touch, counselor." Detective Brian Delahanty rose to end the interview, and his tone was frosty. "And don't go away without telling me."

Nan got up, too. "I asked you before," she noted conversationally, "and you never really answered. Am I under suspicion?"

His smile was thin. "*Everybody's* under suspicion, counselor. And before you get huffy, look at this from my point of view. Two hundred and thirty-one people registered at that reunion last night. Every one of them, by their own admission, was aware of the presence of Brenda Blaine. One of them probably killed her. One or more others probably saw something that could tell us who that was. This is an investigative nightmare, and I'm not what you might call overstaffed."

He leaned back against a file cabinet. "So far we haven't got much in the line of motive. But means, hell, there were three hundred of those damned swords and no way in the world to account for them all. People dropped them, left them at tables, had them stashed already in car trunks. Opportunity? All those people milling around, most of them pretty blasted. Brenda Blaine must have been a pretty noticeable figure, but we can't find anyone who remembers seeing her leave."

"A bit overwhelming," Nan agreed.

"You're an investigator," Delahanty said in a surprisingly cordial tone. "What would you do?"

"Hmmm," Nan said. "Is that a serious question?"

He nodded.

"Well, then. I'd want to find Brenda's son and see what he knows about why she came. I'd get hold of that videotape Grant Kirby was shooting, if you haven't already."

"We've got it," Delahanty said, "but I haven't had a chance to look at it yet. It's four hours long, unedited."

"I'd also check out the people who left early. Where'd they go, and why? I'd look for discrepancies in the lists—people who say they were there at nine, say, but weren't in the class photo." The picture was a panoramic number shot by an outfit that dashed off somewhere to develop and print the photos that same night. The pictures had arrived just after the police.

Nan went on. "I'd try to reconstruct everything Brenda did and everywhere she went. Who saw her last, that sort of thing. Was she staying at the hotel?"

Delahanty nodded. "Under the name Brenda Singer. She has a live-in boyfriend named Bernie Singer out in Vegas. She mention him?"

"Not to me. She just told me she was divorced, no details. Anyway, obviously you'll be going through her stuff. She told me she dealt blackjack at the MGM Grand. I'd want to know more about that, her work, her friends, this boyfriend you mentioned. She said she's not a gambler, just likes the way folks in Vegas live on the edge. I'm not entirely certain I believed that."

Nan hesitated a moment. She'd been ready, she realized, to believe anything Brenda said last night. But this morning much of it seemed vaguely unreal.

"Maybe somebody from Vegas followed her here and killed her. It'd be a great cover. I'd check for people nobody recognized, which is probably hopeless. I'd look over the hotel register. Brenda's mother died a long time ago, but I'd see if her grandmother is still alive and talk to her."

Delahanty was nodding. Brenda wasn't the only show-off in their class, Nan realized suddenly. And Brian Delahanty was sharp enough to run his own investigation. Was he baiting her?

"Then I'd go to the reunion picnic this afternoon at Memorial Park. Everybody who's still in town is supposed to be there, and you can bet they'll all be talking about Brenda." She shrugged. "But you know to do all this stuff. Maybe the smartest thing for you to do right now would be to get some sleep before the picnic." She headed for the door. "And don't forget to call Rosalie O'Brien."

"It's right on top of my list of Things to Do Today," he assured her with a cheerful grin. "Just after 'Find killer.' " He opened the door. "See you at the picnic, counselor."

CHAPTER 4

Nan awoke disoriented, with sunshine streaming into her eyes. It took a moment to realize she was back in her childhood room again. The clock on the dresser said 1:15, but that couldn't possibly be right.

Then it all started coming back: the reunion, Henry Sloane, Brenda Blaine's body sprawled across the front seat of her car. The rental car, now impounded as evidence. Good luck explaining *that* to Hertz.

Nan swung her feet around and slowly got out of bed. This might technically be home, in the sense of when-you-go-there-they-can't-throw-you-out, but it didn't have the womblike comfort that she secretly believed *home* should offer. The place was plenty familiar, but every inch of it was layered with half-forgotten traumas, repressed angers, and the emotional maelstroms her mother was unwilling to acknowledge or address.

To further confuse matters, June Robinson had long since redecorated everything, including Nan's childhood room. The Spring Hill and Stanford pennants were gone, the twin beds replaced with a white wicker daybed. The new wallpaper was a muted paisley in pinks and blues, and the "window treatment," as Mom called it, a complicated arrangement of pleated shades and lace goober-gobbers. Undoubtedly they had a correct name—jalousies, jalopies, swags, swigs, one of those decorator terms Mom was always bandying about. But Nan had no idea what it might be.

A shower helped shake off some of her grogginess. She slipped on shorts and a T-shirt and went downstairs. Mom sat at the kitchen table, smoking a cigarette and reading the Sunday *Chicago Tribune*. She was positively agog.

"You can't believe the restraint I've exercised," Mom told her, with a wide smile that nullified her faintly accusatory tone, "not hauling you out of bed to tell me *everything*. Why on earth didn't you wake me up when you came in? Good heavens, Nan, finding a *body*!"

June Robinson's light brown hair was sleekly styled and lacked even a smidgen of gray, a fine tribute to hometown cosmetology. Even Nan had started to notice the occasional gray hair, though whenever she found one, she yanked it out immediately. Indeed, for a woman of sixty-three with no history of plastic surgery, June Robinson looked mighty fine. All those years of unguents and lotions and nightcreams had paid off; her skin remained remarkably smooth and unlined. She wore just a dab of blue shadow over her cerulean eyes. She wasn't precisely trim, at least not by California standards. But she wasn't fat either, and her church dress was bright and summery, covered with cheerful pansies.

Nan found her mother's fluttery fussing oddly reassuring, a spot of familiarity in a world suddenly gone amok. The more she thought about last night, the more bizarre everything became. What was Brenda Blaine doing in Nan's car, dead *or* alive? For that matter, what was she doing at the reunion? And why would anybody want to kill her? It was impossible to imagine a grudge strong enough to flare up after twenty years.

"I'm sorry, Mom," Nan said. "I didn't see any point in waking you up when I came in at four-thirty. And then when I went out again at quarter to nine, you were already gone." June Robinson customarily attended early services at the First Methodist Church and then taught Sunday School. "I tried to stay awake when I got back from the police station this morning, but I was just bushed."

"Well, of course you were." Mom went into her protective-mother mode, and Nan had to admit it felt good. "But you'll simply have to tell me everything now. There's iced tea in the fridge, or I can make more coffee."

"Iced tea sounds wonderful," Nan told her. "And what about some of that stuff you showed me yesterday from the Bruggentheis bakery?"

As Nan opened the white boxes and browsed, her mother poured two icy glasses of tea, adding lemon slices automatically. You couldn't fault Mom in the hostess department. "Details, Nan, now, all of them," Mom begged. "I have to admit I felt rather foolish this morning, not knowing anything at all. Everybody at church, I mean *everybody*, knew more than I did, and here it was my own daughter who . . . well, you know."

Nan gave her mother a hug and cut a generous slice of cherry strudel. She had dieted for weeks before this reunion, in a form of vanity she found vaguely unsettling. But the damn thing was over now. Full calories ahead. She munched languidly as she told June Robinson everything she knew about Brenda and the murder. It didn't take long.

"Such a terrible, terrible thing," Mom said, finally. "I don't know why she'd even bother to come back and spoil everybody else's good time."

"I don't think she was planning to get murdered, Mom."

Mom had the good grace to look embarrassed. "I think I'll just run upstairs," she said, "and see if I can't extricate my foot from my mouth while I change into something more comfortable."

Nan had polished off two slices of strudel and a custard horn by the time Mom returned in her "gardening clothes": a straw Panama hat banded in silk flowers, neatly pressed khaki slacks, and a many-pocketed pink shirt. It was a safe bet she wouldn't get her hands—or even her white Smith & Hawken goatskin gloves—dirty. This outfit was strictly for show. A yardman took care of the lawn and heavy garden chores, heavy being defined as anything more rigorous than cutting bouquets.

Mom's dog was out in the yard, the latest in a never-ending chain of nervous little yappers. This one was a blond cockapoo with the unfortunate name of Glocky. Even Mom couldn't remember why he'd originally been named Glockenspiel, but the Robinson pups had always sported dingbat names: Alfonso, Murgatroyd, Aloysius, Mehitabel, Hermione. Barefoot, Nan stepped carefully, mindful that Glocky, like his predecessors, had probably left little surprises everywhere.

"I'd love to see little Colleen in this yard," Mom said wistfully. "If only Julie could have come, too."

"She would have liked to," Nan answered diplomatically. Her sister's actual words, as she recalled, had something to do with hell freezing over. "But they've got a lot to catch up on. And Colleen isn't old enough yet to appreciate this." Julie and her family had been through a difficult spring, with a high-risk pregnancy only a small part of the trauma.

"I just miss Julie particularly in the yard," Mom went on.

"I know what you mean," Nan agreed. "I do, too."

This was the yard Nan and Julie had grown up in. Here Julie—now a commercial flower grower in San Diego County—had raised her first flowers and vegetables in a back corner reserved for her dabbling. Here, too, they had grilled hot dogs and burgers at family barbecues, played hide-and-seek and croquet, swung in the tire suspended from a limb of the horse chestnut tree.

Nan's early girlhood memories were largely happy ones. In retrospect, she could acknowledge the imperfections, the tensions, the hushed and furious quarrels her parents conducted behind closed doors. But at the time, it had just been life, and an okay one at that.

When she thought about her father during those early years, she remembered him mostly at the dinner table. As an auto dealer, Phil Robinson worked odd hours, but he never failed to be home for supper. Beyond that, she recalled visits to his auto showroom and the wonderful smell of new car interiors, annual excursions to the auto show at McCormick Place, sitting in Dad's lap and "driving" down the streets of Spring Hill back before anybody bothered with seat belts.

She was still not entirely clear when she had first noticed her father's drinking, or the problems that it created, though the awareness coincided roughly with puberty. Phil Robinson's alcoholism was not a subject his widow would discuss even now, though Nan had tried on several occasions to force the issue. Her mother's denial was absolute and extended beyond the grave. Her husband had died in an automobile accident, Mom insisted, in a way that implied mechanical failure.

Now Mom brought out a pitcher of iced tea and a bowl of dark Bing cherries. They sat in a pair of Adirondack chairs under the willow, and Mom lit another cigarette, the better to appreciate the fine midday air. The yard seemed stunningly lush, full of rich green shrubbery, thick emerald grass, and a flourishing rose garden. Cheerful borders both here and in front were full of daylilies and black-eyed Susans.

"Do you really think they'll go ahead with the picnic, Nan?" Mom asked.

Nan had given this some thought. "I'll be amazed if they don't. In fact, the murder will probably goose attendance a bit. They had us all split up into different groups under police guard last night, so nobody really got to talk about what had happened. Everybody will want to compare notes. And even before Brenda got killed, people seemed pretty jazzed about meeting each other's kids." Nan heard her mistake the moment the words passed her lips.

Mom's predictable sigh rustled the lower branches of the willow. "At least Julie finally has a child." Nan's dereliction in the production of grandchildren was a well-worn topic. "Your father always said . . ."

"My father always said, 'Don't call me to baby-sit,'

that's what my father always said," Nan told her evenly. "Let's give it a rest, okay, Mom?"

The willow branches shifted again with another exhalation. "Whatever you say, dear." Mom brightened. "Ralph is coming by tonight. I told him you were anxious to meet him."

"You bet!" Nan responded cheerfully, grateful to have the subject change so easily. Ralph Salamone was Mom's new boyfriend, and according to Mom he was desperately handsome. Nan and Julie had been tracking this whirlwind courtship—at a distance—with great interest.

Ralph Salamone sounded like the answer to every widow's prayers. Mom had met him in the late spring on a long weekend up in Door County. Ralph was widowed, well-mannered, and retired, living in Naperville. He was spectacularly attentive. He whisked Mom away for weekends in elegant restored Galena bed-and-breakfasts, cooked elaborate brunches, had even rushed Glocky-poo to the vet when the dog went suddenly lame.

"He'll be here around six," Mom said. "He makes sublime Belgian waffles, and he promised to fix them for us."

Nan counted to ten. "Mom, I thought we agreed yesterday that we wouldn't make any plans together for tonight because I'd probably still be tied up with people from the reunion."

"Well, now that there's been that horrible murder . . ."

"I came two thousand miles to see these people, and they're only going to be here through today, most of them. You *know* how anxious I am to meet Ralph, but he'll be around the rest of the week, won't he?"

Mom's backbone stiffened, and she stubbed her cigarette out irritably. Her martyrdom was no act; it was an integral part of her personality, refined during thirty-three years of flawed marriage. "Ralph has to go to Milwaukee to see his sister. She's rather ill. He's leaving Tuesday morning."

"Then why don't we have dinner tomorrow?" Nan suggested.

Mom sniffed. "Fine. In the meantime, Ralph will be making Belgian waffles here this evening." She used her patented wound-me-some-more-I-really-don't-mind-at-all voice. "If you can find the time to join us, that would be lovely. If you're too busy, of course we will understand."

Then she got up and walked slowly and deliberately into the house. In a moment of confused loyalties, Glocky circled her, then gave a sort of doggy shrug and scampered back to yip at a squirrel.

Nan leaned back and considered what she'd learned at the police station. Brian Delahanty had told her precious little, but she could still fill in quite a few blanks.

Nearly everyone at the reunion had been fingerprinted last night, peer pressure and an unwillingness to appear evasive taking ultimate precedence over manicures, dignity, and the Bill of Rights. Presumably somebody would be in jail by now if there'd been any matching prints on the sword or the car. So either the murderer had already left by the time the body was discovered, or everything had been wiped clean. Nan shivered at the image of somebody meticulously cleaning a brass sword in order to stab Brenda to death.

Death by party favor.

Which brought up another point. Brenda Blaine hadn't been the sort of woman who'd lie down in a car and watch you wipe off a sword so you could ice her. She'd kick balls, scratch eyes, put up one hell of a fight. In death she had lain peacefully with her eyes closed. So she must have been unconscious when she was stabbed.

But not dead, or she wouldn't have bled so profusely down the front of her white satin and rhinestone dress.

Nan shivered as she got up to go inside and get dressed for the reunion picnic. Somebody there was likely to be a murderer.

But who? And why?

* * *

Janis Levin looked across at Nan from the driver's seat and grinned. "Think we can peel out in this thing?" Janis was driving a rented compact Pontiac with a model name Nan had never heard of before.

Nan laughed. "We'll be lucky if we can *chug* out in it. Frankly, my dear, this ain't the old Cutlass." Janis had driven her mother's '71 Cutlass in high school, a car with definite muscle.

Janis pulled away from the curb with a minor squeal and turned left at the corner, heading away from Memorial Park where the class picnic was to be held and toward Spring Hill High School.

"So," Janis said, "now that we've ditched your mother, I want the whole story, every last pant and sigh. What happened with Henry?"

"You sound a great deal like Detective Delahanty, you know? And the only reason my mother wasn't asking the same thing is that I guess nobody told her who I was with in the woods."

"In the woods where . . ." Janis prompted patiently.

"Where *nada*, I'm sorry to say." Nan considered. "And I *am* sorry, actually. Last night before we found Brenda, I was having a minor attack of conscience, thinking that if I went off with Henry I'd regret it later. But what I'm regretting right now is that I didn't even have the chance to say no." She paused. "Which I probably wouldn't have, anyway."

"Maybe he'll be at the picnic," Janis suggested.

"Ten to one he won't," Nan told her. "And even if he is, I guarantee he'll be very formal and proper. He's a high school principal, for Pete's sake. Those people have to adhere to *standards*."

Tall deciduous trees on both sides of the street met overhead in a luxurious canopy of greenery. Nan found the lush verdancy of the Spring Hill summer jarring. Summer back home in L.A. was the dry season. Everything shriveled and parched, and the hills turned dusty brown as the chaparral desiccated. Oh, people watered lawns and gardens, of course, and Beverly Hills landscapes thumbed their bright green topiary noses at doomsaying water officials lecturing on drought and civic responsibility. But no amount of southwestern irrigation could equal this effortless display of midwestern greenery, the town's casual woodsiness in all but those newer subdivisions carved out of surrounding cornfields.

At the end of the road up ahead, Spring Hill High loomed: three stories of sturdy red brick, built to survive adolescents and the ages. And doing a fairly decent job of it, apparently.

"It seems like it ought to look different," Nan said, as they turned the corner and approached the main entrance with its massive stairway. "It's kind of scary how unchanged the place is." She felt a rush of unrelated memories. She hadn't been happy here, but the place had unquestionably shaped her.

"Twenty years really isn't that long," Janis noted, circling the building slowly. There were some kids playing softball on the athletic fields and a couple pedaling away on bikes, but no other real sign of activity. She headed out past the small strip of businesses and coffee shops adjacent to the campus. "But I'll tell you, what breaks my heart is seeing Blackie's gone."

Blackie's drive-in had been little more than a shack, but for decades it was *the* Spring Hill High gathering spot. Here social distinctions blurred. *Everybody* went to Blackie's. At lunchtime, after school, following football games, in the evenings after Y-club meetings. Blackie's served milk shakes made from ice cream and gooey double cheeseburgers and the only hot dogs Nan had ever really liked, dressed with onions and fresh tomatoes and optional chili. Five years ago, the ramshackle old drive-in had been razed, and a modern dental office now stood in its place. Somehow it didn't feel like progress.

Janis cut off down a side street. She was headed, Nan realized without asking, for the house where Henry Sloane had lived in high school. Part of Nan's and Janis's teenage driving ritual—having *finally* attained the freedom of a pair of driver's licenses—had been endlessly circling the blocks where various objects of lust or affection lived. Henry's house also appeared unchanged, though the Sloanes no longer lived there and the awnings on the front windows were royal blue now, instead of forest green.

Next Janis headed downtown, past the corner where her father's shoe store had once been. Shoe Town was a video store now.

"What do you suppose ever happened to those X-ray machines?" Nan wondered. "The ones where you'd stick your foot in and look at your own bones?"

"I dunno," Janis answered, "but I'll tell you this. My father lives in continuing terror that somebody's gonna get cancer of the toe and come sue him."

"Oh, come on!"

"Honest. Though I keep telling him if it would happen to anyone, it'd have to be me. I used to *love* to look at my toes, every single afternoon when I came by after school. And apart from one mutant toenail that seems to think it's a hoof, I'm just fine."

Janis continued through town toward Robinson Ford, renamed Friendly Ford when June Robinson sold the dealership after her husband's death. "As if it was hostile before," Mom always sniffed. But she hadn't hesitated at all to sell the place.

"You want to stop?" Janis asked as they approached.

"Nah," Nan answered, staring at an area of the lot that was fenced off with a bunch of major earthmoving machinery inside. There was still plenty of space for the current models, of course, gleaming in the afternoon sunlight. Car dealerships were notorious space hogs, and back when Dad had opened Robinson Ford he had this strip of road pretty much to himself. "What do you suppose they're doing? Construction?"

"Beats me," Janis answered. "Do we care?" She pulled in at Spring Hill Import Motors, Wally Sheehan's place, and turned around to head back into town. "And are we ready? I could probably cruise all afternoon, but if the point is to see people, we probably ought to get to the park."

Once they arrived, Nan noticed quickly that people weren't quite as eager to talk with her as they'd been the night before. A couple of casual acquaintances nodded and moved on quickly. Others chatted briefly, but couldn't quite decide whether or not to mention that Nan's dinner partner had been found dead in Nan's car. Mostly they didn't, though several people muttered something on the order of "How terrible for you." On the whole, it seemed a lot worse for Brenda.

Henry Sloane, Nan quickly ascertained, was not at the park. By now, she thought grimly, he was undoubtedly safely back home, head atom in the nuclear family.

The general atmosphere in the park was jovial but subdued. Some of the guys were grilling burgers and hot dogs near a set of picnic tables loaded with Tupperware bowls of potato salad and cole slaw and red Jell-O, a perennial midwestern fave. In the flat open section of the park—the hollow flooded each winter for ice skating—an informal volleyball game was in progress. Here and there a few folks played with Wally Sheehan's Frisbees, though Nan noticed that today nobody was pretending to fence with reunion souvenir swords, a popular pastime the night before.

Nan and Janis picked up drinks and wandered around, stopping to sit for a moment on a bench near the playground. Pam Webster and some of her friends were coordinating planned activities for the younger kids, children with old-fashioned names that would have been unthinkable thirty years earlier. Though there *were* still some limits. Nan hadn't noticed any Hepzibahs or Beulahs or Berthas or Elmers mentioned as children in the reunion program book.

Mary Lee was inordinately proud of her daughter and

had spoken about her at great length last night. Pam was sixteen, an honor student and, of course, a cheerleader.

"It's kind of a time warp, seeing her," Nan told Janis, with a nod toward Pam Webster. "I feel like I'm watching Mary Lee twenty years ago." Pam looked startlingly like her mother, but the resemblance didn't end there. She also had the same mannerisms, the same revolting peppiness, even the same girlish giggle.

"What *I* can't believe is that Mary Lee said that being a cheerleader was her kid's *birthright*," Janis grumbled. Janis had always been notably short of school spirit. She looked around and grimaced. "Well, I guess I won't be hooking up with Mr. Right today after all."

"Let me guess," Nan said, sipping her Diet Coke. "You had this idea that there'd be somebody you never knew or noticed back in high school, but he'd turned out to be . . . oh, maybe a neurosurgery professor, or a software magnate, something like that."

"Am I that obvious?"

Nan shook her head. "Not at all. I had the same idea. Which, of course, was ridiculous, but hey, stranger things happen. My friend Shannon has an aunt who went back to her *fortieth* high school reunion and ran into her high school boyfriend. They were both widowed with grown kids. *Bam!* Three months later they got married, and when they went back to the fiftieth, they were voted Cutest Couple."

"Oooh," Janis approved. "I *do* like that. But it ain't gonna happen here. Not today. Not with this crowd. And I don't think waiting twenty more years will improve anything, either. Though everybody keeps making a point of how much better they like this than the tenth."

"That makes sense. By now, most of us are pretty well settled into our lives. But ten years out, it was still crazy. A lot of us were still figuring out who and what we were going to be." Nan smiled as she remembered. "I knew for an absolute fact that I'd *never* come back, and it never occurred to me to go to the tenth. But I remember the night of that reunion real clearly. I was in San Francisco working on this big case, just starting to get involved with Leon. I got really ripped and kept playing Paul Simon singing 'My Little Town' on a boom box in my hotel room. Over and over again, *loud*. My God, I was mature."

Janis laughed and peered across the park. "Say, isn't that your buddy the detective by the barbecues?"

Nan followed Janis's gesture. "It surely is. Maybe I'll just mosey over there and see if he's come up with anything. You want to come with?"

Janis shook her head. "Spies do better on their own. I'll go get something to eat, I think. My flight back tonight is only a snack."

"They're *all* only snack flights any more," Nan noted. "Though, actually I think I prefer it. You know where you stand with an apple and a cup of yogurt. Whereas those mystery meat cutlets always seemed like something that got sucked through jet engines." Nan brightened. "Did I tell you the flight attendant on my plane out had OH MISS as her name tag?"

"So did mine," Janis answered. "Now get on with it, will you? I want gossip, details, sordid inside information to dish at the office tomorrow."

"At your service," Nan told her with a crooked salute as she meandered off in the general direction of Detective Brian Delahanty, who was now deep in conversation with Jim Webster in the shade of a massive oak tree.

"Well, hello there," Jim Webster greeted Nan as she sauntered up to the two men. He offered a practiced handshake, not the previous evening's hug. Congressional candidates just couldn't be too careful. He turned back to Brian Delahanty. "Give me an update tonight," he told the detective. "I'll be home." Then he was gone.

Nan smiled at Brian Delahanty. He looked pretty good in daylight, and more at ease outdoors than in his cramped little office. His body wasn't half-bad, either, particularly in comparison to some of her tubbier classmates. Of course, some of the most perfect male bodies Nan had ever seen belonged to intellectual anacephalitics.

First things first. "Did you talk to Rosalie O'Brien?" she asked.

He smiled faintly. "Yeah."

"And?"

"And she said that if you were going to kill somebody, you wouldn't do it in your own car, and you'd make damned good and sure somebody else found the body."

Nan laughed. "Well put. So does that mean I'm not a suspect?"

"All that means," he responded laconically, "is that one detective on another force is your buddy. Thought of anything helpful since this morning?"

"Mostly since this morning I've been asleep," Nan admitted.

"Wish I could say the same thing. Your boyfriend still here?"

"If you mean Henry Sloane," Nan answered carefully, "I don't think so. At least I haven't seen him."

Brian Delahanty gave a twinkly grin. "Too bad. Say," he went on, "I just had a very interesting conversation with a detective in Las Vegas." His tone was vaguely conspiratorial. "The guy had a Brooklyn accent so thick I thought I was in a Scorsese movie. He says Brenda Blaine had a few outstanding parking tickets, but other than that she's clean in Nevada. Lives in a glitzy new development. He's going to check for possible gambling difficulties, underworld connections, what he called 'the usual scumsearch.' "

"Interesting," Nan answered, sweeping her hair back with one hand. The sky was clouding up a bit, and it was starting to feel muggy. "Have you found Brenda's son yet?"

"He's off somewhere in Alaska on a national park wilderness maintenance crew," Delahanty told her. "Now that we know where he is, we're trying to get word to him. I got that from Brenda's live-in boyfriend, Bernie Singer. Says the kid's a big conservationist."

"You talked to her boyfriend?"

Delahanty's face closed. "Yeah."

"And?" Apparently he wanted to be begged.

"And he's a big fat question mark," Delahanty answered with an air of finality.

"Meaning that you don't know anything, or you're not going to tell me?"

Delahanty grinned. "A bit of both, actually. There's nothing obviously wrong with the guy, I can tell you that. He's as superficially clean as Brenda. Plays cocktail-bar piano at Caesar's Palace, and he called in sick last night."

Nan started making rapid calculations in her head: geography, time zones, airline schedules. "So he could have come here? And killed Brenda? Is that what you're saying?"

"Not at all, counselor, not at all. But he didn't answer the phone at Brenda's house until nearly two-thirty this afternoon. Says he's been laid out with stomach flu, that he turned off the phone."

"Are you going to check at O'Hare?" Nan asked.

"As soon as the Vegas guy wires me Singer's photo," Delahanty promised. "And speaking of Singer, he gave me one piece of hot gossip, something you might want to mention to a few folks if you happen to be shooting the shit about Brenda this afternoon."

Nan looked quizzically at Brian Delahanty. He was smiling openly now. "You're sending me out to rumormonger, did I hear that correctly?"

"Perish the thought. But you know, I can't worry too much about muddying the waters of this investigation, since it started out as basic sewer sludge anyway. And sometimes if you throw in a big enough rock, you can scare some bottom feeder into making a move."

"So what's the rock?" Nan asked.

He leaned forward conspiratorially. "Do us both a favor

and don't tell anybody where you heard this. Be kind of vague, but act like you know what you're talking about." He gave a quick grin. "Lawyers are good at that sort of thing. Anyway, Singer claims Brenda was really looking forward to going to Spring Hill, had talked about it for months. That she was planning to see her kid's father."

"Oh *really*?" Nan's eyes widened.

Brian Delahanty's smile became positively beatific. "You heard me, counselor. The boyfriend says Brenda told him Ryan's father is a big shot in Spring Hill."

CHAPTER 5

Nan waved good-bye to Wally Sheehan, pasted a smile on her face, and strolled in her mother's front door, calling out a nice cheery, "Hello!" It was seven-thirty, long past the Waffle Hour.

Mom emerged from the back of the house, frowning at her wafer-thin gold watch. She was followed closely by a man who could only be Ralph Salamone.

"Sorry it took so long to get here," Nan apologized. "I stayed to help clean things up at the park." Surely Mom couldn't fault her for pitching in with the old gang. "Am I too late for the Belgian waffles?" With luck, the answer would be yes.

"The kitchen's closed," Mom sniffed.

Ralph Salamone hovered discreetly back by the doorway to the sunporch. He was handsome to a fault: a full head of silver hair, warm olive complexion, dark brown eyes that glittered in greeting. He wore pale gray slacks with a cream knit sport shirt and expensive Italian loafers. He was physically slight, not much taller than June Robinson, who was shod tonight in flat dress sandals.

"Hello," Nan said, as Ralph stepped forward. "I'm Nan Robinson." She extended a hand, which Ralph stunned her by kissing. Nobody had *ever* kissed her hand before, not even as a joke.

"I'd have known you anywhere," he effused. "You're almost as lovely as your mother. And your mother, I don't have to tell you, is one in a million."

Nan stifled her gag reflex as Mom twittered graciously and suggested they adjourn to the sunporch. It was a room Nan loved. From April through October, louvered windows opened on three sides of screening to catch any possible breeze. In winter, storm windows created the illusion of being outdoors without any nasty exposure to the elements. It was a nice, if not terribly functional place: too cold in winter, too hot in summer, furnished in rattan with a few big houseplants, a couple of dozen needlepoint pillows, and a panoramic view of the backyard. The cribbage board was set up on a table.

"I had no idea it was getting so late," Nan began.

"Please!" Ralph exclaimed, holding up a hand to stop her. "I understand there's been a terrible tragedy, but even so, it must be wonderful to see so many friends after so many years. I feel honored you could join us at all tonight."

Mom remained pouty, the mercury bursting right through the top of the old Martyr-Meter. "I was simply starving. We couldn't wait a moment longer."

"Of course not, and no reason why you should have," Nan said. Enough already. "But there was a ton of food at the picnic. I'm really pretty stuffed."

"How about a cappuccino, then?" Ralph asked.

Mom glowed. "Ralph gave me the most wonderful espresso machine," she simpered. Fool that Mom was for any new kitchen appliance that came around the bend, it was a wonder that she didn't already own three. Though if she did, she'd never tell Ralph.

In the kitchen they made small talk while Ralph cranked up the mini-espresso machine, a streamlined matte-black device that would fit perfectly into one of Mom's oversized cupboards. The cupboards—installed as part of a major remodel—ran floor-to-ceiling everywhere and were crammed with obscure kitchen paraphernalia: pasta extruders, bread bakers, yogurt nurturers, gelato freezers, hundreds of baking pans and molds, and every Cuisinart accessory ever issued.

Most of this stuff had been used once or twice and then shelved, the reality being that June Robinson lived alone and was forever on one goofy-ass diet or another. The cashew-and-cream-cheese diet. The wild-rice-and-mushrooms diet. The Starts-with-P diet. Nothing as plebian as counting calories ever went on at 755 Madison Street. Mom's idea of exercise was brisk hair-brushing, though she attended a low-impact aerobics class. So low-impact, indeed, that she'd probably never moistened any of her color-coordinated sweatbands.

Back on the sunporch with their cappuccinos, they doused the lights. The evening sky to the east was purplish as sunset neared. The Heights was a quiet neighborhood. Crickets chirped while random fireflies lit the evening air. Nan loved fireflies, and had almost forgotten them. She'd never seen a single one in Southern California.

Ralph Salamone, with Glocky contentedly curled at his feet, made good conversation, wandering easily through neutral topics. They commiserated about the pathetic season the Cubs were having, a conversation that made Nan feel vaguely disloyal to her father's memory. Phil Robinson had been a die-hard Cubs fan, always up for an expedition to Wrigley Field. Was this guy a potential stepfather?

Ralph had fresh gossip about the latest Chicago Democratic scandal, a multilevel scam wherein a host of people received big chunks of public money for the construction of municipal facilities that never quite got built. There was a timelessness to the tale; it seemed to Nan that she'd spent her entire life hearing about various Chicago Democrats caught with their hands in public cookie jars.

Ralph's sense of humor was quick and sharp, and he covered a wide range of subjects, carefully avoiding the reunion and murder at Nan's request. As they spoke, evening melded into night, and his arm tightened around June Robinson's shoulders on the love seat they shared. A *love seat*, for crying out loud. This was beyond trite.

When Mom's yawns began to merge, Ralph stood up. Beyond the screens, the fireflies continued blinking.

"I can't remember when I've had such a pleasant evening in the company of two lovelier women," Ralph said. By now Nan was almost accustomed to the flowery hyperbole. "But you must be exhausted, Nan, and of course, you're still on California time."

California time was two hours earlier, but it was as good an excuse as any to end the evening. And a reminder that she needed to make some phone calls, too. After Ralph kissed Nan's hand in farewell, she slipped up to her room and called Rosalie O'Brien in L.A. Rosalie's machine picked up, and Nan left a message of thanks for the character reference her detective friend had given Brian Delahanty.

Next she tried her sister Julie, who was always home at night and answered on the first ring. Julie listened through Nan's brief recap of the murder, then demanded the lowdown on Ralph.

"I don't know," Nan told her hesitantly. "He's handsome and he's charming and he'll talk your ear off, but there's something that's just not quite ... I don't know. He's smarmy, and he kissed my *hand*, for God's sake, but it's more than that."

"Is he after her money?" Julie had a definite practical streak.

"Hard to say. He's dressed well, and they seem to go to nice places. I can't imagine Mom paying his way, or even going Dutch. She'd be deeply offended."

"But she's so *vulnerable*," Julie pointed out. "And I hate to say this, but if he's as handsome as you say, I think she'd be willing to overlook stuff. And I think this nonsense about no pictures is kind of screwy." June Robinson had apologized for not sending her daughters photos of Ralph, saying he was superstitious about having his picture taken.

"I don't like it either," Nan admitted.

"Well, isn't there some way to check on him?"

"She'd kill us if she found out."

"Yeah, but she'd only have to find out if there's something wrong with him."

Julie had a point. "I'll see if I can think of something," Nan promised. Like what? Calling Interpol?

When Nan emerged from her room after ten more minutes of reunion gossip, Mom had already gone to bed. Sleep was out of the question for Nan. Her internal clock was hopelessly snarled, what with jet lag and time changes and late-night interrogations and midday naps. All seasoned liberally with cappuccino. She wandered through the house, turning off lights, and went out into the backyard.

The stars always seemed especially close in this yard. Phil Robinson had shared his love of astronomy with his daughters, had taught them constellation names and the accompanying myths. Father and daughters had risen together at dawn to watch rocket launchings on grainy black-and-white TV, while Mom whipped up French toast out in the kitchen.

Nan looked up into the heavens now, and wondered where her father was, if he was anywhere at all.

Then she went inside, got a cold can of Diet Coke, picked up her graduation yearbook from the kitchen counter, and headed for the attic.

Each steep riser that Nan climbed seemed to carry her back closer to her childhood. The attic had always been her refuge, her sanctuary, a place nobody would follow to harangue or criticize or cavil. Nan had read Nancy Drew up here, Sherlock Holmes and Miss Marple and Perry Mason, with a thermos of lemonade beside her in the summer and one of hot cocoa in the winter. It was years since she'd been in this attic.

She could feel the temperature rising as she reached the top of the stairs. Sometime in the predawn hours the attic might cool off slightly, but right now it was a stifling oven. Midwestern weather alternated sweltering summers and frigid winters, each extreme unbearable in its own unique and charming fashion. Because Phil Robinson had always been skeptical of central air-conditioning, Mom still refused to install it. The house made do with window units in the bedrooms and several freestanding fans that whirred at intervals on the first floor.

The attic was unfinished, full of random piles of boxes, odd little tables, chairs and dressers that had failed to make the decorating cut during various renovations. Most of the furniture was shrouded in sheets.

Nan found her childhood telescope and opened its case, caressed the parts lovingly. She'd take it home with her, she decided impulsively. It would be useless in smoggy L.A., of course, but she could set it up down at Julie's house in Floritas. Which would also give her something to do when she visited, no minor consideration.

She replaced the telescope and set the case by the stairs, then crossed to the corner where a tiny dormer window opened above the table Nan had used as her childhood "office." Between bookends on the table were six years' worth of Spring Hill High School yearbooks, covering the time both Nan and Julie had been students. There was a gap where Mom had pulled out Nan's graduation year, the volume she was carrying now.

Not certain just what she was looking for, Nan plugged in the old black-wire attic fan and set it to HIGH. Then she pulled the sheets off an overstuffed armchair she had always liked, one Dad had used a lot, and carried over her four yearbooks.

Brenda Blaine had come back to Spring Hill specifically to attend this reunion, a reunion her Vegas boyfriend said she was really excited about.

Why?

It seemed logical that she wanted to see the father of her child, the "big shot." She was feeling assertive and confrontational, and if Big Daddy was in town, Brenda would make it a point to see him. But did Ryan's father know he *was* Ryan's father?

Probably.

Was he paying for his knowledge?

Almost certainly. Brenda hadn't seemed the sort who'd be above a spot of mild extortion. And this wasn't even extortion, simply child support.

So then, who *was* Ryan Blaine's father?

The possibilities seemed almost limitless. Brenda got around. No reason to assume it was a classmate, either. Brenda would have been capable of boffing anybody, from the morning paperboy to Old Man McWhirter, the high school principal. And she wouldn't have worried about justifying herself, either.

Nan hadn't watched Brenda continuously at the reunion, of course. But she *had* been continually aware of her, and so had plenty of other people. Even if she hadn't been killed, nobody at that reunion would ever have been likely to forget seeing Brenda Blaine.

She'd done everything to call attention to herself but stand on a table screaming, "I'm happy, dammit. I didn't just survive, I did mighty well, thank you all very much and fuck you, too." Still, apart from the folks at their dinner table and Frank Finney, Nan hadn't noticed her spending any length of time with anybody, though there'd been a stretch when she'd danced with all comers. Maybe Brenda's return was simply a matter of wanting the hometown pooh-bahs to see that she was vivacious and voluptuous and sober and happy.

Nan sighed, blew the dust off the tops of the yearbooks, and opened the book from freshman year. Brenda didn't have an individual head shot, and appeared only with the Frosh Club, an organization inclusive of all ninth graders. She was a skinny brunette in that picture, standing at the end of a row. Her hair was lacquered up into a beehive with a striking blond streak climbing the side. Already, her chin stuck out defiantly.

Sophomore year there was only a class picture. The hairstyle was the same but it was all light now, a darkish honey-blond. She stared at the camera through thick smears of eyeliner and long artificial lashes. Nan recalled Brenda in the girls' room with an eyelash curler—a truly medieval implement—leaning toward the mirror while her cigarette smoldered on the sink.

Junior year Brenda's lipstick was white and her hair very pale. The hairstyle was totally different, no longer lacquered high at all. Now it hung long, straight, and flowing. She looked almost like an entirely different person, but the eyes were the same, raccooned in kohl. In her Typing Club picture, she sat in the front row wearing light tights and a skimpy A-line striped mini-dress. Brenda was constantly testing the boundaries of the Spring Hill High dress code, forever being sent home to put on a looser sweater or a longer skirt.

By her graduation photo, Brenda had stopped smiling.

She looked cold and hard and significantly older than most of the other boys and girls pictured on the same page. She also looked quite pretty, in a cheap, starlet kind of way. She wore a soft, fuzzy black angora sweater that Nan remembered well, often worn over a black and yellow-striped miniskirt with black tights. The outfit gave Brenda the look of a shapely bumblebee.

The entry beside the picture read: BRENDA LOUISE BLAINE: *Frosh Club, 1; Gym Leader, 3, 4; Typing Club, 3. Monroe Secretarial College.* No clues here.

Nan flipped a few pages to her own entry: NANCY LYNN ROBINSON: *Student Council, 1, 2, Secretary 3, President 4; Yearbook Staff, 3, Features Editor, 4; State Leadership Commission, 4; National Honor Society, 4; Quill & Scroll, 4. Stanford University.* An entirely different world.

There was only one more picture of Brenda in the senior yearbook. With the gym leaders in their white shorts, she was almost indistinguishable from the other girls, most of whom also had yards of center-parted, gleaming, flowing hair. Mary Lee was in that picture, too, and Janis Levin.

At a temporary impasse, Nan flipped randomly through the book, hoping for inspiration. Mary Lee was everywhere, her bright eyes glittering, her dark pixie feathered and bouncy around her pretty face. Jim Webster was big and hulking in a dozen pages of football shots, Mary Lee peppy and spirited on the sidelines. Jim crowned Mary Lee Homecoming Queen on the field and danced the first dance with her at the Homecoming Dance. There were all sorts of cheerleading pictures registering various levels of histrionics.

A poignant shot showed Jim clowning with his close friend Jerry Leffingwell, posed as muscle-men outside the gym in their letter sweaters. Nan wondered if Jerry would seem so frozen in time if she didn't know he had died a few short years later. There was an odd quality to pictures when you knew the person was no longer alive.

Janis Levin was in many of the same clubs as Nan—and Nan, who'd been responsible for scheduling most of the group shots, was in just about every club photo but the Chess Team. Brenda's old buddy Frank Finney showed up in baseball and business rep pictures, and Nan noted that his butt was every bit as big as she remembered it. Wally Sheehan was recorded in a dozen goofy poses, and in several group shots had mugged outrageous faces.

Edwin Crosby was in Student Council with Nan, headed the United Fund Drive and the UNICEF Trick-or-Treat operation. Rose was a joiner, a member of groups like the Spanish Club that didn't do anything but gather annually for a yearbook photo. With her lips clamped tightly together in every picture, Rose looked like the last child left in an orphanage.

They *all* looked so incredibly young, so unformed. Some of them—Brenda, for instance—now had children older than they'd been in these photos. But young as they appeared, with the exception of Rose, they carried an aura of invincibility, seemed totally certain of themselves.

If only there were some way to save up that certainty for later on, to apply the self-confidence of seventeen to the endless crises of adulthood.

"Is Jim Webster's business in trouble?" Nan asked her mother over coffee and the last of the cherry strudel on Monday morning.

"Why, whatever do you mean?" Mom asked, wide-eyed.

Nan returned the innocent gaze with one of her own. She'd trained under a pro, after all. "Well, I kept getting the feeling yesterday at the picnic that maybe things aren't quite as rosy at Webster Construction as Jim and Mary Lee kept bragging. That there's some kind of big problem with this new industrial park of his, for instance."

"Oh, *that*," June Robinson coyly waved an airy hand.

"You want me to beg, is that it?"

Mom shrugged. "I wouldn't mind. But no, there was just a kind of silly misunderstanding about the property for a while. I think it's all straightened out now."

Straightening out a misunderstanding about property in the Chicago metropolitan area usually involved the surreptitious transfer of folding money, as Nan recollected. Or a visit from a guy named Vito with a talent for amateur knee rearrangement.

"Tell me about it."

"It really wasn't anything, Nan, honest. Now, certainly construction has slowed down in this area recently, for Jim and everybody else, but there are still some things being built."

"I noticed something going on at the dealership," Nan interrupted. *Which* dealership was, of course, a given. "I meant to ask you about that. What are they doing?"

Mom sniffed. "Well, it's no business of *mine*, though that vulgar Lithuanian who bought the place did come around suggesting I should help pay. Can you imagine?"

"Help pay *what*?"

"Oh, you know the gas pump your father had there?"

Nan nodded. It had always been a real kick to drive into Robinson Ford, fill the tank, and not have to pay.

"Well," Mom continued, a study in forbearance, "it seems that the silly thing is leaking, and they're making them dig it up and dispose of it. All very complicated and, as I said, no concern of mine." She took a brief pause to breathe, then continued. "Now, about Potawatomi Park. It's going up on the old LaForce farm. You know, about a mile beyond the dealership on Highway 273? Well, it turned out that there was an old family cemetery out there that everybody had forgotten about. So things were held up a little while till they figured out what to do with it, whether to move the graves or what."

Yuck. "And did they move the graves?"

Mom shook her head. "They changed the plans instead, to work around them. They're fixing up the plot—which was actually *totally* run down and overgrown—and then they're going to put a little historical museum right next to it, all about the French settlers in this area."

"Victory from the jaws of defeat," Nan noted. "Very Websteresque. You know, we never really got to talk about this. Do you think he's got a chance, running for Congress?"

Mom raised her hands, palms up. "Who knows? If he gets endorsed by the retiring incumbent, old George Whaley, then certainly. A really good chance, actually. He's a very good-looking boy, and he's been extremely successful. People like him, Nan."

"Jim Webster in Congress," Nan marveled. "It'd almost be worth a trip to Washington." Where she could stay with her ex and his new wife, maybe. It was always nice to have something to look forward to. Now, however, it was time to get busy. "Who do I know at the high school?"

Mom shifted gears easily. She was the Spring Hill equivalent of a CIA database. "Right now?" She set down her juice glass and wrinkled her brow slightly.

"Yup. Like a teacher, preferably somebody who'll be there today. Teaching summer school or something. Any ideas?"

"Why?" Mom asked suspiciously.

"I want to take a look at the old yearbook files." Nan explained the previous night's yearbook session in the attic. "When I was on the staff, at the end of each year we'd gather up everything that was left—duplicate photos, outtakes, whatever—and put it in banker's boxes. They stored them down in a corner of the basement."

Mom frowned skeptically. "Surely you don't expect those things to still *be* there."

"Why not? When we'd take the stuff down, there was a little storage room with boxes that went back to before World War II."

"They'll have pitched it all years ago."

"Maybe not."

They hadn't.

True to expectation, Mom had come up with the name of a former classmate of Julie's on the Spring Hill faculty. Maggie Bainbridge was now Margaret B. Dougherty, guidance counselor. Nan found her on the phone behind an ancient wooden desk in the Counseling Center, where not even the bulletin board displays seemed to have changed in twenty years.

Maggie smiled and waved Nan to a chair as she spoke into the receiver. The big room was otherwise deserted. "Mrs. Tucker, the reason that Tom's enrolled in summer school in the first place is because his attendance was so poor last spring. Would it help if I spoke to his boss?" Maggie made a face into the phone as she listened. "I'm not trying to get him into trouble, I'm trying to keep him *out* of it. Mrs. Tucker, I know he needs the job. I understand that. All right." She jotted down a number and hung up.

"Well, hello there!" Maggie spread her arms wide. "Welcome to your past! Does it give you the willies?" Nan had known Maggie only as one of Julie's friends. She was as striking now as she'd been then, with thick dark hair, a perfectly oval olive-complected face, and bright black eyes. She asked about Julie now, and seemed pleased with Nan's answers.

"I'm glad she's doing something unconventional," Maggie said.

"She calls herself a farmer," Nan answered. "Around these parts that's not too terribly unconventional."

"But these people grow corn and soybeans," Maggie reminded, "and Julie grows *flowers*. Which doesn't seem the same at all to me. So. You said when you called that you wanted to find out about Brenda Blaine. I've done some checking. All of her official records have been subpoenaed, so they're at the police station. But the old yearbook stuff, yeah. It's still down in the basement. C'mon."

Maggie had come full circle from her days of patchwork denim and ratty T-shirts. She looked ultra-efficient in a crisp beige summer suit and low-heeled green pumps. She stepped gingerly down the basement stairs and avoided touching anything as she led Nan past the giant boilers in the school's heating plant. A layer of dust lay on all the machinery, which had been shut down for months. There was no central air-conditioning, Spring Hill High being customarily cooled by opening the windows.

Maggie turned a corner and they continued down a corridor lined with ominous-looking gray pipes. At the end of the hall Maggie unlocked a door and pulled a light cord hanging just inside the door.

The storage room was exactly as Nan remembered it, the walls lined with cardboard storage boxes. She located the year of her graduation and the preceding two years. There were six heavy boxes altogether, and Maggie found a dolly to get them upstairs.

In the counseling office, Nan set up shop on an unused wooden desk and began sorting through random photographs and files. It was probably unreasonable to hope that somebody had left a signed note expressing annoyance with Brenda Blaine and noting a plan to bump her off in twenty years. But short of that, Nan had no idea what she was looking for.

She flipped through a sheaf of sports pictures. Nothing. Outtakes from group photos showed glimpses of underwear and a couple of blurs where students had moved unexpectedly. She moved now to a stack of candids, and after ten more minutes came across a picture of Brenda Blaine.

Brenda was in the background, actually, sitting on a low concrete wall and laughing with a girl Nan recognized immediately, though it took a moment to remember her name. Liza, that was it. With one of those Polish names that was all consonants and pronounced entirely differently from the way it looked. Krzyzanowski. Yeah. Pronounced *Zhu-shan-ow-ski*. Nan was virtually certain that Liza hadn't been at the reunion, and a quick check of the group photo and program book confirmed it. Liza Krzyzanowski wasn't even listed as MISSING. Curious.

Liza had been impossibly tiny, one of those girls who manage to pack plenty of curves into maybe ninety pounds. Barely five feet tall, though she'd had a lot of dark curly hair that gave her a bit of extra height.

Most important, she'd been good buddies with Brenda. Memories of the two of them together were coming back thick and fast now. A pair of self-styled rebels who ate lunch together, smoked in the johns, ditched classes regularly, and rode around town in Liza's beat-up Chevy Malibu. Liza had been loose, like Brenda, not somebody who hung out with a Miss Priss like Nan.

Liza was the most promising lead yet to Brenda's past. Surely *somebody* knew where she was. Nan would check with Mary Lee, who'd handled registration, and see if they'd tried to find her for the reunion.

She spent another hour and a half looking through the boxes, but came up empty. On impulse, she slipped the shot of Brenda and Liza into a folder she'd brought, then stacked the boxes by the desk.

"Don't worry about taking those downstairs," Maggie told her. "I've got a student coming in who's working off community service hours. He can take them back."

"In *high school*? Community service hours?"

"You'd better believe it. We're firm believers in nipping juvenile delinquency in the bud here at Spring Hill. There're kids all over town doing hours at the Senior Center and Parks District."

Nan nodded approvingly. "I like it. You know, at the other end of the spectrum, I saw one of your bright stars in action the other day. Pam Webster."

Maggie smiled. "She's a real honey. We've got other kids here whose parents were our classmates, but Pam really shines. Just like her mom did, I guess, though I don't recall firsthand. I was a sophomore when you guys were seniors, and my early high school memories are a bit hazy."

"Hey," Nan said, "it's *all* pretty fuzzy to me."

Maggie looked around theatrically to be sure they were alone, leaned forward, and lowered her voice. "That wasn't exactly what I meant," she said, "though I will deny this on fifty thousand Bibles if you ever blab to the school board. Your sister and I were kind of out of it for a couple years there, stoned out of our minds, listening to the Grateful Dead."

Nan laughed, thinking back. "Well, I knew you were up to no good. And let me guess. They don't let Deadheads be guidance counselors?"

Maggie giggled. "I don't think there's an official policy on it, and I'd just as soon not be the test case. Of course I was never *truly* hard-core. Didn't follow them to Egypt and all that. On the other hand, I didn't miss a midwestern concert for decades."

The imagery was really rather wonderful. The only guidance counselor Nan remembered from her own high school days had been about eighty-five years old and half-deaf. "You ever run into any of your students at concerts?"

"Once," Maggie recalled with a chuckle. "And it was a kid I'd been working with for months. He thought he was hallucinating me."

CHAPTER 6

Before leaving the high school, Nan called the Webster house and was told that both Jim and Mary Lee were at the Potawatomi Industrial Park construction site. She stopped at a convenience store for a Diet Coke and arrived at the site around eleven.

The project might have been slowed down previously, but things seemed to be in full swing now. There was a lot of heavy equipment in action, and work crews busy doing whatever it is that workmen do at such places; Nan had no idea, really.

She parked outside the double-wide trailer offices beside a cream-colored Jaguar with the license plate MLW and a spiffy black Chevy truck that said WEBSTER CONSTRUCTION on its doors. Several older cars and trucks, presumably belonging to the workmen, were parked behind the building.

Inside, Mary Lee was alone, sitting at a desk near the door scribbling on some charts. She beamed, jumped up, and acted as if she'd been waiting all morning, not daring to *hope* that Nan might drop by. She wore crisp white slacks and a navy boat-neck blouse, not exactly construction attire but well enough suited to this casual office.

The office had a mildly disordered feel to it. Several desks were littered with papers, and the furniture was all utilitarian—metal desks, plastic in-boxes, big square wastebaskets. A temporary facility that would move wherever the action was, and probably quite different from the formal office in town. The trailer's most striking feature was the dozens of artists' drawings and photos of past construction projects that virtually covered the walls.

"I was over at the high school this morning," Nan told Mary Lee, "looking through the back yearbook files from when we were there. I ran across a picture of Brenda Blaine with a girl that I remember as being her close friend. Liza Krzyzanowski. I know you spent a lot of time tracking people down for the reunion, and I thought maybe you'd remember something about her." Nan took out the purloined photo and laid it on Mary Lee's desk.

Mary Lee frowned earnestly. "Liza Krzyzanowski? Oh, *right*, I do remember her, now that I see the picture. But I don't recall finding her, or even looking. Oh, wait! I know what it was. Liza never graduated." She made a mildly guilty little face. "I guess I should have tried to find her anyway, 'cause she *was* in our class, but frankly, it was so overwhelming tracking down the folks who *did* graduate, that I just kind of let it slide."

"She didn't graduate?"

Mary Lee shook her head. "Nope. She left in the spring sometime, ran away as I recall."

"Hmmph. I didn't know that." Of course, there was no reason Nan would have known. She didn't remember ever having any classes with Liza, or even speaking to her. And kids *had* run away back then, maybe not often, but with a certain depressing regularity. There had seemed to be so many more interesting things happening outside of Spring Hill than at home. "I don't suppose you have any idea how I might find her?"

"I haven't the foggiest," Mary Lee answered breezily. "She may have family still in town or something. Like I said, it was tough enough finding the people I actually *knew*, the ones who *did* graduate. You have no idea how scattered everybody is, and people's parents have moved away, too. It was really a logistical nightmare."

"What about Brenda's family, then? I know her mother

died a long time ago, but what ever happened to her grand-mother?"

Mary Lee pointed an enthusiastic finger at Nan. "That I *do* know. Her grandma's in the same place my mother is, right here in town. Golden Valley." She swung her pointed finger to one of the artists' renditions—a series of low white buildings surrounded by woods. Her expression appeared truly pained. "We built it about eight years ago, never dreaming we'd need it ourselves so soon. It's really a lovely facility."

Nan wasn't sure what to say. "I hadn't realized that your mom . . ."

"She's got Alzheimer's," Mary Lee answered shortly. "It's really a terrible tragedy."

"I'm so sorry," Nan told her with utter sincerity. Of all the problems she and her contemporaries faced as their parents aged, Alzheimer's was the one she feared the most. It was so insidious and heartbreaking, and so often its victims were otherwise in excellent health. "I didn't know."

"Dad died six years ago," Mary Lee said, "not too long before your father died. He had cancer, and I thought then that was the worst thing that could possibly happen. I was wrong."

"How long has she . . ."

"She's been in Golden Valley two years now, but she was getting steadily worse for a couple of years before that. We didn't know *what* to do, really. My sister's down in Texas and she couldn't take her. Jim wanted to keep her at our house, and have full-time care for her, but it would have seemed like . . . I don't know, like having a prison wing or something. And Golden Valley has a separate Alz-heimer's unit. So she's got a room of her own and round-the-clock attendants, and there's always a doctor on call. She hasn't recognized me for years, but I still feel so *guilty* having her there."

"You shouldn't," Nan assured her. "Just be grateful that you're able to afford what she needs."

Mary Lee rolled her eyes skyward. "Don't I know it! Medicare won't help you till you've exhausted all your resources, and insurance never covers enough. I know of so many people who've just been financially *ruined*." She sighed. "I visit her, of course, but . . ." She visibly straightened her shoulders. "Still, there's a lot of other people at Golden Valley who are really doing quite well, who just need a certain amount of help. I spend a lot of time there, delivering books from the library outreach program."

"That's nice."

"It's the least I can do," Mary Lee told her. "I'm on the library board, of course, but that's just administrative. This can really make a difference for people. Brenda's grandmother, for instance. Mrs. McReedy. She takes two books a week from the large-type collection."

"Did you get Brenda's address from her grandmother? To let her know about the reunion?"

"Oh, no!" Mary Lee answered, shocked. "I did mention the reunion to her, of course, and I asked if she had any idea how to get in touch with Brenda, but she said she hadn't heard from her in twenty years. In a way that made it quite clear that the subject was closed. I don't know *how* Brenda found out about the reunion, actually. I've been wondering about that."

"Could she have called the high school?" Nan wondered.

Mary Lee cocked her finger again. "You know, I bet that's it! Maybe *you* ought to be investigating this instead of the police." Her tone was light. "Or are you already?"

Nan shrugged her shoulders. "Not really. But I *am* curious, I'll admit that. And nosy, of course."

"Well, anything I can help you with, you just give a holler. Listen, we've got to get together for dinner this week, okay?"

"Sounds good. Tonight's out of the question, though. I met Mom's new boyfriend last night and he's coming tonight. I was kind of in the doghouse for staying so late at the picnic, actually."

"Well, I, for one, am glad you did, and not just 'cause you helped clean up. We never get enough time to visit when you're in town."

No accident, Nan thought, since (a) she hardly ever came to Spring Hill, and (b) she had virtually no interest in seeing Mary Lee Webster. "Have you met my mother's, uh . . . suitor?"

"Is he that handsome man she was with at the Baxter wedding?"

Nan smiled ruefully. Mary Lee was at least as good a gossip source as June Robinson, and quite possibly better, being plugged into local government at its highest levels. "Probably."

Mary Lee was on a roll. "White hair, Italian, very handsome, wonderful manners. Ralph . . . no, don't tell me, I've got it . . . Salamone."

"That's the one. You liked him?"

"I thought he was adorable." Mary Lee leaned forward conspiratorially. "Is it serious with your mom and this guy?"

"Who knows?" Nan tried to keep the edge out of her voice. "He seems almost too good to be true."

"So what about tomorrow night for dinner, then?" Mary Lee rattled on. "Say, about six-thirty? I'll see if Wally can come, too, and we can really let down our hair, just like old times." Whatever old times Mary Lee alluded to had never included Nan, but memory could be mighty selective.

"Sounds great," Nan answered.

Just then the door banged open and Jim Webster came in, doffing a hard hat labeled MAYOR JIM in Magic Marker. He looked robust and handsome. The Webster congressional campaign literature would undoubtedly show him with a clipboard on the construction site, Making Progress Happen.

"Hey, Nan!" he greeted her enthusiastically. "What a nice surprise!"

"I just stopped by to check with Mary Lee about some

stuff," she answered. "I was going through old yearbook files at the high school this morning, and I ran across some pictures of one of Brenda Blaine's good friends. Mary Lee didn't remember anything about her, but maybe you do?"

Nan held the picture up, and he gave it a puzzled frown. "Liza Krzyzanowski," she told him. "They were really tight, I think, but Mary Lee tells me she ran away senior year."

"Then that's what happened," Jim answered, crossing to a metal desk at the back of the trailer. "I don't remember her." He looked back at Mary Lee. "Honey, how are we doing on those revised landscape plans?"

"Almost done," Mary Lee told him. She turned to Nan with a look of distinct pride. "I do a lot of the landscape design for Jim's projects. This one is a particular challenge, since we have to work around some parts of the LaForce property."

"You mean the family graveyard?"

Mary Lee raised her eyebrows. "You *do* find things out, don't you? Actually, it's turned into a wonderful opportunity. We're planning a full-blown museum, with the help of the local historical society. What I'm trying to do is keep as much of the original vegetation as possible. I just *hate* it when we have to take out mature trees."

"She's a world-champion tree-hugger," Jim announced from his desk. He picked up an apple and began munching. "A real fanatic, even when it screws up all the rest of the plans."

"Well, I'm with Mary Lee," Nan told him. "I hate those places where they rip out a stand of hundred-year-old oaks and then plant a couple shrubs. Listen, Jim, what have you heard about the investigation, anyway?"

Jim answered seriously, as if measuring a sound bite. "I talked to Brian Delahanty this morning, with Police Chief Bates present. Delahanty will get things cleared up, don't worry."

"He said he's new on the force. Where did he come

from, anyway?" Nan tried to make the question crisp and detached. No point in starting Mary Lee's rumor mill going.

"He used to be on the force in Detroit," Jim said. "When Stan Hardwick retired, we needed a chief detective with better experience than what was already available on the force. So we advertised and Delahanty showed up."

"Does he have family around here?" The question was, Nan hoped, general enough to cover anything from a great-uncle to twin daughters. What she really wondered, she realized suddenly, was whether the detective was married. Good God, did she care?

Jim shook his head. "None at all. He lives in a condo over near the expressway. Divorced, I think, with kids in Schaumburg. As I recall, that was why he wanted to come here, to be near his kids. I know he took a pay cut."

"Did he say who they think killed Brenda?" Nan asked. Mary Lee was listening attentively.

"I know they're looking closely at Frank Finney," Jim offered.

"This is really terrible," Nan said, "but all I can remember about Frank is that he used to work after school at the old Jewel, as a bag boy."

"He was a really great softball player, though he never did very much with it," Jim said without hesitation. "Coaches Little League now. I used to see him all the time when Jamie played."

"His son is on the junior varsity team at the high school," Mary Lee added.

"So he still lives in Spring Hill?" Nan realized that her former classmates were starting to blur in her mind. Even though Mary Lee described them as scattered, at least a quarter of the people at the reunion remained in Spring Hill, and most of the rest were elsewhere in the western suburbs of Chicago.

"He bought one of the first places we finished in Sunny Acres," Mary Lee said. "He's still with Jewel, too. By the time Frank got out of the service, they were starting to

build that big new store in the Northridge Mall. He went
back to work in the old store, and then when they closed
that, he moved to the new Jewel/Osco at Northridge. He's
the produce manager."

"Why is he a suspect?" Nan wondered.

Jim shrugged. "Delahanty was kind of closemouthed
about that, but I heard Frank had some kind of fight with
Brenda at the reunion."

"About what?" Mary Lee and Nan asked simultaneously.
They laughed together, self-consciously.

"You two are like the Snoop Sisters," Jim told them.
"Who knows? I think Frank went out with Brenda for a
while in high school. Maybe they had some unfinished
business. I didn't see this alleged fight, but Wally saw
Frank and Brenda dancing real close at the reunion, and
then a little bit later he said they were off in a corner and
she was yelling at him, really p.o.'d. That's all I know."

Jim looked at his watch. "I've got half an hour before
I'm due at city hall. Planning commission lunch. Would
you like a fast tour of the project, Nan? Or maybe Mary
Lee, you'd like to . . ."

Mary Lee frowned. "I *really* need to get this finished,
Jim, and I wanted to stop by and see Mother later. Why
don't *you* show Nan around? It's your project, after all. I'm
just the cheap help."

Jim laughed, standing up. "False modesty," he told Nan.
"Mary Lee probably knows more about Potawatomi Park
than I do. But hey, grab a hard hat and let's go."

Outside felt muggy. Jim stopped at the edge of the work
area and looked around. "I'm real proud of Potawatomi,"
he said. "This is one of the finest projects we've ever
done."

"Named for the Indians?" Nan asked.

"You bet," he answered, taking off toward the activity
across the field. "This whole area was Potawatomi land
once. I thought it'd make a nice blend of the past and the
future, naming the park for them." He grinned. "And I al-

ways liked the way the name sounded, too, all the way back to Webelos in Cub Scouts."

Up close the earthmoving machinery seemed enormous, massive yellow predators devouring the prairie for Tomorrow. Loud, too. Jim led Nan straight down the center of the construction site, past an area where two cement mixers were pouring foundations.

"Over here," Jim said, "is where the SiliChip factory is going to be. It was a real coup getting that place in here, let me tell you. They're committed to manufacturing in America and wanted to get their assembly plant into the heartland."

Nan laughed. "You mean they wanted to get someplace where it might barely be possible for their employees to live on minimum wage."

Jim frowned. "Such a cynic! Listen, these are highly skilled workers we're talking about, Nan. Many of their employees will come along with the factory, straight from Silicon Valley. It'll be a real boost for Spring Hill. We win two ways: getting new residents and providing more jobs for some of our folks around here. And once SiliChip works out here as well as we expect it to, then we're in a position to go aggressively after more of this type of business. It's clean, doesn't take up much space, and face it, this kind of technology is the future."

He led Nan to an area where a stand of trees was carefully fenced in. "This is where we'll have the historical museum. The farmhouse was in ruins, but we were able to preserve the family plot."

Able to, indeed. He made it sound like the whole project had been designed to highlight a forgotten graveyard. And the rest of the tour maintained the same upbeat feel. When they got back to the construction trailer, Jim looked at his watch.

"I'm almost late, Nan, really need to scurry. Be sure to give my best regards to your mother, now. She's a fine woman, June Robinson. A fine woman indeed." The mayor and congressional candidate smiled his most ingratiating smile. "You'll have to have dinner with us before you leave, Nan. We hardly had a chance to talk the other night."

"Mary Lee and I already made plans," Nan told him. "I'm coming tomorrow night, really looking forward to it." She listened to herself burble, wondered if insincerity was contagious, like chicken pox.

Before going out to Golden Valley, Nan stopped back at her mother's house. Mom rushed to the doorway to greet her, looking decidedly unhappy.

"I didn't know *when* you'd be back," she said petulantly. "I was starting to think I should send out the cavalry. You have *company*."

In the living room, a deeply tanned man in his late forties sat awkwardly on the couch in a cloud of cigarette smoke. His hair was combed sideways across his head, but there was no mistaking the fact that there wasn't much of it. He wore white pants and a slightly shiny pink-on-pink shirt open several buttons to provide a clear glimpse of three gold chains. His chest hair was a lot grayer than what was left on his head. Tan alligator loafers matched a belt that rested just below a slight paunch. He was sockless.

"I'm Bernie Singer," he said, standing up. "But I don't sing, just play the piano." There was nothing remotely spontaneous about the line. "I'm Brenda's fiancé from Las Vegas."

Fiancé?

Nan shook his hand, which was damp. This was not a man accustomed to making small talk with widows in midwestern parlors. She introduced herself, and Mom slipped gratefully back toward the kitchen.

"I don't know what to say," Bernie began awkwardly. His voice had a faint southwestern twang. "I'm, like, in shock."

"I'm so sorry about Brenda," Nan told him. She hesitated a moment, then decided a social lie was certainly forgivable under the circumstances. "She spoke very highly of you." Brenda hadn't, in fact, ever mentioned Bernie Singer's name, or even his existence. Maybe she really *was* his fiancée, though Nan suspected it was a posthumous title.

Why on earth was he here?

"The cops said you sat with Brenda at the reunion," he said, using a gold cigarette lighter to charge up another Marlboro. The ashtray beside him already held half a dozen butts.

As Nan told him briefly about her conversation with Brenda, he fidgeted and rooched and smoked three more cigarettes, lighting one off another. Was he always this nervous?

"That cop—what's his name? Delano?—doesn't seem to like me much," Bernie grumbled after Nan finished.

"Delahanty. What makes you think he doesn't like you?"

Bernie's eyes narrowed. He was really amazingly tan. Of course, if he worked nights, he could spend his days broiling in the Nevada sun. Nan had a sudden image of Brenda and Bernie on matching hot-pink chaise longues beside a turquoise swimming pool, slathered in coconut oil. Brenda would have her suit folded down to the tiniest possible exposure or, more likely, be stretched out in the altogether. Bernie would wear mirrored shades and a towel over his paunch. And they'd both be smoking like steel mills.

"I drop everything," Bernie groused, "fly into town this morning to see about Brenda and what can I do, how can I help. Brenda's my fiancée, right? We're in love, we're supposed to get married at Thanksgiving. And this Delano asshole starts giving me the third degree. Where was I Saturday night, and why wasn't I at work, and did I have any witnesses. Kee-rist!"

"I think he's hoping for an easy solution to her murder," Nan said easily. She wondered what Bernie Singer had told the detective, and wished there were an easy way she could ask the same questions. "How come you weren't at the reunion with Brenda?"

Bernie shook his head. Those poor pathetic hairs were firmly sprayed in place. Not one moved. "I hate that kind of shit. Something's over, it's over. High school, man, it was a drag. It's not like Brenda liked this place or nothing. I couldn't figure out why she wanted to come at all. Unless it was to see her kid's old man."

The hometown big shot.

"Who was that?" Nan asked casually.

Bernie opened both hands and shook his head. "Who knows? Brenda didn't want to talk about something, she was a real clam. The guy had her set up pretty nice though, with the child support."

"Oh?"

"Hey, none of my business, no skin off my nose. Me and Brenda, it was pretty special. I can't believe she's gone. I shoulda come with her, protected her." His eyes narrowed. "You must have some idea who did it."

"I wish I did," Nan said sincerely. "But I haven't got a clue. I'm just as lost as the police."

"That Delano couldn't find his ass with a road map," Bernie snarled. "Small-town moron. I'm gonna go now, but I'm sticking around. Got a room at the Spring Hill Inn, down the hall from where Brenda was." He smiled proudly. "She used my name to sign in, they tell you that?"

Nan nodded.

"That asshole Delano won't even give me her stuff."

"He must consider it evidence."

"Evidence, shmevidence. Won't even tell me when the kid's coming in, I offered to give him a lift from the airport. But I'll tell you something, I get my hands on the asshole killed Brenda, he's gonna wish he moved to Outer Slobbovia while he still had the chance. I got friends," Bernie Singer muttered darkly. "I got friends."

Sweethearts one and all, no doubt.

Nan went upstairs and changed her earrings. It was only three months since she'd had her ears pierced for the very first time—at the mall, by a gum-chewing teenager wielding a staple gun, which was surely an exercise in youthful exuberance, if not downright stupidity.

Back in high school everyone she knew had been piercing their ears; her sister Julie had actually done it in study hall, with the time-honored ice cube–needle–potato combo. But Nan had held back, worried that such impetuousness would only lead to later regret. She'd grow up and be stuck with holes in her ears, ugly disfiguring reminders of youthful folly.

Then one day last spring, she realized that she *had* grown up and that the regret was in missing out on twenty-odd years of earrings. Clip-ons had never been an option. They either pinched like fury or fell off and got lost immediately.

So she thought about it for maybe a week, mentioned it to a few friends who were all wildly supportive, and then decided to go for it. She'd been on an earring bender ever since, buying them all over the place, routinely changing them several times in the course of a single day. Now she removed the gold hoops she'd worn through the morning and replaced them with long danglers that featured dragonflies at their very ends.

What she was planning to do was call Henry Sloane, but she couldn't quite bring herself to make the call. She'd warm up, she decided, by calling Janis Levin at work in Atlanta.

Janis was thrilled to hear from her, of course, though it wasn't even twenty-four hours since she'd left Spring Hill. Janis was fascinated by Bernie Singer and pumped Nan relentlessly for details. Alas, Nan was realizing as she reported, this was a guy whose depth could be measured in millimeters.

After saying good-bye to Janis, she didn't allow herself even to hang up the phone. She just flicked the button and called directory assistance downstate for the number of Henry's high school. He was already back at work, he'd told her, doing whatever it is that principals do in August. Nan hadn't been interested enough to ask.

She got through to him immediately, which was a bit of a surprise. Along with being elderly and socially obsolete, the principals of Nan's recollection had also been wildly inaccessible.

Not Henry. "How nice to hear from you," he said cordially. "Just let me close my office door." He was back in a moment. "To what do I owe the pleasure?"

"Oh, stuff it, Henry," she told him irritably. "Don't be so damned formal." She heard him laugh and felt herself relaxing. "Sorry. It's just that you got to leave and I'm still here in the firestorm. Which continues to blaze unchecked."

She filled him in on what had happened since they were separated by the police on Saturday night. It took awhile. "I don't exactly know why I called," she admitted finally. "I guess it's just that . . . I thought you'd want to know. And I never did get to say good-bye, which pissed me off."

"Me, too. Though taking the long view—in broad daylight at two-hundred-some miles' distance—it may have all been for the best. Not Brenda being killed," he hastened to add. "You know."

"Yeah. I know." Nan hesitated. There were a hundred things she could say, all best left unspoken. "I keep wondering if there's something I missed that night. Something I should have seen, or saw and didn't recognize because I was, um, preoccupied."

"I was equally preoccupied," he reminded her. "Though I've given the whole thing plenty of thought. Like all the way home on Sunday morning when I was trying to figure out just how I was going to explain all this to Amy."

"I take it you found a way."

He laughed. "Sins of omission have always been my specialty. As in leaving out a detail or two. We never got the chance for any real sins of commission," he added softly.

File under OPPORTUNITIES: MISSED. "If you think of something, call me," she told him, reluctant to end the conversation, realizing that it was probably the last one, maybe ever.

"Of course," he answered.

And then the line was empty. Very, very empty.

CHAPTER 7

Terry Cannon

Midday Monday, Brian Delahanty was on the phone with yet another downstate Illinois detective when Bob Stedman from the county prosecutor's office waltzed in.

"Yeah, that's right," Delahanty said. "Really push them on the prints. Shit, I know nothing ever gets solved on prints, you know nothing ever gets solved on prints, but there's always a first time, right? They give you a hard time, tell 'em everybody who was still there when the body was found was printed. Yeah. Except one guy who put up a big song and dance about civil liberties. Ran his name, and guess what? He jumped bail on a DUI in Iowa three years ago. He's wishing he forgot the auld lang syne right about now. Got him locked up downstairs."

Delahanty waved at the coffeemaker, and Stedman poured himself a cup.

"What? No, just emphasize that it's all routine. Check on anything they remember about the Blaine woman. When did they last see her, who did they see her with, anything suspicious, blah, blah, blah. Yeah. Fax me whatever you get. Thanks."

He hung up and looked at Stedman. "The people who left early. It's a real bitch tracking them down."

"No progress?" Stedman frowned.

What the hell did he think this was, TV? It was only thirty-six hours since the body was found. And from the first moment he'd looked out over that crowd of drunks on Saturday night, he'd expected this to be a tough one.

Everybody kept spitting out ideas and theories, but nobody had anything resembling a cold, hard fact.

"I hear her boyfriend's in town," Stedman said. "The one who didn't quite make it to work Saturday night."

"Yeah, you just missed him. A real charmer."

It was probably too much to hope, Delahanty realized, that Bernie Singer actually was the killer. But a boy could dream. And it would keep everything nice and clean, a simple traveling murder that didn't have a thing to do with Spring Hill or class reunions or twenty years' worth of collective histories. Besides, Singer was a real scuzball, the kind of loser Delahanty instinctively detested: smug, smarmy, more than a little stupid, and given to vague rumblings about friends in high places. Friends who were high, more likely.

"Walters got a nice clean shot of Singer on the sly when he was in here this morning," Delahanty went on. "I've got a guy out at O'Hare right now checking for anybody who might've seen him coming in or out on Saturday. But the flight crews are scattered all over the country."

"Hmmm," Stedman said archly.

Brian Delahanty didn't like Robert S. Stedman and hadn't from day one. Stedman was dogged, humorless, and ambitious, with a long narrow face and a nose that brought to mind the Wicked Witch from *The Wizard of Oz*. But Christ, was he connected. Ten years in the DA's office was just the tip of it. He'd put down roots in Spring Hill that dug clear down into Jules Verne–land.

Fresh out of Northwestern Law School, Stedman had moved to Spring Hill and promptly married into one of the town's oldest families. His father-in-law had worked for Webster Construction thirty years, back when Webster Construction was the old man and relatively small potatoes. Tight with old man Webster, too, so tight that they bought it together when a freak storm capsized their sailboat midway between Navy Pier and Benton Harbor a few years before Delahanty joined the Spring Hill P.D.

Stedman's wife was a do-gooder, charity volunteer, hospital pink lady, all that kind of stuff. She'd also put on twenty pounds with each of their three kids and was built like an aircraft carrier. His brother-in-law, Tom Propst, was corporate controller of Webster Construction. The Stedmans and Websters and Propsts routinely vacationed together and played pass-the-cranberries at Thanksgiving.

"Well, what *do* you know?" Stedman asked, in a tone that implied a recitation of the ABCs might be beyond the detective.

Delahanty ticked them off on his fingers, lingering just a moment on the middle digit. "Number one, at eleven-fifteen a couple leaving early for Crown Point, Indiana, saw Brenda Blaine walk out the end door of the lobby, alone. Number two, at eleven thirty-five, Nan Robinson and Henry Sloane found her dead in the car. Number three, she was clocked from behind with a rock, then put in the car and stabbed. We're holding that, by the way. We found the rock chucked under a bush."

"Prints on the rock?"

"Yeah, right. And a business card taped to it with a little confession written on the back. Number four, and this I find really interesting, somebody tossed her hotel room."

Stedman's eyebrows shot up. "Anything missing?"

Delahanty shrugged. "Your guess is as good as mine. Whoever did it didn't worry about putting everything back neat and tidy."

"Maybe she was just a slob."

"A slob doesn't leave a hundred-dollar toothbrush in the toilet," Delahanty said. "But she was traveling light anyway. The desk clerk said when she checked in Saturday afternoon, she just had the one bag, and it wasn't tagged for baggage check so she probably carried it on the plane. She had a return ticket for Tuesday, and she paid for the room in advance with cash through Monday night."

"Tuesday? What in the hell was she planning to do until Tuesday?"

"Maybe she wanted to see the Impressionists at the Art Institute."

"What about the Robinson woman?" Stedman asked. "It *was* her car, and she spent a lot of time that night with Brenda Blaine."

Delahanty shrugged. "She seems clean, and there's an LAPD homicide detective vouches for her. Says she helped solve something for them awhile back, somebody from Spring Hill who got iced in L.A."

Stedman momentarily furrowed his brow. "Oh, yeah. That would be Debra LaRoche. The family had moved to South Bend, actually, but I remember hearing about her."

Ordinarily Delahanty liked to noodle a tricky case with somebody bright, but his distaste for Stedman took all the pleasure out of it. Stedman seemed unduly interested in this case, or maybe not. It *was* a murder, after all, in a town where jaywalking was one of the top crimes. Also, Stedman's buddy the mayor had been sitting at the same table Saturday night as the victim, most embarrassing. But mostly what made Delahanty wish Stedman would get lost was that shooting the shit with him was wasting time.

"We need to clear this fast," Stedman warned. "It's already on the wires, getting a lot of play all over the country. My brother called from Connecticut, wants to know what the hell is going on here. We've got SiliChip coming in here this winter, and we're looking to attract more high-tech, low-pollution–type business. It looks bad if this is the kind of place you check into the local hotel, somebody sticks a sword in your heart."

Delahanty grunted and changed the subject. Why belabor the obvious? "The boyfriend was really pushing to get the Blaine woman's stuff," he said, "which makes me kind of itchy to take another look at it all. Interested?"

He rose, and Stedman followed him downstairs to the evidence room. The crime techs had been over everything three times, and there wasn't much to begin with.

Delahanty spread the final possessions of Brenda Blaine out on a table.

Stedman pawed through her clothes, holding up a pair of red Frederick's of Hollywood G-string panties with a lascivious leer. There was a whole pile of trashy lingerie, but not much in the line of real clothing: some scanty white size-six shorts, a lime green halter top, high-heeled white sandals, and a turquoise shift that she'd probably worn on the plane.

Delahanty opened the big makeup bag and dumped it on the table. It seemed like a lot of cosmetics for a weekend trip; more, indeed, than his ex-wife, Maureen, had ever owned at one time. But it had all checked out to be makeup, pure and simple. And Lucy Waller, the crime tech who went through it all, said the colors and products were all what you'd expect for the Blaine woman.

He idly pushed the button on her Interplak and was surprised to find it still worked despite its immersion in the john. Have to write a glowing letter to the manufacturer. *While working on a murder investigation, I discovered that . . .*

"This is it?" Stedman asked skeptically. "To last through Tuesday?"

"There's four nighties," Delahanty pointed out. "Maybe she wasn't planning to do the sights after all."

"No papers? No address book?"

Delahanty shook his head. "Also no diary, no love letters, no dog-eared paperback books, no medications except a bottle of stress vitamins. No Post-It reminders to call the cops because so-and-so was planning to kill her."

"Diaphragm?" Stedman asked brightly. "Condoms?" He always perked up a little when sex was involved, which was hard to figure once you took a look at his wife.

"Handful of condoms, but not for contraception. The M.E. said she'd had a hysterectomy, remember?"

"Oh yeah." He looked disappointed. "What about fiber evidence?"

"I had my fingers crossed on that one," Delahanty told him, "but so far nothing jumps out. That satin dress was a regular fiber magnet. It's covered with shit. But she probably danced with thirty different guys. We get a suspect, then we can start playing match-the-fiber. Right now, zippo."

"What a mess," Stedman sighed.

"Uh-huh." Delahanty boxed up Brenda Blaine's effects again, and they started back up the stairs to his office.

"You checked with the grandmother?" Stedman asked.

Delahanty rolled his eyes. "Gaga. Lance Thompson went out to the rest home yesterday. She lay there rocking back and forth, singing 'Amazing Grace.' And Grace isn't even her name."

"Too bad. But there's still the kid."

"Yeah, there's still the kid." Delahanty stopped outside his office door, hoping Stedman would take the hint and move on. "He gets in at five twenty-seven."

"Let me know the minute he's here," Stedman ordered. "I have a feeling he's gonna crack this thing wide open."

"This is absolutely ridiculous, Nan," June Robinson fumed. "What on earth do you think you're doing?"

Nan had just finished a bowl of blueberries with the announcement that she was on her way to Golden Valley to see Brenda Blaine's grandmother.

"Just looking into a few things, Mom."

Mom looked petulant. "But this is supposed to be your *vacation*, honey. I thought we'd have a chance to spend some time together."

"We're together right now, Mom."

"Only because you stopped by to use the bathroom and receive visitors. I might as well be running a hotel. And it's not like Brenda Blaine was a close friend of yours, after all."

Nan rinsed her bowl and put it in the dishwasher. "I know that. But you know what else? Brenda sat down next to me on Saturday night and called me a friendly face. I keep thinking about that."

"I'm as sorry as anybody else that the poor girl is dead," Mom said, though she didn't sound terribly mournful. "But it's hardly your responsibility to solve her murder on your vacation."

"I can't help it," Nan said. "I feel responsible, whether it's warranted or not."

"Finding murderers is a job for the police."

"This isn't L.A., Mom, where there are forty murders a week and the police are used to them. Brian Delahanty might be able to help if somebody steals the tape deck out of your car. But I haven't seen any indication he's up to this."

"And I suppose you are?" Only a mother could cut so cruelly to the core.

"Mom, what harm can it possibly do to talk to her *grandmother?*"

June Robinson's sigh as Nan walked out the door could have powered the entire field of windmills on I-10 between L.A. and Palm Springs.

Golden Valley looked remarkably like the drawing on the wall of the Potawatomi Park construction trailer. It nestled in slightly rolling hills southeast of town, in an isolated oak grove along Sutter's Creek. It was well maintained, nicely landscaped, and extremely quiet.

Nan parked under a massive shade tree just outside the front door. The lobby resembled a jungle, full of enormous plants with big glossy leaves climbing trellises to the ceiling. Chairs and love seats were cheerfully upholstered in bold florals. Straight ahead in a communal lounge area, several elderly women watched TV while a couple of old men played cards in the corner.

Just inside was a reception cubicle where a cheerful young redhead with a serious sunburn sat sorting mail. Her nameplate identified her as Donna DeVries.

"Good afternoon," Nan said. "I'd like to see Alvina McReedy." Something brushed along her ankles, and she involuntarily jumped a foot straight up in the air. "Awk!"

Donna, the receptionist, looked down and laughed. A plump gray cat circled Nan's ankles, rubbing and purring and leaving long gray hairs on her pink linen slacks. June Robinson, on a recent visit to L.A., had adopted a sleek black cat on Nan's behalf, going so far as to name the animal (Nefertiti, in keeping with the family tradition of exotic pet names) and pay the preliminary vet bills. But fond as Nan had grown of Nefertiti, she still didn't much care for cats in general. She made ineffectual shooing noises, which the cat ignored.

"Oh, Theodore," Donna said, coming around the corner of her cubicle. She picked up the cat, stroked his ears, and then aimed him toward the lounge. "I'm sorry if he bothered you. We have several pets here, cats and dogs both. The residents enjoy the companionship. You say you want to see Mrs. McReedy?" She frowned, and her pink peeling nose wrinkled. "Is she expecting you? She won't speak to any reporters."

"She's not expecting me. But Detective Delahanty said . . ." Nan trailed off discreetly, leaving plenty of room for misconception. What Detective Delahanty had told her, actually, when she called earlier, was that Alvina McReedy was hopelessly senile and not to waste her time. On the plus side, he'd agreed to check into Liza Krzyzanowski.

"Well, you can probably go on back, then. I don't know if this is one of her good days or not. Some days she's just as bright as she can be, alert as you and I, and other days, well . . ."

"The officer who was here yesterday told Detective Delahanty that he wasn't at all sure that she realized her granddaughter had been murdered."

Donna furrowed her brow. Looking at her sunburn was downright painful. She was a fool to treat her fair skin so cavalierly; by the time she was forty, she'd have a face like a saddle.

"No, she does know, I'm sure of it. What a terrible thing! I'm told Mrs. McReedy was quite upset last night. And then this morning she called the desk and told me very specifically that she wouldn't speak to any reporters. They've been calling like crazy, you know. Maybe she was having one of her bad spells when the policeman was here yesterday. She's halfway down that left-hand corridor. Her name's by the door."

"Thanks," Nan told her, heading down the corridor toward Brenda's grandmother's room, her stomach fluttering.

Minuscule Alvina McReedy was neatly folded into the crisp white sheets of a big hospital bed cranked to a forty-five–degree angle. Her tiny head turned wrenlike toward the door as Nan walked in.

"Hello," she said suspiciously. "Do I know you? You're not a reporter, are you? I told that girl no reporters."

Nan pulled a ladder-back chair close. Apart from the bed, the room was furnished entirely with severe colonial pieces, apparently Mrs. McReedy's own. The walls were hung with cross-stitched scripture and religious decoupage.

"No, Mrs. McReedy," Nan said, "I'm not a reporter. And I don't believe we've ever met. May I sit down?"

"Don't see how I can stop you," Alvina McReedy sniffed.

It wasn't the most gracious response, but Nan sat down anyway. "I'm Nan Robinson. I knew your granddaughter, Brenda. She and I were classmates at Spring Hill High a long time ago."

Alvina McReedy closed her eyes. Nan hesitated.

"You know that Brenda . . ."

The eyes opened. They were small and clear, a pale, cold blue. Before it turned silver, her fine hair had probably been blond. There were thousands of tiny wrinkles in her face, the lines particularly pronounced around her mouth. Her lips were pinched together, as if she'd recently tasted something very icky.

"That Brenda's dead? Yes, I do know. Nancy Robinson, did you say?"

Nan nodded.

Mrs. McReedy smiled for the first time, turning up the pursed corners of her mouth ever so slightly. "I remember you, Nancy. Brenda talked about you when the two of you were friends. And you spoke at her graduation, of course."

The valedictory address? She remembered *that*?

"We were lab partners in chemistry, senior year," Nan said. "Brenda was very good at chemistry."

"She had a good mind, I always did say that. Her mother never recognized it, but I did. I wanted so much more for her." Alvina McReedy fairly oozed rectitude. If Brenda had been subject to the constant force of this woman's disapproval, it was a small wonder she'd left and never returned.

"I saw Brenda Saturday night at the reunion," Nan said carefully. "I sat beside her at dinner and we talked a long time. I think she was happy, Mrs. McReedy."

"Really?" There was raw disbelief in the old woman's tone.

"Really."

Mrs. McReedy harrumphed, clearly unconvinced. "Tell me, Nancy, was Brenda drinking at that reunion?"

So that was what bugged the old lady. Or at least part of what bugged her.

Nan smiled gently, spoke reassuringly. "Not a drop, ma'am. She was very proud that she didn't drink anymore. She told me she'd been in Alcoholics Anonymous for many years."

Mrs. McReedy leaned back and sighed. "If only I could have gotten Louise to do the same thing. But that daughter of mine never wanted to listen to anybody, rest her soul."

Louise Blaine, divorced in an era when Spring Hill considered the condition closely akin to leprosy, had been known as one of the town's hard cases. The three generations of women had lived in a small clapboard house at the edge of town. Brenda's mother had never, to Nan's knowledge, held a job. She died of cirrhosis at a tragically young age, only a few years after Brenda left Spring Hill.

Through all those years in the little white clapboard house, Alvina McReedy had been employed as a secretary at the First National Bank of Spring Hill. When she reached mandatory retirement, she returned frequently to the bank as a temp. Her variety of Calvinism permitted no idle time.

"Mrs. McReedy, did Brenda keep in touch with you?"

The eyes narrowed suspiciously. "Did she tell you she'd been in touch with me?"

"No, she didn't say. I never asked. We talked about our parents, though, her mom and my dad. My dad was an alcoholic, too, Mrs. McReedy. I guess you probably know that."

Nan had spent the first thirty years of her life denying that her father had a drinking problem. It was oddly disconcerting now to make such frequent public declarations of the fact. Repetition wasn't making it any easier, either.

"It's a terrible thing," Mrs. McReedy said, without sounding the least bit sympathetic. "Louise wasn't raised that way, Nancy. And neither was Brenda. My husband, Mr. McReedy, would never permit a drop of liquor in the house so long as he was alive. His father died of drink. I was always grateful he didn't live to see what happened to Louise. She was the apple of his eye. But perhaps he could have stopped her."

Nan shook her head gently. "Probably nothing could have stopped her, Mrs. McReedy. You can't blame yourself. Alcoholics are a law unto themselves. Did you know where Brenda was living?"

"I knew she was in Nevada. But ... Brenda and I were ... I daresay the appropriate term is 'estranged.' Before Brenda left home, I ... I told her she was ... well, the words certainly don't matter now. I told her I never wanted to see her again." The little old lady inhaled deeply and closed her eyes. "And I didn't."

Was she really sorry? It was hard to tell. And did she know about her great-grandson, the dean's-list college sophomore?

Nan waited a respectful moment. Interesting that the old lady's memories from twenty years earlier were so specific. But she *had* been thinking about Brenda, so all these things would have surfaced more easily. "Mrs. McReedy, do you remember a girl named Liza Krzyzanowski?"

The old lady scowled. "She was a bad one, a terrible influence. I had to forbid Brenda to see her, not that it did any good. She was incorrigible. I know for a fact that girl used drugs."

"Did Brenda?"

"Use drugs? Certainly not." Alvina McReedy's righteous indignation meant nothing. She wouldn't have been the kind of adult a rebellious teenager would confide in. Or try to turn on.

"Did you know Liza's family?"

Mrs. McReedy shook her head slightly. "No, of course not." Her tone suggested that the Krzyzanowskis were a class below.

"I understand that Liza ran away from home."

"Good riddance to bad rubbish. Brenda was forbidden to see Liza, not that she paid any attention." Mrs. McReedy frowned, a position her face fell into easily. "It seems to me that Liza's mother called, asking if we knew where she was."

"When was that?" Nan asked.

"Why on earth would I care to remember? Obviously it was before Brenda left herself."

"Except that Brenda graduated first. Liza dropped out of school."

"She was not a girl preoccupied with her education," Mrs. McReedy noted tartly. "I remember clearly telling Brenda that she should stay away from her and associate more with girls like yourself. I was pleased by her friendship with you."

Come again? They were only *lab partners*. Why would Mrs. McReedy think that Nan and Brenda were close friends? The obvious answer was that Brenda had lied. Thinking that Brenda was chumming around with a boring Goody Two-shoes like Nan Robinson might help keep Grumpy Grandma at bay.

"Do you remember anything about Brenda's boyfriends that last year before she left?" Nan asked carefully.

"She used to slip out and meet boys," Mrs. McReedy answered after a moment. "She wouldn't bring them home. I never could be sure where she was, really. It was impossible to enforce rules. Louise invariably undermined my authority. Every time I'd force an issue, Louise would come to Brenda's defense and it would be the two of them against me. I know Brenda spent a great deal of time with boys. They were attracted to her. She knew it, she worked at it, she liked it that way."

Whew!

"Did she ever mention any of her boyfriends by name?"

"She went with a boy named Frank Finney for a while. And there was somebody else named Al, who was older. He was the mechanic down at the Texaco who worked on my car, heaven help us. I forbade her to see that fellow. He was far too old for her."

She shook her head against her pillow.

"I don't know, I guess there were others. She had that one special friend, but I don't guess that's what you mean." A note of wistfulness entered her tone for a moment. Then she tightened up again, waving a tiny hand. The skin clung to her bones, flesh stretched over matchsticks. "I won't besmirch any reputations at this late date. It's all long over. Brenda laughed about the boys, sometimes. She and Louise would talk, put their heads together and laugh. I believe she shared many confidences with Louise that she never told me."

A safe enough bet. "Mrs. McReedy, when did Brenda leave Spring Hill?"

"August fourth, the summer after her graduation. It was a Tuesday. I've never forgotten it. She left a note on the kitchen table. It said: *I won't be home for supper tonight or ever again.* Like a knife in my heart. Louise cried for days."

"Had you and Brenda been arguing?"

"Life with Brenda was an argument from the moment she said her first word."

Nan hesitated. "She was pregnant, wasn't she?"

"I'm sure I wouldn't know."

But the old lady did know. Nan was certain of it. Hadn't she ever stopped to wonder about that baby? Ryan Blaine, her only great-grandchild, her only surviving descendant, was due in Spring Hill any minute now. Nan considered telling Alvina McReedy about Ryan, decided it was not her news to break.

"Do you think Brenda stayed in touch with Louise after she left?"

"Louise got letters sometimes, in Brenda's handwriting. But she kept them locked in a cedar chest."

"Did you find the letters after your daughter passed away?"

"No. They were gone." But she spoke too quickly. Most likely she had read and destroyed them.

"Did Brenda know her mother had died?"

"I sent Brenda's next letter back, marked 'Deceased.' " This woman was *cold*.

"And you didn't hear from her again?"

"Never." Alvina McReedy sighed. Suddenly she seemed weaker, less formidable. "I'm ninety-three years old, Nancy. I was thirty-seven when Louise was born. They'd long since told me I could never have children. Louise was a gift to me, a joyous gift. When I lost Mr. McReedy, she was all I had left. But she was wild, uncontrollable. She made a bad marriage, and I took her in when she came home with Brenda. Brenda was Louise all over again."

She looked up, clearly exhausted.

"And now both of them are gone. Who would have thought I'd live to see such a terrible day?" She lay back. "I'm so tired. So very tired."

Nan had more questions, but they could wait. She patted the old woman's hand. Did anybody ever come to visit her? Had anybody brought a cake when she turned ninety-three?

Nan had no living grandparents. Dad's parents were both dead before she was born, and her maternal grandparents had died of emphysema and a heart attack within two months of each other while Nan was at Stanford. But what if they'd outlived the proper functioning of their bodies, like so many of these Golden Valley residents? Would they be here, or living with June Robinson? Would Mom one day be living with Nan?

"I'll leave you to rest now, Mrs. McReedy," Nan said gently. "But I'd like to talk to you again. Would you mind if I came back tomorrow?"

"If you'd like," the old woman said, unenthusiastically.

She closed her eyes. Nan rose silently and tiptoed out of the room.

Nan still had well over an hour before she'd promised her mother she'd be home. Without stopping to think too much about it, she headed for the Northridge Mall.

She picked up a box of Polaroid film in Osco, then walked across into the companion Jewel supermarket. It was one of those massive stores where you can do all your shopping in a single stop: tampons, carburetor cleaner, artichoke hearts, Spam. And beer, of course, mostly in twenty-four-can boxes, mountains of them. There were staggering quantities of beer all over the place. Nice solid American brands, too, for the most part. None of your pansy imported stuff.

She wound her way through displays of corn on the cob

and peaches and watermelons, then pushed without hesitation through the double doors at the rear of the produce department. A produce clerk in a red apron popped a grape in his mouth and pointed to a table in the rear where Frank Finney was packaging elderly fruits and vegetables for the mark-down table.

"Hi, Frank," Nan said pleasantly. "I didn't get a chance to talk to you the other night."

He looked at her without recognition. "Do I know you?"

"I'm Nan Robinson," Nan said. "I was at the reunion."

Finney looked at her suspiciously. He was medium height and pear-shaped, with short black hair and brown eyes. His hands kept busy, arranging yellowing heads of broccoli and browning cauliflowers on foam trays. "Yeah?"

"I sat with Brenda Blaine," Nan went on.

"Oh, shit," he muttered.

"I've been talking to some of the people who spent time with Brenda at the reunion, and I thought you might be able to help me."

"I'm trying to do my job here," Finney said. "It doesn't look good if I've got cops coming by bothering me at work."

"I'm not officially with the police," Nan said, in what had to be the understatement of the summer. "And I won't get in your way. I just wanted to ask you a couple questions."

"Look," he said, "I don't know anything. I already told the police that. And if you're not a cop, why do you care?"

Nan smiled ingratiatingly. "Because I don't like thinking that somebody killed Brenda. And, selfishly, because I seem to be a suspect in her death. Her body was found in my car."

"Oh." He looked around uncomfortably. There was nobody else in earshot, but he obviously wanted her to leave.

"I spoke with Brenda's grandmother this afternoon out at Golden Valley Rest Home. She remembered you as one of Brenda's special high school boyfriends."

"That's bullshit," he answered shortly.

"Oh, I don't think Mrs. McReedy would have any reason to lie about that, do you?"

"I'm busy right now." He tossed an oozing bunch of grapes into a trash can.

"Don't stop working on my account," Nan said, careful not to show her irritation. "I'm just wondering how it happened that one of Brenda's old boyfriends had a big argument with her just before she died."

"Oh, for Christ's sake," Finney said. "She got a little annoyed at something I said, that's all."

"And what was that?"

"None of your business."

Nan fixed a steely glare at him. "I see. So it *was* a serious argument."

He ignored her and started packing a pile of mushy tomatoes five to a tray. "Customers aren't supposed to be back here. This area is for employees only."

"I'm not really here as a customer," Nan said, still very polite, but with a definite edge in her voice.

"You're not a customer, you're not a cop. I don't have to talk to you."

"If you change your mind, give me a call." Nan took out one of her California State Bar business cards and wrote her mother's phone number on the back. "I'm sorry to have bothered you."

She turned to walk out. From the corner of her eye she saw Frank Finney pitch the card into a trash can and lob a rotten tomato after it.

Ralph wasn't due for forty-five minutes yet when Nan got home, but Mom was antsy anyway. Nan showered quickly, then came downstairs, opened an Augsburger, and stayed out of the way. Mom swept back and forth from the yard with baskets of flowers, which she stripped and arranged in several large vases. She was all gussied up in an aquamarine eyelet-lace dress that matched her eyes and was almost, but not quite, too girlish for her. The dining table was set with her finest linen, crystal, and china.

Ralph arrived promptly at six, carrying grocery bags and brimming over with good cheer. He immediately donned a crisp white full-length chef's apron and began to bustle about the kitchen. Nan slid onto a stool at the kitchen island, sipped her beer, and watched him as Mom went back outside for a few more glads to finish off the floral arrangements.

"I've been telling your mother we should take one of those Princess cruises down to Acapulco," Ralph said conspiratorially. "They depart out of Los Angeles, don't they?"

"Some of them," Nan said.

"Then we could see you there. Perhaps you might like to join us. Your sister, Julie, and her family could come along, too."

Now *that* was an image. "They're not big travelers, Ralph," she said carefully. "But of course, we'd all love to see you anytime. Can I help with anything?"

Ralph rinsed several sheaves of fresh herbs, tossed away the bruised leaves, and spread the perfect ones on paper towels to dry. "You could slice the cantaloupe, Nan. Very thin. And then wrap each sliver in some of this prosciutto." He indicated a slim parcel wrapped in white butcher paper.

Damn! She'd assumed Ralph would decline her assistance, had offered out of simple good manners. One of the benefits of a vacation was being able to meet your meals for the first time when they appeared before you. But she dutifully sliced the melon while Ralph heated court bouillon in Mom's enormous copper fish poacher. A magnificent Alaskan king salmon glistened on the counter.

Ralph sliced mushrooms and Vidalia onions and green peppers and tomatoes for salad and whisked together a dressing out of his fresh herbs, virgin Sicilian olive oil, and balsamic vinegar. As he worked, he chatted knowledgeably about various sources of truly fresh produce in the western suburbs.

Nan found herself idly wondering what this man was like in bed. There was absolutely no doubt in her mind that he and Mom were getting it on, and she rather liked the idea. God knows what Mom's sex life had been like with Dad; it was not the sort of subject ever discussed in the Robinson household. But she could envision Ralph Salamone as a gentle, caring lover.

"Now, where on earth did I put that?" Mom wondered, passing through again. She was incredibly fidgety tonight, and positively kittenish. She simpered, she smirked, she all but dropped her handkerchief in front of Ralph.

"Relax, June, dear. Here, have some wine." Ralph poured her a glass and she took the wine, accepted the kiss that accompanied it, and bustled off again.

"Quite a woman, your mother," Ralph said fondly. "She's one in a million."

It was the same expression he had used last night, and Nan found it less than charming.

"One *on* a million," she suspected he really meant. June Robinson's net worth as the widow of a very successful auto dealer, who had carried loads of life insurance, was substantial.

Nan shook herself and opened another beer. Perhaps her distrust of Ralph was silly. Everyone always said she was exceptionally suspicious, though the most she'd own up to was sensible skepticism. When she was a kid, Mom had called Nan the Eeyore of the Robinson family. It really wasn't true that she always anticipated the worst. She simply noted that pessimists were rarely disappointed. This was due in part, she knew, to being the daughter of an alcoholic, and she could cite chapter and verse in the ACA literature to back up her position.

The kitchen filled up with wonderful smells as Ralph lowered the salmon into the French fish poacher, which had resided in the Robinson pantry forever without—to Nan's knowledge—ever actually being used. Ralph promised he'd try to get back from visiting his sick sister by Friday night, to fix them homemade pasta with sun-ripened tomatoes and pesto. Quite an anomaly for his generation, this man who not only enjoyed cooking but apparently had an entire repertoire of diverse dishes.

Nan excused herself briefly, then returned with the Polaroid. "Smile!" she requested brightly. Mom instinctively preened her hair and beamed fetchingly, but Ralph's protestations carried definite annoyance. Nan ignored him as she took a series of shots and propped them on the counter.

She was, she realized suddenly, in a truly lousy mood. The entire afternoon had been depressing: Bernie Singer, arguing with Mom, Alvina McReedy, and then the capper, Frank Finney. Frank had definitely rubbed her the wrong way. Nan was accustomed to dealing with errant attorneys who wet their pants at the very notion of specific attention from the state bar. Being dismissed by a guy sorting through moldy cucumbers was a distinct comedown.

"I wish I could get through to Detective Delahanty to tell him about seeing Alvina McReedy," Nan complained. She'd just tried again and been told rather curtly that the detective was unavailable. "Nobody will even tell me where he is."

Mom put her hands on her hips. "Enough of this wretched business," she announced firmly. "I don't want to hear one more word about Brenda Blaine for the whole rest of the evening."

Which was, in a way, a blessed relief.

After Ralph Salamone made his flowery good-nights and took his blushing girlfriend outside for a gallant Mediterranean smooch, Nan went straight to the kitchen.

Earlier in the evening, she had leaned the stack of Polaroids against a ceramic canister. The pile looked thinner now. Of six pictures, only two remained, both shots of Mom and the salmon.

Every picture of Ralph Salamone was gone.

She supposed she should feel satisfied, but instead she

felt a gnawing ache in her stomach. She opened a drawer and, beneath boxes of foil and Saran Wrap, pulled out the picture of her mother's handsome beau from where she had stashed it earlier after slipping it out of the stack. At the time she'd told herself that she'd laugh later at her paranoia. She looked at the picture now. Ralph had been facing the camera, pouring herb dressing over the salad. He was a good-looking devil, no question, and photogenic to boot.

She sighed as she took a large Ziploc bag and slid the picture in. Then she opened a cupboard door and reached behind a salad shooter and a potato chipper. Using a napkin, she removed a wineglass and put it in another Ziploc bag. Then she put the whole business in a small Carson Pirie Scott bag and carried it up to her room.

She was about to try Brian Delahanty one more time when the phone rang at nine forty-five. It was the detective.

"I'm sorry I couldn't get back to you sooner," he said.

The ill-mannered lout. Seven messages she'd left in five hours. "I'm sure you're very busy. But I wanted to tell you what happened this afternoon. I spent over an hour with Brenda Blaine's grandmother. She was just as compos mentis as you can imagine. Perfectly okay. I think she knows something about Brenda's past that she's not telling us."

"She was coherent?" Delahanty sounded dubious.

"Totally."

"I'll be damned. I don't think it matters very much, though. You must not have heard that we have a suspect in custody for the murder of Brenda Blaine."

"You *what*?"

"About two hours ago," Brian Delahanty announced smugly, "we arrested Reverend Edwin Crosby of the First Methodist Church."

CHAPTER 8

Rose Crosby was sobbing into a slice of apple strudel at the Robinson kitchen table when Nan came down for breakfast on Tuesday morning. Mom hovered anxiously over Rose, offering coffee, orange juice, Kleenex. Nothing seemed to be working.

"It's just so horrible," Rose moaned. Her hair was stringy, her face red and swollen. She wore a sleeveless cotton dress of no apparent shape or style. "Our whole lives are being ruined because of that ..." She gave another cry and buried her face in her arms.

"How long?" Nan mouthed at her mother.

Mom looked up at the kitchen clock. "Half an hour," she whispered back. Then she spoke in a normal, soothing tone. "Nan, Rose says that Edwin is innocent, that this is all just a huge misunderstanding."

"Well, obviously," Nan agreed. She had known Edwin Crosby since before either one of them was potty-trained, and the idea that he'd killed Brenda was absurd.

Nan poured herself a cup of coffee and sat down at the table. She touched Rose's arm lightly. "Rose? It's Nan. I'm sorry you're having such a terrible time. I talked to Detective Delahanty last night, but he didn't tell me much."

Rose looked up. "Edwin's innocent," she wailed.

"Of course he is. So why don't you tell me what's happening? And maybe then we can figure out what to do."

Rose took a deep breath and looked around, as if noticing for the first time just where she was. "Could I have some coffee?" she asked meekly.

"Of course," Mom chirped, almost tripping in her haste to reach the coffeemaker.

Rose sipped the coffee, wiped her eyes, and blew her nose. Then she tried to smile and flashed those awful teeth. "I'm sorry to be such a nuisance," she apologized.

"Don't be silly," Nan said. Poor Rose had spent her whole life being apologetic. "You're not being a nuisance at all. Now, do you think you can talk about it?" Rose nodded. "Good. Let's start at the beginning. When did they come to arrest Edwin?"

Rose shook her head. "They didn't come. Edwin went down to the police station yesterday afternoon. He'd been beside himself since the picnic, when we found out that Brenda's son was coming to town, and that she'd talked about his father. Edwin realized he had to come forward, to explain. Only by then Ryan was already there, and it was too late."

"Explain what?" Brian Delahanty had refused to tell Nan the reason for Edwin Crosby's arrest, and not knowing was driving her nuts. She'd come close to going down to the police station herself last night.

"Because Ryan Blaine is Edwin's son." Rose choked the statement out.

Good God. Nan saw her shock mirrored on her mother's face. It took a monumental effort to keep her jaw from dropping at the very notion of Edwin Crosby coupling with Brenda Blaine. Turning the calendar back twenty years made it no less implausible.

"You mean that Edwin and Brenda Blaine . . . they, uh . . .?" Nan inquired delicately.

Rose nodded again. "I know it seems strange, but Edwin says it happened. He and Brenda were neighbors. Of course, I didn't know Edwin very well in high school, didn't really get to know him until we were in classes together at Wheaton College. So I never knew anything about whatever had happened with him and Brenda. But of course, I knew that Edwin had a son born out of wedlock."

"He told you that?" Flabbergasted though she was, Nan kept her tone gentle.

Rose stared at her. "Why, certainly. When Edwin proposed marriage to me, he explained that a child had been born as a result of a youthful indiscretion. He had accepted financial responsibility for the child. That was all he told me and all I wanted to know. I was shocked when he told me—horrified, if the truth be known—but I was proud of his integrity, the way he accepted his moral obligation."

"This was when you were still at Wheaton that he told you?"

Rose shook her head. "No. He was in the seminary, then."

Nan had a sudden image of Brenda Blaine baiting Rose at the dinner table at the reunion. *I'd bet old Edwin there is hell in bed*, Brenda had said. Rose's blushing befuddlement had been quite genuine. But Edwin had appeared gutshot.

"But Edwin never told you that Brenda Blaine was the child's mother?"

Rose shook her head. "After that first conversation when he proposed, we never discussed the matter again. All he told me was that the child was a boy and that the mother had moved away from the midwest."

Nan tried to put herself in Rose's position, to imagine blindly accepting such a staggering revelation from a prospective husband. Impossible. Nan would raise holy hell and demand every scrap of pertinent information immediately. It was one thing to have stepchildren; lots of folks did, starting with her own sister. Stepkids were simply one of the realities of a society filled with marital mistakes. But this was hardly the same.

"You never talked about it? Not even in passing?"

Rose shook her head again. "Edwin handles our finances.

Sometimes there were additional expenses that I'd only find out about when my own allowance was cut. But he never gave me any particulars, other than to say he was meeting his moral obligation. I knew what that meant."

When her *allowance* was cut. In her late thirties, and she had an allowance. It made Nan shiver.

"When did you find out about Brenda?" she asked softly.

Rose shuddered. "The night of the reunion. I never *dreamed*, when I saw that vulgar creature coming toward us, that it might be the"—she hesitated, then spoke with total incredulity—"the mother of Edwin's child."

Mom had taken a seat on the other side of the table and was spreading apricot jam on an English muffin. She offered a half to Rose, who waved it away.

"I couldn't possibly eat, I'm just so nauseous," she apologized. "But thank you very much."

Nan had no such problems. She took the muffin. "Exactly when did you find out that Brenda was Ryan's mother?"

Rose closed her eyes and swayed slightly. "I began to realize something was wrong when Edwin got so very tense during dinner. He's usually at his best in a group of between six and twelve people. But he barely said a word all through dinner, and he just stared at his food the whole time. I thought perhaps he had picked up a touch of the flu. He was trying not to look at her, I realized later, but he just couldn't help himself. But *still* it never occurred to me. And then, she made that incredibly coarse remark, and Edwin jumped a mile. And suddenly I knew."

At the first opportunity, Rose had confronted Edwin, who declined to discuss the situation. Rose persisted. "I was being a horrible nag, and I pride myself so on not nagging Edwin. But I simply had to hear it from his own lips. He put me off until after the class picture, and then we left."

Nan tried to remember the last time she had seen the Crosbys at the reunion and couldn't. Folks like Rose and Edwin had a tendency to blend into the woodwork.

"We came back to the house," Rose went on, "and he told me everything. Of course there really wasn't much to tell. But I was . . . devastated. Thank heavens we'd taken the children to Mother's for the night! I couldn't have faced them. I was so terribly upset, absolutely mortified. And then the next morning, we got to church and found out that Brenda had been murdered."

Mom *had* mentioned that Edwin's sermon Sunday morning seemed a bit off.

"What time did you get home from the reunion?" Nan asked.

"Around nine-thirty."

"Did either of you go out again?"

Rose looked indignant. "If you're suggesting that Edwin actually did kill that hussy—"

"Not at all," Nan said hastily. "Not at all. But these are questions the police will be asking you, if they haven't already."

"I was down there till after ten last night," Rose sniffed, "and I told them that neither Edwin nor myself left our house between when we got home from the reunion at nine-thirty and six forty-five the next morning when we came over to the church."

"Thanks for telling me," Nan said. "I certainly don't mean to make this any more difficult for you. But I just can't count on the police to tell me everything I want to know. Now, who's Edwin's lawyer?"

"Why, he called George Carroll, who handles all the legal matters for the church. Mr. Carroll said this really isn't the sort of thing he does himself, but he promised to find Edwin a"—Rose gave a little shiver of horror—"a criminal attorney. And he's going to get Edwin released, he promised that, too."

"Good," Nan said. "I'll do whatever I can to help you, Rose, but I really need to talk to Edwin. Would you take me over to the jail to see him now?"

"But I promised my children I'd come right back."

"I can watch the little ones," Mom offered.

"Oh, that's not necessary, Mrs. Robinson. They're all right. Ryan is with them."

Come again? "Ryan Blaine is at your house?"

"When Edwin . . . called to tell me they'd arrested him, he said that he had seen Ryan and acknowledged his paternity publicly. So of course, Ryan is staying with us. He's Edwin's son."

Oh. Of course.

The Reverend Edwin Crosby had already been released on his own recognizance by the time Nan and Rose got to the jail. The $250,000 bail the prosecutor's office wanted had been denied, and the warden said Mayor Webster himself had driven the preacher home. The warden sounded pretty impressed.

When they got back to the parsonage, Edwin opened the screen door and greeted them solemnly. Nan had never been inside the sturdy brick parsonage before. The furnishings were squeaky-clean but relentlessly shabby, the kind of stuff a first-class thrift shop wouldn't even bother to put out on the sales floor. Everything was in shades of brown.

A young man who had to be Ryan Blaine stood just behind Edwin. Nan was stunned at the physical resemblance. Hard to believe that half this boy's genes came from Brenda Blaine. Ryan was slightly taller than his father and much thinner. But he had the same large ears, the same slightly hunched shoulders, the same thin brown hair, the same facial structure.

Except for the ponytail and the earring, he was a veritable clone.

"You must be glad to be home," Nan told Edwin awkwardly.

Rose Crosby hesitated, then walked past her husband without speaking and headed toward an inner doorway where two young boys and an older girl stood wide-eyed. "Come along, children," Rose said, picking up the smaller boy and shepherding the others down the hall. It was the first natural, comfortable move she had made all morning. It was also a first-class snub.

If the Reverend Edwin Crosby was nonplussed by the abdication of his wife and children, he didn't show it. "Please come in," he said. "I'd like to introduce you to my son, Ryan. Ryan, this is Ms. Robinson, from California."

Ryan shook hands politely with a firm grip. His wide brown eyes reminded Nan of Bambi, hearing gunshots. He wore jeans, a UC Santa Cruz T-shirt featuring the banana slug mascot, and heavy hiking boots. His earring was hand-crafted, a sterling stud set with turquoise.

"Pleased to meet you, Ms. Robinson," Ryan said.

"Call me Nan," she told him. "I'm sorry to meet you under such difficult circumstances." Then she turned to his father. "Edwin, I'm very concerned. Is there someplace we can talk?"

Edwin Crosby rocked slightly from side to side.

"Your office at the church, perhaps?" Nan prompted.

"Why, I suppose. Ryan, will you be all right here?"

"Sure," the boy said. "Sure . . . Dad." He seemed to be testing the word.

Edwin Crosby held the front door open for Nan. "We'll be back a little later, then. *Son.*"

It was a start.

The Reverend Edwin Crosby's office at the First Methodist Church smelled of lemon furniture oil. The wood was rich and dark, the paneling thick solid oak. The walls were covered with cheaply framed photographs, plaques, and certificates. Edwin had attended many a seminar, gotten much additional training, been photographed frequently with local dignitaries, Methodist and otherwise. In various framed photographs, Nan recognized Jim and Mary Lee Webster, Wally Sheehan, even—and this was truly startling—her own father being named Christian Businessman of the Year.

That was just after Edwin had come back to the parish as assistant pastor.

Edwin seated Nan and then sat down in the brown leather chair behind his desk. He stared vacantly out the window.

"When I was a little boy," he began, "I always knew I wanted to be a minister, to do God's work. I dedicated my life to Jesus when I was nine, and I've always tried to live by the Golden Rule. In the back of my mind and heart, I dreamed of coming back to Spring Hill one day and leading the flock at this church. When I got the appointment here, it was perhaps the greatest thrill of my lifetime. And when Reverend McAllister retired and I was asked to step up into his position, I felt that surely all my dreams had now come true."

It was an interesting recitation, though a bit far afield from the subject at hand. Edwin's verbal style had always been discursive.

"I've spent many years, now, looking out this window, planning sermons, talking to the Lord. In the spring, the cherry blossoms in the garden send up the most delicious perfume. But this would have been my last year in Spring Hill." He swiveled the chair to look in Nan's general direction, still avoiding eye contact. "I was about to be appointed to a regional position in the Methodist church. I hated the idea of giving up this parish, but the new position would have enabled me to help make some of the important decisions which face the church in these rapidly changing and morally demanding times." Finally he looked her in the eye. "That won't happen now."

Nan was quiet for a moment. "Edwin, I'm sure this is all some kind of ghastly mistake and we can get it cleared up. But let's be practical here. The first thing you need is a top-notch lawyer. I'm not licensed to practice law in Illinois, and I don't have any personal experience with criminal trials anyway. But I'll be happy to help you find good representation."

"That shouldn't be necessary," Edwin said, "though I appreciate your offer. Jim said he'd see that I had good counsel."

"Jim Webster?" she asked, confused.

Edwin nodded. "Of course. He promised to help with my legal expenses as well."

A mighty generous offer, Nan thought. Any attorney Jim Webster knew would not come cheap. And criminal attorneys always wanted funds up front. Once your client starts serving twenty-to-life, he loses all sense of urgency about paying legal fees.

"Rose came to my mother's house this morning, hoping that somehow I could help you. She told me that you're innocent of Brenda's murder."

Edwin Crosby's eyes widened. Bambi's old man. "But of course I am!"

"Then somebody else is guilty. And the fastest way to get the charges against you dropped will be to figure out who that is."

"I didn't kill Brenda," he said.

"Did you tell the police that?"

He nodded. "Of course. But they didn't seem to believe me." He seemed genuinely befuddled by this.

"Edwin, you just introduced Ryan as your son. Are you certain that he is?" Given the remarkable physical resemblance, it was a silly question, but one that had to be asked.

"Oh yes," he said firmly. "Absolutely. I've seen pictures of him over the years. He looked like me, and Brenda said he was mine. Now that I've met him, there's no doubt at all in my mind."

Nan looked directly at Edwin. "From the police point of view, that gives you a motive for killing her, then. An excellent motive. Would you have been considered for the regional Methodist position if it were known that you were the father of an illegitimate son?"

He didn't hesitate. "No, of course not."

"Does that new job pay more money?"

He nodded.

"And you wanted that job."

He nodded again.

"Then there you have it, from the police point of view. Where were you between eleven fifteen and eleven thirty-five on Saturday night?"

Edwin jerked his head. "Is that when she was killed?"

"Approximately. Where were you?"

"Here. Or rather next door, at the rectory."

"With Rose?"

"With Rose."

"Did anybody else see you after you left the reunion?"

He shook his head. "No. Rose was terribly upset. She'd guessed that Brenda was ... Ryan's mother. It distressed her enormously. We returned to the rectory and talked and prayed for hours. It was well after midnight before we went to sleep. And then in the morning when we went across to the church, we heard Brenda was dead."

Nan wondered fleetingly if the Crosbys were the sort of couple who made love as an affirmation when an argument was over. It was difficult to envision the Crosbys making love ever.

"There's something I don't quite understand," Nan said. "And that's ... well ..."

"Me and Brenda?" Edwin asked quietly.

Nan nodded.

"In some ways," he began, "you and I knew each other very well growing up. We saw each other every Sunday for many years. But in other ways, you were always a stranger to me, a sophisticated girl from the nice part of town. And of course, I was very shy."

Would he ever get to the point?

"You probably wouldn't have been aware of this," Edwin went on, "living in the Heights, but Brenda and I were neighbors through the alley when we were growing up. There weren't a lot of children in the neighborhood, and until perhaps third or fourth grade, we were close friends.

There was a rather dilapidated storage building out behind Brenda's house. The front was a garage, but the back we used as a playhouse."

Finally, something that made sense.

"When Brenda and I graduated from grammar school, we were still friendly. We went to Wentworth, a relatively small elementary school, and neither of us had a lot of close friends there. Brenda was already dating guys from the high school by then, but we were like . . . it's hard to say. Not brother and sister. We were more like cousins."

Kissing, evidently.

The Reverend Edwin Crosby went on, smiling to himself a little, looking out the window as he brought up obviously pleasurable memories.

"I liked Brenda," he said. "Always. She was so vivacious, so tough, so rebellious. All the things I knew I never could be and never would be. By the time we were in high school, she was quite wild, with a truly scandalous reputation. My mother was a very religious woman, and Brenda upset her. But I still met her sometimes. We'd talk, and she'd say what jerks the guys she went out with were."

Had they really been jerks? Except for Frank Finney, Brenda's boyfriends that Nan remembered had a forbidden, slightly dangerous allure, an intriguing macho air, a strong visceral appeal. Good-looking guys, with nice healthy bodies and tight hipslung jeans, fascinating to watch in motion.

She realized suddenly that if you changed the pronouns, the same description fit Brenda. The high-school Nan, painfully conformist, had been fascinated by Brenda's independence, her devil-may-care attitude, her disregard for convention. Just as Edwin had.

"I was a virgin," Edwin continued, with a faint blush. "Brenda wasn't. She was still using the back storeroom area of the garage as a playhouse, but a rather different form of play. She had blackout curtains and candles back there, and sometimes a bottle of Boone's Farm or Annie Green Springs wine. She had an old fold-up twin bed set up like a couch with one of those Indian paisley throw things on it. Lots of pillows. She . . . I realize this sounds preposterous, but I swear to God it's true . . . she seduced me."

"It doesn't sound preposterous at all," Nan told him gently. "I think it sounds kind of . . . sweet. And friendly."

He smiled for the first time, the blush more pronounced. "Friendly, it was. Absolutely."

"How long did it go on?"

"The first time was Thanksgiving night of our senior year," he said without hesitation. "The last time was the Fourth of July, right after graduation. We were together a lot on holidays. Holidays bothered Brenda. Because of her . . . well, her family."

Of course. Thanksgiving at the McReedy-Blaine residence must have been a real treat. Alvina praying till the turkey was stone-cold, Louise passed out in the mashed potatoes, Brenda checking the exits.

"Did you know she was pregnant when she left town?"

He shook his head.

"I didn't even know she'd run away until several days later. There was a place we used to leave messages for each other when we were children, an old metal tackle box in the storeroom. Sometimes we still used it. When I heard she'd left town, I looked in it and found a note. It just said, *'I had to get out. Sorry I didn't say good-bye.'* "

"The note didn't say anything about being pregnant, or about you being the father?"

"Nothing."

"You say she had wine back there. What about dope?"

He shook his head. "Not with me. She offered to turn me on one time, but I said no. She just laughed."

"Did you know her friend Liza Krzyzanowski?" Nan asked.

Edwin's eyes widened. "Why, I'd forgotten all about her! Liza Krzyzanowski." He shook his head. "She came by once when Brenda and I were back there, just talking. She was high on something, I think. But that was the only time

I ever met her." He thought for a moment. "She ran away, didn't she?"

Nan nodded. "Sometime that spring, apparently. Do you remember anything about that?"

"Not really." He hesitated. "But now that I think about it, I remember Brenda being upset after Liza left. She wouldn't talk about it, but I think she missed her. And she spent more time with me after that."

"What do you know about Brenda's other boyfriends?"

"Oh, I was never her *boyfriend*!" Edwin protested. "Just her friend."

"Whatever. Who *was* her boyfriend, did you know? Frank Finney, maybe?"

"Frank? I don't remember. Brenda wasn't the type to name names. Why do you ask?"

"Because if you didn't kill Brenda," Nan explained patiently, "somebody else did. She had some kind of fight with Frank Saturday night just before she was killed."

"Frank Finney?" He shook his head. "That's impossible. He's a devoted family man."

"So are you," Nan reminded him gently. "When did you hear from Brenda again after she left Spring Hill?"

"I was a senior in college," he said. "I don't know how she tracked me down, but I got a letter from her from California, with photographs of Ryan. I was stunned, aghast. Here was this little kid who looked just like me, who almost certainly was my child. I wanted to do the right thing, but I was absolutely destitute. I was on scholarship, working two jobs to stay in school. I took the coward's way out, I'm sorry to say. I ignored her letter."

He fidgeted as he continued. "She wrote me again, and I didn't answer that letter either. Then about two years later, when I was in divinity school, I heard from her again. She was in Las Vegas, and Ryan needed an operation. It was the picture she sent this time that really got me. On top of the piano at my parents' house there was a framed picture of me riding a broomstick horse in a cowboy outfit. She had Ryan posed the same way. It really tore me up.

"So I found a way to send her some money. I took out a loan, and I'd just had a great-uncle die and leave me a small inheritance. I sent it all to Brenda. I prayed incessantly about her. And I knew that I couldn't live with myself if I didn't accept responsibility for this child I had caused to come into the world. I promised Brenda a double-tithe, and she said that would be fine."

A double-tithe of a seminary student's earnings might buy a couple of Big Macs. And ministers made next to nothing. But Brenda had been pragmatic, and apparently genuinely fond of Edwin Crosby. She wouldn't demand more than the traffic could bear.

"Is there any proof of paternity?" Nan asked.

"I gave them a blood sample while I was in jail."

Nan inwardly groaned. "You didn't have to do that, you know."

"I volunteered," he said earnestly. "I'm not guilty of anything. But now that it's all in the open anyway, I wanted to settle this paternity question once and for all."

"Does that mean that Ryan has also had a blood test?"

"They're running them concurrently."

Did Edwin think he was working for the district attorney's office? Still, it probably didn't matter much. A simple look at Edwin beside Ryan was conclusive enough.

"Did you see Brenda in person over the last twenty years?"

"Never."

"Did you speak with her on the telephone?"

"She called me occasionally. Perhaps five or six times over the years."

"Did you ever call her?"

He shook his head. "I never had her number. Or her address, after she moved to Las Vegas. I always sent her checks to a post office box on the first of the month."

"Did she send letters to you?"

"Occasionally. I destroyed them."

"Did you know she was coming to the reunion?"

"Oh, no. I was horrified when she walked in. It seemed like a very bad dream."

"Did you speak with her privately that night?"

He shook his head again. "Rose insisted on remaining for the class photograph, but once I saw Brenda, I only wanted to get away."

"You didn't dance with her?"

"She asked me," he said stiffly, "and I declined." He looked up again, his eyes pleading. "I didn't kill Brenda, Nan. I swear it by my faith in God almighty. But for the sake of my son, her killer must be brought to justice. Can you find him?"

"I'll do my best," Nan assured him, feeling very little confidence.

CHAPTER 9

Nan left the Reverend Edwin Crosby in his sepulchral office and went back to the parsonage. She rapped lightly, and when nobody answered, tried the door and walked inside.

Ryan Blaine sat tensely in a shabby armchair, flipping through *National Geographic*, looking like he was waiting for biopsy results. He tightened further when Nan came in and sat on the nearby edge of an ancient couch. The boy wore his alienation like a shield.

"Ryan," Nan said gently, "I've just been talking with Edwin. I promised him I'd do whatever I could to find out who killed your mother. And I was hoping you'd be able to help me."

"I don't know how," he answered abruptly.

"For starters, I'd like to know more about your mom's life. What she did, who her friends were, what she was like. I spent a few hours with her the other night, and I liked her a lot. But I hadn't seen her for twenty years before that, and when I knew her in high school we weren't particularly close friends."

Just then Rose Crosby appeared in the doorway, with her children hugging her skirts in a tableau that might have come from the prairie frontier in 1853. Rose's hair was recently combed, and she'd applied dark pink lipstick. The shade was wrong for both the yellow dress she wore and her own coloring, but the gesture was important. Rose

Crosby was prepared to put on a public face in defense of her husband.

"You met my children at the picnic, didn't you, Nan?" Rose asked.

"Of course," Nan said. The kids looked dazed and frightened, and the youngest boy seemed to be fighting tears.

"My mother's been keeping the baby," Rose said. "We're going over there now for a while." Nan saw Ryan's face tighten. Going to *his* mother's house was an option lost forever.

"I've switched the phone over to ring at the church," Rose continued. "It's just too hard answering all the ... Miss Miller, the church secretary, is taking all the calls. You can dial out, but nothing will ring here. Will you two be all right?"

"Of course," Nan said easily. "You folks just run along."

They watched as Rose and her children moved as a single centipedal unit through the room and out the door. When they were gone, the atmosphere seemed to lighten dramatically.

"It must be odd," Nan said, "meeting all these people." Instant siblings. An unknown parent. Scary stuff.

Ryan hesitated. "It is. Would you, uh, like some coffee cake or something? The kitchen's full of food."

Nan followed him into the kitchen where he moved his hand slowly along the edge of a long kitchen counter laden with baked offerings from parishioners. A situation that would give even Miss Manners pause: What *do* you do when your minister's arrested for murder? The chicken casserole would be the easy part.

"Such a lot of food," he said, shaking his head.

"When bad things happen to people in Spring Hill, everybody starts baking." Nan had a sudden memory of the Robinson kitchen after her father's death, filled with casseroles and pies in Pyrex dishes with names taped to their bottoms, cakes and cookies on disposable platters. "And folks here care a great deal about the Crosbys."

What did Ryan Blaine think about the Crosbys? For a dual resident of Las Vegas and Santa Cruz—one of the west's least likely combinations—this must feel like visiting Mars.

"So what looks good?" Nan asked. The kitchen had a country motif, with blue tulips stenciled on solid white wooden cabinets. Beside a half-full coffeemaker sat a three-pound can of supermarket-brand coffee.

"There's a nice fruit tart with fresh peaches," he said. "I had a little of that awhile ago."

Nan wasn't really hungry, but she smiled encouragingly. "It sounds wonderful, and this time of year they're probably local peaches. Could you cut me a slice? And have some more yourself, why don't you?"

Ryan already knew where to find plates and silverware, and he seemed pleased to have something specific to do. It must have been a blindingly difficult twenty-four hours. First he was snatched out of the Alaskan wilderness by a helicopter pilot announcing his mother's murder. Then he'd been flown directly to Chicago without so much as a change of socks. In Spring Hill, he had been introduced to the father he'd never known—in a cell because that father was under arrest for killing his mother.

So far, however, the kid seemed to be holding his own.

Nan deliberately made general conversation at first, drawing the boy out on his summer experiences with the National Park Service, for which he had also worked the previous summer, in Glacier National Park. He hoped to make a career as an environmentalist. When he spoke of his summer jobs, he fairly glowed.

"Hardly anybody ever goes through there," he explained, excited by the memory of the road he and his cohorts had been refurbishing in Alaska. "It was originally an Indian trail, and it's still just barely passable with four-wheel drive. The wildlife is amazing, elk and moose and bear. Sometimes I think I'd like to just go off someplace like that and stay forever. It's so humbling to be surrounded by so much natural beauty. The guys I work with call it God's country."

"And you don't?" Nan wondered mildly.

Ryan looked around nervously with a little frown. "I've ... I don't quite know how to say this, particularly here. I'm not sure that ... well, I ... Oh, never mind."

"What?"

He paused, then closed his eyes. "I don't know if I really believe in God."

Nan couldn't help laughing, and after a moment Ryan joined her.

Ryan shook his head with an embarrassed grin. "I can't believe I just told you that, and *here* of all places!"

"Don't worry about it," Nan told him. "You're in a strange place with people you've never met, under awful circumstances. I think you're doing great."

"Great?" He stared at her and the grin seemed to slide down off his face. "My mom's d—"

But he couldn't say the word. His mouth hung open for a moment, and then suddenly something broke inside him and he buried his face in his arms on the table, sobbing. Nan moved her chair beside him and gently stroked his head and shoulders.

It occurred to her that this was the first genuine instance of mourning she had seen for Brenda Blaine. Everybody else had treated the woman's death as a damned nuisance and a massive inconvenience. Nobody, not even Brenda's own grandmother, had shown any particular sorrow or remorse.

But to this boy, Brenda wasn't the town Bad Girl. She wasn't some outrageous Vegas blackjack dealer tricked out in satin and rhinestones, an exotic floozy plunked down in the midst of her old hometown to create a scandal.

She was Mom, and she was dead.

As Nan rode out this emotional release with the boy, she tried to imagine what it would be like to have your mother murdered. There'd be, first and foremost, the incredible pain of a mother's death. Then the added jolt of having that death come suddenly, without warning, with no opportunities to say good-bye or resolve misunderstandings.

And finally there would be the horror of the murder itself, awareness that somebody hated your beloved mother enough to physically destroy her.

June Robinson wasn't likely to be murdered, of course, not here in Spring Hill. But until a few days ago, Nan would have sworn that *nobody* was ever likely to be murdered in Spring Hill. She thought again about Ralph Salamone and her ambivalence toward him. What if someone like Ralph were truly evil? They knew nothing about him except what he had told them. They had taken him entirely on trust.

Brenda Blaine had trusted somebody. That person killed her.

After Ryan regained his composure, he turned to Nan. "Detective Delahanty told me something last night," he said. "He said that Mom's grandmother is in a rest home here. It kind of caught me off guard, because Mom always said she didn't have any family."

"Your great-grandmother is over at Golden Valley," Nan said. "I saw her just yesterday."

Nan remained greatly troubled by the visit to Alvina McReedy. A cross-stitched sampler hanging on the wall beside Alvina's bed had found its way into one of her dreams last night. *Wine biteth like a serpent and stingeth like an adder.* Proverbs 23:32 was painstakingly sewn onto the sampler, which was faded enough to have been in Alvina McReedy's home back in Brenda's childhood. A real fun gal, Alvina.

"Does she know about me?" Ryan asked hesitantly.

"I don't know."

He closed his eyes in sudden pain.

"Could we go see her?" he asked, after a moment.

"Sure," Nan agreed. "But I should warn you, some days she's a little fuzzy. She's ninety-three years old."

"Ninety-three." He shook his head. "Amazing. I have a ninety-three-year-old great-grandmother. I can't believe my mom never told me about her."

"I'm not sure your mom got along real well with her," Nan cautioned.

I sent the next letter back marked "Deceased."

He was still shaking his head. "A great-grandmother. And you think she doesn't even know about me?"

"I didn't say anything about you to her," Nan said carefully, "and she didn't mention you specifically. But . . ."

But Alvina McReedy had almost certainly read Brenda's letters to Louise before destroying them. And Brenda, who laughed conspiratorially with her mother, heads together, would surely have told Louise about her son.

"I want to see her," Ryan said abruptly. "Do they have, like, visiting hours there?"

"I don't know. Why don't we call and find out?"

And see, too, if this was one of the days when Alvina McReedy wouldn't know them from hat racks. Nan located a phone book in a closet by the back door and dialed. Donna, the receptionist, answered.

"Good morning," Nan said. "This is Nan Robinson. I was there yesterday visiting Mrs. McReedy. I wanted to come by again, and I wondered if one time would be better than another to see her."

There was a long silence.

"I'm afraid it won't be possible to see Mrs. McReedy at all," Donna said finally. "Mrs. McReedy passed away in her sleep last night."

The news brought Ryan to the brink of hysteria. It seemed crucial to get him out of the parsonage, into some neutral environment where he could breathe more freely, reestablish some connection with reality as he knew it. After a few moments of awkward confusion, Nan realized that the most controllable environment she knew in Spring Hill was her own mother's backyard.

Mom seemed unsurprised to see them, and Ryan reacted politely, if not enthusiastically, to this new stranger. But as they sat in the Adirondack chairs in the shade of the willow, Nan knew it had been a wise idea to get this boy out of the strained piety of the Methodist parsonage. At a guess, the Crosby household was fairly grim under the best circumstances. Right now it rivaled the atmosphere in an airline lounge where relatives awaited word on plane crash survivors.

"It's funny," Ryan said after awhile. "My mom never talked about where she came from much, but I always had the sense it was way out in the sticks somewhere. And everybody here talks about Chicago as if it were a million miles away. But when I came in from O'Hare, everything seemed built up solid."

"It is far, in terms of miles," Nan answered. "It's forty-three miles from Spring Hill to the Chicago Loop. The land between here and there's filled in since I was a kid. When I was growing up, all those suburbs full of condos and apartments, all those industrial parks you passed along the expressway, they didn't exist. Everything was all cornfields." Like the field being filled now by Potawatomi Industrial Park.

"Yeah, that's what Mom always said. She really hated the midwest. Said it was all cornfields and narrow-minded bigots." He suddenly flushed. "I'm sorry. I didn't mean—"

Nan laughed. "I'm not offended. I left, too, remember? And I have a feeling that your mom was never particularly happy in Spring Hill. Did she talk about it much?"

Ryan shook his head. "Almost never. Only if I was, like, complaining about Las Vegas or something." That made sense. Ryan would not be at one with a town like Las Vegas. "Then she'd say it could be a lot worse, and she'd make some comment about the midwest."

"Did she ever mention Spring Hill specifically?"

"Uh-uh. No names of anything. Not even the state. And like I said, it was almost never."

"But before you got here, we were told that she'd talked to you about your father."

"She didn't talk about him directly to me," Ryan said slowly. "In fact, when I was little, she told me my father was dead."

A harsh untruth to lay on a child. But perhaps it was the easiest way for Brenda to stave off the questions of an intelligent, inquisitive youngster. And it was entirely possible that Brenda herself had been told something similar as a child. According to Mom, nobody had ever known anything about Louise's husband, the mysterious Mr. Blaine. Not even if there'd actually *been* a Mr. Blaine.

It was one of many questions that Alvina McReedy could have answered, and now never would. *Be not deceived; God is not mocked: for whatsoever a man soweth, that shall he also reap.* Galatians 6:7. Another faded sampler on the rest home wall.

"Then how . . ." She allowed her voice to trail away. This conversation was tricky enough, and it seemed pointless to push too hard and have him clam up completely.

"Mom was married for a while," he said. "When I was about eight she married this guy named Joey Latella. I don't know what she told him but sometimes when they'd fight, I'd hear him say things about my dad. 'The hometown hot shot,' Joey always called him. I tried asking her once or twice about it, but she said Joey didn't know what he was talking about and to just forget it."

"She and Joey fought a lot?"

Ryan gave a short mirthless chuckle. "Constantly."

"How long were they married?"

"Just a couple years. Then one day Joey was gone. Mom cried and cried and started really drinking a lot. It wasn't too long after that that she stopped drinking and got into AA. I heard later that Joey was living with some topless dancer from the MGM Grand."

A swell environment for child rearing. "Whatever happened to Joey?"

Ryan shrugged. "No idea. I never saw him again, but that doesn't mean anything. I never spent much time on the Strip."

"You like Santa Cruz better then, I guess."

He brightened significantly. "Oh yeah. It's a whole different world. First time I went there, I thought I'd died and gone to heaven." He blushed suddenly at the inappropriateness of his statement. "Oh, man, I didn't—"

"A figure of speech, big deal," Nan said easily. "My sister lived in Santa Cruz awhile."

"Really?"

She smiled back. "Really. Julie's two years younger than I am. She's a commercial flower grower down in San Diego County now, but she took a long time figuring out what she wanted to do with her life. She'd always say she was living by trial and error. Santa Cruz was one of the places she stayed a long time, waitressing and working at some of the local nurseries. The only reason she left was that she married a guy whose family raised flowers down in Floritas."

"I can understand that," he said.

Ryan would like Julie, Nan realized. Maybe when all this was over, she could figure out a way to get them together.

"I don't know Las Vegas very well," she said, "and I have to admit I don't like it very much."

"Good taste," he said with one of his rare smiles. "Vegas sucks."

"Did you and your mom live near the Strip?"

"For a long time," he said. "We moved into a real nice condo with a pool after Joey left and Mom got straight. She got some kind of settlement from a lawsuit. She had one of those Dalkon Shields, and it messed her up so she could never have more kids. I think that's how she got the condo. Then about three years ago, she bought a house out in a new subdivision. One of those things where they cut the desert into cubes and then put up four different houses, A-B-C-D, A-B-C-D. We're in the top of the line, the four-bedroom, and she got all kinds of upgrades. It's a real nice place, black-bottomed pool and everything. My own bathroom, even. Mom got all sorts of new furniture when we moved in. She had a great time picking stuff out."

"Had she been saving up a long time?" Nan asked. "For the house?"

Ryan rolled his eyes and guffawed. "Not likely. Mom was always real generous, but she wasn't much of a saver." He frowned. "You know, Nan, I don't know where the money came from. It's not like she won big at something, 'cause Mom didn't gamble. I kind of hinted around about it, but she wasn't saying anything. I . . . I always thought maybe it came from my dad."

Neither one of them stated the obvious, that the Reverend Edwin Crosby couldn't bankroll more than a pup tent.

"Sounds like she was good at keeping secrets."

"The best," Ryan agreed. "Like Christmas, I could never figure out what she was going to give me. You could ask her direct questions or kind of sly ones, and you'd never trip her up. And she'd hide my presents with her girlfriends or neighbors or something. I could never find anything." He seemed mildly embarrassed.

"I was the same way," Nan admitted, "always poking around trying to find my presents. I was pretty good at it, too. Of course, that meant I didn't have many surprises."

"Big deal." He shook his head. "Surprises I can do without."

A common link among the children of alcoholics, Nan realized, kids who understand how horrendous surprises can be, who yearn for certainties. Did Ryan know about ACA?

"Speaking of surprises, I met Bernie Singer yesterday. Did you know he's in town?"

Ryan stiffened. "That policeman told me."

"He's very upset about what happened to your mom. He said they were planning to get married at Thanksgiving."

Ryan snorted. "Bernie said that?"

"Uh-huh."

He shrugged. "First I ever heard of it. Mom always told me after Joey that she'd never get married again. She said, why bother? You could have the benefits without the legal aggravation."

"It was a rough divorce?"

"How do you measure rough?"

That one went right to the heart. "I suppose there's no such thing as an easy divorce," she said slowly. She and Leon had been scrupulously civilized, but the oddest little things had turned out to be incredibly painful. "If you love somebody enough to marry them, it has to hurt when you admit that the marriage didn't work out. And if there are kids involved . . ."

"I wasn't involved," Ryan said shortly. "I just lived there. It wasn't like Joey was a real dad to me. He was just like the others, ignored me unless I really got in the way. I learned how to stay out of the way."

"Were there a lot of others?"

He was silent for a while. "You saw my mom," he said finally. "There were always men around her. Sometimes they lasted a while, most of the time they didn't. I never paid a lot of attention unless they moved in."

"Was that . . . often? That they'd move in?" He was close to closing up on her, she could tell. It had to hurt, talking about his mother this way.

"Often enough, I guess. Bernie was better than some of them. But I was out of there by the time Bernie moved in. *I'm Bernie Singer,*" he mimicked, *"but I don't sing, just play the piano. Hey, kid, what's happening?"*

Nan laughed. "Are you going to see him while he's here?"

"Not if I can help it." Ryan sounded very bitter now. "I want him to get his shit out of her house, too. I can do that, can't I? It's mine now, isn't it?"

"I don't know," Nan answered carefully. "Did your mother have a will?"

He laughed. "Mom make a will? She thought she'd live

forever. But she did have a lawyer, I know that. And I remember her saying that if anything funny ever happened to her, he'd take care of everything."

Interesting. *Very* interesting. "Do you know his name?"

"Sal Bonaventure. I told the detective about him."

"Do you know him yourself?"

Ryan shook his head. "Nah. But he's in Vegas."

"I'll try to get in touch with him," Nan promised. "He'll know the Nevada law. Are you aware of any other living relatives?"

He shook his head.

"Then if Brenda died intestate, I'd imagine anything she had would probably go to you."

"If it's mine," he said, in that bitter tone again, "I'll throw that slimy son of a bitch Singer out on the street and sell the damned place and never go to Las Vegas again. I hate that town. I never knew how much I hated it till I got out of there."

Nan was quiet a minute. "You know," she said finally, "that sounds just like the way your mother felt about Spring Hill. She had a friend who felt the same way, a girl named Liza Krzyzanowski." Nan pulled the old photo out of her purse. "Do you remember ever meeting anybody who looked like this?"

Ryan looked at the picture. "This was Mom in high school?"

"Yeah. And that little brunette was Liza."

He shook his head. "I don't think I've ever seen her." He hesitated, then looked at Nan, a bit uncomfortably. "Do you suppose—nah." He shook his head.

"What? Any way I can help, I'd be happy to."

"This afternoon," he said slowly, "I have to go to the funeral home, and I'm kind of dreading it."

"I'd be happy to go with you," Nan offered.

"Thanks," he said, relief clear in his voice. "That would help."

* * *

After dropping Ryan back at the parsonage, Nan drove her mother's car to the Spring Hill Inn and parked in precisely the same spot she had used Saturday night. It was easy to see why her car had been so well situated from the killer's point of view: Abundant shrubbery almost totally hid it from the side door to the parking lot. Less risk of being caught before the job was finished, which would be most inconvenient.

Nan walked slowly down the path she and Henry Sloane had followed toward their brief but intense tryst. In daylight it was far less romantic, far more open. There were some candy wrappers back in the woods where they'd been standing, a couple of empty beer cans tossed under a bush. But even now you could barely see back into the parking lot, so it wasn't surprising that they'd noticed nothing late at night. Distractions notwithstanding.

She returned to the building, which hadn't existed when she last lived in Spring Hill. It looked very modern and glassy and impersonal. For a few years it had belonged to one of the minor hotel chains, then been dumped during a corporate reorganization.

On her way inside, Nan passed a pair of women in business suits arguing about a shinto factor, whatever that might be. They seemed to belong to the motivational seminar taking place at the Inn. The small banquet rooms where reunion guests had waited for police questioning on Saturday night now bore signs saying things like YOU'RE THE BOSS! and TOMORROW'S TOO LATE and CREATIVE CLOSINGS.

She stuck her head into the ballroom, which was being set up for dinner. It looked smaller than it had Saturday night, but offered no clues or suggestions. Then she timed a leisurely stroll from the ballroom to the parking lot, allowed what seemed a reasonable length of time to knock out Brenda, drag her to the car, stab her, and wipe away fingerprints.

She was back in the ballroom in under four minutes. Without even hurrying.

* * *

The southern outskirts of Spring Hill hadn't expanded as aggressively as the northern ones that headed toward the expressway into Chicago. But they still had changed greatly in twenty years, and definitely extended farther than Nan remembered.

Once upon a time, the town had ended just past the sofa factory, and the area immediately adjacent to that factory had been cluttered with the sort of ramshackle houses where Brenda Blaine lived with her mother and grandmother. Now the sofa factory was history, and most of its environs had been cleared for a small, neat industrial park—another Webster Construction project, perhaps? The house where Edwin Crosby had grown up was gone, and Alvina McReedy's clapboard house long razed, along with Brenda's playpen-*cum*-love nest in that infamous back storage room.

One thing that seemed unchanged, however, was Riverside Texaco, where Alvina McReedy had mentioned a boyfriend of Brenda's working. Someone known only as Al. Grasping at straws, Nan told herself. That's what she was doing. But at least she was doing *something*.

Riverside Texaco—which had never been anywhere near a river—wasn't doing much business when Nan pulled in. There was still a single service bay, its door standing open to the street, but the rest of the garage area had been converted into a mini-mart. Nan went inside, bought a Diet Coke, and asked the indifferent teenage girl at the counter if the owner or manager was in.

"That'd be Jack," the girl said, popping a big wad of gum. "Jack Doyle. He's in the garage."

Jack Doyle looked about forty-five, wearing coveralls and scowling at the underside of an old rusted Honda Accord when Nan walked into the garage. He looked up and offered a twisted grin. "Let me guess," he said. "I just won the lottery and you're making a personal delivery."

Nan laughed. "Afraid not. Sorry."

"Then, please God, don't tell me you're with the EPA or some other damnfool government agency, 'cause I've had about all I can handle from them, and I'd hate to have to shoot you."

"Wrong again. But I *am* hoping you can help me with something."

He wiped his hands on a shop towel and stepped away from the car. "I can give it a try."

Nan introduced herself. "I'm looking for somebody who worked here about twenty years ago," she began.

Jack looked confused. "What in God's name for?"

"I guess you've probably heard about the woman who was killed on Saturday night at the Inn? Brenda Blaine?" He nodded slowly. "Well, somebody told me that she used to date a guy named Al who worked here. I know it's been a long time, but I figured there was maybe one chance in a million of finding him."

Suddenly Jack gave a grin wide enough to show some silver in his molars. "Twenty years ago? A guy named Al? You know, I just might be able to help you after all. Just *one* second." He stuck his head into the mini-mart, pulled a Coke out of the glass-fronted icebox, then headed for a back alcove where a metal desk was almost buried by service manuals. "C'mon, sit down a minute. I'm ready for a break anyway." He lifted a box of parts off a chair and took a flick at the seat with a shop towel before offering it to Nan.

"This used to be my dad's place," he explained when they were seated. "Back when you're talking about. And twenty years ago, I was working in Indianapolis for an auto parts company. Came back here maybe twelve, fifteen years ago, when my dad had his first heart attack." He gave a little shrug. "It was gonna just be temporary, but you know how things go."

"Do you remember somebody named Al from back then?"

"We've had a lot of Als through here," Jack Doyle told

her, taking a hearty swig from his Coke and getting up to shift one of the floor fans to aim more directly at them. "Mechanics aren't a real stable workforce, see. Some guys, heck, they're gone before you get a name sewed on their uniform. I'm shorthanded right now, actually, but with all this EPA crap going on, I'm trying to handle it all myself and save a buck or two."

He paused and looked at her. "But you don't care about that. This Al that you're looking for, what do you know about him?"

Nan considered. "Practically nothing, really. That he worked here. That he maybe dated Brenda Blaine when she was a senior in high school. And that if she was going out with him, he was probably"—she hesitated—"kind of studly."

Jack Doyle threw his head back and laughed. There was a *lot* of silver back there. "Studly. That'd be our Al, all right. Actually, he was here for a long time, six, seven years, something like that. Moved away, I guess, or maybe went back to school or something. I don't remember. Like I said, I wasn't here then. But I know somebody who might know. Let me make a phone call."

He flipped through a greasy Rolodex and punched a number on the phone. He actually seemed to be enjoying himself immensely. "Matty? Jack Doyle here. I got a bet going with somebody, maybe you can settle it." He wiggled his eyebrows at Nan as he listened. "Yeah, well, I may be loyal, but I ain't *stupid*. This puppy's not putting any more on the Cubbies *this* season. Not that kind of bet anyway. It's about a flash from our past. Al Tarantello."

There was a long pause now while Jack listened, made occasional grunts, said, "Oh yeah" at intervals. Finally he said thanks, set down the receiver, and raised both thumbs. "Gotcha!"

Nan smiled expectantly.

"Al's in Colorado," Jack Doyle told her, with a wave of his hand toward the west. "Matty says he thinks he's somewhere around Denver, but that's all he knows. Does that help?"

"It may," she told him. "It just may. You remember Al being a ladies' man?"

"I sure do," he said fondly. "Those were the days. Not like now, with deadly diseases. And all these chickenshit regulations and government pipsqueaks got nothing better to do than try to ruin an honest man's life."

He seemed to be begging for sympathy.

"You were afraid I was with the EPA?" Nan asked.

"Take a look out front there," Jack said, pointing toward the pumps. "Looks like a gas station, right?"

Nan nodded.

"Well, you may be surprised to know that it's actually a Hazardous Condition." He almost spat the words out. "I got me a leaking gas tank down there, and they're saying it's getting into the groundwater. So I got to dig it up and take it out." He was really going now. "But that ain't enough, either. We got to pick it apart like boning a trout, lift all the pieces out little bit by little bit, take the whole thing off to a hazardous waste dump. Dirt and all. They got these environmental do-gooders crawling all over the western suburbs making trouble. You know what they used to do in the old days?"

Nan shook her head, stunned by the force of his diatribe.

"They'd just chop 'em up and bury 'em where they lay. And nobody ever came pissing and moaning about the groundwater then."

Precisely how the planet had gotten into such a mess. When Nan spoke, however, it was sympathetically. "My mom was just talking about something like that. At my father's old car dealership."

Jack Doyle squinted slightly and his smile returned. "You're *that* Robinson family?"

"Is there some reason I wouldn't want to be?" Nan asked carefully. One never knew.

He shook his head hurriedly. "Not at all, not at all. I

remember your old man cut me a fine deal one time on a Mustang, first car I ever owned new. Called the bank personal to cut some of the red tape on my loan, too. But your mom don't own the place anymore, does she?"

"No. But the new owner wanted her to chip in on whatever's involved in cleaning up."

Jack Doyle waved a dismissive hand. "I hope she told him to stuff it."

Nan took a moment to picture her mother telling Horace Kobleski, "that vulgar Lithuanian," to stuff it. Truly mind-boggling. "I'm sure she was more polite," Nan told him, "but she did say no. And thanks for helping me track down this mysterious Al."

"You find him, give him my regards," Jack Doyle said. "And tell him Loretta Hensinger weighs three hundred pounds."

CHAPTER 10

Brian Delahanty wasn't sure if he wanted to laugh, cry, or scream when Nan Robinson strode into his office at two-thirty on Tuesday afternoon, all smug self-importance.

He was damn close to wipeout. Sixty-three hours since Brenda Blaine had bled all over the front seat of that nice Ford Taurus. And the last twenty-four had left a bad taste in his mouth.

Edwin Crosby was a nebbish, a dolt, an ineffectual lamebrain. But those weren't capital crimes. And he couldn't bring himself to believe that Edwin Crosby was a cold-blooded killer.

Whoever wasted Brenda Blaine had first clocked her from behind with a rock in the parking lot. He could almost—*almost*—see the preacher doing that in a fit of rage. Not rage. Irritation. Edwin Crosby seemed incapable of rage. But he sure as hell couldn't feature Crosby dragging the unconscious mother of his child into a car and ramming a brass sword into her heart three times.

So why in the hell was Bob Stedman so eager to nail him? The prosecutor didn't seem to have any particular vendetta against men of the cloth. He was active enough in the local Presbyterian church, and certainly conscious that Spring Hill was a town of sturdy Christian values.

The repressed religious types were the worst, Stedman argued, because when they snapped, they really let go. That might be, but it was Delahanty's experience that when preachers wigged out, their arena of sin was more likely to be sexual. They'd find some hooker willing to pee on them, or slip off the old clerical collar and head for a leather bar. Diddle altar boys. They didn't abruptly end a life of piety by breaking the Sixth Commandment.

The other odd thing about Stedman's fixation on Edwin Crosby was that his good buddy, Mayor Jim Webster, was now loudly protesting Crosby's innocence, to the point of leaning on Judge Hawthorne to get the preacher sprung. And the mayor was a man whose right hand always knew precisely what his left was up to.

True, in some ways Crosby looked like a nice ticket to clear the Blaine murder. When the preacher dragged in all hangdog yesterday afternoon with his woeful tale of paternity, Delahanty had thoroughly enjoyed his "confession." An utterly lapsed Catholic, Delahanty loved it when some purported man of God made a great big secular fool out of himself. But being a jackass didn't make somebody a murderer. Besides, Crosby and that dowdy wife both claimed he'd been paying child support all along.

So it took Delahanty by surprise when Bob Stedman jumped all over the preacher. And then when Lance Thompson brought the kid in from O'Hare, Stedman took one look at Ryan Blaine, freaked out, and ordered Delahanty to arrest Edwin Crosby on the spot. It wasn't clear to Delahanty precisely why Ryan Blaine in the flesh was so much more damning than Ryan Blaine in the abstract; after all, the preacher had just spent a weepy hour telling anyone who'd listen that he was the kid's father.

Stedman's reconstruction was that Crosby had taken his wife home and then sneaked back to the Spring Hill Inn to have things out with Brenda Blaine. *What* things were left unexplained, as were the particulars of their meeting. Even Stedman agreed it was far-fetched to assume Crosby had just happened to run into Brenda in the parking lot. But Stedman argued that the preacher had set up an assignation before leaving the reunion.

None of which explained where the key to Brenda

Blaine's hotel room was, or who'd tossed the room. Her room key still hadn't surfaced in a search of both church and rectory, and it hadn't been sent back postage-guaranteed by somebody who picked it up absentmindedly and dropped it in a mailbox later on.

The fiber angle wasn't panning out either. That satin dress was positively fuzzy with fibers, but not a one of them matched the drab polyester suit worn to the reunion by the Reverend Edwin Crosby.

If only he could pin something on that Vegas sleazeball, Bernie Singer. Tony Morantz in Las Vegas was still working on the Singer angle, and Delahanty was in no rush to call him off. The guy had an odor. And if Singer believed that throwing himself around as the bereaved fiancé would deflect attention from himself, he was even dumber than Delahanty thought.

On the home front, there were still no leads on Jamison's whereabouts, and he was starting to face the fact that after six days of absence, the dog probably wasn't coming back. Either he was dead somewhere—a real possibility considering how dumb he was about streets—or he'd been adopted by somebody who hadn't seen the reward posters or was so taken by the mutt that they just couldn't give him up. If the dog didn't turn up by Labor Day, that's the story Delahanty would have to give Laurie. He could already picture her sweet little face, Maureen's face in miniature, dissolving into tears.

What he didn't really need right now was Nan Robinson standing hipshot in his office door, daggers blazing out of her bright green eyes.

"I need to talk to you," she said authoritatively.

He was about to brush her off when Tank Thiswell scooted around the corner holding a sheaf of papers and looking befuddled. Delahanty stood up and took her arm.

"Later, Tank," he said. "Counselor Robinson and I are in conference. Take it to Lance."

She looked at him oddly, but let him lead her down the hall.

"What was that all about?" she asked.

He grinned. "Mental health break." He had just spent half an hour reviewing some of the finer points of report writing with Tank. Since they'd begun writing reports in pencil, there wasn't an eraser in the cop shop that wasn't worn to a nub, courtesy of Tank. Back when they did them in ink, he'd gone through gallons of Liquid Paper. Somebody else's turn for Nitwit Patrol.

"I can't believe you think Edwin Crosby killed Brenda," Nan Robinson told him, wasting no time on pleasantries.

He heard his stomach start to growl and tried to figure out when he'd last eaten anything approximating a meal. "Had lunch?" he asked.

She nodded. "More or less."

"Well, I haven't, and I'm starved. Come down to Myra's and watch me eat."

She smiled. "I'm sure that will be an edifying experience," she said sweetly, heading for the front door. He watched her walk with genuine appreciation. She was a real smart-ass, but she sure had nice legs.

"She was ninety-five years old and she had a hinky heart. The surprise was that she was alive at all."

Detective Delahanty plowed his way through half a fried chicken and a mountain of fries as Nan picked at a salad in a back booth at Myra's, around the corner from the police station. Myra herself had served them and was now fussing behind the counter as she had every day since World War II. Nobody knew Myra's age for sure, but the neatly permed hair under her trademark white hairnet was getting mighty skimpy.

"She was only ninety-three," Nan countered.

"Oh. A regular spring chicken. Her doctor signed a death certificate, counselor."

Nan made her tone reasonable and offered her most appeasing smile. "Alvina McReedy's doctor didn't have reason to consider her death suspicious. I do."

He put down a denuded thigh bone and wiped a smear of grease off his thick blond mustache. Nan couldn't remember the last time she'd eaten deep-fried chicken, ten billion calories to the piece. But dammit, it looked tasty.

"I'll be the first to admit that the timing of her death is odd," he said. "On the other hand, maybe not so odd. You have a bad heart and people start dredging up stuff that's upsetting, that can do it. But that's not the point. You say the old lady told you she didn't know Brenda left town pregnant, and she hadn't heard from her in twenty years. How could she possibly have known anything significant?"

"Brenda's death has something to do with her life in Spring Hill," Nan said. "I'm certain of it. Otherwise there'd be no reason for her to be killed here. Of course, it's possible that somebody in Vegas hated her enough to kill her, or she'd double-crossed somebody in a dope deal or something. But if that were the case, nobody'd bother to follow her here and stab her with a reunion souvenir. They'd drive her out into the Nevada desert and put a bullet in her brain."

"You certainly have a hyperactive imagination."

This time she tried to make the smile self-deprecating. "Right. Ryan said he mentioned his mother's lawyer to you. Bonaventure, I think his name was."

"Yeah. *Sal* Bonaventure, to be precise."

"Have you talked to him?"

His smile was ironic. "You're going to like this," he said. "He's on vacation. In Siberia."

"*Siberia?* Surely you don't mean that literally."

"Surely I do. And there's no way to get in touch with him for another ten days. And he's a solo practitioner. So there you are."

"Damn!" She hesitated a moment. "You know, I stopped by Jewel yesterday and tried to talk to Frank Finney."

"And?"

"And he wouldn't talk to me. He said he'd told his story to the police."

A lazy grin crossed Brian Delahanty's face, but he didn't say anything.

"I know he went out with Brenda in high school," Nan said. "Her grandmother specifically remembered him."

"So did Brenda, apparently. What did the old lady have to say about Finney?"

Nan desperately wished she had more information to barter with. But there was no point in trying to fake it. "Nothing, really. Sorry."

"It happens," Delahanty told her, "that there's videotape of Brenda dancing with Finney on Saturday night. A very slow dance, if you know what I mean."

So the videotape had turned out to be useful after all! Nan would have to call Grant Kirby and get a copy of it. He worked at Argonne Lab and lived in Downers Grove, according to the reunion book.

"I understand they had a huge argument just before Brenda was killed."

"Now, where would you have heard a thing like that?"

She smiled. "I have my sources. Is the fight on the tape?"

"No. And it wasn't the world heavyweight championship, if that's what you're getting at. It was just words. We got a call from somebody in Peoria who overheard the whole thing."

"Somebody who was already gone by the time she was killed?"

"It's a long drive to Peoria. They left early." He dipped some fries in catsup, but offered no further information.

"God," she said, "do you suppose somebody might have actually seen something and still hasn't heard about the murder?"

"Not unless they left at dawn on Sunday to go camping in the north woods. Or Siberia," he added as an afterthought.

"Well?" she said expectantly.

"Well, what?"

"Well, what was the fight about?"

He grinned. "Oh yeah. Mr. Finney told Ms. Blaine that she was the same old cock tease she always used to be, only now she looked like a two-dollar whore. She slapped him."

No wonder Frank Finney hadn't wanted to talk about it. "Where was he when Brenda was killed?"

"Don't get too excited," he said. "After the altercation, Finney went and sat down with his wife and another couple. He and the other guy left the table once and went to the john together. Twenty minutes later, you found the body."

"So he could have done it. There was time."

"Time, yeah. Opportunity, not really. The buddy says Finney was never out of his sight, and the folks at the table swear they were only gone a couple minutes."

"It wouldn't have taken long." She debated telling him about her timing experiment at the Inn and decided against it. "His friends could be mistaken about the time. Or covering for him. It was pretty late, and everybody'd been drinking for hours."

"All that's missing is a motive," Delahanty said laconically.

"They argued, remember?"

"That's not good enough. And Finney's squeaky-clean. No arrests, no traffic violations, not even an outstanding parking ticket. Doesn't womanize, doesn't gamble. Says he hasn't seen Brenda Blaine since high school graduation, and the closest he's ever been to Las Vegas was a grocery convention in Kansas City six years ago. He admits being shocked to see Brenda. He admits dancing with her. He admits being slapped. That's it."

"Hmmph," Nan answered. "You know, it's fascinating to me that one person could be so incredibly disruptive after such a long period of time. But it just reinforces what I've thought all along, that Brenda was killed here because of something that happened here."

"Edwin Crosby knocked her up twenty years ago, remember? Right here in Spring Hill."

"But Edwin is fundamentally decent. Once he knew about Ryan, he paid Brenda child support."

"He's got four other kids here in Spring Hill," Delahanty pointed out. "It's not like he had money to spare." Delahanty didn't seem to speak with much conviction, which was a little confusing.

"If he were going to get rid of Brenda, the time to do it would have been long ago. Ryan's nineteen, for crying out loud."

"You can build up a lot of resentment in nineteen years," Delahanty said mildly. "You told me yourself that Crosby was quiet and uptight during dinner at the reunion."

"Hey, I've known him my entire life. He's *always* been quiet and uptight. Besides, I think that whoever killed Brenda may also have killed Alvina McReedy."

"The ninety-three-year-old pentathlete."

Nan smiled. "Alvina McReedy was a self-righteous tight-ass, and I didn't like her at all. She'd obviously never approved of Brenda. But she was smart and she was observant. She remembered Frank Finney, didn't she? When I saw him yesterday, I told him that. What if he went out to Golden Valley last night and killed her so she couldn't tell what she knew?"

"I don't think she knew anything."

Nan shook her head. "I know she knew more than she was telling me. And she may well have known something that she didn't realize was important, something that would have been damning to the real killer."

The reference, for instance, to a mysterious male friend of Brenda's. *She had that one special friend, but I don't guess that's what you mean*, Alvina McReedy had said wistfully. Nan suddenly realized, in a wave of depression, that Mrs. McReedy had undoubtedly been referring to Edwin Crosby. *I won't besmirch any reputations at this late date*, she added.

"Then why didn't she just open up and tell you?"

"She did. At least by her standards. You don't like the possibility that the old lady might have been murdered," Nan said shortly, "because if she was, there's no way Edwin Crosby could have done it. He was locked up in your very own jail when she died."

"All right, all right." He smiled halfheartedly. "Let it not be said that the Spring Hill police left a single pebble unturned. I'll get an autopsy on the old lady."

"You might want to check on something else, too."

"Like what?"

"Mrs. McReedy told me Brenda dated an auto mechanic named Al Tarantello from Riverside Texaco. I found out he's in Denver somewhere."

"And you think what? That he made some two-thousand-mile turnaround to kill Brenda Blaine?"

"I think he might know something about Brenda in high school."

"He might know the real words to 'Louie, Louie,' too. But somehow I doubt it." Brian Delahanty glanced up at the clock on the wall. "I've gotta get back and show Tank Thiswell how to print his name. We're working on big *T*s this afternoon. Anything else?"

Nan hesitated, then closed her eyes and touched the paper bag beside her on the seat of the vinyl booth. This would all be so easy if she were just at home. She could check everything without asking strangers for help, and when it turned out to be a silly false alarm, nobody would be the wiser. But she wasn't home, and this smug cop was her best and easiest shot.

"I was hoping you could do me a little favor," she said, as nicely as she could. She set the bag on the table and told him what she wanted.

First he chuckled. Then, realizing she was serious, he gave her a long, hard look and asked a series of staccato questions.

And finally, with just a smidgen of a smirk, he agreed.

At four-thirty that afternoon, Nan stood at the rear of a small hushed chapel with Eloise Damone, a sixtyish woman in sensible shoes and a severe black suit. Fifteen feet away, Ryan Blaine spoke softly into his mother's open casket. His words were blessedly inaudible.

Being in this place again was awful. Nan's last visit had been her father's funeral five years earlier, and walking through the arched wooden doors brought back every horrible aspect of that experience. The sickly sweet floral smells, the stagnant atmosphere, the closed doors, the waxy, wizened body of an elderly man they'd passed in the West Chapel. When Dad was here, there'd been an old lady in there.

Nan felt herself transported back to the endless afternoon and evening of her father's wake, the continuous parade of somber people carefully avoiding any discussion of exactly *why* they were gathered so prematurely to mourn Phil Robinson. Virtual strangers had clasped her hand in theirs and murmured sympathetically, reminisced about how cheerful Dad always was, such a jovial fellow. A merry man indeed, and a jolly drunk. Now a dead drunk.

Leon was with her then, the stiff and uncomfortable husband caught in a crowd of strangers, slipping often into some back office to advise L.A. subordinates on whatever lawsuit he was working on. Her sister, Julie, alone because she and Adam were so strapped she'd had to borrow plane fare, had wandered about in a daze, mostly fiddling with the flowers. And Mom was enthroned on a sofa, sobbing.

It had fallen to Nan to greet people as they came in, to accept condolences, to thank strangers for coming, to keep things relatively upbeat by reminding the mourners they'd been fortunate to have jocular Phil Robinson among them for as long as they had.

All the while wanting to scream.

Even now the temptation was overwhelming to really let loose a holler in this place, to rattle the heavily draped windows and maybe jiggle a coffin or two.

"I hope it was all right to let that . . . that gentleman view the remains," Mrs. Damone murmured with a faint sneer, jolting Nan back to the present tragedy. Bernie Singer had put in an unexpected appearance at the funeral home that morning.

Nan regarded Eloise Damone with genuine curiosity. How could she stand to *do* this sort of work, surround herself day after day with raw grief and pain, heartbreak and lamentations? Not to mention the clinical aspects, which Nan knew just enough about to find truly revolting.

"Oh, sure," Nan told her. "They lived together."

"He seemed . . . rather distraught."

"Well, of course he was." Nan yearned to consider Bernie Singer a serious suspect for Brenda's murder. He was *such* an insufferable jerk. But he'd unexpectedly come clean about Saturday night, that he hadn't been suffering stomach flu but was seeing some other girlfriend while Brenda was away. A detective in Las Vegas had confirmed that alibi. So he wasn't just a leech. He was an *unfaithful* leech.

On the plus side, he'd told Mrs. Damone that he was heading home this afternoon. By now he was probably somewhere over Nebraska.

Nan watched Ryan at his mother's casket. What must it be like to say a final good-bye to your mother? Nan was twice Ryan's age and could scarcely bear the thought of her own mother's death. The reality, when it came, would surely be devastating. Difficult though Dad's death had been, there was a certain inevitability to it, a sense they were all acting out a scene which had been written in Cutty Sark years before.

"The police had her effects . . ." Mrs. Damone went on. "It was necessary to provide clothing."

Which was probably the equivalent of a paper doll dress, Nan suspected, a Hollywood false front. Brenda's body wore a simple gray dress that she probably wouldn't have been caught alive in.

At this distance, laid out on satin pillows in a coffin, Brenda looked quite dead, of course. But she also looked young and pretty and innocent, minus that aura of phony glamor from the reunion. Losing the rhinestones definitely helped. Of course, none of them knew what Brenda had looked like in her day-to-day life. Maybe she *always* wore rhinestones. Or maybe she customarily dragged around with no makeup and a bandanna on her head.

"We can have the cremation tomorrow morning, if he's certain that's what he wants." Mrs. Damone sounded dubious. What *she* wanted was a plot and a vault and a lot of expensive accoutrements.

"He's quite certain," Nan assured her. "When will the ashes be ready?"

"By four tomorrow. But before they can be released, it will be necessary to settle the account. The gentleman this morning said her son would handle it." Eloise Damone sounded doubtful, and a tad worried.

"You'll get your money, don't worry."

Nan wanted desperately to leave. But Ryan's good-bye to his mother was just the beginning. Somewhere else in this creepy, whisper-filled building, Alvina McReedy's remains were being tidied up for viewing. Ryan had startled them by announcing on arrival that he also wanted to see his great-grandmother. *Her* funeral was pre-paid, with specific instructions that there be no services or visitation of any sort. About the only contingency not covered was an unknown relative seeking a peek. A study in situation ethics for Damone Brothers Mortuary.

As for Brenda, if Ryan couldn't write a check, Nan was

fully prepared to cover the charges until he could reimburse her. But Eloise Damone had been just a little too snotty. Let her sweat a bit longer.

CHAPTER 11

As Nan drove to the Websters' for dinner, all tricked out in her finest casual-wear, she considered Brenda Blaine's lifestyle.

Brenda wasn't a gambler. Everybody seemed to agree on this. Yet she lived well, far better than one might expect of even a world-class blackjack dealer. She'd been smart enough to put her Dalkon Shield settlement into real estate, but was generally carefree and mildly irresponsible with money. She drove a late-model Corvette and had apparently supported a succession of boyfriends over the years, including a ne'er-do-well ex-husband and Bernie Singer, currently in residence at Brenda's house.

Her top-of-the-line house. Three years ago, with no apparent change in income, she had seriously upgraded her living quarters. Where'd she get the money?

Drugs? A big dope deal might have done it, but nobody seemed to think she was involved with drugs, either personally or as an entrepreneur.

Armed robbery? Unlikely but possible. She was an admitted thrill seeker, had taken up skydiving as a substitute for alcohol.

Embezzlement? Even less likely. Brenda occupied a *very* low rung of a system with a thousand built-in safeguards for management of money. And Vegas casino owners brooked no financial irregularities.

An underworld payoff? There were definite possibilities there, and an infinite number of ways a smart and striking woman could be useful to organized crime. Still, Brian Delahanty's sources with the Vegas police had come up empty.

So what was left?

Blackmail.

It really pained Nan to consider Brenda as an extortion-ist. It was so much nicer to regard her as an independent woman who'd seized control of her life and gotten her act together. But blackmail fit. Maybe she'd gotten her act to-gether with somebody else's money.

Whose?

The circular driveway in front of Jim and Mary Lee Web-ster's custom home led up to a stunning blond brick house sprawled on two acres of prime wooded land at the edge of Jim's most upscale development.

It didn't seem to Nan like a place where a friend of hers might live. It was more like somewhere her parents might have gone for a Christmas party.

Mary Lee opened the massive oak front door, wearing a flowing hostess gown in pale yellow with gold threads woven through the sheer fabric. She wore gold sandals and Egyptian-style jewelry: a hammered gold necklace so thick and heavy it resembled a breastplate, matching bracelet, long oval earrings. She looked tired, with dark smudges under her eyes.

"How wonderful to finally have you here!" she said, as if her weekly invitations had been spurned for years. She spoke quickly, with nervous, fluttery gestures.

"I'll try not to track in mud," Nan said. "This is pretty impressive, Mary Lee."

False modesty had never been Mary Lee's long suit, and she made no attempt to deprecate her home. "I have to ad-mit I just love it," she said. "Thanks. Come on in and take the tour. Jim's showering."

Mary Lee led her first to the kitchen, a vast expanse of granite countertops and oak cabinets, where she opened a

Beck's for Nan. "Now," she said, "I get to play show-and-tell."

She sounded like a celebrity preening for a classy TV interview, explaining as she wandered down corridors and through large, open spaces, that she'd wanted a home that would be *livable*. Comfortable for kids as well as adults, pleasing to her *personally*. "I went through *three* decorators before I was finally satisfied," she confided. Yippee-ti-yo.

The spacious living room was broken into gracious conversational groupings. The furnishings were traditional and timeless; the sofas butter-soft, pale-gray leather; the carpets ankle-deep. Six-foot trees grew out of glazed crimson ceramic pots. There were matching red accents sprinkled elsewhere: lamps, pillows, a pair of comfortable-looking velvet armchairs beside the fireplace.

The house was single-storied and U-shaped, northern and southern wings encompassing a patio. They passed through a family room—where touch football could comfortably have been played without disturbing anyone watching the wall-sized TV screen—then turned left down a corridor. Jim and Mary Lee each had offices in this north wing, hers in white lacquer and lavender florals, his in imposing English-country-manor leather and dark wood. Beyond lay bedrooms, lots of them.

When they passed through the kitchen again, Mary Lee stopped to check something in one of the ovens.

"I hope you're not allergic to crab," Mary Lee said. "These are the most *wonderful* hors d'oeuvres. Marina Stedman's recipe. I used it to lead off the appetizer section of the *Spring Hill Cookbook*, but I don't suppose you've seen that."

"Mom sent me a copy," Nan assured her.

The cookbook, edited by Mary Lee in her capacity as Mrs. Mayor, was a spiral-bound fund-raiser for the Spring Hill Parks & Rec Department. Nan, whose idea of throwing a dinner party was making restaurant reservations, had dutifully located June Robinson's three offerings, only one of which sounded familiar. Then she'd stashed the book in a drawer under some virgin potholders and popped a Lean Cuisine in the microwave.

Jim Webster sauntered in, hair freshly blown dry, smelling ruggedly masculine and wearing manly designer sportswear. He kissed Nan's cheek and poured himself a Scotch.

"Your timing's perfect," Mary Lee said. "I was just about to show Nan the master bedroom."

"Good thing I picked up my dainties," Jim answered. "Kids back yet?"

"Just Karen. Pam plans to make a flying dinner stop and then baby-sit for the Nelsons. I don't know where Jamie went."

Jim frowned a minute, then shrugged. "Beats me." He smiled. "I run a city government and a business with dozens of employees, but the biggest scheduling hassles I have are always with my immediate family. Mary Lee's head of every charitable organization in the county, and the kids are . . ."

"Absolutely incredible," Mary Lee finished sweetly. "C'mon, Nan, before Wally gets here."

"Do you see a lot of him?" Nan wondered.

Mary Lee grinned. "Between his marriages. And since Kris moved to Louisville with the kids, he's practically a permanent boarder. Plus, of course, he and Jim have business stuff going on all the time, from the dealership and God knows what all else. Now, the pièce de résistance!"

Mary Lee led Nan into the southern wing, past a large solarium and an exercise room loaded with state-of-the-art equipment. They lingered for a moment in a small room full of craft supplies, cabinets with hundreds of little drawers, racks of paint bottles, and a computerized sewing machine Mary Lee swore would do everything but the dishes. In this house it was an alcove, but a quick calculation revealed it was the size of Nan's living room in her Venice bungalow.

"What's this?" Nan asked. On a work table, quarter-inch strips of veneer in several different wood grains lay neatly beside a set of Exacto knives. Some of the wood strips had been fashioned into a miniature parquet pattern.

"One of my ongoing projects," Mary Lee answered coyly. "Come see."

She turned right leaving the craft room and opened a set of double doors into the master bedroom. It was immense and stunning. Everything was white and gold, with a thick white carpet that resembled a heavy blanket of snow and some kind of white fur covering the king-size bed. It felt like walking into a Christmas card.

"The rug is really an indulgence, and it's a nightmare to keep clean," Mary Lee confided. "But I always told myself that when my kids were old enough, I'd have a bedroom out of a fairy tale."

Cinderella, Nan decided. Though perhaps the analogy was wrong, since Mary Lee was the one who'd grown up with money. And Jim was no prince, just the son of a hard-working contractor.

"Oh, wow!" The exclamation popped out as Nan spied a three-story dollhouse that covered most of a low table.

"Isn't it great?" Mary Lee asked. "It's my Colleen Moore influence. I could never get enough of her Fairy Castle at the Museum of Science and Industry. I keep thinking it's finished, but there's always something else to fiddle with. Like the parquet floor I'm making. I'll put that in the dining room."

"Have you been working on it a long time?" Nan asked.

"I started with Pammy when she was little. With a much smaller house. But you know," Mary Lee admitted sheepishly, "Pam was never *nearly* as interested as I was. And Karen just wanted to play ball. Finally I just stopped pretending it was for my kids and began to totally indulge myself."

As Nan squatted to examine the dollhouse, the extent of Mary Lee's self-indulgence became clear. The place was decorated to the max and loaded with miniature details. Tiny groceries were scattered on kitchen counters. Every room was wallpapered and either carpeted or inlaid with tile, brick, or wooden flooring. Exquisite miniature paintings hung above microscopically carved Victorian parlor furniture. Minuscule hairbrushes and perfume bottles sat on embroidered dresser scarves. Miniature quilts covered four-poster beds. Bitsy stuffed teddy bears rested in a wee nursery crib, and teeny brass fireplace tools sat beside carefully laid twig fires. And petit point area rugs were everywhere.

"There's a dollhouse museum in Santa Monica," Nan said, "called Angel's Attic. It's full of antique dollhouses, truly amazing stuff. You'd love it. Next time you come to L.A. you'll have to check it out." Nan had taken her mother there once, and remembered clearly the rule of thumb for objects on sale in the gift shop: The cost of an item rises in inverse proportion to its size. A table set with dollhouse china could easily cost more than dinner for four in Beverly Hills. Wine included.

"Oooh, I'd *love* that!" Mary Lee enthused. "You know, I've been thinking about starting another one. A southern plantation house. Now look, here's my pride and joy."

With a fond backward glance at the dollhouse, Mary Lee crossed ten yards of carpet, reached into a hidden recess of a mirrored wall and slid open a door. Nan followed her into a spectacularly organized walk-in closet. Hundreds of dresses, skirts, and blouses hung neatly, arranged by length, color, season, and style. Sweaters were folded into cedar cubicles. Handbags and belts hung on special hooks beside the cedar shoe-wells. On higher shelves, dozens of fabric-covered storage boxes sat tidily full of—what? Old T-shirts and cutoff blue jeans?

It might have been the wardrobe department at a major film studio. Mary Lee strolled through briskly, opened a door at the rear of the closet, then traipsed into a mind-boggling bathroom.

It, too, was gold and white, with gold fixtures and a great

deal of handpainted tile. Dead center, reached by three tiled steps, a tub-*cum*-Jacuzzi large enough for Olympic trials waited under an enormous skylight for a sybaritic adventure. Surely nobody did anything so prosaic as flossing or peeing in here. The toilet was apparently tucked off in a closet.

"I am duly impressed," Nan announced. "I've had smaller apartments. And I hope you're both morning people, because this must be positively blinding when you first get up."

Mary Lee giggled nervously and straightened the hand towels. "It's totally wasted on me in the morning, actually. Jim wakes up nice and peppy, but until I get my second cup of coffee, I'm basically just sleepwalking."

Nan smiled politely, asking herself the big question. Would she want to live like this if she had unlimited money? Unlikely, though it wasn't a dilemma she expected ever to confront.

They left the bathroom through another door that took them through Jim's closet and dressing area, the twin of his wife's and equally crammed with clothing. Back in the bedroom, Mary Lee stopped at a pair of mirror-backed curio cabinets and flicked a switch.

Under the sudden bright light, dozens of crystal figures glittered in groupings inside the cases. Looking closely, Nan could see that many of the crystal figures were—could this really be?—downright tacky. Yes, there were some stunning Steuben objets d'art, but there were also odd little bullfrogs with faceted crystal legs, moated castles, dragons, flamingos, and a replica of the Taj Mahal.

"You might not remember," Mary Lee said, "but I'd already started my crystal collection in high school." Nan didn't even remember ever being in Mary Lee's house. "It's just grown and grown over the years," Mary Lee went on, faintly apologetic. "It's kind of a hodgepodge, I guess. Some of those were gifts from my kids. And folks Jim meets in business sometimes give me things when they learn about my collection."

"It's truly . . . dazzling," Nan said carefully.

Mary Lee rubbed her temples, and Nan realized that she'd already seen the gesture half a dozen times on the house tour.

"Are you all right?" Nan asked.

"Just a little headache," Mary Lee admitted. "I took some Tylenol. Would you like to see the yard?"

Was there a choice? "Sure."

They left the master bedroom through sliding glass doors that opened directly onto a patio with a multi-tiered asymmetrical fountain bubbling merrily in its center. The yard beyond stretched down to a stand of tall evergreens. On one side of a perfect emerald lawn, a swimming pool was discreetly hidden behind shrubs. The other side was a riot of color.

"And this," Mary Lee announced with a flourish, "is my Long Border!"

Nan looked at the yard, puzzled. There were a lot of flowers and yes, they did stretch on, but . . .

"It's very nice," Nan said politely. "Quite long."

Mary Lee chuckled. "You don't know what I'm talking about, do you? I'm sorry. I figured what with Julie growing flowers and all . . ."

"*She* grows them," Nan explained. "I just stick 'em in vases."

"Well, there was this fabulous English landscape designer named Gertrude Jekyll who developed the concept of the herbaceous border. See how this flower bed starts out with cool colors on the ends and then converges with hot yellows and oranges and reds in the middle?"

Nan looked and nodded. She wouldn't have picked up that detail on her own in a million years. And she wasn't sure Julie would, either.

"She took up landscaping when she couldn't paint anymore because her eyes went bad," Mary Lee went on. "I can kind of relate to that. The idea of painting with plants. Actually, I used to do a lot more around our own place before I got so involved in landscaping for the business." She glanced at her watch. "Oops! Better check the crab puffs!" She scooted off.

Nan had barely seated herself in a white wrought-iron chair by the fountain when the door to the kitchen opened and Wally Sheehan bounded out.

"Hello, hello, hello!" Wally burbled, bending down to kiss her. He looked more normal today without all the silly racing clothing. His carrot-colored hair matched some nearby marigolds. "This must be my lucky day, a cute little chick in from the coast."

Nan bristled instinctively. "You know," she noted, ever so politely, "there aren't too many synonyms for 'woman' that I like less than 'chick.' "

"But I bet I can think of a few." Wally grinned. "How about broad? Bimbo? Didn't realize you'd gotten so touchy, Nan."

"Oh, I'm no more touchy than the average chick," Nan answered. "But it's been a tiring couple of days." Mary Lee seemed to feel sorry for Wally, and there was a faint air of pathos about him. Nan sympathized with his failed marriages, but she greatly feared he'd want to talk about them. She'd spent too many hours hearing miscellaneous men apply hindsight to their marital ruins.

"Now don't go away," Wally warned. "I'm going to get me some of Massa Jim's fine Glenlivet, and I'll be right back."

"Bring me another Beck's, would you?"

"At your service, my lady." He swooped low to the ground and backed away, right into a flowerpot. It was exactly the tension breaker they both needed. In the laughter as they righted the terra-cotta planter and tried to replace its contents, Nan was reminded just how much fun Wally actually was.

Mary Lee and Jim joined them, and the talk was light

and easy. Nan finished her second beer and excused herself to find a bathroom. On her way back out, she stopped in the kitchen where Mary Lee's kids were having dinner. Pam, the eldest, was dishing out macaroni and cheese to her younger sister and brother. The sliced hot dogs took Nan suddenly back to her own grade-school lunches.

Was this her equivalent to Proust's madeleine, a plate of Kraft's macaroni laced with Oscar Meyer weiners?

"Hello," she told the kids. "I'm Nan, a friend of your parents from way back. You must be Karen and Jamie." The twelve-year-old girl at the table ventured a quick "Hi" that revealed a flash of braces, and the fourteen-year-old boy merely grunted. Nan turned to Pam, who was slicing fruit at a mid-kitchen island. "I saw you taking care of people's kids on Sunday at the park. You were good with them."

Pam Webster blushed slightly, and Nan was struck again by how strongly she resembled her mother. What would it be like to have a child who looked like you, talked like you, walked like you? What would it be like to have a child, period?

"Thanks," Pam told her. "Did you have kids there?"

Nan shook her head. "Not there or anywhere."

Suddenly Pam yelped. Nan saw a streak of blood on the cutting board and jumped to help the girl.

But Pam brushed her off. "I'm okay, really." She thrust her finger under the faucet as the water momentarily ran pink, then pressed a paper towel tightly against the cut. "It's just a little nick."

"Can I at least get you a Band-Aid?"

Pam nodded. "Top shelf left in the bathroom around the corner."

Nan found the bathroom, which she'd missed altogether on Mary Lee's grand tour, and returned with a box of bandages and a tube of antiseptic. Pam allowed Nan to bandage the cut, which really wasn't too bad.

Jamie looked up from his grub for the first time. He was long and lean, with the best features of both parents. Once his acne cleared up, he'd be a heartbreaker.

"Good thing Mom wasn't here," Jamie said. He feigned dropping his face into his macaroni. "Thunk."

Nan frowned, confused.

"Mom's a little squeamish sometimes," Pam explained.

"A little!" Jamie howled. "How about that time I conked my forehead?"

"You were a mess," Pam agreed fondly. To Nan she said, "Jamie had a gash over his eye, and it was bleeding all down his face. Mom passed out before she could even get her head between her knees."

Nan stayed a moment or two longer with the kids before going out to rejoin the adults. Over at the barbecue grill, Jim critically surveyed a bed of glowing mesquite. "Just about ready to put on the steaks," he announced. "Prime corn-fed Illinois sirloin."

Dinner was served on a glass table on the patio to the accompaniment of soft classical music and the frequent popping of insects that ventured too close to several bug-zappers. They ate steak with fresh herb butter, corn pudding, and sugar snap peas in Dijon vinaigrette, all delicious and all fixed from scratch by Mary Lee, a regular mother lode of domestic talents. No wonder she looked so exhausted.

Much of the dinner conversation centered on Jim's bid for Congress. Jim and Wally worried that getting the nomination would prove tricky in a field left wide-open by the retirement of an incumbent not planning to make primary endorsements. Whoever got the Republican nomination, however, would almost certainly be elected. Democrats were an endangered species in Porter county.

"If anyone can do it, Jimbo can," Wally finally pronounced, raising his glass high again. Wally had put away a prodigious amount of zinfandel since dinner began. Nan wondered what it was about this town that made auto dealers drink so heavily. "Of course, it would help if we could just buy votes, in the time-honored tradition of Chicago politics."

"You mean you can't?" Nan asked, with mock incredulity.

Wally chuckled. "Only if anybody finds out about it. One of many fine traditions of my people. Or maybe we could just pass out shots of whiskey. Another fine Irish tradition."

Nan said nothing, and Mary Lee looked distinctly uncomfortable. How long would it be before Wally landed in rehab?

"I heard a story recently," Wally went on, "about how Bridgeport was settled." Chicago's Bridgeport neighborhood was the Irish enclave that had produced endless political leaders, including various Mayors Daley. "The Irish were pouring in during the Potato Famine, and they'd been digging canals in the east. The Erie Canal, for instance. Great diggers, the Irish. And a lot of the time they were paid in scrip, which could basically only be redeemed for land."

Wally topped off his glass and offered the bottle around. There were no takers. "Anyway, the Illinois & Michigan Canal, which was dug to connect the Chicago and Illinois Rivers, was a hundred miles long, starting at Bridgeport. One sly dog looking to unload a lot of land in Bridgeport poured a barrel of whiskey into a public well by the site of the ground-breaking for the I & M Canal. It was a hot day, and naturally folks started drawing water—with a genuine kick to it. Well, let me tell you, those lots went like hotcakes!"

"And folks have been loaded in Bridgeport ever since," Jim concluded. "A statement I will deny if anyone ever tries to attribute it to me."

"Yet another slippery politician," Nan noted with a

laugh. She raised her wineglass. "To slippery politicians everywhere."

Talk turned then to the current raging Democratic scandal in Chicago, and from there to Spring Hill's relative lack of corruption, and how SiliChip would pave the way for more high-tech business. Finally, inevitably, the conversation wound its way around to Brenda Blaine.

"Old Frank Finney was shitting bricks before they arrested Edwin Crosby, I heard," Wally said. "Everybody from here to Milwaukee heard Frank call Brenda a hooker and saw her deck him."

"I didn't," Nan said, with genuine regret. "Was it pretty dramatic?"

"An Academy Award performance," Wally assured her.

"I saw them dancing together," Mary Lee volunteered suddenly. "If I were Karen Finney, I'd have been furious. Brenda was *all over* Frank."

"Karen is Frank's wife?" Nan asked. Mary Lee nodded. "Where was she when all this was going on?"

"I don't know exactly," Mary Lee said. "But when we were waiting for the police, I noticed she was *really* bombed. I don't think Karen normally drinks very much. She could barely stand up."

"I understand Brenda's boyfriend was here," Jim said. "Did you meet him, Nan?"

"He was over at Mom's house when I got back from seeing you guys yesterday," Nan answered. "I talked to him for a while. He was pretty upset about Brenda."

"I saw him at the Lemon Twist Lounge last night," Wally said. "Looked like some kind of gigolo. And he didn't exactly seem to be in mourning, if you know what I mean. He was putting some pretty heavy moves on Jenny, the bartender."

Jim laughed. "Everybody puts moves on Jenny the bartender. At least, since she got those implants. Seems to me, I've seen you hovering around her, too, Wally."

"Got me a weakness for honeydews," Wally said, "and

Jenny's so tall, they're right at my eye level. The boyfriend was crying in his beer how Brenda should never have come in the first place. Gotta say I agree with him." He was starting to slur his words slightly.

"Why shouldn't Brenda have come?" Nan snapped.

Alcohol made Nan combative, and she realized suddenly she'd put away more than her share. Maybe she'd have to walk home. Or call a cab. Of course, she could—and she stifled a giggle at the idea—call Brian Delahanty for a ride, the way Dad had so often phoned the station house when he was on one of his benders.

Wally shrugged. "She didn't know anybody. Didn't have any friends. No chance to make any business deals. I mean, why bother?"

"Maybe she was just curious," Nan said.

"About what?" Wally wondered.

"About how her early lovers had turned out?" Nan suggested.

"Frank Finney's doing okay," Wally said expansively. "As for the others, she could've just started making random phone calls to the Spring Hill white pages."

"Wally!" Mary Lee sounded shocked.

"Oh, don't be so naive, M.L.," Wally told her, filling his glass once again. "Everybody had a hack at old Brenda Bang-Bang."

"Well, if your memory of her is typical," Nan said, "then maybe she wondered if everybody would still be as narrow-minded as she remembered. If they'd still be mean and rude to her."

"Nobody was mean and rude," Wally argued. "Hell, I danced with her myself."

Nan had a sudden memory flash of Wally and Brenda on the dance floor. Brenda was wearing Wally's racing cap. Wally's shirttail was pulled out, and Brenda was lunging toward him, practically rubbing his face in her breasts.

"I really think if we knew why she came," Nan said,

"we'd be halfway toward finding out why she was killed. I think I've got a lead on her high school friend, Liza Krzyzanowski."

Wally's eyes widened. "Liza K? Lordy me."

"You remember her?" Nan asked.

"Just vaguely," Wally answered. "She was Catholic. We went to catechism class together."

Nan had forgotten catechism class. Catholic students enrolled in public elementary schools had been dismissed early on Wednesdays for religious instruction. "So you knew her!"

Wally shook his head. "Not really, just at church. And I don't remember old Liza K being too terribly pious once she hit high school."

Jim shrugged dismissively. "My main concern right now is poor Edwin. I just couldn't *believe* it when that boy showed up and he was arrested."

"Truly shocking," Mary Lee agreed. "Poor Rose is just *devastated*, and I don't see how they can possibly afford a decent lawyer."

"I'll see that Edwin has proper legal representation, Mary Lee, don't you worry." Jim spoke somberly, once again measuring sound bites. "I've arranged for Jake Moroney to meet with him tomorrow and take the case."

Nan's eyes opened wide. "Jake Moroney? He's got quite a reputation in criminal defense." As being ruthless, cutthroat, expensive, and just a tad sleazy.

Jim nodded. "He even managed to keep a few of the Greylord defendants from making license plates. Really top-notch. If he can't walk Edwin, I figure at least he'll mitigate the hell out of the circumstances." He shook his head reflectively. "Who'd have ever thought a mild-mannered guy like Edwin was capable of murder?"

Nan set her wineglass down suddenly. "Not me. And I still don't. Edwin told me he didn't kill Brenda, and I believe him." She looked slowly and deliberately around the table. "That means," she said finally, "that somebody else killed her. Somebody else who's still walking around free."

Mary Lee took a sudden sharp breath. Jim was suddenly busy with his napkin, and Wally's hand shot out automatically for his wineglass.

Nobody looked very happy.

CHAPTER 12

Nan arrived back at her mother's house shortly after ten. June Robinson was asleep in front of a Bette Davis movie in the sunroom, her knitting lying in her lap.

Nan left her there, went upstairs, and tried calling Colorado again. Although it felt very late, it was only nine in Denver, and the chances of finding Al Tarantello at home were better in the evening. Assuming, of course, that the Al Tarantello from Aurora was the guy she was trying to find. There was only one person by that name in the greater Denver area, according to Directory Assistance, and he hadn't answered his phone when Nan tried before leaving for dinner at the Websters.'

This time a man picked up.

"I'm trying to find someone named Al Tarantello who used to work at Riverside Texaco in Spring Hill, Illinois," Nan began.

"What for?" the man answered suspiciously.

Bingo! Nan, still a bit high from slightly too much beer and wine, raised a silent fist in jubilation. This *had* to be the right guy. Earlier she'd worked out exactly what she planned to say, but now she felt a lot looser.

"You don't know me," she explained. "I'm Nan Robinson, and I went to Spring Hill High with Brenda Blaine twenty years ago. I was told that she dated Al Tarantello before she left town."

"Yeah?" He still wasn't copping to anything, not even

his name. But anyone who had regularly dated Brenda wasn't likely to have forgotten the experience.

"Well, if you're the guy I'm trying to reach, I have some kind of bad news. Brenda was murdered the other night, back here in Spring Hill."

"Holy shit!" His voice lost its studied cool. "What happened?"

"She came to our twentieth high school reunion and somebody stabbed her."

"Are you shitting me?"

"No," Nan said firmly, "I'm not." She gave him a moment to respond. He didn't. "You're probably wondering why I wanted to talk to *you*," she went on. She explained the circumstances of Brenda's death, the arrival of Ryan Blaine, the arrest of Edwin Crosby.

"Are you trying to say this is *my* kid?" he asked finally.

"Not at all, not at all," she assured him. "He looks exactly like Edwin, and they're doing blood tests to confirm it. Edwin always supported him. No, the reason I want to talk to you is that I don't really think Edwin is guilty, and it seems to me that maybe what happened had something to do with Brenda's life here before she left. Her grandmother told me that she went out with you, and frankly, I think somebody she dated would know more details about her life than her grandmother, anyway."

"You've gotta give me a minute," Al Tarantello said. "This is kind of a lot to hit somebody with out of nowhere. I haven't thought about Brenda for years. Spring Hill neither."

"I know, and I apologize. But I wasn't even sure this was going to be *you*, and I didn't know where to reach you during the day." She explained how she'd located him. "I was also hoping you might have some idea how I could reach a friend of hers from back then. Liza Krzyzanowski."

"Liza Krzyzanowski ... Boy, you're *really* pulling out the oldies there. I'd forgotten all about her. Polack name, but her mama was Italian. Tiny little thing, dark. She split, seems to me."

"So I've been told. But nobody really seems to know where she went, or any of the particulars."

"L.A., maybe?" he said after a moment. "Seems like Brenda said she heard from her in L.A. But Jerry's the one who was really bummed when Liza left."

"Jerry?"

"Guy worked at the station after school, went out with Liza. What was his last name, anyway? L-something. I wanta say Lefkowitz, but I know he wasn't Jewish. He's dead now, anyway. Something happened when he was in the service, I forget what. A long time ago."

Nan reached for the Spring Hill yearbook, flipped to the senior pictures. "Leffingwell?" she asked, with virtual certainty.

"Yeah! Leffingwell! How'd you know that?"

"I looked him up in an old yearbook," Nan answered. "He was listed 'In Memoriam' in the reunion book." Jerry Leffingwell, football and basketball star. A literal dead end. "I think somebody told me he was in a military plane crash."

"Damn! In Nam? Nah, he was too young for Nam." He paused a moment. "Listen, I don't know what I can tell you about Brenda. I haven't seen or heard from her since she left town back whenever you say it was. Didn't see all that much of her after Liza left, now that I think about it. Me and her used to double with Jerry and Liza."

"How long did you date Brenda?"

"Hell, I don't remember. It was awhile, I can tell you that. Through a winter, 'cause we went skiing one time. Through a summer, 'cause we went to the drive-in a lot. She wasn't supposed to go out with me, so I never did go to her house. I remember her grandma threw a shit fit when she found I was going out with Brenda. Drove into the station one day and starting screaming at me outta nowhere. Pretty funny, really."

Pathetic seemed a better description, but of course Nan hadn't been there.

"What was Brenda like?"

"Hell, you knew her. Didn't you say you knew her?"

"Yeah, but I wasn't her boyfriend."

"Me neither, I don't guess. We had us some times, though. Brenda would try *anything*. First time she ever went skiing, she went straight to the top of the hard hill. Talked me into going hang gliding some place in Michigan another time. Can't say I much cared for it, but Brenda had the time of her life."

"Were you surprised when she left town?"

There was another pause. "Not really, I don't guess. She hated Spring Hill. And after Liza left, I think she wanted more'n ever to get out. She didn't say good-bye or nothing. I heard about her being gone from Jerry, but it'd been awhile since I seen her."

"Can you think of anything about her—or about her life back then—that might explain why somebody would want to kill her now?"

"Hell, no! But like I said, I hadn't thought about her for a long time."

"Well, if you'd think about her some more," Nan told him, "I'd really appreciate it. And if you think of anything, call me collect." She gave him her numbers in Spring Hill and L.A. "I really appreciate your help."

"Didn't do nothing," he told her.

"No, that's not true. You gave me a little more of a picture of Brenda's life back then. Oh, and something else."

"Yeah?"

Nan swallowed. This sounded *so* degrading. But she'd promised. "Jack Doyle said if I found you to tell you that Loretta Hensinger weighs three hundred pounds."

His laugh was long and loud and hearty. "You tell that SOB Jack Doyle it woulda served him right if he'd married her."

* * *

In the morning, Nan asked her mother if she knew where to find Darlene Leffingwell. Darlene, two years older than Nan, had been Jerry's sister. She'd also, eons ago, been in Nan's Girl Scout troop.

"Why, of course I know where she is!" June Robinson exclaimed. "She has an absolutely darling needlework shop over in Columbia. I *know* I've told you about it. Absolutely wonderful mohairs and some really nice kits, though I don't like kits that much myself. Her name is Lovejoy now."

Nan grinned. "I knew you wouldn't fail me." Her mother *had* mentioned Darlene Leffingwell in the past, though not for several years. Nan just hadn't paid attention.

Mom was frowning over her list of morning errands. "I suppose I ought to stop by and see how poor Rose Crosby is doing." She didn't sound happy about the idea.

"I'm sure there are plenty of people rallying around her," Nan answered. Were there? Or was Rose such a martyred pain in the ass that folks would steer clear when she was glum?

"Well, maybe so, but I wouldn't want to get on her bad side."

"Rose? Rose *has* a bad side?" Nan asked, genuinely surprised.

June Robinson rolled her eyes skyward. "Well, let's just say that Rose doesn't get mad. She gets even."

Nan looked at her encouragingly. There had to be more.

Mom continued, in her best I-don't-mean-to-spread-vicious-gossip-but tones. "Well, there was the time that Patty Morgan suggested Rose try a more flattering hairstyle. *Not* a bad idea, either. I don't know if you know Patty, but she has a bit of a weight problem. Well, *one week later*, the Easter Sunday bulletin, which Rose typed up, listed Fatty Morgan as the soloist."

Nan laughed. It was almost nice to know that Rose had a petty side.

"Then there was the time the McHenry boy beat up Rose's son on the playground. Sally McHenry's been on

KP at church potlucks ever since. And there were those who thought Lorraine Triggs wept just a little too long on Edwin's shoulder when she was going through her divorce. Rose was one of them. There weren't any witnesses, but when Lorraine got to the Christmas bazaar cake decoration judging, it turned out that her Snow White's Cottage had fallen upside down on the floor." Mom smiled slyly. "Grumpy was the sole survivor."

The doorbell rang then, and to Nan's surprise it was Hertz, delivering another Taurus. Nan had all but given up on getting the impounded rental car replaced, having spent several irritating phone sessions working her way up the Hertz chain of command. Finally yesterday, she'd gotten a supervisor who agreed to send out another car with no additional charges, provided—and the woman was both ominous and adamant on this point—that the police confirmed that Nan had no involvement in Brenda's death. Nan had given her Brian Delahanty's number. Then she actually got a laugh out of the woman by noting that if she *were* arrested for murder, her contract with Hertz was the least of her problems.

But now she had her own wheels again, and the feeling of relief was almost palpable. Being a houseguest—even at the home of your youth—required a lot of social energy, and it always helped Nan enormously to know that if need be, she could walk out the door and drive away. Even if it were only around the block.

She got directions from her mother and hit the road. Columbia was about eleven miles to the south, away from the expressway, past the old furniture factory site and Riverside Texaco.

Nan stopped at the Texaco station to thank Jack Doyle and pass along Al Tarantello's message, feeling like a bit player in a third-rate comedy. Next week, boob jokes. But Jack Doyle was delighted, and remembered Jerry Leffingwell, though only vaguely.

"He was just a kid," Jack said. "Didn't work here long, I don't think. But I honestly don't remember."

It was a safe enough guess, however, that Jerry's sister would.

Just past the Texaco station, the road became a sparsely traveled two-lane highway, passing through lush, tall corn-fields on either side. Nan arrived in Columbia five minutes later. It was a pretty, sleepy little town, and Nan had no problem finding Darlene's Needlework on Main Street.

The window was full of pillows and sweaters and other complicated creations of yarn and thread and fabric. It re-minded her a bit of her mother's house, or her sister's. A little bell tinkled as Nan walked into the shop, which smelled of wool and cinnamon.

At the rear of a small room full of yarn bins and hanging samples, a woman sat at a large oak table assembling a group of small buildings out of needlepoint pieces. Three houses stood complete, and a church was under construc-tion. Darlene Leffingwell Lovejoy looked up and smiled the same crooked grin Nan remembered from Girl Scouts twenty-five years earlier.

"Nan," she said, standing up. "I'd have known you any-where. You look wonderful!"

"Were you expecting me?" Nan asked, knowing the an-swer even as the words came out of her mouth.

"Your mother called," Darlene said. "She wanted you to pick up a couple of things for her if you don't mind."

Thanks, Mom. Not that it really mattered, but what if Nan had been counting on the element of surprise? Nothing like a meddlesome amateur to foul things up. She made a fast mental leap. That was probably exactly what Brian Delahanty thought of *her*. All things were relative.

Darlene was very tall and somewhat broad-shouldered, out of proportion to this shop full of delicate doilies and in-tricate lace and fragile whatnots. She wore little makeup, and her long straight hair, brown with many gray streaks, was pulled back into a clasp at the nape of her neck. Her simple shift was embroidered with birds perched on the branches of a graceful tree. Darlene's features were blunt, her cheekbones wide, her chin square. She'd never been exactly pretty, but she'd always cut a striking figure. She still did.

"I was trying to remember just how long it was since I last saw you," Nan said, shaking hands. It was nice to shake hands with a woman who knew how to do it properly, no dainty offering of a few frail fingertips. She wasn't surprised that Darlene hadn't expected to hug her after all this time. This wasn't California, and Darlene had always been reserved. "And I don't think I ever saw you again after you graduated and went off to . . . where was it? Illinois?"

"Northern," Darlene answered. "And you went out west someplace, didn't you?"

Nan had never really thought of Stanford in quite those terms. "Yeah."

"But I feel as if I've been in touch anyway," Darlene told her, " 'cause your mother talks about you all the time. You and Julie, both." Darlene gestured to a chair. "Would you like something to drink? I was about to have a glass of iced tea."

"That sounds great," Nan said.

Darlene served sun tea with lemon in tall green handblown Mexican glasses. She took a sip and began stitching together two walls of a needlepoint church. "After all these years," she said, "I still can't quite get used to doing my Christmas samples in the spring and summer."

"This is all pretty overwhelming to me," Nan said, sweeping a hand around the shop. "I'm strictly a paint-by-numbers type myself. Give me a needlepoint kit and a couple of years, and I'll give you a half-finished pillow."

Darlene laughed, a clear and hearty peal muffled only slightly by all the softnesses of the shop. Then she looked at Nan thoughtfully. "Then, if you don't mind my asking, why on earth are you here?"

Darlene had always been pretty direct when she and Nan were in Girl Scout troop 335 as elementary school students. Darlene was an undisputed star among the Scouts, particularly where the out-of-doors was concerned. Darlene could pitch tents and tie knots and blaze trails and whip up pocket stew. She knew birdcalls and animal tracks and celestial navigation. The year Nan requested Barbie's Dream House for Christmas, Darlene got a Swiss army knife.

"I'm sure you heard about Brenda Blaine being killed the other night," Nan said.

"Of course. This is big news in these parts, Nan. People don't get murdered around here."

"So I keep hearing." In Los Angeles, on the other hand, the annual murder rate usually topped two thousand by Halloween. Shortly before Nan had left for Spring Hill, a story in the *Los Angeles Times* had announced the astonishing news that nobody had been murdered in L.A. the previous day. "Actually, part of why I wanted to talk to you was that your brother, Jerry, apparently dated a friend of Brenda's back when they all lived here, and I was hoping you might know her, or have some idea where I could find her."

"I was away at college when Jerry graduated," Darlene reminded Nan.

"I know, but it's worth a shot. Liza Krzyzanowski?"

Darlene's brow furrowed momentarily, and then she smiled. "Oh yeah, Liza. I didn't really know her, just met her when I was home at Christmas, that kind of thing." She grinned wryly. "She was about half my size, literally. Normally it doesn't bother me too much being, well, *big*. But when I was younger I noticed more. And there's a certain kind of little-bitsy woman that makes me feel like a Green Bay Packer. Liza was like that."

"Do you remember anything else about her?"

"You mean beyond that they forgot to blow her up to full size? Not really. Jerry was going out with her for a while, and then he wasn't. I wasn't all that interested in his girlfriends, really. He had kind of trashy taste in women."

Nan hesitated. "You know, I'm really embarrassed, but I can't remember when it was that he died. I just remember that I was away at school and my mother wrote me about it."

"You sent me a card," Darlene remembered.

Oh yeah? This really *was* embarrassing. And it cast in a new light the fact that so many people didn't remember things about Brenda or about twenty years ago. So much minutiae occurs in everybody's lives that a lot of it gets jettisoned when it's time to make real memories.

But Darlene didn't press the issue. "It was three weeks after his twenty-first birthday. He was in the air force, stationed somewhere in California. What they kept stressing at the time was that it was all terribly routine, the flight he was on." She grimaced. "Except, of course, that it crashed into the side of a mountain."

"Was Jerry the pilot?"

"Oh, heavens no! He was a mechanic. He was being sent somewhere to fix something. Only he didn't get there."

"I'm sorry. I can't imagine what it would be like to suddenly lose Julie."

Darlene smiled gently. "A sister would be harder, I think. But I never had a sister." Her smile grew fonder. "Jerry was two years younger than me, but he shot up early. We were a real pair of beanpoles, I'll tell you. I had my full height by the time I was fifteen. Five-eleven. It didn't help much knowing that Jerry was taller." She chuckled. "It wasn't like I could go out with him, after all. And once we were in high school, we didn't hang around together much. I look back, and I think that being tall was probably the main reason I stayed in Girl Scouts so long."

The standard pattern in Spring Hill had been for Brownies to fly up into Intermediates, then drift out of scouting altogether by seventh or eighth grade. It had been decidedly uncool to be a Girl Scout after that. Darlene was the only girl from Nan's troop to stick with scouting after puberty, and she'd had to go to St. Charles to find a Senior troop.

"I always figured it was because you liked camping so much," Nan said. "Remember Butternut Springs?"

Darlene laughed. "How could I ever forget? But the really great camping was with the Seniors. We'd backpack into the woods up in northern Wisconsin, set up a real camp, the whole bit. I'm a troop leader now, you know."

Nan hadn't known, but she liked the idea. "That's great, Darlene. Is your daughter a Scout?"

"Heaven forbid. She's fourteen now, dropped out of scouting ages ago. Not what the in-crowd does, I guess. I'm not sure she's any more a part of the in-crowd than I was, but she tries harder."

Nan switched tacks. "You know, I saw a picture of Jerry and Jim Webster in their letter sweaters when I was going through the old yearbook files the other day. Were they pretty good friends?"

"More when they were little, I'd say." Darlene smiled. "Jim was a neighbor, and they used to play together in grade school. It's funny, I know Jim Webster is a big muckety-muck now, but I always picture him as being about seven years old with his nose running and his zipper at half-mast. What the little boys called having their barn door open."

Nan chuckled at the image. It was hard to think of Mayor Webster—soon to be Congressman Webster—as somebody's grubby little neighbor. She and Darlene and Jerry and Jim had all gone to the same grade school, but the Leffingwells and Websters had lived way off in the opposite direction beyond the school.

Nan looked at Darlene, remembered her admiration for the tough, independent, outdoorsy girl she had been. She had liked Darlene then, but she'd never really felt close to her. Darlene had been a loner as, to a far more limited degree, had Nan herself. But they were loners with a shared history, and somehow she felt closer to Darlene now than she ever had as a child.

"Listen," Nan said, after a few moments, "I need to get

going, so maybe we ought to gather up whatever my mother wanted. But why don't you come over and have dinner with us before I go? I know this isn't much notice, but is there any chance you could come over to Spring Hill tonight?"

"As a general rule," Darlene said, "I'm free Monday through Sunday. I'd love to, Nan."

CHAPTER 13

Nan found Detective Brian Delahanty nursing coffee and a slice of cherry pie in a back booth at Myra's when she got back to Spring Hill. He wore a pale tan sport coat over a white tennis shirt and brown cords, giving him a deceptively low-key air. He waved, a smile lighting up his face, then watched appreciatively as Nan walked toward him.

He was somebody, she realized, that under other circumstances she might have been interested in knowing better, maybe dating. Of course, cops were trouble. Even detectives. Nan thought fleetingly of Rosalie O'Brien's partner, C. J. Bennett. Rosalie always defended the faintly Neanderthal C. J., but she *had* let slip that on his back door he had a sign: THESE PREMISES GUARDED BY SHOTGUN THREE DAYS A WEEK. YOUR GUESS WHICH THREE. Brian Delahanty probably had a framed poster of Gordon Liddy in his bedroom.

"Good morning," he said warmly. "You look great."

"Thanks," she said, slipping into the booth opposite him. "I guess clean air agrees with me."

"That isn't all that agrees with you," he told her, his tone becoming grim. "I got the medical examiner's report. Alvina McReedy didn't have a heart attack after all. She was asphyxiated."

Nan's eyes automatically narrowed. "Hmmm."

"Hmmm, indeed," Brian Delahanty agreed. "I think this is where you say, 'I told you so,' counselor."

"I'm far too well brought up to do that, detective."

He raised his eyebrow. Myra herself bustled over to the table and filled a cup of coffee for Nan.

"That's all?" Myra asked doubtfully. In her eyes, any woman under 150 pounds was anorexic.

"Do you have any eclairs?" Nan asked, in a sudden burst of self-indulgence.

"We *always* have eclairs, dear," Myra answered. "I'll be right back."

"So what did the M.E. say?" Nan asked the detective.

"Alvina McReedy's breathing was interrupted permanently, probably by somebody holding a pillow over her face. There's no evidence that she put up a struggle."

"She was probably already asleep."

He nodded. "That's the M.E.'s guess. Based on the stomach contents, he fixes the time of death at between nine and eleven P.M. Monday night."

"After visiting hours were over."

"After visiting hours were over. Exactly. The doors are all locked at eight. Which is not to say that it wouldn't be easy to get into the place. Except for the Alzheimer's wing, it's not designed with security as a consideration. All the rooms are on the first floor with great big windows and pop-out screens. There's lots of shrubbery around the windows."

Myra set down an eclair, gave a little wink, and departed.

Brian Delahanty scowled. "It gets worse. Residents can control the heat or air-conditioning in their own rooms, just like in a hotel. A lot of them prefer open windows and fresh air. Including, wouldn't you know it, Alvina McReedy. Apparently she was a fresh-air fiend who hated air-conditioning and kept her windows open wide all summer."

"You've been out there since you found out?" Nan asked. She sampled the eclair, which was everything she had hoped for. So what if she were making a pig out of herself? She'd read somewhere recently that midwesterners weighed nearly twenty-five percent more than folks in other parts of the country. At least until she got home, she'd seem skinny in context.

Brian Delahanty nodded. "The M.E. called me last night, and I swung by to see the lay of the land. If this were a high-crime area, Golden Valley would be in big trouble. I was able to wander around the grounds for half an hour without anybody noticing or stopping me. It took another five minutes of banging on the front door before some night attendant showed up. With chenille marks on the side of his face."

Nan smiled at the image. "What if there were a medical emergency?"

"The residents all have panic buttons by their beds," he answered. "But in general, anybody who's really sick is moved either to the hospital or to a hard-core nursing home. They stretch the rules a little to accommodate people like Mrs. McReedy who have trouble getting around but aren't actively ill. Golden Valley's not really intended to be a medical facility."

"She had a hospital bed."

"That's a standard option. Doesn't mean anything."

Nan considered for a moment. "Who found her body Tuesday morning?"

"The woman bringing her breakfast tray. Again, folks normally eat in the dining room, but room trays can be arranged. They tell me that Mrs. McReedy's arthritis made it hard for her to get going in the morning, but that usually by lunch she was able to make it to the dining room."

"Did they do CPR or anything?"

He shook his head. "According to the kitchen aide, she was stone-cold dead, which, of course, fits the autopsy report."

"Did anybody *look* for signs of a struggle?"

"Unfortunately, no." He shrugged. "Hey, it's an old people's home. Old people die. Golden Valley has a standard routine they follow when a resident kicks. They try to be discreet for the sake of the other residents."

That made sense. It would be depressing enough to live in a community of geriatrics without having to regularly watch your friends being carted down the halls in body bags.

"Who knows this?" Nan asked.

"You, the police department, the M.E., the D.A.'s office, and the folks out at Golden Valley. Which means by now, everybody in northern Illinois."

"Has anybody told Ryan Blaine?"

He was immediately defensive. "I found out at eleven o'clock last night, less than twelve hours ago. I have four men out at Golden Valley interviewing anybody who might have seen or heard something, and a crime scene tech going over Mrs. McReedy's room. But no, I haven't told Ryan Blaine."

"Don't bother," Nan told him. "I will." She paused a moment and looked Brian Delahanty straight in the eye. "You know, this presents something of a problem. Somehow I don't think Alvina McReedy was murdered because she cheated at cards or she tattled on somebody who took two desserts. I think she was murdered because she knew something, or because somebody was afraid she *might* know something. She may be gaga half the time, but there was that other half the time to worry about. I know she wasn't telling us everything she could have."

"Most people don't," he noted pleasantly.

"Most people don't have their granddaughters reappear after twenty years and get promptly murdered, either. It stands to reason that the same person killed both Brenda and her grandmother. Which leaves Edwin Crosby out. He was locked up in the Spring Hill jail Monday night. He *couldn't* have been skulking around the shrubbery at Golden Valley with a pillow in his hand. Maybe it's time to drop the charges against him."

"You're a fine advocate for your client, counselor. But let's not forget that he had the means, the motive, and the opportunity. And his only alibi is his wife."

"He's not my client," Nan answered mildly, "and he never was. But I do happen to know that Edwin's retained counsel. Jake Moroney."

Delahanty whistled softly. "Stony Moroney, eh? I'm surprised the Methodists would go for a guy like that."

Nan shook her head. "The Methodists probably wouldn't. Jim Webster's paying for Moroney. He believes Edwin deserves the best representation."

He raised an eyebrow. "He thinks Jake Moroney is the best?"

Nan smiled sweetly. "He mentioned that Jake Moroney hasn't lost a murder trial in three years."

Delahanty smiled back. "Then perhaps Counselor Moroney is due for a change."

Nan laughed. This detective was flirting with her, she was quite certain of it. And it was fun.

"I looked up the Missing Persons report on Liza Krzyzanowski," Delahanty told her, after a moment's pause, "and there's not much there."

Nan waited. "Do you want me to beg?"

"I might enjoy that," he answered slowly.

Nan put two fists under her chin and woofed softly, à la Glocky.

His smile widened. "I *do* enjoy it! On April twenty-sixth of her senior year at Spring Hill High, Liza Krzyzanowski was reported missing by her parents, Tadeusz and Anna. She'd been gone for five days then. She was seventeen. It was treated as a standard juvenile runaway, which was fairly common at the time. The hospitals were checked, the jails. Her teachers didn't know anything, her friends said she'd been talking about running away."

"What friends?"

He smiled. "Brenda Blaine, for one. A boyfriend, Jerry Leffingwell, for another. Also her younger sister. She didn't have much reason to stick around, it seems like. She had a juvie record for drugs and curfew violations. She was on probation and never checked in again with her probation officer. She was failing three courses in school, truant more often than she showed up."

"How depressing," Nan said. Strange to think that she'd been totally unaware of classmates living such lives. "You know, I never asked. Did Brenda have any kind of a police record?"

"She'd been picked up on some curfew violations. Nothing else, which is surprising when you think about it." He shrugged. "Anyway, back to your little runaway. Pictures went out, the usual routine. The parents had no idea where she'd gone. And nothing ever turned up."

"And nobody ever heard *anything*?"

He shook his head. "Nope. Not that made it into our files, anyway."

"Are there relatives still around?"

"Now, how in the hell would I know that?"

Nan smiled demurely. "I assume you have your ways."

"Yeah, well, you assume wrong. This has nothing to do with anything. But I can tell you this much, there aren't any Krzyzanowskis still in Spring Hill. Elsewhere around Chicago, I'm sure there are plenty. Chicago's got the biggest Polish population this side of Warsaw."

"Thanks," Nan said. "I guess. Let me ask you something else. Why are you so stuck on Edwin as Brenda's killer?"

He answered without hesitation. "He stood to lose out on a big promotion if Brenda Blaine told his church superiors about Ryan."

Nan leaned back and looked at the detective scornfully. "Why on earth would she do *that*? He was already paying her child support, voluntarily. A double-tithe, he said. More money for him, more money for Ryan. Hell, you know how hard it is to enforce court-ordered child support. Edwin Crosby hadn't even been to court. He was paying her because it was the right and proper thing to do."

"He says."

"And there were *hundreds* of people with the means and the opportunity to kill Brenda."

"But only one with a motive."

"What about Frank Finney?"

"Because she slapped him? I don't think so."

"Where was he Monday night, do you know?"

Brian Delahanty smiled. "Monday is Little League night in Spring Hill, and he coaches the Cardinals. He was at Memorial Park."

"Do you know that for a fact? He seemed awfully upset when I told him that Mrs. McReedy had brought his name up."

"No, I don't know it for a fact. Yes, I'll check it. Look, this is really enjoyable, but I've got paperwork backed up from here to Botswana." He frowned and spoke almost to himself. "Plus Jamison."

"Jamison?" Nan asked, puzzled.

He looked mildly embarrassed. "My dog. He ran away last week, and I haven't been able to turn him up yet."

"That's too bad," Nan answered automatically. A lost dog didn't seem like a terrible calamity to her, but there was something in Brian Delahanty's eyes that made her want to be sympathetic. "Have you had him long?"

"Couple years. He's just a pound mutt, but he means a lot to my little girl. Sometimes I'm not sure if it's me she comes to see, or Jamison."

"That seems like an odd name for a dog." This from the daughter of someone whose cockapoo was called Glockenspiel? Whose own cat was named Nefertiti? This flirting business could get out of hand. And who exactly was his little girl?

He gave a kind of distant smile. "I named him for a partner of mine in Detroit, Ken Jamison. Jamison used to grouse a lot, complain that everything was named for somebody. The Joe Louis Sports Arena. Gabriel Richard Park. St. Ignatius Church. Cadillacs, Fords, Oldsmobiles. Said nobody would ever name anything for him."

"He must have liked it when you got the dog, then."

"He was already dead," Brian Delahanty said shortly.

"And I really need to go. I'll talk to you later." He put some bills on the table, got up, and left.

Nan sat for a moment and wondered how Ken Jamison might have died, hoping his namesake dog hadn't done likewise. Then she turned her attention back to Alvina McReedy.

If Frank Finney were out and around on Monday night, he could easily have stopped by Golden Valley and let himself in Alvina's window. She realized, with a sinking sensation of guilt, that she had specifically told him where Brenda's grandmother could be found.

But Frank Finney hadn't been charged with anything. Edwin Crosby had. And a nagging question had been eating at her. Edwin's supposed motive—preventing Brenda from revealing Ryan's paternity and queering the Methodist promotion—would apply equally to Rose Crosby. Rose could have slipped out of the parsonage and returned to the Spring Hill Inn that night just as easily as Edwin might have. And where had Rose Crosby gone when she left the jail after visiting her husband on Monday night?

When Nan had first tried to imagine Rose Crosby stabbing a virtual stranger in the heart, she had found the idea ridiculous. Rose, she was quite certain, didn't have the gumption.

That was until Mom had revealed Rose's hidden vengeful side at breakfast this morning. Now Nan pictured Rose snubbing her husband and crossing the threadbare parsonage carpet to her solemnly waiting children, recalled the protective way she shepherded them away. She remembered the children huddled around Rose's skirts as they stood in the kitchen doorway.

To protect her family, there was no telling *what* Rose might be capable of.

Nan went to the library and checked all the Chicago area phone books. There were a lot of them, and they held a staggering number of Krzyzanowskis, on pages that positively shimmered with consonants. There were Krzyzewskis and Krzyzanskis and Krzeminskis and Ksiezaks and Krczkas and Krzaks and Krwkas. The Chicago directory alone had a dozen Krzyzanowskis, and there were lots more scattered through the suburbs.

Nan photocopied the relevant pages, went home and started punching in numbers on the phone, beginning with the area near Spring Hill and working her way out.

She got no-answers. She got machines. She got children. She got elderly ladies who spoke only Polish. Now and again she connected with adults who spoke English, but they knew nothing about a Krzyzanowski family who'd lived in Spring Hill.

Finally, when she was ready to give up, an old man with a thick accent said, "Spring Hill? You mean Tad and Anna?"

Nan was so stunned she almost spilled her drink. "Yes, do you know them?"

"Tad my brother," he told her.

"Do you know where I can reach him?" Nan asked excitedly.

"Ach, he gone," the old man told her.

"He died?"

"No, he go back to Poland. He retire, go to Wroclaw, him and Anna. Live pretty good there on the social security, he say. Me, I tell him we were lucky to get away the first time, for why we want to go back."

A reasonable enough sentiment, Nan thought. "What about his children? Are they still here?"

"How come you want to know?" The suspicion in the old man's voice was not unreasonable. People who had fled oppression tended to regard paranoia as a life skill.

"I went to school with the children," Nan told him. "I wanted to see them again."

He seemed satisfied. "Mischa, he go to Wisconsin. Six children, good, no? Elizabeth, she go long time ago, broke her mother's heart. Only Maria in Chicago still."

"Do you know where I could find her?" Nan actually had her fingers crossed. She felt incredibly silly and really, really nervous.

"West Chicago," the old man told her. "A hairdresser, she is. Married a roofer."

Nan thanked him profusely, got an address and phone number for Maria Fazio, took a deep breath, and called Maria's home. She decided against leaving a message on the machine and tried Hair Creations in West Chicago. Maria, she was told, would be in at two.

Nan made an appointment for two-thirty.

Hair Creations was in a strip mall on Highway 59 and smelled strongly of chemicals. When Nan walked in, she spotted Maria Fazio instantly, carefully cementing silver-blue curls in place for a lady in a lavender polyester jumpsuit. Maria was about five-one and weighed maybe 160, with great cascading masses of shiny black curls. Her features were delicate and pretty, her dark eyes heavily made-up. Nan took a seat to wait, and watched. The woman moved lightly for her size, seemed cheerful and interested in her client.

Ten minutes later, Nan was seated in Maria's chair. The hairdresser cocked her head and regarded Nan's hair critically. She fluffed it a bit. "So!" she said. "I'm Maria. What would you like today? You just had a nice trim, looks like."

Nan nodded with a smile. Her L.A. hairdresser, Alistair, had sculpted her reunion haircut barely a week earlier. "How about a shampoo and a blow-dry?"

"Sure thing," Maria told her brightly. "I don't think I've seen you in here before, have I?" She shrouded Nan's body with a maroon wrap and led her back toward the shampoo sinks.

"I'm just visiting," Nan answered. "From L.A."

"Really!" Maria's dark eyes lit up.

Nan watched her. "I came to my high school reunion."

It startled the woman. "How nice," she answered automatically, withdrawing into caution.

"Of course, we had a little excitement," Nan continued. "Maybe you heard about it. There was somebody murdered there. Over in Spring Hill," she added.

"How awful," Maria Fazio said. She clearly knew all about it and had no interest whatsoever in chatting. "Here, sit down now and just lean back."

Nan sat down but she didn't lean back. She kept watching Maria Fazio. "I think you knew the woman who was killed," she said, "a long time ago. Her name was Brenda Blaine, and she was a friend of your sister Liza."

Maria Fazio backed away slowly. "Who *are* you?" she asked, so softly it was almost a whisper. A very anxious whisper. There was something haunted in her eyes—fear, bad memories, it was hard to say what.

"I'm Nan Robinson," Nan told her. "I was sitting with Brenda at the dinner, and her body was found in my car. I got kind of involved despite myself."

"You don't want your hair done." The statement was flat, uninflected.

Nan half smiled. "Not particularly, I guess. But I thought this would be a good way to meet you and ask about your sister."

"How did you find me?"

Nan broadened the smile. "I let my fingers do the walking, tried all the Krzyzanowskis in the phone book till I found your uncle."

"Uncle Lud?" She sounded surprised.

"Uh-huh. He told me your parents went back to Poland."

Maria looked sad. "Yeah."

"How come?"

"I honestly don't know. My mom didn't really want to, particularly when it meant leaving her grandkids behind. But my father made his mind up, and that was that." Maria sighed and looked distant. "I *really* miss my mom." She shook herself back and looked at Nan suspiciously again. "Why are you asking about Liza, anyway?"

Nan shrugged. "I'm not entirely sure myself. It's just that nobody seems to know anything about her except that she was Brenda's good friend and she ran away. I guess I was hoping you'd know where to find her. It seems to me that she might know something about Brenda's past that would explain why she was killed here and now."

Maria Fazio shook her head slowly. "Liza never came back. She went to Hollywood, but then we never heard anything from her."

"She hasn't been in touch?"

Maria looked around. There was nobody else in the back of the shop. She pushed over a wheeled stool and sat down on it, looking at her hands.

"Do you know where she is?" Maria asked slowly. "Is Liza dead, too?"

Nan looked at her quizzically. "Why do you ask that?"

"Because I . . . I don't know. I guess I've thought for a long time that Liza must be dead, that something bad happened to her out there." The woman made *out there* sound like some very alien planet. Of course, she *was* talking about Hollywood.

"Actually," Nan told her, "I don't have any idea at all where she went. Or why, for that matter."

"Why was to get out," Maria Fazio said. "That part's easy."

"You weren't surprised when she left?"

Maria shook her head slowly. "She'd had a big fight with my father. *Another* big fight." She hesitated. "Liza was always in trouble, seems like. And she'd run away before, but she always came back."

This was news. "When she ran away before, where did she go?"

Maria shrugged. "Chicago, I think. She knew some people she'd go crash with in Lincoln Park when things got too heavy at home. And I think sometimes she crashed at Brenda's, too."

"At Brenda's?" It was hard to imagine Alvina McReedy taking in a girl she'd described as a "terrible influence." Of course there was always that shed behind the garage. Which apparently did more business than some hotel chains.

"That's what she told me."

"What else did she tell you?"

"Not much," Maria said. "I'm four years younger than Liza. She didn't have a lot of time for me, really. I just tried to stay out of the way when she got into it with my dad."

"He was strict?"

Maria Fazio threw her head back and laughed. "He was a *terror*! But Liza was his match, I'll say that for her. He'd whip her, and she'd just laugh at him. I guess the wonder is, she didn't split sooner."

"Was there something in particular that happened when she left the last time?"

"Not that I knew of," Maria answered. "It was always kind of the same."

"Did you know she was doing drugs?"

"Oh, sure." The answer was easy, offhand. "Everybody was, back then."

Well, almost everybody. Edwin Crosby probably hadn't been. Or Rose Jenner. Nan's own drug experimentation had been cautious to the point of absurdity. "What kind of drugs?"

Maria answered without hesitation. "Downers mostly, I think. Reds."

"Was she dealing?"

Maria shrugged. "I don't know. It wouldn't surprise me. She always seemed to have money, more than she'd make working at Burger Boy. She liked new clothes. That was one of the things my old man got so mad about."

"You said you heard from her from Hollywood?" As leads went, this was hardly solid, but at least it was a start.

A false start. "I didn't. Brenda did. She told me Liza was gonna be a movie star." Maria closed her eyes. "I guess it didn't happen."

"It doesn't happen for most people who try," Nan told her gently. Southern California was full of people who had followed their dreams to Hollywood, then stayed after the dreams faded and reality intervened. For young girls, that reality could be harsh indeed. "What do you remember about Brenda?"

Maria ran her fingers back through her thick glossy curls. "Not all that much. They didn't hang around the house a lot, of course. Mama didn't like Brenda."

A common characteristic of adult women in Spring Hill, it seemed. "Where *did* they hang out?"

"Well, Blackie's, of course."

"Anyplace else you knew about?"

Maria's smile was wry. "Liza wasn't exactly confiding in me. I was just the kid sister."

"She was going with Jerry Leffingwell, I understand. Do you remember him?"

The smile this time was broad and warm. "Well, sure! Jerry was a basketball star, *everybody* knew who he was. He used to work on my mom's car at the house when my dad wasn't around. I'd kind of hang around and watch."

"Was that the car that Liza drove?"

"Uh-huh."

A woman with a high-swept frosted hairdo appeared in the doorway. "Maria?" she sounded puzzled and a bit annoyed. "Your three o'clock is here."

"Tell her I'll be right with her," Maria answered. She turned back to Nan. "Do you really want your hair done?"

"I guess not," Nan admitted. "But I'll be happy to pay for your time."

Maria shook her head. "Don't worry about it. Just promise me one thing." She hesitated briefly. "If you find out anything about where Liza is, would you let me know? Not knowing all these years has been . . . hard."

"Of course," Nan assured her. But the promise sounded hollow.

Darlene Leffingwell Lovejoy was knitting with Mom on the sunporch when Nan arrived back at the house, having picked up both Ryan Blaine and a copy of the reunion video shot by Grant Kirby. Mom and Darlene, needles clicking briskly, looked like the distaff side of a frontier barn raising.

"What can I get everybody?" Mom asked, swinging into her gracious-hostess mode and setting aside the needle-work.

"I'd like a beer," Nan announced. "And I'm ready to call for the pizza anytime. I'm absolutely ravenous. Ryan's offered to make a salad."

Everyone moved into the kitchen, where Nan began pulling vegetables out of the refrigerator.

"You know, Ryan," June Robinson said thoughtfully, "it occurs to me that things must be pretty crowded over there with the Crosbys. It's none of my business, or course, and certainly no reflection on Edwin and Rose, but if you'd like to stay here for the rest of your visit, I have a spare bedroom all made up."

Ryan looked genuinely surprised. "That's very generous of you, Mrs. Robinson," he said. "And to be perfectly honest, I'd like very much to stay here. Nan . . . Nan's been real good to me, and I like being around her." He hesitated a moment. "But I can't. As long as they believe my father . . . killed Mom, I feel like I have to stay with him. I know he didn't do it, and if I were to leave now, it might look like . . ."

"Of course," Mom soothed. "But if you ever change your mind, the offer's open."

He nodded politely, commandeering a cucumber and

starting to peel it. "Thanks, Mrs. Robinson. I'll keep that in mind."

"We have some wonderful cold salmon," Mom announced, putting the leftovers from Monday night's feast on the table. "If you'd like to add it to the salad." She pulled out a cut glass cruet and smiled. "And look! Here's some of Ralph's special homemade Italian herb-and-garlic salad dressing."

"Ralph?" Darlene asked with a raised eyebrow. She had taken a seat at the kitchen island, out of the line of direct traffic.

"A special friend of mine," Mom simpered.

"When's he due back?" Nan asked carefully.

"He called just this morning," Mom burbled, "when you were out. He hopes to be back late this evening, and he said to save him a slice of pizza." She turned to Darlene. "If I do say so myself, I'm quite a good cook, and I'm mighty embarrassed to have Nan invite you over and then order out. I simply can't understand why it is she insists on ordering pizza, pizza, pizza whenever she comes to town."

Nan laughed. "Mom's spoiled, Darlene. She doesn't understand that it's almost impossible to get decent pizza in Southern California. The Italians all settled around San Francisco." She grimaced. "What they call 'Chicago-style' is a particular travesty. You wouldn't believe it. It always has a crust that's about eight inches thick and weighs forty pounds. Nobody ever believes me when I tell them we grew up on big flat thin-crust pizzas with chunks of sausage, not those dumb little slices. And cheese," she added rapturously, "tons of thick gooey cheese dripping off every slice."

Mom just shrugged. "I was starting to say that Ralph suggested we might all have dinner at the Wagon Wheel tomorrow night. Darlene, Ryan, you're welcome to join us if you'd like."

"Sounds great," Nan said, momentarily setting aside her

doubts. Ralph Salamone was, in general, a thoroughly enjoyable man.

"I'd like that very much," Ryan said. "Thanks."

"My Girl Scout troop meets on Thursdays," Darlene said, "or else I'd love to."

"That's a shame," Mom told her. She turned to Ryan. "The Wagon Wheel is the oldest restaurant anywhere in the county. It was founded in 1872 by Austrian immigrants, and there's a wagon wheel in the lobby that came off the covered wagon they used to get here from Pennsylvania. Now, Nan, if you absolutely insist on this pizza, let's get our order together and I'll run out to Petricelli's." She sighed. "I *wish* they'd start a delivery service!"

After the sort of major haggling and negotiation normally associated with an international trade agreement, the group finally settled on a large sausage and mushroom and a medium with the works, no anchovies. Nan could feel her stomach rumble in anticipation.

While they waited for Mom to return with dinner, Nan took Grant Kirby's videotape out to the sunporch and stuck it in her mother's almost virgin VCR. She had given the machine to Mom one year for Christmas, discovering too late that June Robinson had little interest in renting movies and even less in recording off the TV. She claimed, in fact—this woman who had mastered every kitchen appliance from the pressure cooker to the convection oven—to be incapable of taping anything, even with the number programmer Nan had added on a later birthday.

And so it sat, a big Japanese paperweight shelved beneath the TV.

"This could be very boring," Nan warned Darlene and Ryan. "There's hours of tape. Grant plans to edit it down, but I told him I wanted everything."

The tape began with Mary Lee and Rose Crosby setting up in the lobby, then showed endless shots of people in registration lines, including Nan. He'd even captured the Spring Hill Motors Frisbee that clipped her ear. Frank

Finney registered with a thickset woman in an unbecoming green dress. There were shots of people at the bar, laughing in groups, sitting at tables.

"This is fascinating," Darlene said with genuine enthusiasm. "I haven't seen or thought of so many of those people for so long. Of course I didn't know a lot of them, 'cause they were younger."

"Funny how that works," Nan agreed. "I noticed the same thing when I went through the old yearbooks. People in classes ahead of me I was pretty familiar with, but after my class, I hardly recognized anybody except Julie's close friends." She frowned at the video. Grant was making his leisurely way around the ballroom as people found tables. "This really is interminable. I know it's taken longer to get everyone to dinner than it did at the actual reunion. I hope you're not too bored, Ryan."

"Not at all," he demurred. He sat cross-legged on the floor and absentmindedly scratched Glockenspiel's ears.

"It's no wonder the police were so happy to arrest Edwin and be done with it," Nan sighed after a while. "I was *there*, and I still don't know who some of these people are." A number hadn't been pictured in the group photo, but they couldn't all be spouses. There was at least one table where she didn't recognize a soul.

Then Brenda Blaine arrived.

Grant Kirby had noticed her almost immediately, had captured her entire breathtaking walk across the dance floor to the dinner table, breaking only after Brenda took her seat between Nan and Rose Crosby. It was a real star turn.

"She loved that," Ryan said softly, "having people watch her."

Then why in the hell hadn't somebody been watching when she was killed? She *must* have sneaked out, Nan decided, to some sort of assignation. But that was hardly news.

"Be sure and tell me," Nan told him, "if you see your mom do anything that surprises you or seems out of character. You knew her so much better than any of us, and we were all preoccupied with a lot of other people at the time." Like Henry Sloane. When would he appear?

Nan stopped the tape and rewound it briefly, freezing the frame on the stunned faces at the table. "Too bad he didn't come in closer," she lamented.

"He didn't know Brenda was going to be killed," Darlene reminded her. "I'd say that so far he's done a more than thorough job. Everything's all in focus, and goodness knows there's plenty of it."

"Those cameras focus automatically. But look. Check out our faces."

The angle at which Grant Kirby had been shooting showed Nan and Janis Levin from behind, with their faces turned. Nan thought, irrelevantly and to her internal embarrassment, that she looked very good indeed, and not at all surprised by Brenda's arrival. She'd refined a pretty good poker face in her years of legal work.

Jim Webster, too, was impassive, though beside him Mary Lee's jaw dangled. Wally Sheehan did look surprised, with a certain measure of amusement. Rose Crosby, staring into her vichyssoise, was apparently oblivious.

The Reverend Edwin Crosby, on the other hand, appeared to have just been keel-hauled.

Nan started the tape again. The next part was relatively dull. Grant Kirby dutifully recorded each course of the meal as it arrived, but shot no other film during dinner until Wally Sheehan began his remarks. In his racing jacket and cap, Wally looked downright silly, and jokes that had seemed mildly amusing at the time were now incredibly lame.

Jim Webster's speech was recorded beautifully. Jim was a natural in front of the camera, which loved him. He was a gifted speaker as well, certain to distinguish himself in Congress. Nan had little trouble picturing him in the Senate after a few warm-up terms in the House.

Then Grant's camera panned the room, lingering for a

moment on Mary Lee Webster's radiant, cheering face. In doing so, he also captured Brenda. Nan remembered the apparent reluctance with which Brenda had joined the standing ovation, waiting until almost everyone in the room had already risen, applauding in dirgelike half-time.

What she hadn't seen then, and what shocked her now, was the expression on Brenda's face. She froze the picture again.

Brenda was obviously and unaccountably furious. You didn't need to know this woman to see the anger smoldering under her barely civilized smile, to feel the fury going into each slow clap.

What on earth had upset her so?

Late that night, after everyone had gone home and Mom had retired, yawning, Nan wandered around the backyard aimlessly.

All those numbing hours of videotape hadn't jarred loose any forgotten memories or given her any startling new information to work with. Even the shots of Brenda dancing with Frank Finney were disappointing. Yes, they were undoubtedly very close to each other. But Frank and Brenda were on the far side of the dance floor, with the focus on a couple in the foreground doing an Arthur Murray–style ballroom dance. Lessons to enhance a floundering marriage, at a guess. *Nobody*'d danced like that in high school.

Nan knew she was running out of time. It was already one A.M. on Thursday, and she was supposed to leave town on Sunday, to be back at her desk in Los Angeles on Monday morning. If she couldn't figure out what had really happened quickly, Edwin Crosby might well be convicted for a murder she was certain he hadn't committed.

It wasn't enough to hope that Jake Moroney could get an acquittal. That would still leave Edwin under a lifelong cloud, still ruin his ministerial career. His only hope was total exoneration, and the only way to assure that was her old buddy, the SODDI defense. Some other dude did it.

But who? If Bernie Singer had truly been in Las Vegas
the night of the reunion, he was out and the killer home-
grown.

Nan thought about the videotape. The first thing that
Brenda had done when she entered the ballroom was stop
and look carefully around the room, scanning the tables as
if she were looking for somebody. Then she headed directly
for the table where Nan had been sitting.

She had spoken first to Nan on arriving at the table. But
Nan had been facing away from the door. It was ridiculous
to think that Brenda would recognize the back of Nan's
head after twenty years.

So she was coming because of somebody else she saw at
that table.

CHAPTER 14

Brian Delahanty hung up the phone and stared glumly at the printout on his desk. This was truly the pits. The euphoria he normally felt on taking out a scam artist totally eluded him. And he couldn't legitimately take credit for it anyway. The entire thing had been dropped in his lap.

A red herring, that's what he thought it was when Nan Robinson brought him the cockamamie proposal, the Polaroid, and the dirty wineglass on Tuesday. She was trying to divert his attention from the preacher, that was all. A noble—if transparent—effort, one that somewhat lessened his opinion of her. If she thought he was some rural rube whose attention could be so easily diverted, then she wasn't as sharp as she had first appeared to be. He'd come close, in fact, to simply chucking both glass and photo in the trash, figuring to later assure her that there was no need to worry.

Christ, what if he'd actually *done* that?

He read the printout again and sighed, picking up the still warm telephone receiver. His friend and sometime hunting buddy, Detective Mike Wainwright of the Naperville P.D., already had Antonelli's apartment there staked out. There was a woman with him, Mike reported, a local divorcée in her sixties whose attorney husband had recently dumped her for his young secretary. In a commendable display of good manners, Mike was planning to wait until after the divorcée's departure to bust Antonelli.

The Naperville woman wouldn't know about Antonelli's

wives in Cleveland and Huntington and Grand Rapids, the extortion warrants out of Allentown and Wilmington, the lady friend in Spring Hill. She wouldn't know about the wealthy wife with Alzheimer's in the Miami nursing home who had signed a power of attorney and was providing the seed money for the entire merry-go-round.

Delahanty sighed. There were probably dozens of other lady friends fleeced and abandoned throughout the northeast and midwest, women too embarrassed to come forward and confess their witlessness and vulnerability to smirking cops. Women who preferred to swallow their humiliation and take their financial reverses and hang on to their memories.

A guy like Antonelli would leave them with some good memories, too. Nan had described him as charming, the photo showed a looker, and it was a safe bet he was a real piece of work in the sack. That type always was.

Christ, what a mess.

Nan herself answered the phone, a lucky break. He told her only that he needed to see her in person and that he'd pick her up in five minutes. When he pulled up the unmarked car in front of her mother's big old brick house in the Heights, she was waiting on the steps, reading a magazine. She wore khaki shorts and a scoop-necked T-shirt, and she didn't look glad to see him.

"Come for a ride," he told her, leaning over to open the passenger door. "We need to talk."

She stiffened slightly and got in without a word. She knows, he thought. She's expected this all along. He drove out the road that led to the Golden Valley Rest Home and pulled off in a grove of old oak trees.

She turned and stared at him. "What's up?" she asked. Her voice was a little uncertain, and he would ordinarily have expected a wisecrack.

He handed her the file, watched her bite her lip and suck in her breath as she saw the photograph and read the name. She went through all of it, then turned to him.

"A carny," she said flatly. "My mother's in love with a carny who's got a rap sheet as long as the Mississippi River."

"He got out of the carny business a long time ago," Delahanty told her.

"Yeah, when he went into the full-time victimization of old women."

"Your mother's not an old woman, counselor."

"She's not today's hip young lassie, either. And stop calling me counselor." Her fist was clenched white, and she slammed it into her thigh, leaving a red welt. *"Goddammit!"*

Then he truly startled him. She started to cry. He knew she wouldn't want to be touched or comforted, but when he opened the glove box and handed her a pack of tissues, she took it. After a couple of minutes she blew her nose.

"I'm sorry," he said, and he realized he meant it.

"I didn't want this." She spoke quickly now, talking almost in double time the way his cousins in Massachusetts did. She rubbed absently at the red mark on her thigh. It was a nice thigh. "You may not believe this, but I really wanted to be wrong. I wanted you to tell me, hey, you're a real jackass, wasting my time this way. The guy's clean, he's just what he seems like, a nice old man who likes to cook. Not some goddamned bunco artist. Not a bigamist wanted for extortion."

She shook her head. "Of all the rotten, miserable ... What's going to happen, detective?"

"He'll be arrested this afternoon in Naperville. And you could call me Brian."

"Yeah, sure, right. Brian." She looked off out the passenger window. "Why couldn't he have picked on some other rich widow?"

He smiled at her gently. "The Widow Robinson's a very attractive lady, Nan. Like her daughter."

"And she's rich."

"There's that, too," he conceded. Was she tough enough?

Yeah. "I remember hearing about a case like this out east somewhere, with a nastier twist to it. Same M.O., only he didn't just take their money and marry them. He killed them, too, for the insurance."

Nan sniffled a little, wiped her nose again, and frowned. "I didn't think you could get away with that these days, with everything computerized and cross-referenced and all."

His laugh was a bit grim. "You can get away with a hell of a lot if you look and act normal and don't do anything to excite suspicion. You ought to know that, doing the work you do."

"I guess I ought to. But dammit, Brian, that's all abstract. You know—good versus evil, right versus wrong, shady versus aboveboard. And it's not my *mother*."

Delahanty felt a sudden, totally irrational urge. He would bundle her off to a motel somewhere, make love to her until she forgot all about her mother and the grifter, break down what remained of those icy reserves, and get inside her emotions while they were still cracked open.

He exhaled slowly. Nice image. But it wasn't practical and it wasn't ethical and he was on duty and she'd probably be like that goddamned Detroit DA once he got her in bed anyway, spewing orders and instructions. Sleeping with the Detroit DA had been like fucking a drill sergeant.

"I can tell your mother, if you want," he offered. "She doesn't need to know you were involved at all. I can tell her Antonelli got picked up as a result of an investigation in Naperville and had ID on him that linked him to here. That I remembered you mentioning that your mother saw him, blah, blah, blah."

Nan shook her head and offered him a half smile. "Thanks, Brian. It's a really nice offer, and I wish I could take you up on it. But I started this, and I have to finish it. That's something I got from my dad. If you start something, make damn sure you're prepared to finish it, he always said." She clenched her fists. "Dammit, why did he have to pick on *her*? There have to be a million rich widows out there."

"Look at it this way, Nan." He liked the way her name sounded. "If he'd picked on some other rich widow, he probably wouldn't have gotten caught. So he'd have another wife, and then one after that. For all we know, the guy's got women from here to Tokyo, and he may be married to half of them."

She laughed shortly. "That'd be a swell approach to take with my mother. Say, Mom, not only did you fall for a con artist who's got a few wives already and at least two other girlfriends we know of, not to mention those extortion warrants back east, but there're probably lots more women." She shook her head. "She's going to feel like such a *fool*. And that's not the half of it. I know she's been sleeping with him, and I'd be willing to bet anything she's never slept with any other man besides my father."

"Anybody can make a mistake, Nan. Anybody can get conned. And without casting aspersions on your mother's morality, she might have had a few rolls in the hay she neglected to mention to her daughter. And if she did, so what?"

Nan bit her lip and looked doubtful. He reached over and took her hand.

"Hey. You did the right thing. Sometimes doing the right thing hurts people. But that doesn't make it less right."

"Maybe I *should* let you tell her," Nan answered with the shadow of a smile. "You make it sound so reasonable. But it's *not* reasonable, Brian. She's a lonely woman in a small town, and she's been made a royal fool of."

Enough already. "Would you rather he'd stolen all her money?"

"Of course not." She jerked her hand out of his.

"Would you rather he'd killed her?"

"How can you say such a thing!"

The anger seemed a good sign, though he hated to see

her vulnerable side tucked back behind that shield of California brass-balls lawyer.

"That's more like it," he told her mildly, leaning back against his door. "Keep your perspective. Pretend this guy's some scumbag you uncovered while you were investigating an ambulance chaser. Don't cut him any slack because you happen to have met him or because he happens to have charmed somebody you know. When are you leaving town?"

She frowned at his abrupt transition. "Sunday afternoon, I told you. But what—"

"I was hoping I could buy you dinner before you go."

Her face closed up again, and he saw the muscles at her jaw clench. She looked as if she wanted to cry again. Real smooth, Delahanty.

"Sorry, that just slipped out. Forget I mentioned it."

"But I—" She hesitated, looked away grimly.

"No big deal," he told her easily. Like hell.

"You don't understand," she said after a moment. "It's nothing to do with you. I just remembered we were all supposed to go out for dinner with Ralph Salamone tonight. Or John Antonelli, or whatever the hell his name is. And even though she'll want to boil me in oil, I wouldn't feel right leaving my mother tonight." She glanced sideways at him. "Maybe tomorrow night? What's that, Friday?"

He nodded. "It is, indeed. I'll pick you up at seven." He stared at her hard. "You sure you don't want me to tell her? It's all in the line of duty."

"Thanks," she told him, meeting his eyes and smiling slightly. "But I'll do it. Just take me home quick, before I lose my nerve."

After he dropped off Nan Robinson, the day was effectively shot. Delahanty sat at his desk a few more hours, shuffled paper, juggled ideas, endured another visit from Bouncin' Bob Stedman of the DA's office. Finally he gave up and left.

Outside it was still hot, still bright. He drove the streets of Spring Hill aimlessly for half an hour looking for Jamison, no longer nursing much hope for the mutt's return. But he went through the motions. He checked to see that his REWARD posters were all still in place. He called all the pounds one more time.

Then he went home and ran his trains.

After Maureen left him the last time, the time he knew was for good, he had found himself teetering on an abyss of impossibly empty time. A marriage, even a marginally functional one, took up a lot of time, and a child, even one as quiet and shy as Laurie, took up plenty more.

Suddenly both were gone, first from his immediate life, and then from Detroit as well. The salesman Maureen left him for was transferred to the western suburbs of Chicago. For a while after his wife and daughter left town, Delahanty drank, which wasn't particularly satisfying but did fill the time. He tried exercising more, but it bored him. Three miles each morning, before he was really awake, was enough.

He wasn't ready for women yet. And he had his twenty in, was eligible for retirement. So he moved. He found the job in Spring Hill near Schaumburg, where Maureen and Laurie and the cuckolding salesman were living. He filed the papers and retired. Then he moved to the Chicago suburbs and started seeing Laurie on alternate weekends again, began patching up the ruptured bond between himself and his daughter. He got Jamison as an enticement for Laurie, and was surprised to find how much he liked having the fool dog around.

And then, in the cruelest twist of all, Maureen's new husband got transferred again, this time to Pittsburgh.

So Brian Delahanty went to the attic of his mother's house in Lansing and brought out all the boxes of his boyhood H-O train set, remembering with a stabbing pain how he had once planned to set up trains with a son and how

Laurie had politely run her Christmas starter set a few times, then abandoned it.

He set up a huge table that filled the dining room of his condo and built mountains and tunnels and bridges and towns. He ran rail lines off onto shelves that circled the living room. He built the wet bar into the outfit, and with great difficulty and many false starts, turned the faucet into a waterfall.

Before he realized what had happened, the entire living area of the condo had turned into a railroad line, all but his bedroom. On her quarterly visits, nine-year-old Laurie called him "cuckoo," but she said it fondly.

He rarely brought friends back to his place, and never women.

He wondered now what Nan Robinson would think about the trains.

When it was all over, Nan realized that she had almost no specific memories of the confrontation. The moments she remembered were snapshots: Mom's initial indignation, a magazine hurled across the sunporch, a glass of tea spilled onto a needle-pointed butterfly pillow, alternating waves of fury and hysteria.

Brian Delahanty had loaned Nan the file with the printout on John Antonelli and the photograph of the man they'd known as Ralph Salamone. At first Mom refused even to look at it, preferring to focus instead on Nan's hideous betrayal, her appalling sneakiness, her vilely suspicious mind, her wildly unfair accusations. In some ways that was the easy part.

"You're a fine one to lecture *me* on men," Mom wailed at one point. "Thirty-seven years old, divorced, without even a child to comfort you in your old age, as if having a child is *any* comfort at all." Then she started howling again.

"It could have happened to anybody," Nan reminded her gently, using tissues to sop the tea up from the pillow.

"But it didn't. It happened to me, and here I am stuck with the proverbial serpent's tooth, and you—you've betrayed the man I *loved*. Sent him off to *jail*. How could you do this to me? Do you have *any* idea how hard it is to find a man when you're a sixty-two-year-old widow in a small midwestern town, anyway?"

Actually, Nan reflected without commenting, it was hard to find a man when you were any age, any place.

June Robinson was blubbering now, her makeup washed away, her face puffy and haggard. "Ralph was my last chance, and now you've seen to it that he's gone. Poor Ralph."

"Poor *Ralph*?" Nan had no trouble working up her own little head of righteous indignation. "Poor Ralph indeed! Poor Ralph—or should we call him Poor John?—would have stuck around just long enough to separate you from your money, Mom, and then he'd have disappeared, off to that alleged sister who was always so mysteriously ill." She forced herself to be calm. "Mom, it's ugly, I know, and I hate it that this happened, but it *could* have been worse. Would you rather have married him as Wife Number Four, or Seven, or whatever it really is?"

"I'd rather never have been born," she sobbed, and her mother's regression to the quintessential wail of adolescence tore at Nan's heart. As her mother crumbled, all of Nan's anger melted into compassion. She could not remember having felt more miserable or helpless.

When it became apparent that her mother wanted nothing whatsoever to do with her, Nan trudged slowly upstairs to her room for a good cry of her own, taking little comfort in the awareness that her mother would later regret having tried to slay the messenger of bad tidings. She called Julie in California, grimly reported on the afternoon, and suggested that her sister wait a day or two before speaking directly to Mom.

Then she tried—with minimal success—to read, finding it necessary to return repeatedly to the top of the page, unable to concentrate on even the simplest homogenized articles in her mother's *Reader's Digest*. At last she dropped off into an uneasy nap.

The ringing phone beside her was jarring, disorienting. Nan groped for the receiver. "Hello?"

"Nan Robinson?" The voice was old, female, quavery.

Nan shook herself and sat up. The clock on the dresser said 6:35, and long streams of warm late afternoon sunlight filtered through the maple leaves outside the bedroom window. Waking from daytime sleep generally left Nan groggy and befuddled. But then, in a stomach-churning flash, she remembered the afternoon's anguished confrontation with her mother, and she was wide awake.

"This is Nan," she answered slowly. Serpent's tooth in residence.

"I'm afraid," the voice went on, in a sort of half whisper, almost like rattling tissue paper. "You mustn't tell anyone I called. I don't want them to get me, too."

Had she missed something? "Who is this?"

"Never mind that," the woman told her. "Alvina McReedy was my dear friend. She told me she talked to you. She knew much more than she told you, you know. That's why I'm so afraid."

Nan's pulse raced. Was this a genuine breakthrough, or a septuagenarian crackpot? "Are you at Golden Valley?" she asked slowly.

"Well, of course I am," the woman hissed irritably. "I live right down the hall from Alvina, or rather from where Alvina used to be. Before *they* got her."

"Before *who* got her?"

"You surely don't think I'm foolish enough to let them hear me say anything now, do you? I *saw* what happened that night."

Nan slipped into her shoes, tightened the laces. She could get to Golden Valley in less than ten minutes. "You mean the night Mrs. McReedy died?"

"Well, of course that's what I mean. And it just isn't *right*." She hesitated a moment. "I'm just so afraid."

"I'll come right now," Nan offered, stretching her legs. Her mother didn't want her around anyway. "There's visiting hours till eight, aren't there?"

"No, no, no!" The woman sounded distraught. "You *mustn't!*"

"Then I don't understand what you . . ."

"You can't come through the lobby. Then they'll *know*." This was beginning to sound like world-class paranoia. Or maybe not. *They* could be purple extraterrestrials, or entities all too corporeal. Two people were dead, after all. "Come to my window later, when everything gets quiet. I'll stay awake and watch for you. Nine-thirty. But you mustn't let them know. You *mustn't!*"

Nan rested her forehead on one hand. "Where will I find you?"

"Around the side in the north wing," the woman whispered. "I'm in the fifth room, the fifth window. There's a lilac bush outside my window. You just rattle my screen, and I'll be right there."

"I wish you'd tell me your name," Nan said gently. "If you're worried, I'm sure I can get you police protection."

"*No!*" The voice rose, then fell again to almost a whisper. "Just come, dear. *Please.*"

Then there was a click.

Nan realized with a guilty and belated start that she'd never called Ryan to tell him there would be no happy family dinner at the historically significant Wagon Wheel Restaurant. She herself had no appetite at all. But when she heard the unmistakable disappointment in his voice, she realized she'd actually been looking forward to the evening herself. That even though she'd pretty thoroughly cooked his hash, she had *liked* Ralph Salamone, the man who'd been introduced as a potential stepfather.

On impulse, she invited Ryan to join her for a different

dinner altogether, at Myra's. She was suddenly starving, a
vision of Brian Delahanty's plate of fried chicken floating
just ahead of her like a heavenly golden mirage.

And dinner was almost fun. Ryan was coping pretty well,
all things considered, and he was a bright boy with a lot of
opinions. More importantly, the dinner—and its three or
four thousand calories of crisply fried, juicily flavorful,
cholesterol-laden chicken—filled the anxious early evening.

It was nearly nine when she dropped Ryan off at the parsonage, coming inside just long enough to tell Edwin about
her mother and Ralph Salamone. When the dust settled a
little, Mom would probably welcome some consolation—or
even better, an assignment of great urgency to promote the
community good—and Edwin seemed pleased to confront a
parish problem in which he didn't personally star. Nan left
feeling rather smug, as if she'd masterminded a successful
blind date.

She considered calling Brian Delahanty to tell him where
she was going and why. But time was short, and she didn't
feel the strength to argue with him. That he would argue,
she didn't doubt. Besides, how much trouble could she get
into by talking to an old lady at a nursing home?

It was 9:32 when she pulled into the parking lot at
Golden Valley and parked at the north end, away from the
main door and lobby, in an area where several other cars
were parked. She cut the engine and stepped into the humid, quiet night. The moon hung low over the horizon. The
evening air was only slightly restless, and it felt a lot like
the night she had walked into the woods and her past with
Henry Sloane.

An owl hooted in the woods behind the compound and
she smiled, wondering if the elderly residents could hear or
appreciate it. Hearing was one of the senses that seemed to
go first.

She moved quietly across the lawn beside the north wing
of the building. The building was a single story, slightly

raised over basement windows. Between the lawn and the building ran thick shrubbery about four feet high.

She counted windows. Flickering lights in the first two came from televisions. The first changed intensities and muted sounds so quickly that someone had to be channel-surfing on a remote control. A man, no doubt. A deodorant commercial was playing in the second room, where the TV sound was turned up high and seemed even louder, given the raised window sash.

So this was how Alvina McReedy's killer had gotten in. It was disturbingly easy to sneak up. The parking lot was deserted, visiting hours were over, and even Brian Delahanty hadn't been able to get a prompt response at night from the minimal evening staff. Plus, any residents still awake were likely to suffer major hearing deficiencies.

Nan oriented herself quickly in her head. Yes, this was the very wing in which she'd visited Brenda's grandmother.

The third window was closed tightly but there was a bright light on, and Nan could hear a baseball game playing on either radio or TV. The fourth window was dark.

And so was the fifth.

She moved in closer, pushing aside the bushes to get to the screen. Rattle the screen, the woman had told her. But she hadn't said her room would be dark. She *had* said the fifth window, though. Nan was certain of that.

As she rattled the screen and peered upward into the dark room, Nan could see the shadow of a ladder-back chair, make out the outline of a picture on the wall beside the hallway door. Her eyes had been adjusting to the darkness, and she realized suddenly what the picture was: a framed sampler.

Wine biteth like a serpent and stingeth like an adder, it would say if she could get close enough.

This was Alvina McReedy's room.

In the split second before she realized that she'd been set up, Nan heard a rustling in the bushes behind her. Smelled a sharp, acidic odor. Felt a sudden blow on the back of her head.

Then darkness.

CHAPTER 15

Pitch-black. An overwhelming acidic smell. Confinement.

Nan's eyes burned, and her chest felt as if someone were tightening a wide metal band around it. She fought a wave of nausea, began to cough, fought that, too.

The strongest impulse was to let go, release herself, fall back into semiconsciousness. But even in her state of muddled bewilderment, she knew that was the most dangerous thing she could do.

Where *was* she?

It was dark, confined, confusing. There was a noise, a rumble, a motor. A car. The trunk of a car.

How? What?

Never mind that. Inventory. Take inventory.

Item. She was curled in the fetal position, her knees near her head, resting on her left side. She tried to move her hands forward. No go.

Item. Her hands were twisted behind her, and she couldn't get them free. Tied, maybe? She wiggled her fingers as best she could, thought she felt a rope. She could lock her thumbs together, but that was it. Next.

Item. Her left hand was partially numb, probably from the pressure of her limp body cutting off the circulation. She shifted slightly, tried to lift the pressure off that arm. It was too cramped to move much.

Item. There was something wrapped around her mouth, wet and sharp-smelling, like bleach. *Bleach?* Got to get rid of it. She pushed her nose down against her shoulder, rubbed. No good. Tried to rub it against the carpet on the floor of the trunk.

Item. Fumes. Acidic fumes coming from the cloth around her nose and mouth. Her eyes burned when she opened them. Better to keep them shut.

A major jerk as the car stopped suddenly. A stoplight? Where were they? She couldn't tell, had no idea how long the car had been moving before she came to. It was hard to differentiate noises, too. The sound of the motor was loud, and she felt a kind of ringing in her ears.

Sleep. Sleep would make it all go away.

No! Sleep would be disastrous. She *had* to stay awake, had to get her wits about her.

She twisted her head now, fought to stay awake, brought her knees up. Used the knees to push and flatten the tip of her nose. To push the cloth down away from her nostrils.

Victory! Cloth dislodged from nose. Car moving again now, too. Horn honking somewhere, not this car.

Limited victory. Nausea still coming in waves, the cough pushing up from deep inside her constricted chest. Uncover the mouth, got to uncover the mouth. *Do it.* She twisted further, yearned for bonier knees, finally managed to rub the cloth down below her chin. *Yes!*

Felt the nausea begin again.

A sudden jolt, throwing her upward, bumping her head on the inside of the trunk's roof. Then another bump. Potholes. Had to be. The car was turning now, going left. Wherever she was headed, it had to be bad. Not much time, either.

Another left turn, then a right one. The car stopping, the sound of a car door opening, a rasping squeak outside. The car door closing again, car moving forward, roadway much bumpier.

Think!

Nobody to rescue her. Nobody knew where she was going. Should have told Ryan at dinner. Should have left a note for her mother. Should have called Brian Delahanty. Should have stayed in bed.

Should have ... the hell with *should have*. Now was now, and later might not happen at all.

Many bumps and then a sudden stop. Engine off, car door banging. She braced herself, tried to figure if she could get her feet high enough to kick when the trunk lid swung up. Waited.

Nobody came.

Footsteps walking away, vague sounds in the distance, nothing obvious. Silence.

Heavy-duty silence. Wherever they had stopped, it was away from street noise. There'd be no passersby, no accidental discovery.

Footsteps again, this time coming back to the trunk.

Nan used her knees to push the cloth back up slightly over her mouth, breathed shallowly to avoid the fumes that permeated the cloth. Closed her eyes, feigned unconsciousness.

Heard the turn of a key in the trunk, heard and felt the car move as the trunk lid lifted. Trunk light going on, sudden brightness. Buried her face and fought the nausea. *Limp.* Stay limp.

Felt hands give her body a shake. Stayed loose, disjointed. Waves of nausea rising again. Held them back.

Felt her legs lifted, pulled out over the rear opening of the trunk. A strong arm around her knees, lifting, pulling her slack body out of the trunk.

Her head had moved back into the deeper recesses of the trunk as her legs were pulled and her body shifted position. She stayed limp, tried to avoid inadvertently squinching her burning eyes tight against the sudden brightness. The trunk light was right by her head, like a spotlight.

No idea who was out there, pulling at her legs. Tried to open one eye slightly as her body moved farther out of the trunk. Impossible to tell without opening wider, revealing her consciousness. Just a figure in the darkness, a vague dark shape against the greater blackness of the night.

Hands under her hips now, pulling her backward, a jolt as her head bumped on something. Her hands caught against the rim of the trunk as her body was pulled forward. A grunt from the assailant and a hand reaching under Nan's body, trying to free the obstruction.

Now!

She brought her knees up sharply, felt the right one bang into a chin, opened her eyes wide and saw the assailant fall backward with a grunt of surprise.

Keep moving.

She braced her hands behind her and pushed up with all her strength, managed to get her body up and out of the trunk. Her legs were stiff and felt somehow disconnected from the rest of her body, but she didn't dare stop to think about it. She fought another wave of nausea as she turned to face her attacker.

Got a fast blurry view of the assailant's face, stopped a microsecond to process the astonishing information, then lost her balance as the attacker lunged at her.

Her feet weren't trustworthy. Her hands were tied behind her back. Her wits were dulled by the events of the past half hour and by whatever had soaked into the cloth around her nose and mouth. There was only one thing left she could do, only one weapon that remained.

She vomited.

She let the nausea go in a single massive projectile that exploded onto the face opposite her, stunning both of them equally, bringing forth a cursing howl of indignation. The foul smell was sudden and overwhelming. Gagging, Nan backed away and sidestepped, choked back a second wave of nausea.

This would be the only chance she'd get. The attacker retched involuntarily and swept an angry forearm across face and cheeks, wiping away the dripping goo. Now was the moment.

Nan brought her right foot up sharply behind the assailant's knees. Watched in a sort of slow motion as the attacker tried to simultaneously maintain balance, avoid reflexive vomiting, and remain on the offensive. Stepped carefully out of the way. Saw the assailant teeter in a slick puddle of Myra's finest half-digested fried chicken, lose footing, fall backwards with a decided *thunk* as head connected to the sharp metal edge of the open trunk, lie motionless on the ground at the back of the car.

It was impossible to fight the second wave of nausea now, and Nan didn't even try. She turned away, stumbled half a dozen steps and leaned over, felt as if her innards were twisting themselves upward, forcing themselves through her raw and anguished throat. When at last she finished retching, she leaned for a moment against the side of the car, then moved cautiously around behind the trunk.

Looked down on the unconscious figure of Mary Lee Webster, dressed all in black, drenched in vomit.

Now, finally, Nan looked around, discovered where they were.

They were at the Potawatomi Park construction site, on the far side, near the fenced area where the old LaForce farmhouse had stood, where the family graveyard remained. The gate hung open.

Across the field sat the silent earthmoving machines, massive monsters stilled for the night. She could see the trailer where Jim and Mary Lee had their on-site offices. It looked to be a million miles away, but it was her best hope for getting help. Mary Lee would revive sooner or later, and if it turned out to be sooner, Nan had pretty well blown her wad, both literally and figuratively. She was weak and disoriented, and her head was starting to blaze with pain. For the first time, she noticed a throbbing behind her left ear.

She looked down at Mary Lee again, not getting too close, seeing that the woman's chest rose and fell rhythmically. There was probably something she should be doing to disable her further, but Nan's hands were still tied behind her back, and she felt herself weakening by the moment.

So she started trudging across the field, one foot ahead of the other, not daring to think how far it was. Reducing the twelve-step credo even further, taking one step at a time. One step, then another. Moving on, not daring to count. Every ten steps or so, she looked back to be sure that Mary Lee hadn't arisen, wasn't sprinting across the field in pursuit. Nan had no idea what she'd do if that happened. Her mind was blanking out now.

She got to one of the giant machines, one with some sort of massive blade on its front, and tried for a moment to cut the rope holding her hands together. Hopeless. The blade was too large, too dull. Her fingers were too numb. She continued across the field, slinking now from the shadowed protection of one machine to the next. Each time she set out for the next one, she checked back to see that the dark figure on the ground beside the trunk hadn't moved.

But now she was too far away to tell for certain.

Finally, she neared the trailer. She could go no farther, that much was clear. Her knees were starting to buckle with almost every step. She was dizzy, and her head raged with pain. Her hands were numb and tied behind her. A homicidal maniac was somewhere out on the field. Possibly already slipping up behind her. There was nobody within earshot, probably nobody within half a mile.

And the trailer was locked anyway.

But wait. There was a little decal on the door of the trailer office, a metal wire going around the window. An alarm system.

An alarm system, she *hoped*. There didn't seem much reason to wire a trailer in a locked construction site in a low-crime area, except to discourage teenage vandals. The alarm might well be a dummy, the fake kind sold to cheapskates trying to outwit morons.

She looked around on the ground for a rock, something

large enough to break glass but small enough to pick up and hurl backwards at an upward angle. Found one that looked about right.

The first time she tried to heave it upwards and backwards, it bounced off the metal wall below the window with an appallingly loud bang. The second time it clanked weakly against the window, but didn't break the glass.

She was running out of strength. She picked the rock up again, leaned forward, took a deep breath and hurled the rock up behind her.

Heard the delicious sound of breaking glass, followed almost immediately by a piercing siren. Knew that the sound might well arouse Mary Lee, that help could still be a long time in coming, that there was no guarantee that the alarm was actually wired to the police or anybody else.

She slipped back into the shadows, moved past several machines, and slipped beneath a bulldozer, inside the protective haven of two massive black rubber tires, each one six feet tall.

The siren continued to pulse into the night, but now there was another sound. A car engine, coming nearer, crossing the field from the old homestead.

Damn! She should have thought to take the keys.

Nan crouched fearfully beneath the machine, saw the dark shadow of Mary Lee's car move, without headlights, slowly toward the gate. Saw Mary Lee swing the gate open, race back to her car, drive through, and speed away into the night, turning on her lights only after she entered the roadway.

It was another five minutes, easily, before the Spring Hill patrol car came, sans lights and siren, stopped cautiously at the open gate, then crept inside to the trailer office. Nan saw the squad car door open and a uniformed cop step out into the night, gun drawn, bright flashlight slashing arcs through the darkness. In the moment before he closed the door, she saw his face. It was the young guy who'd been first at the hotel when she found Brenda's body.

She thought. Tried to think, anyway. Everything was starting to get murky. The cop was young and twitchy. If she made any sudden moves, scared him, he was likely to shoot her. But if she didn't make herself known, she might pass out and be overlooked completely.

She stayed behind the gargantuan tire, which seemed capable of stopping bullets, or at least slowing them down.

"Help me," she called. It was the first she'd tried to use her voice, and it came out hoarse and weak.

The light swung around toward the bulldozer. "Don't move," the cop ordered. His voice sounded a little shaky, too.

"I'm under the bulldozer," she called. "I've been hurt."

She could see him hesitate. "Come out with your hands up, slowly," he ordered.

"I can't," she started to explain. "My hands are . . ." And then she passed out.

Lights everywhere, shining into her face, swirling on the top of police cars and ambulance. Nan squinted against the painful brightness, pulled a hand up to shield her eyes. They were all talking at once, a swirl of faces over her. There was something over her mouth.

"Nan!" She recognized the voice. Brian Delahanty. "Nan, can you hear me?"

She tried to nod her head, held the hand over her eyes. *Her hand was free.* "Too much light," she murmured. She brushed at the obstruction over her mouth, an oxygen mask. A hand held it there, gently moved her own hand away, spoke reassuringly. It hurt to breathe.

She heard Brian arguing with the paramedics, saw his face move down close to hers. Felt strong fingers take hold of her hand.

"Who did this?" he asked. "Can you just tell me who did it?"

"Mary Lee Webster," she croaked out, one rasping syllable at a time, watching his face register the political nightmare he was stepping into.

"Shit!" he answered. "You're sure?"

She nodded again. Talking *really* hurt. But Mary Lee had gotten away, was probably home already, showering off Nan's dinner, washing the evidence of her attack down the drain of her palatial bathroom.

"Trunk of her car," Nan whispered. It was a little easier to talk now, but not much. "Threw up on her. Over there. By the old homestead."

This time he worked through the incredulity faster. Then he threw back his head and laughed out loud. "Well, ain't you a pistol!" he told her, with a squeeze of her hand and a mighty Irish grin. "I'll see you at the hospital in a little while, counselor. You're gonna be just *fine*."

Then he got to his feet, and the paramedics started loading Nan into the ambulance.

CHAPTER 16

They'd never actually left her alone through the night, but the day's activity in Nan's hospital room began officially with an orderly banging galvanized buckets and mopping the floor at six A.M. It was a semiprivate room, the other bed mercifully empty.

Nan negotiated the bed controls and raised herself to a sitting position. In the frigid room her hospital gown—faded blue and yellow diamonds, so threadbare it was probably the one she'd worn for her tonsillectomy at twelve—was worthless. Shivering, she pulled the skimpy blanket up, managing twice to catch her arm in the oxygen tubing that led to a little jobbie stuck up her nose. It hooked over her ears, and they had removed her earrings, which infuriated her further. If the holes closed before she got home, she'd be tempted to file a malpractice suit.

Her nose, chin, and cheeks felt rough and rashy. The cloth wrapped around her face after Mary Lee knocked her out had been soaked in a mixture of household bleach and ammonia. It was a combination that spoke almost touchingly of Mary Lee's homemaker roots—deadly when inhaled in confined spaces by the super-hygienic who sometimes actually died in the pursuit of cleaner toilets.

What had saved Nan was the relatively short period she'd been exposed to the combined chemicals. The skin irritation, they'd assured her last night, would clear up quickly. Already it felt less sore. And the concussion was mild, or so they seemed to think.

An unbearably chipper nurse wearing oval gold-rimmed, mother-of-pearl earrings responded to her call button and scrounged a couple more blankets. She brought cream and applied it gently to Nan's sore face. But the nurse was firm: nothing to eat or drink until the doctor arrived at some unspecified hour in the future, probably high noon. Nor could Nan remove the oxygen tube to use the bathroom, and she bore the indignity of the bedpan in silence. She wanted desperately to complain, of course, but her throat was still sore.

She had been an unbelievable dolt, she realized, to fall for Mary Lee's great-granny impersonation. The should-haves were piling up again. She should have told somebody where she was going, not that it would have helped much; her rental car had been left behind at Golden Valley and held no clues. She should have taken somebody with her, Ryan for instance. But the caller really *had* sounded like a scared old lady, and there wasn't much point in such self-flagellation anyway.

The smartest tack would have been to stay in L.A. and skip the whole damn reunion.

The doctor showed up around seven-thirty, a brisk young woman who agreed that Nan was bouncing back splendidly and could surely be released later that day if she developed no alarming new symptoms. She could remove the oxygen tubing. And she could have breakfast, which should, the doctor promised, arrive momentarily.

Nan was still waiting, chewing desultorily on the bedsheet, at eight-thirty, when June Robinson walked in with an enormous arrangement of garden flowers in her favorite Orrefors crystal vase. It was an obvious and unabashed peace offering.

"Oh, my poor baby," Mom murmured, leaning over to hug and kiss Nan. She clucked softly as she touched the reddened areas of Nan's nose and chin. "The rash is *so* much better, darling." A superficial observer might have believed that her resentment and anger from the previous

day had disappeared. Fat chance. It would take more than
a brief hospitalization to make June Robinson forget her life
had been *ruined* by her daughter's duplicitous betrayal. The
matter was hardly closed. "You precious, silly girl, you
could have been killed."

"I wasn't, Mom."

June Robinson had sobbed endlessly in the emergency
room last night, and even in her dazed state, Nan had understood that Mom wept both for her saved daughter and
her lost love. This morning the tears were gone and Mom
was her customary cheerful, animated self—bustling around
the room, fussing with the blinds, wondering at the dark
side of Mary Lee Webster, Perfect Suburban Mom.

Half an hour later, Edwin Crosby and Ryan Blaine arrived with a bouquet of daisies just as the breakfast tray finally appeared, stone-cold and stunningly unappetizing.
Gelatinous sunny-side-up egg. Carcinogenically charred ba-
con strip. Stale whole wheat bread and a dollop of sour
plum jam. Tepid tea. Small wonder that the hospitalized so
often lost weight.

Edwin and Ryan stayed just long enough to get a brief
version of the previous night's action, then left, shaking
their matching heads in unison. They hadn't been gone ten
minutes before Darlene Leffingwell Lovejoy arrived, with
Detective Brian Delahanty on her heels. Brian carried a
dozen red roses and looked exhausted. He said hello, met
Darlene, then went to find more chairs.

"This is incredibly embarrassing," Nan said. "I make a
big fat fool of myself, and everybody I know within a
twenty-mile radius shows up instantly."

"Be grateful you're alive," Darlene chided, hopping up
on the neatly made second bed and opening a bag of knitting. "I dropped a pitcher of orange juice on the kitchen
floor when it came on the TV news this morning."

TV news. Swell. Nan wondered grimly how detailed the
report had been. CALIFORNIA LAWYER TOSSES COOKIES ON
MAYOR'S WIFE. Did they have film?

Brian Delahanty returned with a pair of chairs from the nurses' station. He offered one to Darlene, who declined and remained perched on the bed, then pulled his own close to Nan's bed and sat on it backwards.

"The skinny at the nurses' station is that you'll be doing cartwheels on the way out of here," he told her with a smile. "Fit as a fiddle and right as rain, I believe they said."

"I know just who said it, too," Nan muttered darkly. She felt unbearably peevish. Hunger, no doubt. She looked around hopefully. "I don't suppose any of you folks are carrying a spare Quarter Pounder with cheese?"

Brian made a show of feeling all his pockets and triumphantly brought a bag of M&Ms out of his jacket. "Will this do?"

Nan snatched away the bag with a smile. "You bet." She popped a handful into her mouth and chomped the pellets into little sugary splinters. There. Much better. With her mouth full, she half smiled. "Are you as tired as you look?"

He shrugged. "I haven't been to bed yet, if that's what you're asking. It was a busy night."

"Can you tell us what on earth happened?" Mom asked, choosing to ignore the role Detective Delahanty had played in her own recent heartbreak. Of course, she might not remember; her focus had been clearly on her perfidious daughter, not the instruments of Ralph/John's apprehension.

"I can try," he answered with a genial smile.

"Did Mary Lee confess?" Darlene asked.

Brian Delahanty shook his head. In this early morning light there appeared to be flecks of silver in his thick dark-blond hair. "Hardly. She was all shampooed and curled up in her nightie by the time I got to the house last night. Shocked and outraged at the very notion of an arrest." He grinned. "When she realized it was really going to happen, she kind of lost it. Started shrieking, throwing things. Cursing Brenda Blaine, interestingly enough." The grin widened. "The lady's got a mouth on her I wouldn't have believed. Then she clammed, and there hasn't been another peep out of her."

"So it's just my word against hers?"

"Not entirely. Fortunately, Nan, you left a wealth of evidence, so to speak. There's bleached-out spots on the carpet inside the trunk of the mayor's Lexus. And we've been picking bits of vomit out of all sorts of interesting places. The washing machine we shut off with her clothes in the wash cycle. The laces of her Nikes. The treads of her tires where she backed through the scene of the, uh, regurgitation."

Mom was the one looking embarrassed now. And Nan felt a little sheepish herself. It would have been so much nicer to leave a quietly dignified clue—a trail of toothpick tidbits, perhaps, or artfully placed threads—than to upchuck half a fried chicken.

"But what was she trying to *do*?" Darlene asked. "At the construction site, of all places?"

Delahanty looked angry. "There's an area out there they're restoring into some kind of a museum. A family graveyard that they had to work around."

"Oh, right," Darlene said. "I remember there being a fuss about that. But what does that have to do with last night?"

"The old farmhouse is long since gone," the detective told them, "but the old well is still there. Nobody's used it for decades, I don't think, and it's boarded over. Or it was until last night. The boards were pried off, and a crowbar with Mrs. Webster's fingerprints all over it was lying beside the well. Nan, you said she was pulling you out of the trunk when you, uh, fought back?"

Nice use of euphemism, Nan thought. "Yeah."

He looked uncomfortable. "Naturally she's not providing any enlightenment on the subject, but an educated guess is that she was planning to dump Nan in that well and then just board it over again. No reason for anybody to ever check it out. And Nan's trail would end at Golden Valley."

June Robinson gasped and reached over to clutch Nan's

hand. Her fingernails bit into Nan's palm, but Nan kept quiet.

"I'm sorry, Mrs. Robinson," Brian Delahanty told her. "It's all conjecture, of course. And you raised a quick-witted daughter, so that's all it will ever be." He smiled at Nan. "I told you last night, but it's worth repeating. Nicely done, counselor."

"There must be an easier way," Nan told him, "to get praised by the police."

"Indeed," June Robinson agreed. "And just what does Mary Lee have to say about all this?"

"Nothing," the detective admitted. "As I said, after a couple of indiscreet, semihysterical remarks about the late Ms. Blaine, she clammed up big-time. Just as I was reading her her rights." He looked at Nan. "The mayor was highly indignant, as you might imagine. And by the time we'd finished booking her, the legal cavalry had arrived. Also big-time."

"Let me guess," Nan said. "Jake Moroney?"

"Bingo! Which may or may not be a conflict for the good counselor, depending on what happens with the charges on Edwin Crosby."

"Are you charging Mary Lee with Brenda's murder?" Nan asked hopefully.

He shook his head. "The only charge against Mrs. Webster at the moment is the assault against you. Which maybe we can stretch to attempted murder. As for the rest of it, all I can say is it's a whole new ball game."

"The radio said she was released," Darlene put in accusingly.

"No choice, really," Delahanty told her. "Purely the judge's call. Let her go on her own recognizance. Not that raising bail would be any hardship."

"Speaking of conflicts, what about the local prosecutor's office?" Nan asked.

"Interesting you should mention that," he answered. "Of course, there's no way Bob Stedman can handle it." He looked at Nan. "You might be interested in knowing, for whatever it's worth, that the one who really pressed to arrest Crosby in the first place was Stedman. And Stedman's connections to Webster Enterprises run deep. His wife's father worked with the mayor's old man, and his brother-in-law's the company controller. There's no way to prove anything, but I suspect some pressure behind the scenes to get Crosby charged."

Nan considered. "Which effectively stopped you from looking for another suspect."

"Officially."

There was nothing to suggest he'd devoted a moment to any unofficial search, but Nan let it go. "So you think Jim suspected Mary Lee?"

"No comment, counselor." His grin was crooked and cynical. "Hell, I don't even know if *I* suspect her. Like I said, this just reshuffles the cards. But there is one little thing I think you'll find interesting. The search warrant we got last night gave us a lot of latitude in looking through the Webster residence. And guess what we found in the handbag Mary Lee Webster carried to her high school reunion?"

He had their total attention now. Darlene even stopped knitting.

"A confession?" Nan asked hopefully.

"Almost as good." He smiled, milking the moment, then made his triumphant announcement. "The key to room two-forty-seven at the Spring Hill Inn."

Nan caught it first. "Brenda's room!"

"Exactly. Her missing key."

Nan frowned. "Why on earth would Mary Lee hold on to something so incriminating?"

Brian shrugged. "I asked. She didn't have anything to say. But you know, maybe she just forgot. It happens."

"Now what?" Nan asked.

"Now I get back to the detecting business. And you try to stay out of trouble."

"Maybe I'm just really dumb," Darlene said, joining a skein of white angora to the black whatever-it-was in her lap, "but why on earth would Mary Lee Webster kill Brenda Blaine and Brenda's *grandmother*?"

"Beats the shit out of me," Brian Delahanty answered cheerfully. "Begging your pardon, ladies. And now, much as I've enjoyed this, I need to amble along." He stood and smiled down at Nan.

"Oh, no you don't," Nan told him. "I can tell you've got more you're not telling me. Like motive, for starters. Why would Mary Lee kill Brenda? I didn't think she even *knew* her."

Brian Delahanty hesitated. "I can't really say anymore about that right now, but as I understand it, she *does* have a motive, and it's not half-bad. I'm in kind of treacherous political waters here. I promised our mayor I'd let him tell you about it himself."

"Don't be ridiculous," Nan snapped. "I want to know *now*."

"Sorry. I'd tell you, I really would. And I'd even trust you to act surprised later. But I'm a public servant and I'm already pushing it. The man's my boss, more or less. He said he'd be in here to see you later this morning. At ten."

"This is absurd," Nan fumed.

"Patience, counselor," he told her mildly. "And now, I need to get back to headquarters." He smiled. "Ladies."

Then he was gone.

Jim Webster showed up precisely at ten, also carrying an enormous floral arrangement. The room was beginning to feel positively funereal. All that was missing was Frank Finney with a fruit basket.

Mom and Darlene were both still waiting, and the three of them were running out of small talk. Any minute now, they'd be back to Ralph Salamone.

Jim looked haggard. He wore a beige sport coat over tan slacks and an aqua tennis shirt. There were lines on his face that hadn't shown at dinner on his patio two nights earlier. He seemed truly surprised to find Darlene, though he swung into political autopilot and greeted her graciously, by name. But he carefully avoided making eye contact. With anyone.

"Nan," Jim said awkwardly, seating himself in the chair Brian Delahanty had vacated, "I don't know what to say to you. I can apologize, of course, but that hardly seems adequate. Naturally I'll cover your medical expenses."

Money seemed the least of it. "I have insurance," Nan told him, "and I'm not feeling litigious. Just baffled. What the hell happened last night?"

"Mary Lee—" He hesitated. "She's not herself. Something's snapped in her." Laying the groundwork for the insanity plea. Distancing himself at the same time. The scumbucket. "And in a strange way, I guess it's all my fault."

"Oh?" Nan's voice was stronger now. The M&Ms had helped, but a Coke Classic that Darlene had fetched from the 7-Eleven around the corner had really turned the tide. Chocolate and caffeine, the perfect head-injury diet.

"This is . . . embarrassing. I'm not quite sure how to begin." He buried his head in his hands a moment, then looked up in raw pain. The *appearance* of raw pain, anyway. The guy was a politician, after all. "Back in high school, Mary Lee and I started dating as juniors. I think I fell in love with her even before that. And I've never stopped loving her for a moment since then. She was always so . . . so perfect."

Mildly flawed, at least. Perfect people didn't try to throw other people into abandoned wells.

Jim was at his most disarming now. "I was a normal teenage boy with a normal teenage boy's drives and urges. I wanted . . . I wanted to get laid. And Mary Lee was very adamant on the subject of premarital chastity."

Maybe in high school. As Nan recalled, this adamance

had undergone a later adjustment, resulting in the Websters' hasty collegiate marriage and Pam Webster.

"God, this is so hard to talk about!" Jim shook his head. He still wasn't making eye contact, but who could blame him? In fact, it was hard to figure why he'd come at all. "I wanted sex and Mary Lee said no, and she wasn't changing her mind. Spring break of senior year, Mary Lee was in Florida with her family. Maybe you remember, they went every year."

"Uh-huh." Nan hadn't thought about it for twenty years, but a clear image of Mary Lee's freshly sunburned face appeared. Folks who could afford to go to Florida in the spring had always made her vaguely jealous, flaunting their tans while the last grimy snows of March and April melted in Spring Hill.

"Anyway, Mary Lee was gone, and I was going somewhere with your brother, Darlene. Jerry. We were buds from way back."

Darlene nodded. "I remember."

"Well," Jim went on, "Jerry had this girlfriend, the one you were asking about earlier, Nan."

"Liza Krzyzanowski."

He smiled. "Yeah. Liza, that was her name. She brought along Brenda, who was not exactly like anybody *I'd* ever dated! She'd had a fight with her boyfriend or something, I don't know. The four of us were hanging out, having some tequila shots, you know. To make a long story very, very short, Brenda and I wound up at a motel. And we spent a lot of the next week together, till Mary Lee came back." He paused. "I'm not sure what was in it for her, but for me it was . . . really pretty amazing. But once Mary Lee got back, that was it."

Nan had a pretty good idea what was in it for Brenda. A chance to prove her power over someone she'd have regarded as a "socialite." To best that snotty Mary Lee Constantine by reducing her boyfriend to a lump of quivering gonads. To prove the class president had feet, ankles, and legs of clay.

Jim Webster grimaced. "I *thought* that was it, anyway. I'd see Brenda at school sometimes, and she'd just kind of smirk at me. But she was cool, never said or did anything to give it away." He looked down at his hands, twisted his simple gold wedding ring. "Then the summer after graduation, she called me up and said she had to see me. I went down to her house late one night after I dropped off Mary Lee. She was waiting for me in the little room behind her garage, and she told me she was pregnant with my baby."

In a charming display of generational mores, June Robinson gasped. Nan almost laughed out loud.

Jim seemed not to hear. "I was stunned. She'd told me she was on the pill, and hell, I believed her. But I didn't want to risk having her go to Mary Lee, or make a fuss to my parents. She said she was going to leave town and go someplace where she could have an abortion. So I gave her the money she asked for and I thought that was it. I heard she'd left town."

A thin sheen of sweat covered his face, even in the frigid chill of the hospital room. "Then she wrote me from Denver and told me she just couldn't go through with it, that she'd decided to have the baby instead. I was a freshman at Illinois by then, and I *totally* panicked. My dad loved Mary Lee, and my mom had just died. I knew my dad would be devastated if I hit him with this. Fortunately, I had a little money of my own, some savings. I sent Brenda what she asked for. That was just the beginning."

"You really thought she had your baby?" Nan had trouble imagining Jim Webster gullibly accepting the word of a girl whose reputation was as tarnished as Brenda's. It was much easier to picture Jim bluffing her into dropping her demands altogether. The contraceptive failure seemed odd, too. Nan and Henry Sloane had been fanatics about birth control, but of course, they were both cautious, college-bound prisses. And things *had* been fairly loose back then.

Safe sex mostly meant you weren't doing it on a moving motorcycle.

He lifted his hands to shoulder height, palms up. "She sent me a birth certificate that had me listed as the father. I don't know, maybe she just dummied that up. Maybe she had another one she sent Edwin Crosby with his name on it." That *did* sound like Brenda. He shrugged. "The baby's last name was Blaine, in any case."

"You didn't know she'd been in touch with Edwin?" Nan asked.

"Of course not! I just figured I might as well bite the bullet and pay her. I never had any *idea*! It wasn't till just this week, when Edwin got arrested and I found out he'd paid for the same doctor bills and tonsillectomies and stuff that I had, that it ever *occurred* to me she was putting the screws to us both. Not only that, from what Ryan says, half that stuff never even happened. He didn't have braces, or a broken wrist, or music lessons, none of that." Jim Webster sounded downright indignant.

But something didn't fit here. "Mary Lee knew that Brenda was bleeding you?"

He shook his head firmly. "No way. I always handled the money in our family. *Always.* And for the first fifteen years or so, Brenda wasn't unreasonable in her demands. It seemed easier to pay her than to risk having her show up on my doorstep with a son." Ever the pragmatic politician.

"And *did* she ever show up?" Nan asked.

He shook his head with a small wry smile. "She kept that part of the bargain, but how hard was that? Brenda *hated* Spring Hill. Then about three years ago, I went to a convention in Vegas and I ran into her. It was the damndest thing. I sat down at a blackjack table and looked up, and my God, *there she was*. The *dealer*. She recognized me at the same time, and this big strange grin grew on her face. It was like running into the Cheshire Cat."

Indeed. "Was Mary Lee with you?"

Jim shook his head. "Nope. Usually she comes along,

but the kids were sick or something. I figured . . . what the hell. Mary Lee would never need to know. Of course, I wanted to see Ryan, but Brenda wouldn't let me. I swear, I never intended to get involved, but it was just like twenty years ago. Once she got me started, I couldn't keep away from her. I blew off the convention, and she called in sick, and we spent three days in bed. Which would have been bad enough, and of course, it was unfair to Mary Lee. I'd always been faithful to her, always."

There was just a tad too much self-righteousness in his tone. Nan didn't believe him for a second. The Jim Websters of the world could always seduce some comely little cupcake when they wanted. And they frequently wanted.

"I made a mistake that weekend, though," Jim went on. "I let Brenda realize how successful I'd been. Bragging a bit, I guess. I'd just gotten elected mayor, and the Webster Center was nearly finished. I was negotiating for the Potawatomi Park tract. I was full of myself." He shook his head in dismay. "I was a damned fool, is what I was."

"So she tightened the screws." Nan had no trouble at all picturing that. And it fit Ryan's tale of suddenly improved means.

"Did she ever! She told me Ryan was about to start college, and that was going to cost a bundle. Plus, she said, me being in real estate, I could appreciate how a house would be a *much* better investment than her condo. She laid it all out and I paid. What choice did I have?"

Not much. Men who fathered the bastard children of Las Vegas blackjack dealers had limited political futures in Republican Porter County.

He shrugged with a touch of arrogance. "I guess it didn't matter that much. I had the money. She needed it. Of course, I still *did* believe Ryan was my son. And Mary Lee would never have needed to find out, if I hadn't gotten sick." He shook his head in irritation. "I went down to Cabo San Lucas on a fishing trip and picked up some damn virus. It nearly *killed* me. I spent almost a month in the hospital, right down the hall from this room. It was another three, four months before I really got my full strength back. Well, when Mary Lee went to pay our bills, starting sifting through things, right off she discovered how much I'd been sending Brenda. She went berserk."

"When was that?" Nan asked.

"A year ago last Thanksgiving."

"So you told her everything?"

He nodded. "It was the worst moment in our marriage. I can't begin to tell you how horrible it was. We even considered marriage counseling." He said it with a tinge of horror. The midwestern prejudice against therapy still ran deep. "But I really thought we'd worked things out. I thought she'd forgiven me. And of course, I never *dreamed* Brenda would come back to Spring Hill."

Nan stared at him. He looked smaller than when he'd come into the room, less certain of himself. "Do you think Mary Lee killed Brenda?"

His eyes were anguished. "I can't *believe* she'd ... No, of course I don't believe it. But I can't believe what she did to you, either." His sigh was deep, heartfelt. "I just don't know what to believe about *anything* anymore."

After everyone left, Nan waited for the doctor to return and sign her out, looking out of the window and thinking about Jim Webster's tale of penitence and woe.

Could Mary Lee have lost it and killed Brenda in a rage? Sure. How *dare* this harlot turn up to ruin both the reunion and Jim's congressional announcement? Nobody would pay much attention if Mary Lee quietly slipped outside to discuss the situation with Brenda. And Mary Lee could be discreet when she wanted.

She might not be strong enough to kill without a struggle, but Brenda had been knocked out from behind. The lump on Nan's own head proved Mary Lee was no slouch at striking from the rear. She was also demonstrably strong enough to put an unconscious body into the nearest open car. And then? The triumph of furious passion, an attack with whatever happened to be handy.

The hotel key would be in Brenda's little rhinestone bag, and Mary Lee would want to know if Brenda had anything in her room that might tie Jim Webster to her life. Keeping the key was sloppy, but maybe Brian Delahanty was right and she'd simply forgotten.

And Alvina McReedy? Mary Lee knew Brenda's grandmother and visited her own mother frequently at Golden Valley. Where she'd told her husband she was planning to go on the very afternoon that Nan saw Mrs. McReedy. Nan remembered Mary Lee mentioning it when she first visited the construction trailer at Potawatomi Park.

Mary Lee must have felt incredible relief once Edwin Crosby was in custody, accepting paternity of this Nevada mystery child. But Alvina McReedy might very well know something damning about her granddaughter's illegitimate child. And if Alvina could tie Jim Webster to Brenda Blaine, she was both dangerous and expendable. Having killed once, how difficult would Mary Lee find it to hold a pillow over a sleeping old lady's face?

It all fit.

What disturbed her the most, Nan realized, was not these sordid revelations, though God knows they were plenty depressing. Rather, it was the knowledge that Brenda Blaine had been a double-dipping extortionist.

Nan had romanticized Brenda. She had struck out on her own, raised a child, made a living, given up drinking, straightened out her life. That image of the fiercely independent, struggling single parent had no room for this newly revealed slice of sleaze.

An even grimmer thought struck Nan. If Brenda had been double-dipping with such great aplomb, was there any reason to suppose she had limited Ryan to *two* fathers?

Had other "daddies" from Spring Hill been silently supporting their "love child"?

CHAPTER 17

Nan lay ensconced with a glass of iced tea on a chaise longue on the sunporch Friday afternoon, flipping through one of her mother's women's magazines. She felt hideously depressed.

The magazine didn't help, loaded with whole-grain microwavable casserole recipes, and updates on obscure diseases, and profiles of women who whipped up haute couture from old rags while nursing twins and managing $200,000-a-year businesses out of the breakfast nook.

While Nan was hard-pressed to handle one simple job and keep her house presentable; even fixing dinner was usually too much trouble. She shook herself irritably. She should be feeling euphoria at survival, not melancholy because her life failed to attain some nebulous, impossible standard of perfection.

Then Mom came out onto the sunporch, handing over a cordless phone and smiling coyly. "Detective Delahanty's on the line," she chirped, in the same coquettish tone she'd used decades earlier when Henry Sloane would call.

Nan smiled and took the phone. The connection crackled as if the call were being routed from Beijing via Murmansk. Mom kept this phone only because it had been one of the last presents Phil Robinson ever gave her. She'd probably have preferred to exercise her nostalgia over a nice diamond necklace, but Dad had always liked gadgets.

"They told me you went home right after lunch," Brian Delahanty said.

Nan shuddered involuntarily. Somewhere in North Dakota was a factory that manufactured hospital meals from well-aged silage: pulverized, tinted, and shaped to approximate legitimate foodstuffs. With a sister plant in South Dakota to service the airlines.

"I was afraid it would be followed by dinner," she said. "What's new?"

"A lot." There was real satisfaction in Brian Delahanty's voice. "Spring Hill is in an uproar, and my office seems to be the heart of the firestorm. But we've made mucho progress. News travels fast in a small town. Everybody knows Mary Lee's been arrested, and now people are remembering things they didn't really think about at the time. Mostly useful—apart, of course, from the goofball who saw Mary Lee swooping down out of a silver spaceship the night of the reunion."

"Somebody said that?"

"Somebody said that. Last March, he confessed to murdering the pope and grinding him into kielbasa. He showed me the frozen links. But there's some good stuff coming in off the streets, too."

"Such as?" Nan leaned back expectantly.

"Such as, Mary Lee Webster usually doesn't drive that Lexus she had you stashed in. That's the mayor's party car. Mrs. Webster generally drives a cream-colored Jaguar, well known around town. The night Alvina McReedy was killed, Mrs. Webster was at a library board meeting. But she only stayed about twenty minutes, and when she left, one of the librarians noticed she was headed in the opposite direction from her house, toward Golden Valley. A gas station attendant saw her drive by, again headed toward Golden Valley, about eight-thirty. And here's the clincher: One of the biddies out at Golden Valley told us earlier that she saw a 'light-colored roadster' drive into the lot with its lights off the night Alvina died. The old lady wasn't sure what time it was, but she knew it was during a commercial break of a show that runs from eight-thirty to nine. We showed her some car pictures today, a lot of different models. She pounced on the Jag."

"That all sounds pretty circumstantial, so far."

"For God's sake, we haven't even been on the woman for twenty-four hours yet!" Exasperation crackled through the miserable connection.

He was awfully touchy, Nan thought. Lack of sleep, no doubt. "I'm not casting aspersions on your investigation," she said mildly. "Just looking at it as a lawyer. Have you found anything to tie her to Brenda's murder? Besides the key?"

She could almost see his grin. "I'm *so* glad you asked. We got a real interesting break there. This morning Martin Erskine came in. From Erskine dry cleaners. You know him?"

"Of course. He's had that place as long as I can remember. I'm surprised he's not retired by now. Or dead."

"Looks older than Methuselah, but he's still pretty spry. Anyway, he said Mrs. Webster brought in a bunch of dry cleaning on Monday morning, including the dress she wore Saturday night to the reunion."

Nan pictured the crimson and cream silk flapper dress that had clung to Mary Lee's trim, toned body. "And?"

"And he says anytime Mrs. Webster wants special attention given to a stain, she puts a safety pin on it. There was a safety pin on that dress. She told old man Erskine that she'd spilled spaghetti sauce on it. He says she'd already worked at the stain a bit, trying to get it out, but it didn't seem like spaghetti sauce to him. He says it seemed more like a bloodstain."

"Are you trying to tell me that Mary Lee had a *bloodstain* on her dress? And nobody *noticed*?"

"Look at the picture of that dress in the class picture. Or the video. I understand Grant Kirby gave you a copy of it." He sounded a little miffed. "Erskine says it wasn't a big stain, more like a smear. She might not have even noticed it until later."

"Why didn't she just get rid of the dress?"

He laughed. "You're way ahead of me. She picked it up on Tuesday afternoon. And guess what? It's vanished into thin air. We searched very thoroughly, let me tell you. The garbage was picked up on Wednesday. I have two very unhappy men in gas masks out sifting through the county dump even as we speak. Leaving no disposable diaper unturned."

"What does Mary Lee say about the dress?"

"Mrs. Webster isn't saying anything at all, about the dress or the murders or whether it looks like rain. Under strict orders from Jake Moroney."

"That's his job, Brian. Protecting his client." It would be interesting to meet Jake Moroney. The really successful criminal attorneys had an aura to them, a sense of cockiness that dissipated into eternal weariness as you worked your way down the legal daisy chain to the PDs who handled nasty and pointless street crimes. "But why are you worried?"

"You know," he said, "one of the reasons I left Detroit was because I was sick of politics getting mixed up in my work. So how does it happen that I'm here in burb-land, trying to find evidence that the mayor's wife committed murder?"

"Just lucky?" Nan suggested.

"That's me." He hesitated a moment. "You may have forgotten this, what with the head conk and all, but we talked about dinner tonight, you and me."

"I hadn't forgotten," Nan told him. A date with a cop? It would take more than a knock on the noggin to push such incongruity out of her head. "But I've got a kind of conflict. My mother's out in the kitchen making every kind of comfort food I ever liked." Like rice pudding with cinnamon and raisins. "Could we maybe make it tomorrow?"

"You bet," he told her. "Talk to you later."

She hung up, lay back, and considered what Brian had told her. Somehow it just didn't feel right. For starters, why would Mary Lee bother to kill Brenda? The Websters had tons of money, and Jim had already been paying Brenda for twenty years.

True, Mary Lee *had* attacked Nan, intending to reduce her to an obituary note in the Stanford alumni magazine. But that attack had come at the end of a wildly jumbled week, when everyone was pretty thoroughly wiped out.

Back up. Could Mary Lee have somehow learned that Brenda was also taking money from Edwin Crosby? That *Edwin* was really Ryan's father? That Brenda wasn't merely a blackmailer, but a *dishonest* blackmailer? That made more sense. Blackmailers got murdered all the time. From an actuarial viewpoint, the field probably had a mortality rate to rival inner-city gang members and the folks who scrub out melted-down nuclear plants.

Jim had paid without complaint for years. He was a businessman, a no-nonsense kind of guy with money to spare. What if *Jim* had found out Brenda was also bleeding Edwin?

Nah. Jim wouldn't kill Brenda for that. He'd cut her off, for damn sure, and he might find some behind-the-scenes way to punish her: get her fired, have her house repo'd, or something. But he wouldn't risk his political career by killing her at a public gathering.

His political career. Now *seriously* compromised by Mary Lee's transgressions. But Jim would weather the storm, Nan was sure. People in Spring Hill would be sympathetic, though he might not make it to Congress for a while.

Time would pass, however. People would forget. Jim wasn't permanently damaged politically, just slowed down. Hell, he wasn't even forty yet. If Jim Webster wanted to go on to higher office, he'd ultimately succeed. In fact, Mary Lee's best hope might be to have Jim become president and then pardon her.

Mom came in then with a tray. "Ranger cookies, dear."

Nan grinned as she took one. It was *years* since she'd

had Mom's ranger cookies, which featured the unlikely combination of oatmeal, Rice Krispies, and coconut. These were still tantalizingly warm.

"I was going to run down to Shop & Save," Mom announced. "I was thinking maybe some nice loin lamb chops for dinner?"

Nan smiled appreciatively. Perhaps her mother really *was* ready for an armistice. "Sounds terrific," Nan told her. "I may go over and see Ryan for a few minutes. I wanted to ask him something about Brenda."

"Oh, for heaven's sake. Haven't you had enough of this whole bloody business?" June Robinson chided.

Nan bristled, then flashed back to the moment when she'd first opened the door of her car, first seen the bloody front of Brenda's white satin dress. All that vivid crimson fluid drenching the rich, shiny fabric, the rhinestones sparkling amidst the gore . . .

That was it!

She sat bolt upright. "Mary Lee *couldn't* have killed Brenda," she told her mother excitedly. "Because of the blood."

Mom frowned. "What on earth are you talking about?"

"Mary Lee's incredibly squeamish." Nan reported her stop in the Webster kitchen while Pam was slicing cantaloupe for her younger brother and sister, Pam's accidentally cut finger, and the kids' reaction to the injury.

"None of them were freaked out by the blood," she said. "In fact, they were kind of blasé. But they were all definite about Mary Lee. Mom, she passes out on her kids when they get hurt, and a Supermom like Mary Lee would *never* do that if she could avoid it. You'd expect her to be setting their broken arms, not sitting with her head between her knees."

"She might not have intended to stab Brenda," Mom pointed out, clearly not convinced. She concentrated for a moment. "Though you're right, it really doesn't seem in character for Mary Lee. Even if blood didn't bother her. I'd expect something tidier, something nice and neat, like a little rat poison in the Midol."

A half-forgotten conversation popped into Nan's mind. "Wait a minute!"

Mom sat down and took a cookie. "What?"

"Mary Lee got her period at the reunion, I just remembered. At some point that night, I was walking into the john and Mary Lee was just leaving, with one of the Harrigan twins. Cory Harrigan Whatever-it-is-now."

"Mathews," Mom said automatically. Trust her to catch the irrelevant detail.

Nan went on. "Mary Lee was complaining about her period being early." What she'd said, actually, was that her little friend had showed up early.

"So?"

Nan told her about the bloodstain on Mary Lee's dress. "If she got her period at the reunion, she'd be embarrassed, maybe even lie about the stain to old Mr. Erskine. And it explains why it looked like a bloodstain to him. It *was* a bloodstain. It even explains why she'd get rid of the dress if the stain didn't come out entirely. I've done that myself."

"Good heavens, Nan!"

Nan's mind was racing. "But it doesn't explain what the key to Brenda's hotel room was doing in her purse. That doesn't fit at all."

"I'm totally lost, Nan." Mom started to stand up. "Maybe I should just run on down to Shop & Save . . ."

"No, wait. Let me bounce this off you for a second. If Mary Lee didn't put that key in her purse, then somebody else did, probably after the reunion. The cops looked in everybody's bags, at least perfunctorily. They practically slit the lining open on mine. And Jim was being so egalitarian that night, he would have insisted they search his wife and himself."

"Would Mary Lee have put away a handbag without emptying it and checking its contents?" Mom asked, clearly aghast at the notion. Mom had over a hundred purses and sometimes changed bags several times in the course of a day.

"No, of course not," Nan agreed. "I can tell that by just looking at the way her closet's organized. On the other hand, if somebody wanted to frame her, that would be a nice place to stick it. The bag she carried the night of the murder."

"Somebody like who?" Mom asked.

"Her husband, for one."

"Now, Nan, surely you don't think . . ."

"I think he made a big point of coming to tell me a lot of stuff that there was no reason to blab about," Nan said. "That his lawyer would be *furious* to know he told me. I don't understand why, and that makes me suspicious."

"You were *born* suspicious," Mom noted, taking another cookie.

"Okay, then. Say it *wasn't* Jim. There seems to be a lot of traffic through the Webster house. Wally Sheehan and I were there the other night, and they may have entertained others since last Saturday. I remember Mary Lee mentioning some meeting in the living room earlier in the week. And people stop by with papers for Jim and stuff. That happened twice just the night I was there. Plus the kids and all their friends. And whoever takes care of their house-cleaning and yardwork."

Nan looked at her mother glumly. "So anybody could have planted that key. Assuming she didn't put it there herself. If you were going to hide something in somebody's house, hoping it would be found later but not right away, where would you put it, Mom?"

"Well, I certainly wouldn't put it anyplace as obvious as a handbag! No woman would." Mom hesitated a moment. "Unless she wanted it to seem as if a man had hidden it."

Nan grinned. "That's pretty devious, Mom. You're good at this. But it seems more likely to me that a man actually *did* hide it. But who? Jim?"

"Why would he try to implicate his own wife? That's nonsense."

"I suppose it's too much to hope that Frank Finney delivers groceries," Nan said. She couldn't believe how much she disliked the produce manager, having no real reason for her distaste other than the fact that he'd snubbed her. She thought for a moment. "Mom? Do you have some clothes to go to the dry cleaner's?"

Nan drove slowly and aimlessly down the familiar streets of Spring Hill. Here in the Heights there was a timelessness, a sense of serenity, a feeling that whatever might happen in greater Spring Hill or Chicago or the world beyond didn't really matter a whit.

A few children played on wide front lawns, but for the most part there weren't many people out. The weather was hot and muggy, the kind of air you could almost physically bisect with a sweep of the hand. Gathering gray clouds in the northwest signaled what might—if she was lucky—turn into a magnificent summer thunderstorm.

Nan loved midwestern electrical storms. There was nothing like them at home in L.A. What rain came to Southern California arrived only in winter, storms that had crossed the Pacific Ocean for thousands of miles picking up water and fury. When they struck the mainland, they were driving and relentless, flooding roads, washing out gullies, triggering horrendous mud slides. Those storms were long, gray, monotonous. They went on for days.

But the thunderstorms of Nan's youth could spring up in an hour's time, gathering intensity and then launching wild, fantastic displays of thunder and lightning. The skies would be purple and royal blue against stunning streaks of lightning, the claps of thunder would send pets skittering beneath beds and children yowling for the comfort of their mother's arms. Hundred-year-old oaks toppled.

Tornado watches turned into tornado warnings, and everybody waited for the eerie yellow-green atmospheric thickening that meant a twister might actually sweep through. Dorothy and Toto had plenty of company around Chicago. When Nan was seven a twister had swept through Columbia and leveled an elementary school, half a dozen houses, and a Dunkinburger.

She deliberately kept the car windows open and air-conditioning off as she drove. In a few days she'd be back in the L.A. summer smog, these sensations already foreign and removed. But for now she wanted the full sense of this place.

She made a final turn and wound up close to where she had begun her drive, at the little enclave of old stores that had served the Heights since the turn of the century. A dusty hardware store with endless bins of nails and screws, a drugstore where the pharmacist knew everybody's name and ailments, Shop & Save where prices were higher than Jewel but children could be sent with lists of last-minute shopping needs and both delivery and monthly billing were available.

Beside the grocery store stood Erskine dry cleaners. Nan wondered fleetingly why Mary Lee brought her cleaning here, when there were other, more modern cleaners nearer to her home. But as she walked in the door, she understood perfectly. This, too, was a home of sorts.

Martin Erskine was stooped and frail, but his lined old face broke into a wide, gold-toothed smile at the sight of Nan.

"Little Nancy Robinson!" he exclaimed. "What a treat for tired old eyes you are, my dear. Your mother told me you were coming in for a visit this week. I'm sorry about your terrible experience last night."

Was there anyone in the county unaware of what had happened at Potawatomi, of how stupid Nan had been?

"I figured it would be fun to go to my high school reunion," Nan said, "only it turned out to have more excitement than I bargained for."

He shook his head. "Such a business. Forty-seven years

I've lived in this town, and never have I heard such a thing. A beautiful young girl struck down that way." He shook his head again. "Such a business. And you were the one found the poor thing, I hear."

"It was horrible," Nan admitted.

She spread out Mom's dry cleaning on the counter, and the next few minutes were spent writing up the order. Mr. Erskine's sharp eye examined every garment carefully as he catalogued and tagged the clothing, noticing a missing button here, a strained seam there, a smear of dirt near a pant-leg hem.

"I understand there was a stain on Mary Lee Webster's beautiful red-flowered dress," Nan remarked casually when the order was written up. "Detective Delahanty mentioned it."

Mr. Erskine looked distressed. "I would never want to get that lovely little Mrs. Webster in trouble," he said. "So lovely she is whenever she's in here, friendly and polite, not like so many these days. But when I heard what happened to you, oh, my. And my son, he said, Pop, you've got to tell them, no matter who gets hurt. And now, who knows?"

"The detective said you thought it might have been a bloodstain."

Martin Erskine seemed to teeter on the cusp between professional pride and customer loyalty. Professional pride won out. "All my life I've been in the cleaning business," he said. "First the laundry in Chicago, then out here with the first dry cleaning plant in the county. Old I may be, but my eyes are as sharp as the day I was born. Mostaccioli, she said it was. A customer tells me something, I'm not going to contradict her, but your tomato-based Italian sauce has grease in it, and there's no way to mistake it for your bloodstain."

"It was a bloodstain, then?"

He nodded authoritatively.

"And she had it marked?"

He nodded again. "Mrs. Webster's very particular, always pinning problem areas so we can spot things properly."

"Were there other things she'd pinned for spotting when she came in Monday?"

Mr. Erskine thought a moment. "A button missing on one of her husband's sport coats. Some iced tea on a blouse. And she hadn't marked them, but there were some small stains on another suit of his."

"What kind of stains?" Nan asked.

Mr. Erskine shrugged. "Hard to know for sure on a dark gray wool. Coke, she thought it probably was."

Jim Webster had worn a dark gray suit to the reunion. "And the stain on her dress. Do you remember where on the dress that stain was?"

He frowned. "The policeman asked the same thing. It was the skirt."

"I don't suppose you recall if it was the front or the back?"

"That dress with its cut, no zipper and such, the front and back were a lot alike," he said after a moment's hesitation. "I couldn't tell you for sure."

"There wasn't a label?"

He gave his glittery smile. "Mrs. Webster, she cuts the labels out of all her clothes. Scratchy, she says they are. But such beautiful things she has, you can tell they're always fine goods."

"So the stain might have been on the back of the dress?"

He nodded and shrugged. "Maybe."

Nan hesitated. She had contemplated phraseology carefully. "Mr. Erskine, do you think there's a chance that the stain might have been feminine blood?"

He looked away, a flush rising from his throat. "It's possible," he said, with obvious embarrassment. He hastily gathered the clothing Nan had just brought in, turned, and placed the articles in a bin. When he turned back, he was not so pink, but the subject was quite clearly closed.

"These will be ready Monday morning, tell your lovely mother," Martin Erskine said. "And you have a safe trip back to California, my dear."

There was nobody home at the Methodist parsonage. Nan started back toward her mother's, then on impulse made a right turn and went out to the Websters' house.

An earnest-looking young man in his late twenties swung open the massive oak front door. Pale brown hair, already thinning. Gray-tinted lenses in expensive metal frames. Charcoal slacks and a sport shirt, though he'd be more at home in a full suit, preferably vested. His eyes opened wide behind the glasses as Nan introduced herself and asked to see Jim.

"I'll see if he's available," the young man said neutrally, then closed the heavy wooden door firmly in Nan's face, like some marginally trained *Masterpiece Theatre* servant, off to present a calling card on a silver tray.

Moments later Jim Webster himself swung the door open.

"Nan! Come on in, for goodness sakes. Mac shouldn't have left you standing out here. Shouldn't you be home resting? I didn't even realize you were out of the hospital."

"I'm fine, really," Nan said, stepping into the front hall. "You've had a lot of people by?"

"I'll say!" Jim shook his head. "All sorts of media riffraff and ghouls. Neighborhood kids just ringing the bell and hiding in the bushes. Not to mention the phone calls. I had to bring in one of my secretaries to take messages." Life could be *such* a bitch.

He led Nan past the entrance to the living room. She could see Mac and a couple of other men off to the right, earnestly huddled around the big stone coffee table. "Back in a few minutes," he called to them, without breaking stride.

He did stop in the kitchen, where he pulled a Diet Coke out of the refrigerator. "Something to drink?" he asked, taking a swig from the can. "Soda? Beer?" When Nan shook her head, he led her out onto the patio.

Flowers bloomed gaudy and cheerful in their terra-cotta pots, oblivious to the crisis in the big troubled house. At the far end of the patio, the sliding glass doors to the master bedroom were closed, the inside curtains tightly drawn.

"How's Mary Lee holding up?" Nan asked softly when they were seated.

Jim Webster shook his head. "She's in shock, Nan. So am I, for that matter. So are we all. I'm sure she has no idea what happened, what she did last night. The doctor gave her some sedatives, and she's been resting most of the day."

"I think we're all in shock," Nan agreed. "How are the kids handling it?"

He winced. "I don't know. I'm not sure I even know how to tell. Jamie, of course, he's fourteen and a kid that age doesn't want you to think he has any feelings at all, anyway. Karen's been crying and crying, holed up in her room ever since Mary Lee came home. I go to talk to her, and she just tells me it's all a horrible lie and to go away."

There was probably no good age at which to have one's mother arrested for assault and suspected of multiple murder. But twelve would undoubtedly be one of the worst. "The poor little thing. What about Pam?"

He smiled. "Pam's a trouper," he said. "She's a real rock, taking care of Karen as much as anybody can right now, and keeping things moving around here. We don't have any family here, of course. My folks are both dead, and you know about Mary Lee's mom."

Nan could hear a vacuum cleaner faintly humming in the wing where the kids' rooms and spare bedrooms were. "Pam's a very special girl. I'm real impressed with her, Jim."

"She's just like Mary Lee," he agreed, then winced again. "Tough, I mean, and smart and competent. It's hard for me to realize she'll be starting college in another year."

"When I talked to her the other night, she said she'd like to go back east. I gave her a big pitch for Stanford."

Jim shrugged his shoulders. "Who knows? Illinois was plenty good enough for her parents, but she's got a stack of bulletins from the Ivy League two feet tall." He looked as if he wanted to cry. "First, she's got to get through this mess. We all do." He offered a shadow of a smile. "Jake Moroney's a top lawyer, best of the best. I keep telling Mary Lee we'll take care of her, but she's so withdrawn, I'm not sure I'm always getting through."

Nan offered a low sympathetic moan. This was awkward as hell. Why had she come?

Jim leaned forward and spoke softly and confidentially. "I'm worried about her, Nan. This may sound crazy, but I'm afraid she might do something . . ." His voice trailed off.

Mary Lee had already done plenty, it seemed to Nan.

"You mean," she murmured, ". . . self-destructive?"

He nodded. "I hate myself for even thinking it, but she's just so terribly depressed. I'm keeping her medication where she can't get at it herself. She tosses and turns and moans in there. Naturally we're keeping a close watch on her."

"Do you suppose I could see her for just a moment?"

He frowned, then shook his head. "She's asleep, Nan. And Jake Moroney says not to let her talk to anybody but family, anyway. We both know he wouldn't want you talking to her. Sorry."

Nan stood up. "I should run along, anyway, Jim. Is Pam around here somewhere?"

"Of course," he said, rising. "Let me go find her."

Nan stared at the closed glass doors to the master bedroom and wondered about Mary Lee. Jim returned quickly with Pam. The girl looked lost and frightened. Without thinking, Nan opened her arms, and just as instinctively Pam Webster fell into them. After a moment, Nan nodded to Jim, who nodded back and slipped away. She stood holding his eldest daughter for several minutes, feeling the girl tremble, unable to tell whether or not she was actually crying. Poor kid. She'd led a charmed life for sixteen years, and now all her markers were being called in at once.

When Pam finally broke away, she was dry-eyed but looked definitely embarrassed. For the first time, her resemblance to Mary Lee really hurt. She was barefoot in a pair of baggy blue shorts with a Harvard T-shirt knotted at her waist.

"I'm sorry," Pam said. "I didn't mean . . ." She turned away. "And, oh, God, I'm sorry about what my mom . . ."

"This has to be just awful for you." Nan smiled gently. "But I thought I'd put in one last plug for Stanford before I left town." When it came time for college, Pam would surely opt to go far, far away.

Pam smiled weakly as Nan led her over to a wrought-iron settee and sat beside her. For half an hour they talked colleges. Pam seemed pleased to discuss something besides the realities of the present. But she did finally mention her concern over her sister Karen, barricaded in her bedroom with a five-pound box of Fannie May chocolates.

"At least she won't starve," Nan told her. "I'd say to just check on her now and then, and when she's ready, she'll come out."

"I suppose." Pam sighed and looked around the patio. "I guess I ought to cover up this furniture. It looks like rain."

"Let me help," Nan suggested. Pam brought out heavy canvas covers and they bustled about, both pleased by the artificial sense of doing something important.

When they were finished, Nan looked at her watch. Four-thirty, but the sky was so dark, it might have been winter. "I should be going," she said. "Is there anything I can do?"

"I wish there were," Pam sighed. "Thanks for coming by. Mom's friends have called and come by, but I don't know what to say to them, and they stare at me with these awful looks on their faces. It should have been worse with you, on account of . . . but somehow it was almost easier."

"You're keeping a close eye on your mom, I know. Do you suppose she's still sleeping?"

Pam raised one shoulder in a half-shrug. "Let's check," she suggested, crossing the patio and cautiously sliding open the door. "I haven't looked in for a couple hours."

A rush of cool air came through the opened doorway. The master suite was air-conditioned to Alaskan frigidity.

"Mom?" Pam whispered as she pushed aside the curtains and held them for Nan to follow her. "You awake, Mom?"

In the chilly darkened cavern, Mary Lee lay in the absolute center of her king-size bed in the fetal position. She had kicked the white fur cover to the ground. She wore a lightweight cotton nightgown and was covered only by pale, lace-trimmed sheets, but sweat glistened on her face, shoulder, and arm. Her breathing was slow and shallow.

Mary Lee looked pitiful, suddenly and irreversibly old. There were bags under her eyes, furrows on her face. Her skin tone was ashen, and her hair drab and lifeless.

Pam whispered again softly to her mother. Mary Lee shifted position slightly, but showed no signs of rousing. Nan had a sudden, urgent sense that Mary Lee was in great danger. Irrational? She wondered.

"Leave her," Nan whispered to Pam. "Don't try to wake her up if she's resting all right."

They retreated to the patio and Nan rummaged in her bag. She scribbled on the back of one of her business cards. "This is the phone number at my mother's house," she said. "I want you to call me there anytime, day or night, if you need help. Or if your mom does. This may sound strange, after everything that's happened, but I'm worried about her."

"Me, too," Pam admitted. "But what can I do?"

Nan hugged the girl's shoulders. "Hang tight. Is there any way I can call you without having to bother your dad?" That was neutral enough.

Pam smiled. "Sure. I've got a line in my room. And a message machine, in case I'm not within earshot."

Mary Lee as a teenager had also had her own phone line, Nan remembered. Pam wrote down the number, then led Nan back through the oppressive silence of the confused and troubled house. Jim and his cohorts had disappeared, and the living room sat empty.

As Nan drove away, she felt as if knives were turning inside her.

CHAPTER 18

Nan shivered as thunder rumbled in the distance. She still wasn't quite sure what to make of her irrational, frantic worry about Mary Lee's safety. The woman had tried to *kill* her, for God's sake. But Nan was certain there was more going on here than anyone yet realized.

She had used up her quota of bonehead moves for several years to come in last night's episode, and she knew the doctors would be aghast to learn that she wasn't home safe in her own bed. Her mother would not have approved either, but her mother had finally collapsed in exhaustion and would probably sleep for the next fifteen hours. And if Mom *did* happen to wake up, Nan had left her a note.

As for Brian Delahanty, she could only imagine his outrage and incredulity. She didn't think she could explain her fears to him, and she wasn't sure he'd want to hear them anyway.

She had left her car several blocks away from the Webster house, camouflaged in a cluster of vehicles parked outside a house where a party was apparently in progress. Now, dressed in jeans and a dark T-shirt, she walked toward the Webster home with an easygoing nonchalance suggesting to any casual observer that she was simply an unfamiliar neighbor out for her evening constitutional.

She approached the Webster home, walking briskly up the hedge along the edge of the property, past the closed curtains of the living room, and into a four-foot-wide walkway, a secondary and largely unused route to the backyard. Security at the Webster house was surprisingly lax: no electronics, no watchdog, only a simple five-foot wooden fence Nan was able to scale on her second try. Had she not been recently hospitalized, she assured herself, she could have done it the first time.

Once technically in the backyard, Nan moved quickly along the outside wall of the master bedroom wing. Light flowed through the open curtains in what she believed to be Mary Lee's craft room, and she ducked as she passed the window. Then she stopped and sneaked a quick peek inside. A gooseneck lamp burned on the table by the unfinished dollhouse parquet floor, and the door to the hallway stood open. The room was empty. The next stretch of wall was blank, the outside of the bedroom itself.

As Nan cautiously began to round the corner of the building onto the patio, a jagged bolt of lightning suddenly turned the sky purple and illuminated the entire backyard. She jerked back behind the corner of the wall. The thunder that followed was deafening and almost instantaneous. Any moment now, it was going to *pour*.

A single outside light burned on the far side of the patio, near the door to the kitchen. The kitchen itself was dimly lit, and she could see through it to the family room, where Mayor Jim Webster sat in a big leather recliner watching TV. The kids were nowhere in sight, but there were lights behind closed curtains and blinds in the opposite wing where their bedrooms were located.

So far, so good.

When she'd helped Pam Webster put waterproof covers over the patio tables and chair earlier in the day, Nan had noted the proximity of a circular table to the sliding door leading into Mary Lee and Jim's bedroom. Now, if her luck held, she'd be able to sit in relatively dry comfort beneath that table and keep watch through the curtain she had pulled aside on her way out of the bedroom.

The curtain remained as she had left it, open a few inches. Inside the bedroom, a single low-wattage lamp burned on Mary Lee's bedside table, with another faint light coming from inside the open door to the bathroom. That light also glowed softly through the high bathroom window.

Nan could see Mary Lee huddled in the center of the bed, motionless.

The table she had planned to use as cover was farther away from the doorway than she remembered, and raindrops were starting to spatter noisily onto the tile. Nan felt certain that any moment the sky would open and drench her thoroughly. She didn't hesitate. She picked up the round wrought-iron table, cover and all, and hauled it to within a foot of the curtain opening in the window.

Then she ducked underneath the dark green waterproof cover, moments before rain began to seriously rattle on the patio. The loud individual drops pounding on the covered glass above her sounded almost like pellets of hail.

Once beneath the table, she realized that the space was far more cramped than she had anticipated. It was going to be a real challenge to spend any length of time under there without emerging as a permanently twisted pretzel.

She couldn't sit upright without bending her neck at a grievously uncomfortable angle, and the central support curved out into four wide-spreading legs. After much wiggling, Nan determined that her best position was circling the central support core, resting on one elbow. The opaque green cover didn't fall to the ground, tablecloth fashion, but was snugly fitted in a tailored cylinder. After a bit of experimentation she realized there was no way to keep the cover lifted without getting even more drenched than was already inevitable.

And drenched she was. Cascades of water washed across the patio tiles with little regard for aboveground obstacles, and Nan could feel that her jeans and shoes were already thoroughly saturated.

Now, though, came the real test. How could she see into the damn bedroom? She dug in the fanny pack that rested on her abdomen and pulled out an old pocket knife she'd found in the odds-and-ends drawer on her mother's back porch. Opening a blade, she made a twelve-inch slit in the cover.

Now, finally, she could see. But not much. She could see only part of the bed, and that at such a low angle, only the curve of Mary Lee's hip and legs was visible.

With a sudden loud *swoosh*, the sky opened. Rain began pouring onto the patio in heavy, relentless sheets. Which provided, Nan noted grimly, both good news and bad news. The good news was that nobody in the house was likely to notice her hovering under the table. The bad news was that she might well drown.

Time passed. Ten minutes, fifteen, half an hour. She made it a game not to check her watch until she thought at least ten minutes had passed, and after an hour, she was getting pretty good at it. As the minutes crawled past, her mind wandered over the events of the past few days.

The more Nan thought about Mary Lee's attack on her, the more perplexing it became. As was the original crime. Mary Lee was a hemaphobe. Would she really be able to plunge a brass dagger repeatedly into Brenda Blaine's unconscious body? A body gushing blood?

It seemed almost impossible.

But what if Mary Lee hadn't killed Brenda, and suspected that her *husband* had? Would she confront Jim with her suspicions? Not necessarily. She might not even confront him if she were certain. Confrontation didn't seem to be a big part of Mary Lee's style.

But she'd damn sure want to tidy things up. And in the process of that tidying, it took no leap of imagination whatsoever for Nan to envision Mary Lee smothering Alvina McReedy. Mary Lee *had* known, in her faked phone call, just which window belonged to Brenda's grandmother. And how to approach that room unnoticed at night.

Suddenly Nan's attention snapped back to the present.

Her view of the bedroom was obstructed by a pair of

dark denim-clad legs. In the racket of the rain, she hadn't even heard anyone approach.

Now she held her breath as she saw and heard the glass sliding door open, admitting the legs and whoever was attached to them. Then the door to the patio slid closed again.

Nan considered quickly. She was certain she hadn't been observed. It was still pouring rain, and it seemed unlikely that an intruder wouldn't somehow react to another unexpected trespasser who got in the way.

Nothing inside the bedroom seemed changed. Mary Lee still lay in the same position on the bed, and the intruder had vanished from Nan's line of vision.

Time to get wet, it seemed. Nan slid out from under the table and flexed her arms and legs. She'd been contorted under the table long enough to send showers of prickly surprise through sections of her body as she twisted, trying to return normal sensation to her various appendages. The rain still fell steadily, though the occasional sudden deluges were less frequent.

She moved right up to the glass door, but the intruder was no longer visible. A wet black rain slicker lay on the carpet just inside the door, and damp footprints led in the general direction of the bathroom.

Nan looked around. The bathroom window was too high to look through without standing on something. She pulled the waterproof cover off one of the sturdy wrought-iron chairs that matched the table she'd been crouching under, then carried the chair over to the window.

She stood on the chair, balancing against the wall, and carefully lifted her head to peer into the bathroom. The room was empty, but water was thundering into the big square raised bathtub beneath the skylight in the center of the room. Through the window she could hear the water as well as see it, differentiate that aquatic rumble from the downpour that surrounded her. Already the tub was more than half-full.

Huh?

Nan got down off the chair and went back around to the doorway. Nothing seemed changed. Mary Lee still lay in bed, the slicker lay inside the door, and nobody else was in sight.

What to do? Nan quickly circled the patio, jumping in terror when a sudden thunderclap exploded almost simultaneously with a heart-stoppingly close bolt of lightning. Through the kitchen window she could see into the family room. Jim Webster remained sprawled in his recliner in front of the television, oblivious to the storm outside and the intruder within.

So whatever else was happening in that master suite, it seemed unlikely that the mayor was running himself a tub. What *was* going on?

Nan returned to the window in the sliding door, and her heart jumped.

Mary Lee's bed was empty, her cotton nightgown discarded on the floor beside the bed.

Nan jumped back onto her chair, miscalculated, slid off onto the slick patio tiles, and twisted an ankle in the process. *Damn!* She stepped tentatively on the ankle, decided it would have to work. Like a good athlete, she would play through the pain. Then she climbed laboriously back up on the chair and looked again into the bathroom.

What she saw filled her with horror.

Wally Sheehan was lowering Mary Lee's limp, naked body into the nearly overflowing bathtub.

Now he picked up a slim silver object, wiped it carefully with a washcloth, and placed it in her right hand. He lifted her left hand out of the water and moved the hands together. He was wearing racing gloves, and she suddenly recognized the silver object as one of Mary Lee's Exacto knives from the craft room.

Nan jumped down off the chair, felt a howl of protest from her ankle, and stumbled around to the sliding patio door. She felt as if she were moving in super-slow motion. She pulled the door open, giving herself a second to close it and turn the lock. Then she ran across the white carpet and darted into the bathroom, yelling as she went.

"Stop!" she screamed. "Stop!"

Raw panic filled Wally's pale freckled face.

He abruptly let go of Mary Lee and frantically looked around for an exit. Nan was blocking the door into the bedroom, and he hesitated only a moment before opening a side door and fleeing into one of the huge walk-through closets.

At that moment, Nan saw Mary Lee's unconscious body slide under the deep bathwater.

She hobbled up the steps to the tub and stuck her hands in Mary Lee's armpits, pulled the unconscious woman out of the water. Mary Lee was slippery and slack, but at least she wasn't terribly heavy. Nan twisted the flaccid body to hang jackknifed over the tub's edge, head down. She pulled the plug.

Then she followed Wally. By the time she reached the bedroom he was at the sliding door to the patio, pulling on the handle, holding the black rain slicker he had earlier abandoned on the floor.

He turned and looked back at her, clearly panicked, trying to weigh his options, realizing how limited they had suddenly become.

Without thinking about the absurdity of her action, Nan raced across the room and jumped upon his back.

They were fairly evenly matched in height, but Wally had fifty pounds on her, two good ankles, and the added advantage of terror. He bucked like an obstreperous bronco, and sent Nan flying back across the room, smashing into Mary Lee's prized dollhouse. He abandoned the sliding door to the patio and headed now toward the interior door leading into the house.

A bolt of lightning brightened the room as Nan stumbled to her feet and looked frantically around for some kind of weapon. The massive dollhouse, knocked off its table, was too heavy to lift. But there was a standing lamp beside it. She yanked the lamp from its socket and swung it at Wally's head.

The lamp glanced off his shoulder, and he turned toward her again. His eyes were desperate and feral. He gave Nan another shove that knocked her crashing back into the wall.

The door suddenly opened, and Jim Webster stood framed in the light from the hallway. Nan saw him look swiftly from Nan to Wally and back again, saw decision move into his eyes as he strode toward Wally, reaching for the small man.

But Wally was fast. He backed away, banging into one of Mary Lee's two tall crystal curio cabinets. The cabinet rattled, shook from side to side.

Wally bounced off the wall, momentarily losing his balance, stumbling backward again. Nan backed away, slipping across the room, trying to find a phone. 911, she kept thinking, as if that would help right now. As if anything would.

Now Jim lunged forward, tripped on the fallen lamp, and grabbed the side of the nearest cabinet for support. It leaned toward Wally, who caught the cabinet and pushed it away. Then the heavy piece of furniture overbalanced and smashed into its twin.

An incredible, deafening crash sent broken glass flying in every direction as both cabinets and their contents exploded into the room. As Nan instinctively ducked beside the bed, she saw Wally leap backward out of the path of the cabinets, eyes wide, face blanched in naked terror.

In the center of the room, Jim Webster appeared to dance in slow motion for a moment. He teetered gingerly back and forth, eyes wide. Then fell forward, landing first on his knees squarely in the midst of the wreckage, giving an anguished yelp as he struck glass. He thrust his hands forward to break the fall, then screamed again as shards of broken glass sliced into them. He lifted his hands involuntarily, slipped, then landed face down with another horrible scream. Nan watched bright red splotches of blood fleck Mary Lee's perfect white carpet all around him.

She rose from where she'd been cowering behind the bed, moved forward slowly. Wally stood paralyzed against the opposite wall, watching in horror.

Jim moved slightly and a sudden torrent of vivid scarlet blood poured onto the rug from underneath his head. His body gave two shuddering convulsions, the second smaller than the first, then lay utterly still in its spreading crimson pool.

Wally finally moved.

He raced to the doorway and ran down the hall. Nan debated following him, decided there was no point. She looked at her heavy sneakers, then stepped tentatively into the sea of broken glass. Leaning down, she gently lifted Jim's right shoulder. With effort, she pushed him up onto his side.

Blood continued to drain out of his throat, and now she could see what had caused the ghastly hemorrhage.

A six-inch chunk of glass, roughly an inch in diameter, stuck at an angle out of the base of his throat. Nan lowered him slowly to the ground again.

By the time the operator answered her 911 call, the bloodstain had stopped growing.

Brian Delahanty had been to grislier crime scenes. He'd seen more extensive gore, broader splatter patterns, larger numbers of bodies, more disgustingly horrific settings.

But he'd never encountered anything that offered quite this level of drama.

There was the lifeless husk of the town's mayor lying drenched in blood amid a sea of glittering glass shards on what had obviously been a spotless white carpet.

There were paramedics working on the naked body of the mayor's wife in a bathroom that looked like something from a bad miniseries on the squalid lives of the tacky rich.

There was Wally Sheehan, sobbing in handcuffs at the

kitchen table under the wide but watchful eyes of young Jack Pukowski, who'd seen more violence in the past week than he might have expected to encounter in an entire career on the Spring Hill police force.

There was Nan Robinson, a blood smear on her cheek and some nasty-looking cuts on her bare arms, soaked to the skin, and shivering uncontrollably.

And the whole damn thing was punctuated by a thunderstorm that had already washed out a couple of roads in town and turned the front lawn of the Webster residence into a swamp.

So much for the quiet life in suburbia.

Four hours later, Delahanty sat in his office and drummed his fingers on the desk as he listened to Nan tell her story one more time. It was just ridiculous enough to be true. But there were some strange holes in it, too, some odd inconsistencies in what she'd observed. He wondered if she noticed them as well.

"I really expected Jim to try something," Nan was saying, "after the big song and dance he gave me about worrying that Mary Lee was suicidal. And after he'd made such a point of telling me the whole story about Brenda claiming he was Ryan's father." She frowned. Once the paramedics pronounced her cuts superficial and bandaged them, Delahanty had allowed Pukowski to drive her home to change clothes before taking her to the ER for an X ray of the ankle, now Ace-bandaged. The dressings on her arms were covered now by a long-sleeved shirt. "He was obviously up to something. Did you know already about him paying Brenda?"

Delahanty shook his head. "But we were about to start on his financial records. There are plenty of ways he could have covered up whatever he was paying her, of course. Ways you'd need a whole platoon of accountants to uncover. But if Mary Lee knew, she was the weak link."

"Still," Nan said thoughtfully, "that doesn't explain why

he came to me. I can see him maybe sending flowers, possibly even making a courtesy call to the hospital. But this went way beyond that, and he didn't mind having witnesses, either. I *knew* he was up to something. Guys like that never give you anything without a reason. And I just didn't trust him.

"You know what else doesn't make sense," Nan went on, "is when Jim first came into the bedroom, he didn't say anything. *Nothing.* Now think about this. If you think your wife is secure in the bedroom, sedated even, and you hear a noise from that wing, you can't exactly ignore it. So. You come into the bedroom, and number one, your sedated wife isn't there. Number two, there are two other people there, and they seem to be fighting. One of your business partners and some woman you barely know from California. What are you going to do?"

Delahanty gave her a look.

"He didn't say a *word*," Nan told him. "Nothing. Not *What's going on?* or *Where's Mary Lee?* or *Aren't you people lost?* He just went straight for Wally, in attack mode. Now, Jim Webster was a guy who could think fast when he had to. I could practically *see* him processing it all, warp speed, and then he cut out after Wally. *Attacked* Wally. He pretty much just ignored me."

"So you're saying . . . what?"

"That Jim *knew* Wally was in there. He didn't look a bit surprised to see him. *Me*, now, that was a surprise. But he was perfectly aware that Wally was in there, and he must have known why. They had to have planned it together."

"Webster sent Sheehan to kill his *wife*?"

"It would have cleared the slate, wouldn't it?" Nan asked thoughtfully. "We already knew Mary Lee attacked me, and it was pretty easy to extrapolate from that that she killed Alvina McReedy. The only death left to account for was Brenda, and you gave him the opening to pin that on her too, with the menstrual blood on her dress. Even though I *know* she couldn't have stabbed Brenda, because of her aversion to blood. Has there been any word from the hospital about Mary Lee's condition?"

"Just that she has about three times the prescribed dose of barbiturates in her system, and she's still out cold."

"Will she be all right?"

He smiled. "How are we defining *all right*? If you mean will she regain consciousness, they say yes, almost certainly. And there shouldn't be any lasting effects from the overdose. But you and I both know that Jake Moroney is *never* going to let her open her mouth in public again."

The phone rang and Delahanty picked it up. He listened a moment, then smiled, hung up, and rose. "Pleasant as this is, I'm afraid we'll have to cut it short, counselor. Sheehan's lawyer is here—local boy—and they say Sheehan's ready to talk."

"Can I come along?" Nan asked, matter-of-factly.

He threw back his head and laughed. "If you don't beat all! *No*, you can't come along. You're a *witness*, for Chrissake. Credit me with some intelligence, all right?"

"If you insist," she murmured, looking sideways at him. Looking downright sexy for somebody who'd been battered as much as she had in the past twenty-four hours.

"Look," he told her, coming around the desk and putting his hand lightly on her shoulder. "Go home. I'll get somebody to give you a ride. Get some sleep. And in the morning *maybe*—no promises, just maybe—I'll be able to tell you more. But right now I need to get downstairs. I smell a plea bargain in the air." He smiled at her. "And there's nothing that warms my heart like the prospect of a nice confession. It's the Catholic in me."

CHAPTER 19

Wally Sheehan was a natural talker.

Brian Delahanty remembered that from the night of Brenda Blaine's murder when Sheehan, the reunion chairman, had been almost impossible to shut up, blathering on and on about seating plans and classmate lists and just exactly what had been on the dinner menu.

He could be really funny, too. Delahanty remembered *that* from a city awards program for municipal employees—a function guaranteed by definition to be deadly—that Sheehan had raised almost to enjoyability by serving as emcee. God knows why, maybe a favor to the mayor.

But tonight he wasn't funny.

He sat at the table in the little conference room, looking like anything but the stereotypical jolly fat man. He looked more like something that had just washed up after six months at the bottom of Lake Michigan. He was in the clothing that he'd worn when he was arrested, rumpled blue jeans and a baggy navy T-shirt. Under the fluorescent light his hair looked bright orange and his skin greenish-white. Except around his eyes where the skin was still red and swollen from the blubbering he'd been doing.

Sheehan's lawyer was Ken Durant, who made a decent living handling DUIs and the occasional felony around Porter County. Durant was really pissed that Sheehan insisted on talking, but he couldn't stop him. His client had a compulsion to tell all, and that was that. Too darn bad, Mr. Defense Attorney.

"Don't be a fool," Durant told Wally one last time as they set up with the stenographer and the pot of fresh coffee and the audio- and videotape machinery silently whirring behind the one-way mirror on the wall. "You shouldn't be doing this."

"It's the only way, Kenny," Sheehan told the lawyer, rubbing his knuckles in his wiry red curls. "I *have* to. I've already *done* the fool bit." He looked across the table at Delahanty. "You know, I quit smoking years ago, but I sure could do with a cigarette right about now."

Delahanty turned to Tank Thiswell, who sat just inside the door wearing a faint leer and a cheap leather sport coat. Lance was still out at the Webster house, but it had seemed like begging for trouble to leave Thiswell unattended at a crime scene.

"Could you find Mr. Sheehan a pack of cigarettes, please?" Delahanty asked the junior detective cordially. He turned to Wally. "What's your brand preference?"

"What the hell," Wally answered. "Bring me Marlboro reds. And man, don't call me Mr. Sheehan. That sounds too much like my father. Thank God he isn't here to see this."

"No prob, Wally," Delahanty answered immediately.

Tank started to say something, thought better of it after a brief glower from Delahanty, and departed.

"Could we begin?" Delahanty asked. "Or would you rather wait for the cigarettes?" Cordial to the max.

Wally shrugged. "Let's do it."

A faint groan from the lawyer. Sorry, Shyster.

Delahanty did all the identifications, read him his rights again, let the lawyer go on record abhorring the entire session. Then he leaned back.

"Where would you like to start, Wally?" Like they were sitting around chewing the fat at the Lemon Twist Lounge. Where Sheehan was a serious regular. Too bad they couldn't bring a fifth in, loosen him up even more.

Wally shook his head. "I gotta go all the way back or

none of this will make sense." He ran his fingers through that kinky shock of hair. "Maybe it won't, anyway."

Tank came in with the cigarettes and an ashtray then. Delahanty held his breath, fearing the moment was lost, but Wally lit up, coughed once, then started over without hesitation.

"It was senior year in high school," he said, looking at the ashtray as intently as if it had next week's lottery numbers written on the bottom. "Spring break. Jim and I were gonna go up to my folks' place at Lake Lenore, up by the Wisconsin border. My family had a summer cottage. Mary Lee was on vacation with her family, so Jimbo was kind of at loose ends. Anyway, we promised my folks we'd be good little boys, and after all kinds of fussing they said we could stay there alone for a couple of days. What can go wrong, right? He's the fucking class president. So we had some tequila and Bud, and Jerry Leffingwell was gonna get us some grass. No big deal.

"Well, me and Jim get up there in the afternoon and it's pretty deserted, none of the folks in the other cottages are around. Perfect for a couple of guys screwing around and getting high. And then Jerry shows up. With his girlfriend and Brenda Blaine. Now, we were *not* expecting that. Thought it was gonna be just a boys'-night kind of thing. But right away I could see that Jim didn't mind a bit Brenda being there. He was kind of cagey, but I had the idea that maybe the two of them had spent some time together before. Made me wonder.

"So the first night we party big-time, everybody totally wasted. Jerry and his girlfriend Liza go off in one of the bedrooms kind of early on, and then it's Jim and Brenda and me, with Brenda coming on hard to Jimbo and him acting like he doesn't know what to do about it. Finally I take him aside and tell him, hey, man, I don't care, and for sure I won't go blabbing to Mary Lee. He seems all relieved, and the next thing I know he and Brenda are off in the other bedroom, and it's just me out on the couch. At *my* family's place."

He smiled slightly. "But that was okay. I just kept drinking and smoking reefer and man, I didn't care. I was a party animal, you know? So morning comes and everybody comes out, and it all starts over all again. Brenda's wearing Jimbo's football sweatshirt, and it comes to her knees and looks like that's *all* she's wearing. Music's blasting, and breakfast is tequila sunrises—big jokes about that—and the girls had pills, too. I think the shit was Brenda's, actually. Jerry used to get his stuff from her, I know that. Day two goes on in the same general vein, and by late afternoon I'm passed out and God knows what the rest of them are doing.

"Except then in the middle of the night Jimbo wakes me up and he's all panicked. *Totally* freaked. Liza's OD'd on tequila and reds. And I don't mean she's had too much, I mean she's stone-cold dead like it happened hours ago but Jerry was too wasted to notice. She's lying there in my mother's bed. *Naked.* Man, we didn't know *what* to do. It was too late to do anything to save Liza. She was *gone*. And the rest of us were totally fucked if it came out what happened. Brenda's hysterical and Jerry's barely coherent himself and Jimbo's outside throwing up. Bad scene. Very bad."

Delahanty thought about the Missing Persons report on Liza Krzyzanowski. It had been easy to read between the lines. Nobody'd done much with it at the time because she was exactly the kind of girl who'd run away.

But she was also exactly the kind of girl who'd OD in some stranger's bed, and nobody would bother to try to track it down.

Wally stopped, stubbed out his cigarette, lit another. Delahanty considered asking a question, decided to wait. A moment later Wally began again.

"What I remember about that night is being more scared than I'd ever been in my life. I mean, here I'd promised my parents it'd just be me and the class prez, making plans for the prom, keeping the kitchen neat. And here we were, with a dead girl that I hardly even *knew* and all kinds of drugs and booze, and the place was pretty thoroughly trashed, too. Jimbo kept pacing back and forth, and Jerry passed out again, and Brenda sat in a corner in that football sweatshirt. She made herself some coffee, I remember that 'cause it seemed so crazy. Kids didn't drink coffee, and that was all we were. Kids.

"It was Brenda who came up with the plan. And it was so obvious that we all fell in with her right away. There was no good to come from turning ourselves in, and a world of trouble. But Brenda kept saying Liza wouldn't want us all getting fucked over on her account. She'd been talking about running away anyway. She was flunking out, and her old man beat her or something. So we'd just act like nothing happened. Clean up the cottage and go home, and let Liza's family just think she'd gone to L.A. The only problem was, what could we do with her body?

"It was Brenda who came up with that, too. She'd been going with some friend of Jerry's who worked at the Texaco station with him, and she knew they were putting in a new underground gas tank that week. The hole was dug and everything. It was like it was meant to be. I remember she kept saying that, and I'd think, wait a minute. *Meant to be?* But it was her friend and her plan, and I was too scared shitless to do anything but run around wiping up the spilled beer, hoping I was gonna wake up from some shitty dream and it would just be me and Jimbo, getting ready to grill us a couple of steaks.

"Jerry was pretty shaky, even after we got him sobered up, but Brenda got him convinced there was no other way. He was all . . . shit, Liza'd been his *girlfriend*, and now she was *dead* and he was having a hard time keeping from losing it. I remember him yelling at Brenda, telling her she was too fucking cold to be believed, and her yelling back it was damned lucky for him that she was, 'cause otherwise we'd all be going to jail and we were old enough they'd try us as adults."

Wally looked over at Delahanty now. "You know, I always *did* wonder about that, but I never dared ask anybody. Would that have happened?"

Delahanty shrugged. "Maybe. Hard to say now, though. Those were different times." But still times when it was a major social and legal blunder to turn up with a dead girl on your hands. "So what did you do?"

"We followed Brenda's plan. She and Jerry went in his car and took Liza's ... body with them. In the trunk, wrapped up in the sheets that she died on. They were supposed to be putting the tank in the next day at the gas station. Jerry'd actually helped get the pit ready, shoveling the gravel flat at the bottom. So they waited till night and took her down there and put her under the gravel, and the next day those folks from Texaco came and dropped that gas tank in, right on schedule." He took a deep drag, looked at Delahanty, expecting something.

No problem. "Liza Krzyzanowski's family reported her missing," the detective said, careful to pronounce the name properly. *Zhu-shan-ow-ski.* "So that part of the plan worked."

"You *know* about that?" Wally appeared genuinely shocked.

Delahanty nodded. No need to credit Nan Robinson just now. And it pleased him to have Wally wondering just what else he knew. Which was just about exactly nothing.

"Yeah, and that Brenda told everybody that Liza'd run away. To Hollywood, I believe she suggested. Was there any kind of follow-up? Like your parents noticing a problem at the cottage?"

Wally shook his head. "They never even missed the sheets. By the time Jimbo and I cleared out of there, the place was immaculate." He looked regretful. "But I could never enjoy going there again." A real sensitive guy.

"So what happened? Brenda put the squeeze on you guys?"

Wally nodded. "Not right away, though. Brenda was smart. It was her word against ours, and we were the class leaders. *She* was the class slut and well-known drug dealer. But she screwed us right from the beginning. When they left with the body that night, she made us give her our school IDs. They were plastic, like credit cards. She said it was just insurance, in case we decided to do something stupid like call the cops and tell them to check out Riverside Texaco that night before the tank got put in. But when we saw her afterward, she told us she'd buried them with Liza. Who by then was under a tank full of lead-free. And later on, when Brenda wanted money, we didn't have a choice."

Ken Durant was listening to this tale with incredulity. Mildly surprising, given his line of work. A criminal lawyer pushing forty must have heard a lot of far-fetched yarns in his time. It was clear the lawyer had no idea where this tale was going, but Delahanty was starting to get a pretty good idea.

"Jim Webster told Nan Robinson that Brenda had hit him up for child support, told him that Ryan was Jim's son from some one-night stand."

Wally gave a brief and joyless laugh. "That was always his cover story, just in case anybody asked. And yeah, he *did* fuck her, that week and maybe before, I could never tell for sure. But nobody ever asked until last year when Jim got sick and Mary Lee found out he was sending Brenda money. Brenda never asked for anything till after she left town. Like I said, she was smart. Street-smart, anyway. But once she had some distance on her, she got in touch with us both." He considered. "She was never totally unreasonable. At least not till Bigmouth ran into her in Vegas and got into her pants again. After that it got truly ugly. She wanted more from me, too, but shit, I didn't have anything to give her but my Visa bills. My ex-wives took everything but the dental floss."

Something was bothering Delahanty about the gas station angle. "Isn't that Texaco one of the stations where they're getting ready to dig up the underground tanks?" Leakage from underground gas tanks had been a raging issue in the Spring Hill area for well over a year.

Wally nodded grimly. "Yeah, and Jimbo and me've been shitting bricks about it. He did everything he could as mayor to stall the whole underground tank issue, without being real obvious. Even tried to find some way he could have his company do the digging. But there's special ways it had to be done, special companies have to be hired, all kinds of bullshit."

He lit another cigarette off the one in his hand, gave a cough. "Look at me. Chain-smoking like some slug in a De Niro movie. I'll get lung cancer by the time I hit jail." He gave a short laugh. "So anyway, that's that."

"Not entirely," Delahanty pointed out conversationally. "What you're telling is an interesting background story, but it doesn't have much to do with what happened in Spring Hill this week."

Ken Durant perked right up, but Wally waved him silent.

"There's where you're wrong," Wally answered without hesitation. "It has *everything* to do with it. Once Brenda showed up at that reunion, something started that took on a life of its own. 'Cause we *knew* they were gonna be digging that tank out sometime soon. With a body under it. And it wouldn't take a rocket scientist to figure out who went missing around the time the tank got buried. There's records on that kind of shit. *Plus*, we knew the tank was leaking, which was why they were going after it in the first place, but there was no way to know what effects the gasoline would have on whatever was left of Liza. Or our goddamn high school ID cards. I tried to find out, soaked a credit card in gasoline for a couple months and nothing happened, but shit, this is twenty *years*."

An interesting variant on the high school science fair project. Had he placed the Visa card in a little petri dish?

Put half in regular and half in high-test? "Did she bury Jerry Leffingwell's school ID with Liza, too?"

Wally frowned. "What for? Brenda *trusted* Jerry. They did it *together*. Wouldn't matter anyway, on account of he's been dead for maybe fifteen years himself."

"So Brenda showed up at the reunion," Delahanty reminded him gently. "You weren't expecting her?"

The light eyes went wide. "Shit no! I saw her come walking across that floor, and I thought I'd piss my pants for sure. It was my worst nightmare come to life. And then she started *saying* things, making cute little comments. I didn't know what to do."

Delahanty let him stop, light another cigarette, refill his coffee cup. The lawyer started looking restless and nervous, but Wally held him off when he tried to interrupt. Finally, restoked, Wally started up again.

"We couldn't wait, Jimbo said. She was a loose cannon and she was making remarks, and we were both fucked if we let it go on a minute longer than necessary. He made the plan, and I just went along with it. Hell, what choice did I have?"

Delahanty decided it would be imprudent to interrupt with a list of alternatives.

"We waited till later, when everybody was pretty loose and people had kind of lost track of who was where, that kind of thing. Jim arranged to meet her outside, but he didn't tell me what he was doing till it was over. Then he comes up to me, slips the key to her room in my pocket, and tells me Brenda won't be any further problem and to quick go find out if there's anything in there that will mess us up. Tells me nobody'll find her for at least an hour." Here Wally gave another wry smile. "Guess he hadn't figured on Henry Sloane and Nan fixing to have a little backseat auld lang syne. Damn! I'd just barely got downstairs from checking the room when Nan comes charging in, all wild-eyed, and the shit hits the fan."

Wally looked Delahanty right in the eye. He'd been

relaxing as he talked—natural talkers often did—and relief at having told his story fairly flowed off him. He gave a smile. "And here we are, Officer Shit-on-the-Fan."

Detective Shit-on-the-Fan to you, Delahanty thought. "Not quite," he answered mildly. "Are you saying that Jim Webster killed Brenda Blaine?"

"Got it in one," Wally answered, lighting another cigarette. He really *would* do himself some damage at this rate.

"Then what happened to Brenda's grandmother? Alvina McReedy?"

Wally looked unhappy. "That was Mary Lee, acting on her own. It was a hell of a fix for Jim. Mary Lee never knew about Liza, any of that. But he did have to give her the story about child support for Ryan Blaine once she discovered he was sending all that money to Brenda. Mary Lee has spent a *lot* of time out at Golden Valley, cause her mom's there with Alzheimer's. Mighty depressing. Makes me glad my own folks died quick. Anyway, she knew Mrs. McReedy, used to bring her books from the library's Shut-In program. She knew that Nan had been out there to see her. And she was panicky, thinking Mrs. McReedy knew Jim was the father of Brenda's son." He lifted his eyes toward the ceiling. "Which of course he *wasn't*, but there was no way to tell her that at this point without getting everything a *whole* lot more complicated."

"Do you know for a fact that Mrs. Webster killed Mrs. McReedy?" Delahanty asked.

"You mean like, did I stand there and watch her do it? No. But she told Jimbo, and he told me."

Delahanty considered. Multiple hearsay, but with the circumstantial evidence, they'd probably be all right anyway. He felt a little bit sorry for Mary Lee Webster, but not sorry enough to let her skate. Besides, she had Jake Moroney on her side. She'd come out of it with a Congressional Medal of Honor. A damn good thing Moroney wasn't representing Wally Sheehan. Moroney would have smothered his client personally rather than let him run his mouth this way.

"This is all very helpful," Delahanty said genially, "and I guess that brings us to tonight. How did you happen to be visiting the Webster home?"

But Wally wasn't as dumb as he'd allowed himself to appear. "I'm really wiped out," he said. "I think I've said all I want to for the moment."

Ken Durant visibly exhaled at that and sprang to life. "I guess that wraps things up," he said briskly, leaning forward. "Detective, I believe it's time to let my client get some rest. He's clearly exhausted, probably incapacitated."

"Let the record show," Brian Delahanty said, "that we're all mighty tired."

CHAPTER 20

As Nan sat in the candlelit restaurant booth and listened to Brian Delahanty's abbreviated report on the previous night's confession, she was struck by the number of victims the week had produced.

Three people dead. No, four, when you counted back twenty years.

Ryan Blaine, who would have to live with both the loss of his mother and the realization that she was not what she had seemed or what he had believed.

Edwin Crosby, probably forever blocked from further progress in the Methodist hierarchy.

The Webster children, effectively orphaned.

Various Sheehan ex-wives and children, stripped of financial support and pride.

Not to mention June Robinson, who might never allow herself romantic dreams again.

The past twenty-four hours had provided resolution galore, but not much peace, except perhaps for Maria Fazio and the rest of the Krzyzanowskis. At least they now knew what had happened long ago, would finally be able to lay the missing sister and daughter to rest. Nan wondered if Tad and Anna would return from Poland to do so, suspected not.

For herself, Nan felt quite certain it would be a long time before she again felt the slightest interest in visiting Spring Hill. And she could not imagine ever again attending a high school reunion.

"You know," she said, "I really can't believe that Jim would risk everything to kill Brenda."

Brian Delahanty frowned slightly. "What do you mean?"

She shrugged. "Just that he was so good at getting other people to do his dirty work. Is there any way to *prove* that Wally's telling the truth?"

He shrugged back.

"Because it's easier for me to picture Jim telling Wally to go get rid of Brenda than it is to see him doing it himself. She'd go meet Wally without any hesitation. What's to be afraid of? He's the class clown. I'm not so sure that she'd turn her back on Jim, though."

She picked up her fork, fiddled with her cannelloni. She had tasted enough to know that it was exceptionally good, but her appetite was shot. "Although I suppose it doesn't matter all that much. Wally's ruined. And you've got an *excellent* witness to both his assault on Mary Lee and that fight in the bedroom. Which resulted in what at the very *least* ought to be voluntary manslaughter." She shook her head. "What's going to happen to Mary Lee?"

Brian stopped a forkful of linguine with clam sauce inches away from his mouth. "Well, I think she's probably off the short list for PTA Mother of the Year," he said. "And that lawyer's gonna have to hustle a bit to earn his big fat fee. But I know we can nail her on your assault, and I think we can put it together on the old lady, too. If we don't, it won't be for lack of effort."

Nan set her fork down, pushed the plate away. "I wish I could feel better about all this," she told him.

"You will eventually," he reassured her, reaching across the table, taking her hand. "It's been ugly. If it didn't bother you, I'd worry."

She intertwined her fingers in his. "I just keep remembering all the blood," she said softly. "I close my eyes and I see it."

"Look," he said, "give it *time*. You want dessert? They do a mean cheesecake here."

She shook her head.

"Then let's go. We can have coffee back at my place. There's something that I'd like to show you."

Nan cocked her head and looked at him, puzzled. "Some other time that might sound really appealing," she said slowly, "but right now I'm not exactly in the mood—"

"It's a train set," he told her, with a grin. "H-O. As in Ho-ho-ho. As in forget your troubles and be a kid again. And if that doesn't work, I've got a bottle of mighty nice brandy we can try in the coffee." He looked wonderfully boyish.

Nan smiled despite herself. "I guess it's worth a shot," she told him.

And it was.

Nan Robinson is back.

A POCKETFUL OF KARMA

by Taffy Cannon

Hollywood playgirl Debra LaRoche has
disappeared, confounding her ex-boss,
Nan Robinson. Debra is simply too
responsible to do that. Facing police
apathy, Nan must track Debra down.
But between Debra's many boyfriends
and her spaced-out friends at the Past
Lives Institute, Nan doesn't find out
much. She'd better act fast, though, since
there may be another disappearance
soon...Nan's, that is.

For a sample of the first Taffy Cannon mystery, read on...

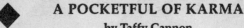

◆ A POCKETFUL OF KARMA ◆
by Taffy Cannon

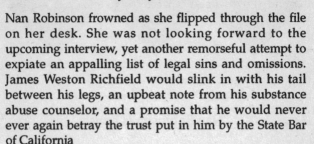

Nan Robinson frowned as she flipped through the file on her desk. She was not looking forward to the upcoming interview, yet another remorseful attempt to expiate an appalling list of legal sins and omissions. James Weston Richfield would slink in with his tail between his legs, an upbeat note from his substance abuse counselor, and a promise that he would never ever again betray the trust put in him by the State Bar of California

They all did.

They were starting to run together in her mind, Nan realized, these fortyish fellows who flushed away promising legal careers as they frantically juggled the demands of creditors, ex-wives, office overhead, miscellaneous addictions, and the clients who invariably ended up on the bottom of the heap.

Richfield, for instance, had maintained a solo plaintiff's personal injury practice uneventfully for eleven years before his own downward slide began. Then he started missing appearances and stopped returning phone calls. He settled one case against his client's wishes and held the payment for six months before passing along the client's share. He blew the statute of limitations for another client, leaving the poor sap in financial limbo and setting himself up tidily for the inevitable malpractice charge. By the time he checked into Betty Ford, his practice was in shambles.

Nan raised her head at a tentative rap on her office door. "Nan?" Violet Thomas looked worried. "You have a minute?"

"Of course, Violet," Nan told her. "Come on in. What's up?"

The office manager for the State Bar Trial Division had been, for years, the spiritual center of the entire operation. Violet knew everything about "her" people—the attorneys and investigators and support staff. She remembered their birthdays and their children's birthdays, knew whose marriages were floundering and whose illnesses were truly serious. A widow with Missouri grandchildren, she worked far longer hours than she was expected or paid to. Violet was tall and angular, with the kind of posture that could only be called "good carriage." Her neatly permed white hair had just enough silver rinse to highlight the dark violet-blue eyes for which she'd been named.

A worry line deepened now between those eyes. "This letter came in the morning mail," Violet said, laying an envelope carefully on Nan's desk. "I'm not exactly sure what to do with it."

The address was handwritten to Mrs. Debra Fontaine at the State Bar Trial Division. The return address was on a tiny white sticker featuring an American flag: Mrs. Peter LaRoche on an unfamiliar street in South Bend, Indiana.

But Debra hadn't worked at the State Bar since she married Tony Fontaine and moved out to Canyon Country. What's more, she'd taken back her maiden name, LaRoche, the moment she filed for divorce. Her mother might have chosen to ignore the latter, but she certainly should have known the former. Why on earth would she send mail to her daughter in an office where Debra hadn't been employed in over three years?

"Very strange," Nan agreed.

"I was just going to forward it," Violet said, "but then I realized that I don't have a current address for Debra anymore. I thought you might know...." Her voice trailed off delicately.

"Sure, I've got her address, assuming she hasn't moved again in the last three months." Not likely, since Debra was living in a Hollywood bungalow purchased with the first installment of an enormous insurance settlement. "I'll get it to her."

"Thanks," Violet said with some relief. "It just seemed so...so...peculiar."

"Don't give it another thought," Nan told her.

After Violet left, Nan turned the envelope over and over in her hands, feeling guilty. She hadn't really even thought about Debra for months now, since that lunch they had after Debra's first meeting with her divorce lawyer back in May.

And she should have.

Debra had been through hell in the past year. Her eighteen-month-old son, her pride and joy, the glue she hoped would hold together an already faltering marriage, had been hit by a car. Timmy lingered in intensive care for seven horrible days before he died. Nan did what she could at the time—precious little, really—but didn't keep in touch afterward the way she could have.

Should have.

She owed Debra at least that much.

Nan had first known Debra LaRoche as a pig-tailed border-line tomboy with perennially skinned knees, a peppy little girl who climbed trees and roller-skated backward and raced her two-wheeler fearlessly down the quiet streets of Spring Hill, Illinois. She was called Debbie then, a doted-on only child with limitless energy and a bright, cheerful smile. The LaRoches lived a few doors down from the Robinsons. The two families weren't exactly friends, but everyone in the neighborhood got along reasonably well, and Nan occasionally baby-sat for Debbie.

Debbie LaRoche was barely ten when Nan left Spring Hill for Stanford. At some point during Nan's college years, the LaRoche family moved to South Bend, and apart from her mother's sometime references, Nan never thought about them again. Then, when Nan was twenty-six, the midwestern old girls' network swung into action. Debra's mother wrote to Nan's mother, who called Nan, who said sure, have Debra get in touch when she got to LA.

Published by Fawcett Books.
Available in your local bookstore.

TANGLED ROOTS

by Taffy Cannon

Nan Robinson must help her sister, Julie, out of a messy situation: Julie's husband, Adam, is accused of shooting Shane Pettigrew, the heir to a Southern California flower-growing dynasty—in his greenhouse. Since Julie had an affair with Shane, Adam's good reputation could clearly be...soiled.

Reporter Hollis Ball is the kind of woman Nan Robinson
would respect: She's divorced, single, and proud of it.
She's also a part-time sleuth.

SLOW DANCING WITH THE ANGEL OF DEATH
by Helen Chappell

Think a bad marriage and a worse divorce are over
when death (finally) takes your ex-spouse?

Think again!

When Hollis Ball finds out that her hated ex-husband,
Sam Wescott, died in a boating accident, she is surprised
to find herself shedding even one tear. But she really
wants to cry when he comes back as a ghost to coax
her into finding his killer!

SLOW DANCING WITH THE ANGEL OF DEATH
Published by Fawcett Books.
Available in your local bookstore.